Praise for *Funny Girl*

"As befits a novel about a popular sitcom, this novel packs in lots of laughs, but it's also got more heft than Mr. Hornby's readers may expect." —*The New York Times*

"A smart comic novel that . . . induces binge-reading that's the literary equivalent of polishing off an entire television series in one weekend." —NPR

"Engaging . . . Hornby's fictionalized evocation of the era is spot-on." —*Entertainment Weekly*

"Funny and fast-moving, perceptive and sharp." —*Los Angeles Times*

"At its best moments, Hornby's novel shows precisely the same quality [as the best television comedy]." —*The Boston Globe*

"Hornby's fluency in script-like breeziness and crisp banter makes *Funny Girl* a pleasurable read. So does page after page of perfectly timed and delivered humor, the subtle and understated kind that starts with the first line." —*USA Today*

"[Hornby's] most ambitious novel to date. . . . [H]e makes the reader care for his characters as much as he does." —*Kirkus Reviews* (starred)

"[A] light, fond, funny tale by the author of *About a Boy*. . . . [A] fizzy delight about the likable oddballs who po~~~ showbiz."

"Theera and the theme (surfi~~ getting dumped in its wake) ~ warmth and sprightly dialogu~ ~~ture

"Beautifully captures the thrill of youthful success and of discovering your own talent." —*Daily Telegraph*

"*Funny Girl* may be read as Hornby's latest defense of popular entertainment against high-culture elitism. *Funny Girl* makes his case for him eloquently and entertainingly . . . both hugely enjoyable and deceptively artful." —*The Spectator*

"I loved this hymn to the 1960s, their infinite creative possibilities." —*Scotsman*

"Endearing, humorous, and touching. Hugely enjoyable." —*Sunday Mirror*

". . . As with any Hornby book, you'll close [*Funny Girl*] thinking it's his best." —*Metro*

"Hornby has transplanted us into an era where funny was also controversial. He allows us to see beyond the actors, but to the creation as a whole—the lives onscreen as well as those off." —*Books & Whatnot*

"A sweet sojourn to 1960s London. . . . [Hornby] has a knack for crackling dialogue and well-defined characters." —Associated Press

"[*Funny Girl*] fits squarely in Hornby's tradition of offering quality entertainment that respects readers' intelligence without making novels feel like homework. Consider it comfort food, prepared by a master." —*Christian Science Monitor*

"Fast, funny, and real." —*Time*

"[*Funny Girl*] skips effortlessly like a stone skimmed across the water . . . it's hard to put down." —*Newsweek*

FUNNY

GIRL

FUNNY GIRL

NICK
HORNBY

RIVERHEAD BOOKS | New York

RIVERHEAD BOOKS
An imprint of Penguin Random House LLC
375 Hudson Street
New York, New York 10014

Originally published in Great Britain by Penguin Books Ltd.

The Library of Congress has cataloged the Riverhead hardcover edition as follows:

Hornby, Nick.
Funny girl : a novel / Nick Hornby.
p.   cm.
ISBN 978-1-59420-541-5
I. Title.
PR6058.O689F86   2015   2014038381
823'.914—dc23

First Riverhead hardcover edition: February 2015
First Riverhead trade paperback: February 2016
Riverhead trade paperback ISBN: 978-1-10198-335-5

Printed in the United States of America
1 3 5 7 9 10 8 6 4 2

Book design by Gretchen Achilles

For Amanda, with love and gratitude, as ever.

And for Roger Gillett and Georgia Garrett.

AUDITION

1

She didn't want to be a beauty queen, but as luck would have it, she was about to become one.

There were a few aimless minutes between the parade and the announcement, so friends and family gathered round the girls to offer congratulations and crossed fingers. The little groups that formed reminded Barbara of licorice Catherine wheels: a girl in a sugary bright pink or blue bathing suit at the center, a swirl of dark brown or black raincoats around the outside. It was a cold, wet July day at the South Shore Baths, and the contestants had mottled, bumpy arms and legs. They looked like turkeys hanging in a butcher's window. Only in Blackpool, Barbara thought, could you win a beauty competition looking like this.

Barbara hadn't invited any friends, and her father was refusing to come over and join her, so she was stuck on her own. He just sat there in a deck chair, pretending to read the *Daily Express*. The two of them would have made a tatty, half-eaten Catherine wheel, but even so, she would have appreciated the company. In the end, she went over to him. Leaving the rest of the girls behind made her feel half naked and awkward, rather than glamorous and poised, and she had to walk past a lot of wolf-whistling spectators. When she reached her father's spot at the shallow end, she was probably fiercer than she wanted to be.

"What are you doing, Dad?" she hissed.

The people sitting near him, bored, mostly elderly holidaymakers, suddenly went rigid with excitement. One of the girls! Right in front of them! Telling her father off!

"Oh, hello, love."

"Why wouldn't you come and see me?"

He stared at her as if she'd asked him to name the mayor of Timbuktu.

"Didn't you see what everyone else was doing?"

"I did. But it didn't seem right. Not for me."

"What makes you so different?"

"A single man, running . . . amok in the middle of a lot of pretty girls wearing not very much. I'd get locked up."

George Parker was forty-seven, fat, and old before he had any right to be. He had been single for over ten years, ever since Barbara's mother had left him for her manager at the tax office, and she could see that if he went anywhere near the other girls he'd feel all of these states acutely.

"Well, would you have to run amok?" Barbara asked. "Couldn't you just stand there, talking to your daughter?"

"You're going to win, aren't you?" he said.

She tried not to blush, and failed. The holidaymakers within earshot had given up all pretense of knitting and reading the papers now. They were just gawping at her.

"Oh, I don't know. I shouldn't think so," she said.

The truth was that she did know. The mayor had come over to her, whispered "Well done" in her ear, and patted her discreetly on the bottom.

"Come off it. You're miles prettier than all the others. Tons."

For some reason, and even though this was a beauty contest, her superior beauty seemed to irritate him. He never liked her showing off, even when she was making her friends and family laugh with some kind of routine in which she portrayed herself as dim or dizzy or clumsy. It was still showing off. Today, though, when showing off was everything, the whole point, she'd have thought he might forgive her, but no such luck. If you had to go and enter a beauty pageant, he seemed to be saying, you might at least have the good manners to look uglier than everyone else.

She pretended to hear parental pride, so as not to confuse her audience.

"It's a wonderful thing, a blind dad," she said to the gawpers. "Every girl should have one."

It wasn't the best line, but she'd delivered it with a completely straight face, and she got a bigger laugh than she deserved. Sometimes surprise worked and sometimes people laughed because they were expecting to. She understood both kinds, she thought, but it was probably confusing to people who didn't take laughter seriously.

"I'm not blind," said George flatly. "Look."

He turned around and widened his eyes at anyone showing any interest.

"Dad, you've got to stop doing that," said Barbara. "It frightens people, a blind man goggling away."

"You . . ." Her father pointed rudely at a woman wearing a green mac. "You've got a green mac on."

The old lady in the next deck chair along began to clap, uncertainly, as if George had just that second been cured of a lifelong affliction, or was performing some kind of clever magic trick.

"How would I know that, if I was blind?"

Barbara could see that he was beginning to enjoy himself. Very occasionally he could be persuaded to play the straight man in a double act, and he might have gone on describing what he could see forever, if the mayor hadn't stepped up to the microphone and cleared his throat.

I t was Auntie Marie, her father's sister, who suggested that she should go in for Miss Blackpool. Marie came round for tea one Saturday afternoon, because she happened to be passing, and casually dropped the competition into the conversation, and—a sudden thought—asked her why she'd never had a go, while her dad sat there nodding his head and pretending to be thunderstruck by the brilliance of the idea. Barbara was puzzled for the first minute or two, before she realized that the two of them had cooked up a plan. The plan, as far as she could work out, was this: Barbara entered the pageant, won it, and then forgot all about moving to London, because there'd be no need. She'd be famous in her own hometown, and who could want for more? And then she could have a go at Miss UK, and if that didn't work out she could just think about getting married, when there would be another coronation, of sorts. (And that was a part of the beauty pageant plan too, Barbara was sure. Marie was quite sniffy about Aidan, thought she could do much better, or much richer, anyway, and beauty queens could take their pick. Dotty Harrison had married a man who owned seven carpet shops, and she'd only come third.)

Barbara knew she didn't want to be queen for a day, or even for a year. She didn't want to be a queen at all. She just wanted to go on television and make people laugh. Queens were never funny, not the ones in Blackpool anyway, or the ones in Buckingham Palace either. She'd gone along with Auntie Marie's scheme, though, because Dorothy Lamour had been Miss New Orleans and Sophia Loren had been a Miss Italy runner-up. (Barbara had always wanted to see a photograph of the girl who had beaten Sophia Loren.) And she'd gone along with it because she was bursting to get on with her life, and she needed something, anything, to happen. She knew she was going to break her father's heart, but first she wanted to show him that she'd at least tried to be happy in the place she'd lived all her life. She'd done what she could. She'd auditioned for school plays, and had been given tiny parts, and watched from the wings while the talentless girls that the teachers loved forgot their lines and turned the ones they remembered into nonsense. She'd been in the chorus line at the Winter Gardens, and she'd gone to talk to a man at the local amateur dramatic society who'd told her that their next production was *The Cherry Orchard*, which "probably wouldn't be her cup of tea." He asked whether she'd like to start off selling tickets and making posters. None of it was what she wanted. She wanted to be given a funny script so that she could make it funnier.

She wished that she could be happy, of course she did; she wished she wasn't different. Her school friends and her colleagues in the cosmetics department at R. H. O. Hills didn't seem to want to claw, dig, wriggle, and kick their way out of the town like she did, and sometimes she ached to be the same as them. And wasn't there something a bit childish about wanting to go on television? Wasn't she just shouting, "Look at me! Look at me!" like a two-year-old? All right, yes, some people, men of all ages, did look at her, but not in the way that she wanted them to look. They looked at her blonde hair and her bust and her legs, but they never saw anything else. So she'd enter the competition, and she'd win it, and she was dreading the look in her father's eyes when he saw that it wasn't going to make any difference to anything.

The mayor didn't get around to it straightaway, because he wasn't that sort of man. He thanked everyone for coming, and he made a pointless joke about Preston losing the Cup Final, and a cruel joke about his wife not entering this year because of her bunions. He said that the bevy of beauties in front of him—and he was just the sort of man who'd use the expression "bevy of beauties"—made him even prouder of the town than he already was. Everyone knew that most of the girls were holidaymakers from Leeds and Manchester and Oldham, but he got an enthusiastic round of applause at that point anyway. He went on for so long that she began to try and estimate the size of the crowd by counting the heads in one row of deckchairs and then multiplying by the number of rows, but she never finished because she got lost in the face of an old woman with a rain hat and no teeth, grinding a piece of sandwich over and over again. That was another ambition Barbara wanted to add to the already teetering heap: she wanted to keep her teeth, unlike just about every one of her relatives over the age of fifty. She woke up just in time to hear her name, and to see the other girls pretending to smile at her.

She didn't feel anything. Or rather, she noted her absence of feeling and then felt a little sick. It would have been nice to think that she'd been wrong, that she didn't need to leave her father and her town, that this was a dream come true and she could live inside it for the rest of her life. She didn't dare dwell on her numbness in case she came to the conclusion that she was a hard and hateful bitch. She beamed when the mayor's wife came over to put the sash on her, and she even managed a smile when the mayor kissed her on the lips, but when her father came over and hugged her she burst into tears, which was her way of telling him that she was as good as gone, that winning Miss Blackpool didn't even come close to scratching the itch that plagued her like chicken pox.

She'd never cried in a bathing suit before, not as a grown woman anyway. Bathing suits weren't for crying in, what with the sun and the sand and the shrieking and the boys with their eyes out on stalks. The feeling of wind-chilled tears running down her neck and into her cleavage was peculiar. The mayor's wife put her arms around her.

"I'm all right," said Barbara. "Really. I'm just being silly."

"Believe it or believe it not, I know how you're feeling," said the mayor's wife. "This is how we met. Before the war. He was only a councilor then."

"You were Miss Blackpool?" said Barbara.

She tried to say it in a way that didn't suggest amazement, but she wasn't sure she'd managed. The mayor and his wife were both large, but his size seemed intentional somehow, an indication of his importance, whereas hers seemed like a terrible mistake. Perhaps it was just that he didn't care and she did.

"Believe it or believe it not."

The two women looked at each other. These things happened. There was no need to say anything else, but then the mayor came over to them and said something else anyway.

"You wouldn't think so to look at her," said the mayor, who was not a man to let the unspoken stay that way.

His wife rolled her eyes at him.

"I've already said 'believe it or believe it not' twice. I've already admitted that I'm no Miss Blackpool anymore. But you have to come clomping in anyway."

"I didn't hear you say 'believe it or believe it not.'"

"Well I did. Twice. Didn't I, love?"

Barbara nodded. She didn't really want to be drawn in, but she thought she could offer the poor woman that much at least.

"Kiddies and cream buns, kiddies and cream buns," said the mayor.

"Well, you're no oil painting," his wife said.

"No, but you didn't marry me because I was an oil painting."

His wife thought about this and conceded the point with silence.

"Whereas that was the whole point of you," said the mayor. "You were an oil painting. Anyways," he said to Barbara. "You know this is the biggest open-air baths in the world, don't you? And this is one of the biggest days here, so you've every right to feel overcome."

Barbara nodded and snuffled and smiled. She wouldn't have known how to begin to tell him that the problem was exactly the opposite of the one he'd just described: it was an even smaller day than she feared it would be.

"That bloody Lucy woman," her father said. "She's got a lot to answer for."

The mayor and his wife looked confused, but Barbara knew who he was talking about. She felt understood, and that made it worse.

Barbara had loved Lucille Ball ever since she saw *I Love Lucy* for the first time: everything she felt or did came from that. The world seemed to stand still for half an hour every Sunday, and her father knew better than to try and talk to her or even to rustle the paper while the program was on, in case she missed something. There were lots of other funny people she loved: Tony Hancock, Sergeant Bilko, Morecambe and Wise. But she couldn't be them even if she'd wanted to. They were all men. Tony, Ernie, Eric, Ernie . . . There was nobody called Lucy or Barbara in that lot. There were no funny girls.

"It's just a program," her father would say, before or after but never during. "An American program. It's not what I call British humor."

"And British humor . . . That's your special phrase for humor from Britain, is it?"

"The BBC and so forth."

"I'm with you."

She only ever stopped teasing him because she got bored, never because he cottoned on and robbed the teasing of its point. If she had to stay in Blackpool, then one of her plans was to keep a conversation like this going for the rest of his life.

"She's not funny, for a start," he said.

"She's the funniest woman who's ever been on television," said Barbara.

"But you don't laugh at her," said her father.

It was true that she didn't laugh, but that was because she'd usually seen the shows before. Now she was too busy trying to slow it all down so she could remember it. If there was a way of watching Lucy every single day of the week, then she would, but there wasn't, so she just had to concentrate harder than she'd ever concentrated on anything, and hope that some of it sank in.

"Anyway, you make me shut up when they're reading out the football results on the wireless," she said.

"Yes, because of the pools," he said. "One of those football results might change our life."

What she couldn't explain without sounding batty was that *I Love Lucy* was exactly the same as the pools. One day, one of Lucy's expressions or lines was going to change her life, and maybe even his too. Lucy had already changed her life, although not in a good way: the show had separated her from everyone else—friends, family, the other girls at work. It was, she sometimes felt, a bit like being religious. She was so serious about watching comedy on the television that people thought she was a bit odd, so she'd stopped talking about it.

The photographer from the *Evening Gazette* introduced himself and ushered Barbara toward the diving boards.

"You're Len Phillips?" her father said. "You're not pulling my leg?"

He recognized Len Phillips's name from the paper, so he was starstruck. Dear God, Barbara thought. And he wonders why I want to get out of here.

"Can you believe that, Barbara? Mr. Phillips has come to the baths personally."

"Call me Len."

"Really? Thank you very much." George looked a little uncomfortable, though, as if the honor had not yet been earned.

"Yes, well, he probably hasn't got a staff of thousands," said Barbara.

"It's just me, and a lad sometimes," said Len. "And today's a big day for Blackpool. I'd be daft to let the lad do it."

He gestured at Barbara to move back a little.

"Say cheese," her father said. "Or is it only amateurs who do that?"

"No, we do it too. Although sometimes I shout 'Knickers!' just for a change."

George laughed and shook his head in wonder. He was having the time of his life, Barbara could tell.

"No boyfriend?" Len asked.

"He couldn't get the day off, Len," George said. He paused for a moment, clearly wondering whether he'd got too familiar, too soon. "They're short-staffed, apparently, because of the holidays. Her auntie Marie couldn't come either, because she's gone to the Isle of Man for a fortnight. Her first holiday for seven years. Only a caravan, but, you know. A change is as good as a rest."

"You should be writing all this down, Len," said Barbara. "Caravan. Isle of Man. A change is as good as a rest. Is it just her and Uncle Jack, Dad? Or have the boys gone too?"

"He doesn't want to know all that," said her father.

"Where does she work?" Len asked, nodding his head toward Barbara.

"I don't know. We could ask her," said Barbara.

"She's in the cosmetics department at R. H. O. Hills," her father said. "And Aidan's in Menswear. That's how they met."

"Well, she won't be there much now, will she?" said the photographer.

"Won't she?" said George.

"I'm always taking photographs of Miss Blackpool. Hospitals, shows, charity galas . . . She's got a lot of responsibilities. It'll be a busy year. We'll be seeing each other a lot, Barbara, so you'll have to get used to my ugly mug."

"Oh, Lord," said her father. "Did you hear that, Barbara?"

Hospitals? Charity galas? An entire year? What had she been thinking? Auntie Marie had told her about the shop openings and the Christmas lights, but she hadn't thought about how she'd be letting people down if she just disappeared, and she hadn't thought about how she'd still be Miss Blackpool in three hundred and sixty-four days' time. She knew then that she didn't want to be Miss Blackpool in an hour's time.

"Where's she going?" said Len.

"Where are you going?" said her father.

Fifteen minutes later, the runner-up, Sheila Jenkinson, a tall, dopey redhead from Skelmersdale, was wearing the tiara, and Barbara and her father were in a taxi on their way back home. She left for London the following week.

2

Saying good-bye to her father was hard. He was afraid of being left alone, she knew that, but it didn't stop her. On the train down, she didn't know whether she was more upset by his grief and fear, or her own ruthlessness: she never once came close to changing her mind. Saying good-bye to Aidan was easy, though. He seemed relieved, and told her that he knew she'd cause trouble for him if she stayed in Blackpool. (He married someone else the following spring, and he caused her trouble for the next fifteen years.)

And London was easy too, as long as you didn't expect too much. She found a bed-and-breakfast near Euston

Station, paid three days' lodging out of her savings, went to an employment bureau, and got a job in Derry and Toms in Kensington High Street, on the cosmetics counter. All you had to do, it seemed, was ask for an inferior version of the life you'd had before and London would give it to you. London didn't mind where you came from either, as long as you didn't mind the tobacconist and the bus conductor laughing and repeating your words back to you every time you opened your mouth. "Toopence!" "Piccadelleh!" "Coopa tea!" Sometimes other customers and other passengers were invited to join in the hilarity.

A girl called Marjorie, who worked in Ladies' Shoes, offered her a double room in Earl's Court, much nearer to the store, and she agreed to take it before she'd realized that Marjorie would be in the double room with her.

She felt even more religious now: Lucille Ball had turned her into some kind of martyr to ambition. The kitchen window looked down over the railway line, and when a train went past, soot fell from the window frames onto the floor. In London, nearly all the money she earned went on food, rent, and bus fares. Marjorie was every bit as lonely as Barbara, and she never went out anywhere, so the two of them spent too much time together. They lived off tinned soup and toast, and they never had enough sixpences for the gas fire. She couldn't watch Lucy, because she didn't have a TV set, so on Sunday afternoons her longing for home was particularly sharp. It didn't help, reminding herself that if she were back in Blackpool she'd spend the afternoon aching to be in London. It just made her feel that she'd never be happy anywhere. Sometimes she stopped and looked in the windows of employment agencies, but nobody seemed to need a television comedienne. Some nights she lay in bed and wept silently at her own stupidity. What had she thought was going to happen?

Marjorie told her that she should buy *The Stage* for the advertisements. There were a lot of girls, she said, who'd worked at Derry and Toms and read *The Stage* during their tea breaks, then disappeared.

"Would I have heard of any of them?" Barbara asked.

"Probably only Margie Nash," said Marjorie. "You must have heard us talking about her."

Barbara shook her head, anxious for news of anyone who had found some kind of secret show-business tunnel out of the store.

"She was the one who was caught messing about with a customer in the gents' lav on the third floor, and then she owned up to stealing a skirt. She used to buy *The Stage* every week."

And, undeterred by the cautionary tale of Margie Nash, so did Barbara, every Thursday, from the newspaper stall by Kensington High Street tube station. But she didn't understand a lot of it. It was full of notices that seemed to be written in code:

CALLS FOR NEXT WEEK

SHAFTESBURY—*Our Man Crichton.* Kenneth
More, Millicent Martin, George Benson, David
Kernan, Dilys Watling, Anna Barry, Eunice Black,
Glyn Worsnip, Patricia Lambert (Delfont/Lewis/
Arnold).

Who, precisely, was being called for next week? Not
Kenneth More and Millicent Martin and the rest of them,
surely? They must all have known that they were about
to appear in a West End play. Was Barbara herself being
called, or girls like her? And if there was any way that these
mysterious calls might involve her, or anyone like her, how
was she supposed to know how to respond to them? There
was no date or time or job description. Lots of shows
seemed to need soubrettes, but she didn't know what a soubrette was, and she didn't have a dictionary, and she didn't
know where her nearest library was. If there wasn't an English word for it, though, then it was probably work best
avoided, at least until she was really desperate.

The vacancies in the back of the paper were more
straightforward, and she didn't need to look anything up.
The Embassy Club in Old Bond Street wanted smart and
attractive hostesses. The Nell Gwynne in Dean Street
needed showgirls and/or dancers, but "only lovely girls"
were invited to apply. The Whisky A Go Go in Wardour
Street required Pussies, minimum height five feet, six
inches, but she suspected that height was not the only

requirement, and she didn't want to know what the others might be.

She hated having to think about whether she was lovely enough to be a Pussy or a hostess or a showgirl. She feared that she wasn't as lovely as she had been in Blackpool; or rather, her beauty was much less remarkable here. One day in the staff restaurant she counted on her fingers the girls who looked like real knockouts to her: seven. Seven skinny, beautiful creatures on her lunch break, in Derry and Toms alone. How many would there be on the next lunch break? How many on the cosmetics counters at Selfridges and Harrods and the Army and Navy?

She was pretty sure, though, that none of these girls wanted to make people laugh. That was her only hope. Whatever it was they cared about—and Barbara wasn't sure that they cared about very much—it wasn't that. Making people laugh meant crossing your eyes and sticking your tongue out and saying things that might sound stupid or naive, and none of those girls with their red lipstick and their withering contempt for anyone old or plain would ever do that. But that hardly gave her a competitive edge, not here, not yet. A willingness to go cross-eyed wasn't much use to her in Cosmetics. It probably wasn't what the Whisky A Go Go wanted from its Pussies either.

Barbara began to imagine the pretty girls working in Derry and Toms as beautiful tropical fish in a tank, swimming up and down, up and down, in serene disappointment, with nowhere to go and nothing to see that they hadn't seen a million times before. They were all waiting for a man. Men were going to scoop them up in a net and take them home and put them into an even smaller tank. Not all of them were waiting to *find* a man, because some of them had already found one, but it didn't stop the waiting. A few were waiting for a man to make up his mind and fewer still, the lucky ones, were waiting for a man who'd already made up his mind to make enough money.

Barbara wasn't waiting for a man, she didn't think, but she no longer knew what she was waiting for. She'd told herself on the train that she wouldn't even think about going home for two years, but after two months she could feel all the fight and the fire in her dying away, until the only thing she wanted was access to a TV set on a Sunday. That was what work had done to her—work and the tinned soup, and Marjorie's adenoids. She'd forgotten all about turning herself into Lucy; she just wanted to see her on the screen somehow.

"Do you know anyone with a television?" she asked Marjorie one night.

"I don't really know anyone full stop," said Marjorie.

It was Friday evening. She was draping stockings over the clotheshorse by the gas fire. "But most of the girls live like us."

"Some of them must live at home," said Barbara.

"Yes," said Marjorie. "You can befriend them and go to the pictures with them and go out dancing with them and one day they might invite you home for Sunday tea and you can watch their telly."

"So it has to be a boyfriend."

"You can go out with them and go dancing with them and go to the pictures with them and wrestle in doorways with them and . . ."

"All right," said Barbara gloomily. "I get the idea."

"I'd say that the quickest way to a television is a gentleman friend. They're hard to find, but they exist."

"You mean a rich man with a wife?"

"You said you were looking for a TV set, not eternal love. They've got flats hidden away. Or they can afford hotels. Nice hotels have television sets in their bedrooms."

So Barbara was waiting for a man too, it turned out. Of course she was. What on earth had led her to believe that she could do something without one? Why did she always think she was different from everyone else? There was no point complaining about it. Or rather, she could complain all she wanted, as long as she was trying to meet a man at the same time, and as long as she kept the complaints to herself. Whoever this man was, he probably didn't want to spend all evening listening to her banging on about how unfair the world was. He wouldn't be that sort of chap, from the sound of it. She needed to change something, anything. She needed to meet someone who wasn't a bus conductor or a salesgirl. There were opportunities somewhere. But they weren't in Cosmetics, and she didn't think they were in the Nell Gwynne.

"How do you know all this?" she asked Marjorie, who didn't strike her as someone who'd had a string of gentlemen friends.

"I used to have a friend in Coats and Furs," said Marjorie.

"Some of the girls there had gentlemen friends. It never happens to anyone in Shoes, of course."

"Why 'of course'?"

"You must have noticed."

"Noticed what?"

"Well, that's why we're in Shoes in the first place. Because we don't look like the sorts of girls who'd find themselves a gentleman friend."

Barbara wanted to tell her not to be so silly, but she flicked through a few faces in her mind and recognized the truth of the observation. All the good-looking girls were in Cosmetics and Ladies' Fashion. There was a selection process that nobody had ever mentioned.

"Can you get yourself a couple of days in Perfume?" said Marjorie.

"Why Perfume?"

"Cosmetics isn't so good. You don't get men buying lipstick and mascara so much, do you?"

Marjorie was right about this as well. Barbara couldn't remember the last time she'd served a man.

"But they buy perfume as presents. They get all flirty when they're buying it, too. They want you to spray it on your wrists and then take your hand so they can sniff."

Barbara had seen this back home in R. H. O. Hills, but not often, and it was never done with any real intent. People were more careful in a small town. If somebody's husband tried something on, his wife would find out soon enough.

"Listen," said Marjorie. "A gentleman friend isn't interested in wrestling. I just thought I should warn you."

Barbara was surprised. "What is he interested in, then? If he's not interested in, you know, *that*."

"Oh, he's interested in *that*. Just not the wrestling part."

"I'm not sure I get you."

"He won't want to wrestle. Wrestling's for kids."

"But if he's a gentleman . . ."

"I think the word 'gentleman' in 'gentleman friend' is like the word 'public' in 'public schools.' It actually means the opposite, when you put it with something else. You're not a virgin, are you?"

"Of course not," said Barbara.

The truth was that she wasn't sure. There had been some sort of business with Aidan, right before the beauty pageant. She had decided that she wanted to be unencumbered before coming to London. He'd been hopeless, though, and she was consequently unsure of her official status.

"Well, be warned, that's all. They're not messing about."

"Thank you."

Marjorie looked at her, apparently exasperated.

"You do know what you look like, don't you?"

"No. I thought I did, before I came down to London. But it's different here. There's a different scale. All those girls in Cosmetics and Ladies' Fashion, and then when you go out on to Kensington High Street . . ."

"All those little stick insects?" said Marjorie. "You don't

DEMONSTRATES
THE WORLD'S
FINEST
PROJECTION
EQUIPMENT
....HER
BELL & HOWELL
HEADLINER
COLOUR SLIDE
PROJECTOR

need to worry about them. All right, you're not very with it. But men don't care about that. You're ridiculous."

"Oh," said Barbara. "Thank you."

"You're like Sabrina."

Barbara tried not to roll her eyes. She hated Sabrina, the girl who just stood in front of the camera on the *Arthur Askey Show*, smiling and showing off her silly bust. She was and did the opposite of what Barbara wanted to be and to do.

"You've got the bosom, the waist, the hair, the legs, the eyes . . . If I thought that murdering you with a meat cleaver, this minute, would get me half what you've got, I'd slice you up without a second's thought and watch you bleed to death like a stuck pig."

"Thank you," said Barbara.

She thought she'd focus on the compliment, rather than the terrifying glimpse she'd been given into her flatmate's soul. She found herself particularly worried by Marjorie's willingness to do all that, the slicing and the bleeding and the murdering, for only a percentage of the advantages she envied. There was something in this compromise that made it seem more real than Barbara wanted it to be.

"You shouldn't be in of an evening, watching me dry my underwear. You should be entering beauty competitions."

"Don't be daft," said Barbara. "What would I want to do anything like that for?"

The next day, Barbara asked a girl she knew on the perfume counter to swap with her for an afternoon, just to see how easy it was to find a gentleman friend. The results of the experiment were startling: you just had to turn on the light indicating that you were looking for one. Barbara was glad she hadn't known where the switch was during her teenage years, because she'd have got herself into all sorts of trouble in Blackpool—trouble caused by married men who owned seven carpet shops, or who sang in the shows at the Winter Gardens.

Valentine Laws wasn't much of a catch. She should probably have thrown him back in, but she wanted to get on with it. He was at least fifteen years older than her, and he smelled of pipe tobacco and Coal Tar soap. The first time he came to the perfume counter, he was wearing a wedding ring, but when he came back a couple of minutes later, apparently for a longer look at her, it was gone. He didn't speak to her until his third lap.

"So," he said, as if the conversational well had momentarily run dry. "Do you get out much yourself?"

"Oh, you know," she said. "Not as much as I'd like."

"'Mooch,'" he said. "Lovely. Where are you from? Let me guess. I'm good at this. I know it's somewhere oop north, but where, that is the question. Yorkshire?"

"Lancashire. Blackpool."

He stared, unembarrassed, at her chest.

"Sabrina comes from Blackpool, doesn't she?"

"I don't know who Sabrina is," said Barbara.

"Really? I'd have thought you'd all be very proud of her."

"Well, we're not," said Barbara. "Because we've never heard of her."

"Anyway, she looks like you," said Valentine Laws.

"Bully for her."

He smiled and plowed on. He was clearly not interested in her conversational skills. He was interested in her because she looked like Sabrina.

"Well, Miss Blackpool." She looked at him, startled, but it was just a line. "What sort of places would you like to go to?"

"That's for me to know and you to find out."

She could have kicked herself. That was a tone she'd

have used back home to slap away a Teddy Boy at the Winter Gardens, but it was no use to her here. She was wrestling, and Marjorie had warned her not to wrestle. Luckily for her, and perhaps because he wasn't accustomed to the snap and snarl of Saturday night dance halls, he ignored her little flash of haughtiness.

"I'm trying," he said patiently. "But I have a proposal to make to you."

"I'll bet," she said.

She couldn't help herself. All her life, or the part of it in which men were interested, she'd been trying to fend them off. Now, suddenly, she had to be different and suppress the reflex she'd needed for years.

"And you'd be right to bet. You'd win money. I wouldn't be talking to you if there were no proposal, would I?"

She appreciated the brutal clarification and smiled.

"I'm meeting a friend for dinner. A client. He's bringing a lady friend, and suggested I should too."

In her past life, she would have mentioned his wedding ring, but she had learned something.

"That sounds nice."

She was still a long way from a television set, but it was a start.

Marjorie advised her to borrow something to wear from work. That's what all the other girls did, apparently. She went upstairs in her lunch hour with a bag, had a word with one of the girls, took away a smart knee-length red dress with a plunging neckline. When she was getting ready to go out, she remembered what she could look like, when she made an effort, put on some lipstick, showed a bit of leg. It had been a while.

"Bloody hell," said Marjorie, and Barbara smiled.

Valentine Laws had booked a table at the Talk of the Town to see Matt Monro, Auntie Marie's favorite singer. On the posters at the entrance, Barbara saw that on other nights it might have been the Supremes, or Helen Shapiro, or Cliff and the Shadows, people who the girls at work would have wanted to hear all about. Matt Monro was from another time, the time that she'd left Blackpool to escape. As she was shown to the table, she noticed that she was easily the youngest person in the room.

He was waiting for her at a table for four at the side of

the stage. His other guests hadn't arrived. He ordered her a Dubonnet and lemonade without asking her, and they talked about work, and London, and nightclubs, and then he looked up and smiled.

"Sidney!"

But Sidney, a small, bald man with a mustache, didn't seem pleased to see Valentine, and then Valentine's face became too complicated for Barbara to read. There was the smile, then the smile vanished, and then there was a quick, shocked widening of the eyes. And then a smile returned, but it contained no warmth or pleasure.

"Audrey!" said Valentine.

Audrey was a large woman in an extremely purple and inappropriately long dress. She was, Barbara guessed, Sidney's wife. And as Barbara watched, she began to see that there had been some kind of misunderstanding. Sidney had thought that it was a night out with one kind of lady ("the ladies," "our good lady wives," that sort of thing), but Valentine had invited Barbara on the assumption that it was another sort of night out altogether, one involving *ladies* but not *the* ladies. Presumably they had enjoyed both kinds of evening in the past, hence the confusion. The lives of married men with money were so complicated and so deceitful, the codes they spoke in so ambiguous, that Barbara wondered why this sort of thing didn't happen all the time. Perhaps it did. Perhaps the Talk of the Town was full of tables at which women of wildly different ages were sitting, all glowering at each other.

"Valentine and I have a tiny bit of business to discuss at the bar," said Sidney. "Please excuse us for five minutes."

Valentine stood up, nodded at the women, and followed Sidney, who was stomping away angrily. It was a misunderstanding with consequences, obviously. Sidney's good lady wife would realize who Barbara was and what she represented; she would presumably work out that there had been other, similar evenings to which she hadn't been invited. If Valentine had been quicker on the uptake he could have introduced Barbara as his cousin, or his secretary, or his parole officer, but he'd allowed himself to be dragged away by Sidney for an ear-bashing, and left the two women to come to their own conclusions.

Audrey sat down heavily opposite Barbara and looked at her.

"He's married, you know," she said eventually.

Barbara very much doubted that she'd still be around to hear Matt Monro sing, so she thought she may as well have as much fun as she could. She looked at Audrey and laughed, immediately and scornfully.

"To who?" she said. "I'll kill her." And she laughed again, just to show how unconcerned she was by Audrey's news.

"He's married," said Audrey insistently. "To Joan. I've met her. He's been married a long time. Kids and everything. They're not even kids anymore. The lad is sixteen and his daughter's at nursing college."

"Well," said Barbara, "he can't be doing a very good job of bringing them up. He hasn't spent a night away from home for two years."

"Home?" said Audrey. "You live together?"

"Oh, it's not as bad as it looks," said Barbara. "We're supposed to be getting married next June. Although obviously if what you're saying is true, he's got some sorting out to do first." And she laughed for a third time, and shook her head at the preposterousness of it all. Valentine! Married! With kiddies!

"Have you met these 'children'?"

"Well," said Audrey, "no." A tiny worm of doubt had crept in, Barbara noted with satisfaction. "But I've talked to Joan about them. Sidney and I have two teenagers of our own."

"Ah," said Barbara. "Talking. We can all talk. I could pop fifteen children out, talking to you now. Pop, pop, pop, pop, pop . . ."

Fifteen children meant way too many pops, she now realized. She'd seem insane if she kept going, so she stopped.

"Five anyway," she said.

"What do you mean?"

"Talking's not the same as seeing, is it?"

"Are you saying that Joan made them up?"

"To be honest, I think this Joan might be made up."

"How can she be made up? I met her!"

"Yes, but you know what they're like. Sometimes they want an evening out without us, if you know what I mean. It's harmless enough. Well, I think so."

"You're saying that Joan was some sort of . . ."

"No, no. He just wanted some company. I was probably at the pictures or somewhere."

"She wasn't a young woman," said Audrey.

"Well, that's quite sweet, that he wanted to spend an evening with someone of his own age."

Audrey contemplated the elaborate fraud that had been perpetrated on her and shook her head.

"I can't believe it," she said. "What an odd thing to do."

Sidney and Valentine came back to the table, friends again.

"I should introduce you two properly," said Valentine. "Audrey, this is Barbara. She works in my office and she's nuts about Matt Monro. So when Joan fell ill this afternoon . . ."

Sidney's wife looked at her, confused and then outraged.

"Nice to meet you, Audrey," said Barbara, and she went to get her coat.

There had been a strange enjoyment in the few minutes she'd spent talking to Audrey because they'd allowed her to appear in a comedy sketch that she'd written herself, on the spot. It had been a half-decent performance too, she thought, considering the thinness of the material. But then the adrenaline left her body, and as she queued for the cloakroom, she felt as blue as she'd ever been in London. Since her conversation with Marjorie, she had been telling herself that her choice was clear, if dismal: she could work behind cosmetics counters, or she could pick up men like Valentine Laws, in the hope that they would take her somewhere a few inches closer to where she wanted to be.

But she had picked up a man like Valentine Laws, and she'd ended up feeling cheap and foolish, and she would be back behind the cosmetics counter the following day anyway. She wanted to cry. She certainly wanted to go home. She'd had enough. She would go home and marry a man who owned carpet shops, and she would bear his children, and he would take other women to nightclubs, and she would get old and die and hope for better luck next time around.

And on the way out of the Talk of the Town, she met Brian.

She nearly bumped into him as she was walking up the stairs to the entrance. He said hello, and she told him to bugger off, and he looked startled.

"You don't remember me, do you?"

"No," she said, and she was glad that she didn't. He clearly hadn't been worth remembering. He was handsome enough, and he was wearing what looked like a very expensive suit, but he was even older than Valentine Laws. Everything about him was untrustworthy.

"We met at the first night of that Arthur Askey film you were in."

"I've never been in any film."

"Oh," he said. "Sorry. You're not Sabrina, are you?"

"No, I'm bloody not bloody Sabrina. Bloody Sabrina is bloody *years* older than me. And yes, she comes from the same place, and yes, she's got a big bust. But if any of you ever looked above a woman's neck, you might learn to tell us apart."

He chuckled.

"I'm so sorry," he said. "I'm glad you're not her. It wasn't a very good film and she was hopeless in it. Where are you going anyway?"

"Home."

"You can't go home yet. Matt Monro hasn't even started, has he?"

"Why can't I go home?"

"Because you should stay and have a drink. I want to know all about you."

"I'll bet you do."

She could wrestle with this man, because she wanted nothing from him and she was sick of all men anyway.

"I'm not who you think I am," he said.

"I don't think you're anybody."

"I'm very happily married," he said.

Suddenly there was a smiling, attractive woman by his side. She was a little bit younger than him, but nothing scandalous.

"Here she is," said the man. "This is my wife."

"Hello," said the woman. She didn't seem to be angry with Barbara. She just wanted to be introduced.

"I'm Brian Debenham," he said. "And this is Patsy."

"Hello," said Patsy. "You're so pretty."

Barbara started to imagine what this could be about. A husband and wife trying to pick her up came from some-where right on the fringes of her imagination. She didn't even have a word for it.

"I'm trying to persuade her to have a drink with us," said Brian.

"I can see why," said Patsy, and she looked Barbara up and down. "She's right up your street. She looks like Sabrina."

"I don't think she likes it when people say that."

"I don't," said Barbara. "And I don't like it when a man tries to pick me up while his wife is watching."

That seemed the safest interpretation. If she didn't have a word for the other thing, she wouldn't try to accuse them of it. She was definitely going to find out what a soubrette was. For all she knew, they were trying to turn her into one.

Brian and Patsy laughed.

"Oh, I'm not trying to pick you up," he said. "It's not sex. It's something even dirtier. I want to make money out of you. I'm a theatrical agent."

Barbara went back to the cloakroom with her coat, and that's when it all started.

3

A t Brian's insistence, she didn't go back to Derry and Toms.

"I have to give two weeks' notice."

She had already phoned in sick so that she could visit Brian in his office. She couldn't take any more time off.

"Why?"

"Why?"

"Yes, why?"

"Because . . ." She couldn't think of a reason, other than that those were the rules. "Anyway, how will I pay my rent?"

"I'll find you work."

"I need money now."

"I'll sub you for a couple of weeks. A month, even. What are you earning, twenty quid a week? I'm not having you turning down work for the sake of eighty quid."

She wasn't earning anything like twenty pounds a week. She'd only been on twelve since she'd finished her probationary period.

"But what work am I turning down? I've never acted in anything in my life."

"That's the beauty of it, darling. No experience necessary. No acting necessary, even. I won't mention Sabrina ever again after this. But you may have noticed that she's not exactly Dorothy Tutin. Sweetheart, you only have to stand there and people will throw money at me. Some of which I'll pass on to you. Honestly, it's the easiest game in the world."

"Sounds like the oldest game in the world."

"Don't be cynical, darling. That's my job. Listen. Do you know what a soubrette is?"

She sighed and rolled her eyes. She was going to find a library the moment she'd left Brian's office.

"You are the very epitome of a soubrette. And everybody wants them. But really, you don't even need to do that. People will pay you a lot of money just to be you. Just do what I tell you to do and we'll all be happy."

"What are you going to tell me to do?"

"I'm going to tell you to meet people, and these people will tell you to do things. Smile. Walk up and down. Stick your chest or your bottom out. That sort of thing. We'll have you under contract to a studio in no time. And before you know it, every man under the age of seventy will have a picture of you wearing a bikini on the wall of his potting shed."

"As long as they let me act, I'll wear anything they want."

"Are you telling me you actually *want* to act?"

"I want to be a comedienne," said Barbara. "I want to be Lucille Ball."

The desire to act was the bane of Brian's life. All these beautiful, shapely girls, and half of them didn't want to appear in calendars, or turn up for openings. They wanted three lines in a BBC play about unwed mothers down coal mines. He didn't understand the impulse, but he cultivated contacts with producers and casting agents, and sent the girls out for auditions anyway. They were much more malleable once they'd been repeatedly turned down.

"The way I remember it, Lucille Ball wasn't left with much choice. She was knocking on a bit, and nobody was giving her romantic leads anymore, so she had to start making funny faces. You've got years before we have to start thinking about that. Decades, probably. Look at you."

"I want to go to auditions."

"What I'm trying to tell you is that you won't need to go to auditions. You could be a model, and then you can be in any film you want."

How many times had he given the same little speech? They never listened.

"Any film I want as long as I don't open my mouth."

"I'm not going to bankroll you forever."

"You think if I open my mouth you're going to have to bankroll me forever?"

"I didn't say that."

"Send me to auditions."

Brian shrugged. They would have to go the long way round.

The next morning, she had to explain to Marjorie that she wouldn't be going into work with her because a man she'd met in a nightclub was paying her not to.

"What kind of man?" said Marjorie. "And are there any more where he came from? I know I'm only in Shoes, but you can tell him I really would do anything."

"He's an agent."

"Did you see his license or whatever it is you need to be an agent?"

"No. But I believe him."

"Why?"

"Because I went to his office today. He had a secretary, and a desk . . ."

"People do that all the time."

"Do what?"

"Get secretaries and desks. To con people. I wonder if the desk will still be there if you go back today."

"He had filing cabinets."

"You can be very naive, Barbara."

"But what's he conning me out of?"

"I'm not going to spell it out."

"You think people get secretaries and desks and filing cabinets so that they can seduce girls? It seems like an awful lot of trouble."

Marjorie wouldn't be drawn on that, but Barbara was clearly being invited to reach her own conclusions.

"Has he given you any money?"

"Not yet. But he's promised to."

"Have you done anything to earn the money?"

"No!"

"Oh dear."

"But that's good, isn't it?"

"I wouldn't have thought so. If he's giving you money already, God knows what he's expecting."

Barbara would have started to feel foolish if Brian hadn't sent her out to auditions immediately. She didn't have a phone, so she would begin the day with a pile of three-penny bits and a trip to the phone box on the corner; if he had nothing for her, he'd instruct his secretary to say so straightaway so she didn't put a second coin in the slot.

The first audition was for a farce called *In My Lady's Chamber*. It was about . . . Oh, it didn't matter what it was about. It was full of young women in their underwear and lustful husbands caught with their trousers down, and their awful, joyless wives. What it was really about was people not having sex when they wanted it. A lot of British comedy was about that, Barbara had noticed. People always got stopped before they'd done it, rather than found out afterward. It depressed her.

The play was being staged in a theater club off Charing Cross Road. The producer told Brian that the Lord Chamberlain's Office might have banned it from a proper theater.

"Utter nonsense, of course. The Lord Chamberlain

wouldn't give two hoots. But that's what they want you to think," said Brian.

"Why do they want you to think that?"

"You've read it," he said. "It's desperate stuff. It wouldn't last two nights in the West End. But this way they can sell a few tickets to mugs who think they're getting something too saucy for legit."

"It's not at all funny."

"It's not the remotest bit funny," said Brian. "But it is a comedy. This is what you told me you want to do."

She was being punished, she could see that. He'd put her up for a handful of terrible jobs, and then she'd be in a swimsuit on a quiz show and he'd be happy.

She read it again the night before the audition. It was even worse than she'd thought, and she wanted to be in it so much she thought she might faint from the hunger.

Her character was called Polly, and she was the one who the central character, the husband with the prim, grim wife, was prevented from making love to, over and over again. She sat down at one of the tables in the dingy little club, and the director, a tired man in his sixties with nicotine-stained silver hair, read in for Barbara's scenes. She started to deliver her lines—with some confidence, she thought, and a bit of snap.

"'We can't do it here. Not with your wife upstairs.'"

But he started shaking his head immediately, the moment she'd opened her mouth.

"Is that actually you, or are you trying something?"

She'd never been in a room with someone as posh as

him. Her father would take this meeting alone as evidence that Barbara's life in London was an astonishing social triumph.

She started again, without doing anything different, because she didn't know what he was talking about.

"It is you, isn't it?"

"What?"

"That." He nodded at her mouth. "The accent."

"It's not an accent. It's how I talk."

"In the theater, that's an accent."

He sighed and rubbed his eyes.

"I'm sixty-three years old," he said. "I was the second-youngest director ever to work at the Bristol Old Vic. This is the worst play I've ever read. We meet at perhaps the lowest point of my professional life, and there is no evidence to suggest that there are better days ahead. I could be forgiven for not caring, I'm sure you'd agree. And yet I do care. And if I cast you, it would show that I'd given up, d'you see?"

She didn't, and she said so.

"Why are you resisting?"

"I'm not."

"In the play. You're resisting. And before I go on, I should say, yes, yes, Albert Finney, Tom Courtenay, Richard Burton, kitchen sink, marvelous, marvelous. But there isn't a kitchen sink to be seen, unfortunately. The play is called *In My Lady's Chamber*. So. Why are you resisting? You sound as though you've spent your life selling tuppenny bags of chips. You'd let a man like Nigel have whatever he wants, surely? I need the audience to believe, you see. I'm doomed, I know. I'm a dinosaur. These things are important to me."

She was shaking with rage, but, for reasons that remained opaque to her, she didn't want him to see.

"Anyway. You were a darling to come in and try."

She wanted to remember this man. She had a feeling that she'd never see him again, because he was tired and old and useless, and she wasn't. But she needed to know the name, in case she was ever in a position to stamp on his hand when he was dangling perilously from his chosen profession.

"Sorry," she said sweetly. "I didn't catch your name?"

"Sorry. Very rude of me. Julian Squires."

He offered a limp hand, but she didn't take it. She had that much pride, at least.

She went to see Brian and she burst into tears. He sighed, and shook his head, and then rummaged in his desk drawer until he found a red folder with the words VOICE IMPROVEMENT PROGRAMME written on the cover in large letters. It looked a bit like the book Eamonn Andrews consulted in *This Is Your Life*.

"This won't do you any harm whatever happens," he said. "I've recommended it to a lot of actresses. It's very good, apparently. Michael Aspel and Jean Metcalfe. How Now Brown Cow and all that. She does speak beautifully."

Her father loved Jean Metcalfe. She was on the radio,

VOICE IMPROVEMENT PROGRAMME

Side 1
VIP 2

VIP

Lesson 3
Clearness and
Distinction

JEAN METCALFE
MICHAEL ASPEL

and she spoke in the sort of BBC voice that nobody in the whole of England, north or south, had in real life.

"I could never sound like her in a million years."

"You don't have to sound exactly like her. Just . . . a little bit . . . less like you. If that's what you want. And if it isn't, then let someone take all your clothes off and kill you by spraying gold paint all over you. You break my heart. Every girl on my books would kill to have your assets. And you want to ignore them."

"They're not going anywhere. Can't I be funny and have assets?"

"It's not me, you know that. It's them."

She examined the Voice Improvement Programme. She was the one who wanted to act, and acting was all about turning yourself into someone else, so what did it matter if she did that even before anyone gave her a job?

"And while we're about it," said Brian, "I wonder whether it's time to stop being Barbara from Blackpool."

He was thinking about the next phase of her career, of course. Nobody making a BBC play about unwed mothers down a coal mine would care whether she was called Barbara. But Sabrina had once been Norma Sykes. Steps had to be taken.

"I thought that was what we were talking about."

"We're talking about the Blackpool bit. We're not talking about the Barbara bit."

"What can I do about that?"

"You don't have to be Barbara."

"Are you serious?"

"Not . . . deadly serious."

"I'll leave it, if it's all the same to you."

"A bit deadly, then. Not . . . life-threateningly. But intimidatingly."

"You want me to change my name?"

"You can always change it back, if it doesn't work out."

"Oh, thanks."

That was all it took for her to decide that she never wanted to be Barbara again: it would be a mark of failure, and she wasn't going to fail. It didn't matter. She could change her name and change her voice and she would still be her, because she was a burning blue flame and nothing else, and the flame would burn her up unless it could find its way out.

"Have you got a name for me already?"

"Of course not. I'm not that much of a little Hitler. We choose it together."

So Barbara chose Honor and Cathy from *The Avengers*,

Glynis and Vivien and Yvonne from the movies, even Lucy from the television. And when all the names she liked had been turned down, they settled for Brian's very first suggestion, Sophie Straw. Sophie sounded posh, she understood that.

"Why Straw?"

"Sandie Shaw. Sophie Straw. It sounds good."

"But why not Sophie Simpson?"

"The shorter the better."

"Smith, then."

"What's wrong with Straw?"

"What do you like about it?"

"I'm a happily married man."

"You've told me before."

"But if even I, a happily married man, somehow end up thinking about rolls in the hay, imagine how all the unhappily married men will feel."

Sophie Straw wrinkled up her nose.

"That's a bit creepy."

"I don't want to be the bearer of bad news, my sweet. But there are some aspects of this business that are a bit creepy."

NICK HORNBY

The following day, Brian sent Sophie Straw up for a part as a young housewife in a soap commercial. She was pretty sure that he was trying to break her spirit. She'd spent the evening listening to Brian's elocution records on Marjorie's record player and practicing her best Jean Metcalfe voice, but this time they stopped her even before she was asked to speak. A man from the soap manufacturer's was sitting in the room with the director, and he smiled and shook his head.

"I'm sorry, Sophie," said the director. "Not this time."

"Can I ask why not?"

The man from the soap manufacturer's whispered into the director's ear and the director shrugged.

"He says you're nobody's idea of a housewife. You're too pretty, and your shape is all wrong."

"What's wrong with my shape?"

The soap man laughed. "Nothing," he said. "That's what's wrong with it. We're looking for something a little mumsier."

She remembered the mayor of Blackpool: kiddies and cream buns, kiddies and cream buns.

"I could have just got married recently," she said, and once again she was sickened by her own hunger. She should have walked out, tipped the table over, spat at them; instead she was begging.

"It's an advertisement for soap, darling. We haven't got time to explain how long you've been married and where you met your husband and how you're still watching your figure."

"Thanks for coming in anyway," said the director. "I'll certainly remember you if I'm doing something that's a better match."

"What would that be?" she asked.

"Oh, you know. A glamorous drink. Babycham, Dubonnet, that sort of thing. Maybe cigarettes. Something that isn't, you know, the opposite of you."

"I'm the opposite of soap?"

"No, no. I'm sure you're lovely and clean. You're the opposite of domestic, though, aren't you?"

"Am I?"

"Are you married, Sophie?"

"Well. No. But I think I could pretend to be married, for two minutes, in a soap advertisement."

"I'll walk you out," said the soap man.

The director smiled to himself and shook his head gently.

When they were out of earshot, the soap man asked her out to dinner. He was wearing a wedding ring, of course.

She was approaching the end of her third week of unemployment. She had failed to convince men in studios, clubs, and theaters all over the West End that she could be a housewife, a teacher, a policewoman, a secretary . . . She had even failed an audition for a part as a stripper, despite being more or less told by everybody else that she looked like one. She looked too much like an actress playing a stripper, apparently. The irony of this particular obstacle to employment as an actress was lost on them. The rejections, it seemed to her, were becoming more and more inventive, more and more humiliating, and Brian didn't have a lot left for her anyway. Everything he made her go up for seemed to prove him right. She wasn't cut out for this. And anyway, if she was prepared to play strippers in horrible little theaters, she could hardly pretend that Brian's plans for her were sordid. There wasn't much difference between playing strippers in vulgar plays and stripping.

"There must be something."

"The only script I've been sent that even contains a young female is a *Comedy Playhouse*."

Comedy Playhouse was a series of one-off half-hour shows that the BBC used as a launching pad for new comedies. If the crits were good and the BBC were happy, then sometimes the shows became a series. *Steptoe and Son* had started on *Comedy Playhouse* and look what had happened to that.

"I'd love to do a *Comedy Playhouse*," said Sophie.

"Yes," said Brian. "I can imagine you might."

"So why not?"

"It's the lead."

"I'd love not to get a lead. It would be a step up from not getting Secretary Two."

"And it's not very you."

He went through the very small pile on his desk, found the script, and began to read.

"'Cicely is well-spoken, petite, varsity-educated, the daughter of a vicar. She is utterly unprepared for married life, and struggles even to boil an egg.' Shall I go on?"

"That's me. I struggle even to boil an egg. What's it about?"

"It's about . . . Well, not much, really. Marriage. She's married to a man. They make a bit of a mess of everything but they muddle through. It's called *Wedded Bliss?*"

"Does it really have a question mark, or are you just saying it like that?"

"It really does have a question mark."

"You wouldn't think people could be unfunny with punctuation, would you?"

"It's pretty wretched stuff, I'm afraid. The sad thing is, the writers are actually quite good. Do you ever listen to *The Awkward Squad* on the radio?"

"I love *The Awkward Squad*."

She hadn't heard it since she left home, and she felt a sharp pang of homesickness: she loved listening with her father to the Sunday lunchtime repeat. It was the only program on television or radio that they both found funny. They tried to time the washing-up for 1:30, and for thirty minutes they were perfectly happy, probably the only family in Britain—if two people could qualify as a family— who enjoyed cleaning the plates more than they enjoyed eating off them. Neither of them could cook a roast, but they could scrub the crusted pans with Brillo pads and laugh. *The Awkward Squad* was about a group of men who'd ended up working in the same factory after doing National Service together, and replicating the roles that they'd carved out for themselves in the army. The chinless, clueless captain was their boss, the owner's son, and the loud, dim sergeant major worked as the foreman. The lads on the shop floor were shiftless or dreamy or crooked or militant. There wasn't a single woman in the program, of course, which was probably why Barbara's father loved it, but Barbara forgave them that. It might even have been one of the reasons why Barbara loved it too: most female characters in comedy series depressed her. She couldn't put her finger on how they managed it, but it seemed like each episode of *The Awkward Squad* was about something. There were daft jokes and silly voices and complicated con tricks, but the characters lived in a country she knew, even though nobody in it was from up north.

"*The Awkward Squad* was written by Tony Holmes and Bill Gardiner, and produced by Dennis Maxwell-Bishop," she said, in her best BBC announcer's voice. "The part of Captain Smythe was played by Clive Richardson, Sparky was—"

"All right, all right," said Brian. "Can you do that for every show on the radio?"

She reckoned she probably could. Why wouldn't she? Other girls dreamed of meeting Elvis Presley or Rock Hudson; she had always wanted half an hour alone with Dennis Maxwell-Bishop. It was not a fantasy she could share with many people.

"That one just sticks in my mind, for some reason."

"Well, this is the same lot," said Brian. "The writers, Dennis, Clive—"

"And if I went to the audition they'd be there?" she said.

"In person?" said Brian. "Good Lord, no. They're much too grand for that."

"Oh, well," said Sophie.

"I was being sarcastic," said Brian. "Yes, Tony Holmes and Bill Gardiner, the obscure radio writers, will be there, in person. And Dennis Maxwell-Bishop, the junior comedy producer. And Clive Richardson is playing the part of the husband, so he'll be there to read. They're trying to launch him as a TV star, apparently."

"Then I want to go," said Sophie.

"It's a rotten script and you're completely wrong for it. But if you really have nothing better to do, be my guest. Next week you're mine."

She took the script home and read it through three times. It was even worse than Brian had made it sound, but when she was back at home doing the washing-up, probably in a couple of months' time, she'd be able to tell her father that she'd met the writers of *The Awkward Squad*. It would be the only memory of London worth keeping.

The auditions for *Wedded Bliss?* were in a church hall in Shepherd's Bush, just around the corner from the BBC. There were four men in the room, and two of them looked at each other and burst out laughing when Sophie walked in.

If this had been any other audition, she would have turned straight round and walked out, but she couldn't tell her father she'd met Tony Holmes, Bill Gardiner, or Dennis Maxwell-Bishop until all three of them had looked her in the eye.

"Charming," she said instead of leaving.

One of the two who had managed to keep a straight face looked pained. He was the oldest of the four, she guessed, although he probably wasn't even thirty. He had spectacles and a beard, and he was smoking a pipe.

"What on earth has got into you two idiots? I'm so sorry, Sophie."

"It's not what you're thinking," said one of the idiots.

"What am I thinking?" said Sophie.

"Good point," said the other idiot. "What was she thinking, idiot?"

Both idiots had London accents, which made Sophie warm to them, despite the unpromising start. They couldn't throw her out because she was common, at least.

"She was thinking, Oh, they're laughing at me because I look so wrong for the part. But it wasn't that at all."

"What was it, then?" said Sophie.

"You look like someone we know."

The fourth man, who was neither idiot nor pipe-smoker, looked at her properly for the first time. Up until that point he'd been smoking and doing the crossword in the newspaper.

"She was probably too distracted to be wondering why you were all laughing," he said.

"We weren't all laughing, thank you very much," said the pipe-smoker.

Sophie had sorted out who was who, to her own satisfaction anyway. The crossword-puzzler was Clive Richardson, the pipe-smoker was Dennis the producer, the idiots were Tony and Bill, although she didn't know which one was which.

"Why was I distracted, then?" said Sophie.

"Because you were too busy worrying about how wrong you look for the part."

"You're Clive, aren't you?" said Sophie.

"How did you know that?"

"I recognized your voice. Because of Captain Smythe."

Captain Smythe from *The Awkward Squad*, the factory owner's dim-witted, public-school-educated son, spoke in a ridiculous voice, like the Queen if she'd been born simple.

This time all three of the other men laughed, although Clive was clearly stung.

"Have you actually read your own work?" he said to the idiots. "Well-spoken, petite, varsity-educated, the daughter of a vicar."

"You don't think I'm petite?" said Sophie. "This duffel coat makes me look bigger than I actually am."

She made her Lancashire accent broader, just to make sure she got the laugh. She did, from three of the four. Clive, on the other hand, looked as though he might never laugh again.

"All this laughter," said Clive. "It's ironic, really, considering the script we have in front of us."

"Here we go," said Tony or Bill.

"Excuse me," said Sophie. "Which one are you? Bill or Tony?"

"I'm Bill."

He was the older-looking one of the two. He wasn't necessarily older, but Tony had a young face, and his beard wasn't as bushy.

"Sorry," said Dennis, and he introduced everyone.

"Clive thinks this is the worst comedy in the history of television," said Tony. "That's why the laughter is ironic."

"And he's right. We haven't laughed much today," said Bill gloomily.

"Well, I enjoyed it," said Sophie. "It must have been fun to write."

The writers both snorted, at exactly the same time.

"'Fun to write,'" said Bill. "Ooh, that was fun to write, Tony!"

"Wasn't it just," said Tony. "I'm so glad I'm a writer!"

"Me too," said Bill. "It's just fun all day!"

They both stared at her. She was mystified.

"It wasn't," said Tony. "It was horrible. Torture. Like everything else we do."

"And before you say anything," said Bill, "the question mark was Dennis's idea, not ours. We hate it."

"I do wish you'd stop going on about the wretched question mark," said Dennis. "That's the first thing you've told everybody who walks through the door."

Dennis began to bash his pipe furiously against one of the half-dozen ashtrays on the table. All of them were overflowing, and the hall smelled like a smoking carriage on a train even though they were occupying only one small corner.

"Our names are underneath your bloody question mark," said Tony. "We are trying to make a living writing comedy. You've made us unemployable."

Dennis sighed.

"I've agreed it was a mistake, I've apologized, we're going to get rid of it, now let's try and put it behind us."

"But how can we, when you're supposed to be a comedy producer, and we now know what you think comedy is?"

"What do you want me to do? Tell me, and I'll do it."

"It's too late," said Tony. "It has been sent out to our fellow professionals."

"Like Sophie here," said Clive. She knew he was being sarcastic again.

The annoying thing, Sophie thought, was that he was very handsome. Actors who looked like him didn't usually speak in silly braying voices on radio comedy shows; they were always too busy rescuing busty damsels in distress on the television or in the cinema. He was, she thought, even better-looking than Simon Templar. He had the most disconcertingly bright blue eyes, and cheekbones that made her envious.

"Did you think it was funny, Sophie?" said Dennis.

"The question mark?"

"No," said Bill. "We know that's not funny. The script."

"Oh," said Sophie. "Well. Like I said. I enjoyed it very much."

"But did you think it was funny?"

"Funny," she repeated, as if this were a quality that she hadn't previously considered in her assessment of their comedy script.

"Jokes and things."

"Well," she said. And then, because she'd now met them all and she wasn't going to see them again, "No."

For some reason, this answer seemed to delight Bill and Tony.

"We told you!" Bill said to Dennis.

"You always say everything's awful," said Dennis. "I never know when to believe you."

"What do you think is wrong with it?" said Bill.

"Can I be honest?" she said.

"Yes. We want honesty."

"Everything," she said.

"So when you said you enjoyed it . . ."

"I didn't," she said. "Not at all. I'm not being funny . . ."

"You're not the only one," said Clive.

"But . . . I didn't understand what it was supposed to be about."

"Fair enough," said Tony.

"Why did you want to write it?"

"We were asked," said Bill.

"Asked to do what, though?"

"We were asked to come up with a show about marriage," said Dennis.

"Oh," said Sophie. "So why didn't you do that?"

Bill laughed and clutched at his chest, as if Sophie had just stabbed him in the heart.

"See, in *The Awkward Squad*, the people seemed real, even the sort of cartoonish ones. These two, the husband and wife, they seem like cartoons even though they just say normal things without jokes in."

Bill leaned forward in his seat and nodded.

"And all the stuff about marriage . . . It's like it's just been stuck on. I mean, they're always arguing. But there's no reason for them to argue, is there? They're exactly the same. And he must have known she was a bit dopey before he proposed."

She got her first laugh from Clive then.

"You can shut up," Bill said to him.

"And why is she a vicar's daughter? I know her father's a vicar. But . . . it never gets mentioned again. Are you just saying she's got iron knickers? What's she going to do with them, once she's married? They'll have to come off."

"Right," said Bill. "Thanks."

"Sorry," said Sophie. "I've probably said too much."

"No, this is all very helpful," said Tony.

"And why is she so dopey anyway? It says in the script she's been to college. How did she manage that? She couldn't find her way to the bus stop, let alone university."

"Well," said Clive, with an air of satisfaction. "There's nothing left to audition for. You've destroyed it."

"I'm sorry," she said, and she stood up to leave. She had no intention of going anywhere until they threw her out, but if nobody said anything to stop her, at least she'd know it was over.

"We can read through it, and then Bill and Tony can go off and do another draft."

"Another draft of what, though?" said Bill. "It's like Clive said. There's nothing left."

"Let's read through it anyway," said Dennis. "Please. We're recording it in just under two weeks."

There was a lot of grumbling, but no dissent. Everyone turned to the first page. Sophie was torn. She wanted to read as well as she could; she also wanted to read at a snail's pace. She was desperate to make the afternoon last as long as possible; she wanted to stay in this room, with these people, forever.

COMEDY
PLAYHOUSE

4

Tony Holmes and Bill Gardiner met in a holding cell in a police station in Aldershot the week before Christmas in 1959. The local police wanted the military police to take them back to the barracks; the military police didn't want anything to do with them. While the two sets of authorities wrangled, they sat there for twenty-four hours, talking, smoking, and not sleeping, both of them feeling stupid and very afraid. They ascertained that they had both been arrested in the same place in the same street, two hours apart; they didn't even tell each other what they had been doing wrong, or where precisely they had been doing it. They didn't need to. They just knew.

Neither of them had ever been caught back at home, in London, but for different reasons. Bill hadn't been caught because he was smart, and knew the places to go, the clubs and the bars and even the public conveniences, although he didn't use them very often. The evening's events had reminded him why. The policeman who'd arrested him in Aldershot may well have been an agent provocateur, one of those officers who hated his kind with such a peculiar and obsessive passion that they were prepared to spend entire evenings trying to catch them. There were plenty of them in London too. Tony had never been caught in London because he'd never tried anything in London, or anywhere else for that matter. He wasn't sure about a lot of things, including who and what he was, but he had no clear idea why he'd decided to try and find the answers to these questions right before the end of his National Service. Loneliness, certainly, and boredom, and the sudden desperate need for the touch of a fellow human being, of any gender, though admittedly he was only likely to find one of the two in the gents' conveniences in Tennyson Street.

In the end, nobody had the stomach to prosecute them, and the following day they returned to the barracks to complete the rest of their National Service. Whenever they looked back on that evening—which they did frequently, although never together, and never out loud—there wasn't much they recognized about the circumstances of their arrest. Had they really been desperate enough to get so near to humiliation and possible ruin? But the content of their twenty-four-hour conversation stayed reassuring and familiar, even years later: they talked about comedy. They discovered their mutual passion for Ray Galton and Alan Simpson within minutes of meeting, they could quote whole

chunks of *Hancock's Half Hour* at each other, and they tried to remember as much as they could of "The Blood Donor" so that they could perform it. They were pretty sure they were word perfect on the hospital scene, with Bill playing Hancock and Tony, with the higher, more nasal voice, taking on the Hugh Lloyd part.

They kept in touch when they were demobbed. Tony lived in east London and Bill was up in Barnet, so they used to meet in town, in a Soho coffee bar—once a week, at first, when they were both still working in the jobs they were trying to escape. (Tony was helping his father in the newsagent's he owned, Bill was a pen-pusher at the Department of Transport.) They spent the first few months talking, and then eventually overcame their embarrassment and started trying to write together, on two notepads. Later, when they took the leap into unemployment, they met every day, in the same coffee bar, and would continue to do so until they could afford an office.

They never talked about the other thing they may or may not have had in common, but Bill was still shocked when Tony got married. He'd never even mentioned seeing someone. Bill went to the wedding, and Tony's bride, a sweet, quiet, clever brunette called June who worked at the BBC, seemed to know all about her husband's partner, or as much as she would have wanted to know anyway. And maybe there wasn't anything else to find out. Bill and Tony wrote comedy scripts together; that was who they were, and Aldershot Police Station had nothing to do with anything.

They did much better than they had dared to hope. They sold a few one-liners to some of the older radio comedians almost immediately. They were employed full-time to provide material for Albert Bridges, whose only remaining listeners were still grateful to him for his company and good humor during the Blitz. When first the people of Britain and then, eventually, the BBC came to the conclusion that Bridges was past his best, Bill and Tony sold *The Awkward Squad*, a comedy series inspired by their National Service experience—or the parts of it they felt they could draw on, anyway.

And now they had been invited to write for *Comedy Playhouse*. They had been itching to try their hand at TV, but when Dennis took them for a drink in Great Portland Street one evening and told them that he wanted a breezy, lighthearted look at contemporary marriage, they were a little cowed by the brief. After Dennis had gone home, neither of them said anything for a while.

"Well," said Bill, "you're married."

"I don't know if my marriage is going to help us very much. It's quite, you know. Particular."

"Can I ask you something about your marriage?"

"What about it?"

"Did June know when she married you?"

"I don't know what there was to know."

"You got nicked for importuning in a men's lavatory. She might want to know that."

"I was released without charge. And I didn't importune anybody, if you remember."

"So you didn't think that was information worth passing on?"

"No."

"And what about the . . . well, the practical side?"

"Is this going to help us come up with an idea?"

"No. I'm just interested."

"Too bad."

"You'll have to be helpful somehow, though. I don't know what it's like to sleep with someone night after night. Or argue with them about what side to watch. Or what it's like to have a mother-in-law."

"We always agree about the television. We have exactly the same tastes."

"Do you think he knows I'm queer?" said Bill. "And he's playing an elaborate practical joke on me?"

"How would he know?"

Bill was extremely careful. He always made sure that he knew the Test score, and that he dressed badly, and sometimes he made careful reference to girls. But then, he was afraid, like a lot of men in his position. He was always one mistake away from prison.

They decided, like God, that if they got the man right, the woman could somehow be made out of him. And the man in *Wedded Bliss?* wasn't too bad, they thought. He was sort of odd, and oddly lovable, prone to fits of surreal rage provoked by everything in England that drove Tony and Bill insane—a sort of sitcom Jimmy Porter from *Look Back in Anger*. But Sophie was right about Cicely, the woman. She turned out to be hopeless, a cartoon sketch. This was unsurprising, seeing as they had borrowed her wholesale from a cartoon, the Gambols comic strip that appeared in the *Express*. The character of Cicely was as close to Gaye Gambol as they could get in script form. She didn't look anything like her, though: Cicely, they imagined, was going to be sweet-looking, rather than curvy, probably because all the actresses that Dennis had suggested seemed very BBC, and BBC actresses all had big eyes, sweet natures, and flat chests. They certainly weren't sexy. But they extracted all of Gaye's feminine idiocies from her and sprinkled them liberally over the script. Cicely lusted after mink coats, burned dinners, overspent her housekeeping allowance, and made complicated, childlike excuses for doing so, missed appointments, failed to understand the simplest mechanical instrument. It wasn't as though Tony and Bill ever believed that Gaye Gambol was

real, or true, and nor did they believe that there were any housewives (or women, or people) like her. But they knew she was popular. If they didn't have the nerve to produce somebody original and fresh, then at least they wanted a safe bet.

At which point Sophie walked in. She had Gaye Gambol's WASP waist, large bust, blonde hair, and big, fluttery eyelashes, and Tony and Bill burst out laughing.

Sophie and Clive ended up performing the script from beginning to end, mostly because Tony and Bill wanted to keep Sophie in the room. They loved her. She delivered her lines with an ease and a sense of timing that had been beyond the reach of every other actress they'd seen that week, and she even got a few laughs out of the script, much to Clive's chagrin, although some of the laughs were derived from her decision to read Cicely in her Jean Metcalfe voice. Sophie smiled politely at a couple of his lines, but that was the most she could manage.

"That's not fair," said Clive.

"What isn't?" said Bill.

"You might at least have pretended to laugh. I have been reading the bloody thing all bloody day."

"The thing is," said Bill, "you hate comedy."

"He does," Tony said to Sophie. "He's always moaning about it. He wants to do Shakespeare and Lawrence of Arabia."

"Just because it's not my favorite thing doesn't mean I don't want laughs," said Clive. "I hate the dentist, but it doesn't mean I don't want fillings."

"Nobody wants fillings," Tony said.

"No, but . . . if they need them."

"So laughs are like fillings to you?" said Bill. "Painful and unpleasant, but necessary? What a bundle of joy you are."

"You're good at comedy, though," said Sophie. "You're very funny as Captain Smythe."

"He hates Captain Smythe," said Tony.

"Well, forgive me if I'd rather play Hamlet than some twittish upper-class ass."

"Sophie, what would you like to do?" said Tony.

"How d'you mean?"

"What character would you like to play?"

"Well," said Sophie uncertainly, "Cicely, really."

"No," said Tony. "Cicely's dead. Gone. Chucked out of the window."

"Oh, Christ," said Clive.

"What?" said Bill.

"You're offering to write something for her?"

"We're just chewing the fat."

"You are. You're offering to write something for her.

Bloody hell. You've never asked me what I want to do. You just say, 'Here's an upper-class twit with a silly voice. Make him funny.'"

"Because you've made it very clear that you're destined for better things," said Bill.

"Well, I wouldn't mind having my own series."

"Oh, that would dull some of the pain, would it?"

"Yes. It would, rather."

"You see, we can't even tell if you're joking," said Tony.

"Which is why we're not rushing to write you your own comedy series," said Bill.

"Where are you from, Sophie?" said Dennis.

"I'm from Blackpool."

"You see, that's interesting," said Dennis.

"Is it?" Sophie was genuinely surprised.

"Coming from Blackpool is more interesting than being a vicar's daughter."

"Couldn't she be a vicar's daughter from Blackpool?" said Tony.

"She's no vicar's daughter," said Clive.

"I'm assuming that's rude," said Sophie.

There was something in the room, Dennis thought. It had been a long day, with unsuitable actresses reading from a very average script, but Sophie had energized everyone, and she and Clive were sparky with each other.

"What's interesting about her coming from Blackpool anyway?" said Bill.

"There hasn't been a North–South romance in a comedy series that I know of."

"Would anyone buy it, though?" said Clive.

"It's an odd-couple romance. That would be the fun of it."

"Stone me, Dennis," said Bill. "Two people coming from different parts of the country means they're an odd couple?"

"He thinks anyone's odd who hasn't been to Cambridge."

Dennis looked momentarily embarrassed.

"I take your point. Their geographical roots would form only a small part of their incompatibility. When did you first meet someone from London, Sophie?"

She hesitated.

"Not until . . . Well, quite recently."

"When you moved down?"

"A bit before that."

And then, just because she felt safe in the room, she decided to tell them the truth. "I entered a beauty competition back in Blackpool. There was a girl from London who'd gone in for it too. A holidaymaker. Is there somewhere called Gospel something?"

"You're a beauty queen? Oh, that's just perfect," said Clive with glee.

"She only said she entered," said Bill.

"I won it," said Sophie before she could stop herself. "I was Miss Blackpool. For five minutes."

"Well, this explains everything!" said Clive.

"What does it explain?" said Dennis.

"Look at her!"

"I think she won a beauty competition because of the way she looks," said Dennis. "I don't think she looks like that because she won a beauty competition."

"Why only for five minutes?" Tony asked.

"Because then I realized I didn't want to be a beauty queen and I couldn't live in Blackpool anymore. I wanted to come to London and . . . Well, I want to be Lucille Ball."

"Ah," said Bill. "Now you're talking."

"Am I?" said Sophie.

"Of course you are," said Bill. "We all love Lucy."

"Really?"

"We're students of comedy," said Tony. "We love anyone who's funny."

"Lucy is one of our people," said Dennis. "Galton and Simpson are our Shakespeare, obviously. But she's our Jane Austen."

"And we're literally students," said Bill. "We watch and listen to things over and over again. We prefer the repeats, because then we can start to take things apart."

Sophie burst into tears, suddenly and to her intense embarrassment. She hadn't known she was about to cry and she couldn't really explain the intensity of her feeling.

"Are you all right?" said Dennis.

"Yes," she said. "I'm sorry."

"Do you want to call it a day? You could come in tomorrow and we could all talk some more."

"No," she said. "I'm fine. That's the thing. I'm having fun."

They were all still there two hours later.

"How about this? Alan is a handsome, snobbish, angry Conservative. Cicely is a beautiful, chippy, Labor-voting northerner," said Bill.

"She's hardly likely to be called Cicely, is she?" said Clive.

"Fair enough," said Bill. "What shall we call her?"

"What goes with Blackpool?" said Tony.

"Brenda," said Clive. "Beryl."

"What about Barbara?" said Dennis. "Barbara from Blackpool?"

They all looked at Sophie, who seemed to have lost interest in the conversation and was staring hard at the ceiling.

"I like it," said Tony. "Not too common. Just common enough. Alan and Barbara."

"I don't like Alan," said Clive.

"What on earth is wrong with Alan?"

"I think what Clive is saying is that if she gets a name change, he should too," said Bill.

"It's not that at all," said Clive crossly. "My best friend at junior school was called Alan. He was killed in the Blitz."

"I'm betting that's an awful lie," said Tony.

Clive smirked.

"It was the word 'friend' that gave it away," said Bill. "You've never had any. What do you want to be called, then?"

"Quentin."

"Nobody wants to watch a program about someone called Quentin."

"Jim, then."

"Oh, I don't care," said Bill. "Jim is fine. Jim and Barbara. So how did they end up together?"

"He knocked her up," said Clive.

"I think you'll find he didn't," said Sophie firmly.

"I don't think it would go down so well upstairs either," said Dennis.

"Oh, here we go," said Bill.

Bill and Tony loved Dennis, and not just because he loved them. He was clever, and he was enthusiastic, and he was endlessly encouraging. But he was a Corporation man to the tips of his brown suede boots, and his playfulness tended to disappear if he thought that the future of the BBC, or his own future within it, was under any threat, real or imagined.

"O.D. would go for it."

O.D., or Other Dennis as he was known only in their very small circle, was Dennis Main Wilson, another BBC comedy producer, much more experienced and successful than T.D.—This Dennis. When Tony and Bill were bored, or felt that they weren't getting anywhere with an idea, they would drop the possibility of Other Dennis into the conversation, and spend a few minutes painting an idyllic word-picture of what their working life would be like with him.

"Say what you like about O.D., but he'll always go in to bat for his writers," said Bill, mock-wistfully.

"Oh, this really is too much," said Dennis. "I have always gone in to bat for you. Always. Even when the match is lost, and the bowling is fast and hostile. Even when . . . Even when the bat's got ruddy great holes in it. Like this one did."

Tony and Bill hooted joyfully.

"Remember, I'm a real person," said Sophie.

They all stared at her.

"I mean, I have come down to London from the North. And I have met a stuck-up snob. And I could have met him somewhere else."

"Oh, really?" said Clive. "Such as?"

"I used to work in Derry and Toms," said Sophie. "Have you ever been anywhere like that?"

"Many times," said Clive. "And I have managed not to marry anyone who served me."

"Or a nightclub? I could have been a Pussy at the Whisky A Go Go. I thought of it."

"Oh, yes. That's what those girls are for, taking home to mother."

"Your character doesn't have to be exactly like you, though," said Sophie. "You could have human blood in your veins. You could be an intellectual who doesn't meet pretty girls very often."

"Yes," said Bill. "She's right. You could try acting."

"I meet pretty girls all the time," said Clive. "And they meet me back."

"I think he was talking about the intellectual bit," said Tony.

"Could you ever fall in love with someone who poured you a beer in a pub?" said Dennis.

"It's funny you should say that," said Clive. "There's a girl who works behind the bar in the Argyll Arms to whom I have in fact proposed. I was drunk at the time. But I was deadly serious."

"So there we are," said Dennis. "Barbara works in a pub and Jim comes in to meet a friend . . ."

"I refuse to be a bloody Tory, though," said Clive. "Nobody in London with half a brain is going to vote for that lot next week. Anyway, what happened to him working at Number Ten?"

Tony and Bill had forgotten that the hapless husband in *Wedded Bliss?* was originally going to be some kind of thrusting young politico, a press secretary or a speechwriter. That had been dropped when they had turned to the Gambols for inspiration, and the scripts had become so generic that he could only be employed in some unspecified, I'm-off-to-the-office-now-darling white-collar capacity.

"Bloody hell," said Tony. "I'd forgotten all about that. It was just about the only decent idea we had when we started."

"And by the time it reaches the screen, Harold will be in," said Bill. "Jim will be in at the birth of our brave new England."

"My dad would kill me if I were Labor," said Sophie. "He says he's worked too hard to give it all away to the work-shy and the trades unions."

Tony looked at Bill, and Bill looked at Dennis, and each could tell that the other was thinking the same thing. Here was everything they wanted to bring to the screen, in one neat and beautifully gift-wrapped package, handed to them by a ferocious and undiscovered talent who looked like a star. The class system, men and women and the relationships between them, snobbery, education, the North and the South, politics, the way that a new country seemed to be emerging from the dismal old one that they'd all grown up in.

"Thank you," said Bill to Sophie.

"Will you let Brian know, then?" she said.

"Let him know what?"

"About, you know . . . Whether you think I'm right for it."

The men all laughed, a lot, even Clive.

"You *are* it," said Bill.

"But you'd let me do it?"

"We *want* you to do it," said Tony.

"I've never done anything like this before."

"None of us had, until we did," said Dennis. "I didn't know the first thing about producing comedy when they gave me *The Awkward Squad*."

"It's not even worth making a joke," said Tony.

"Like fish in a barrel," said Bill.

"You never learn, Dennis, do you?" said Clive.

Dennis rolled his eyes.

"But . . . Shouldn't I go and be a funny secretary in a terrible play first?"

"If that's what you want to do, be our guest," said Bill.

"And come back and see us in five years. But we haven't really got time to plot out your career, because we urgently need someone to play Barbara. So if you're not interested, clear off."

"I think I could do it," said Sophie.

"You?" said Bill, mock-surprised. "Well. That's an idea. What do you think, Tony?"

"Hmmm," said Tony. "I'm not sure. What's she been in?"

Sophie knew they were joking, but she was much closer to tears of desperation than to laughter.

"Stop torturing the poor girl," said Dennis.

The two writers groaned with disappointment.

"Here's the thing," said Tony. "If you're lucky, you meet the right people at the right time."

"And we've met the right person at the right time," said Dennis.

It took a while for Sophie to understand that he was talking about her.

She went in to see Brian the next morning.

"I've got a job," she said.

"You didn't have to do that," he said. "I told you. Do things my way and you'll be fine."

"I thought I was allowed to do things my way for a month."

"Yes," he said. "But I didn't want you going back to Barkers of Kensington afterward."

"Derry and Toms."

"That may be a step up, I don't know. But it seems like the same thing to me."

"No," she said. "I used to work at Derry and Toms. I'm not going back there. I got the *Comedy Playhouse* part."

"The part of the wife?"

"No, they're taking a chance and giving me the husband."

"Oh, for God's sake," said Brian.

"I thought you'd be pleased."

"Of course I'm not pleased. It wasn't a very good script, you're not right for it, it won't go to series, and it'll take me that bit longer to get you spray-painted."

"They're changing the script."

"Why?"

"I told them it wasn't very good."

"They liked that, did they?"

"They seemed to. They're writing a new one for me."

Brian stared at her.

"Are you sure any of this actually happened? Who was there?"

"Clive, Dennis, Tony, and Bill."

"And have they cleared this with Tom?"

"Who's Tom?"

"Tom Sloan. The Head of Light Entertainment."

"Not yet."

"Ah."

"What does that mean?"

"Maybe we shouldn't call off the bikini-shopping expedition on Monday after all."

"You were going to take me bikini shopping?"

"Not me, dear. Patsy. I'm not interested in looking at curvy young women in bikinis. I'm deeply in love with my wife and I'm only interested in money."

She now understood that Brian emphasized his feelings for his wife over and over again for the same reason that people with a fear of heights told themselves not to look down when they were at the top of a tall building: he was afraid. Every time she went into his office, another beautiful young woman was coming out. It was sweet, really. He actually was deeply in love with his wife and he wanted to keep it that way.

Tom Sloan told Dennis that he wouldn't dream of casting an unknown actress in the role of Cicely.

"Well," said Dennis, "she's not called Cicely anymore. She's called Barbara and she's from Blackpool. It's a whole new script."

"Who on earth are you going to get to play someone called Barbara from Blackpool?"

"Sophie Straw," said Dennis.

"Who's Sophie Straw?"

"She's the woman you said you wouldn't dream of casting."

"Right," said Tom. "So your only argument is a circular one."

"It's what the boys want."

"Really? What about you?"

It was what Dennis wanted, but whenever he was in Tom Sloan's office, the words "yes" and "no" seemed impossible to say. They contained none of the ambiguity that meetings with his superiors seemed to require. In the past, he had found himself watching what everyone else was doing before committing himself firmly and irrevocably to tea or coffee, if it was being offered. But he did want Sophie. He thought she was funny, and magnetic, and beautiful. And also he thought she'd be brilliant in the role that the boys were creating for her. They would all regret it if Tom put his foot down.

Oh, to hell with it.

"I think it's an interesting idea," he said. He could feel his pulse start to race.

"A good idea?"

He hesitated.

"Well. On balance, I don't think it's the worst idea in the world."

He hadn't known he had it in him.

Sloan sighed.

"You'd better give me this whole new script, then."

"It doesn't exist yet. They only met Sophie on Thursday."

Tom shook his head impatiently.

"Well, you'd better bring this Sophie up to see me, then."

Dennis took her up to the fourth floor the following afternoon. She looked enchanting, he thought. When she'd come in to audition she looked like a film star, but she'd toned it all down a little for Tom, who was a stern Presby-

terian. The dress was longer and the lipstick wasn't as bright.

"You look terrific," Dennis said as they were waiting for the lift.

"Thank you," she said.

"For the interview, I mean."

"Oh."

"And . . . in life. You look terrific in life and appropriate for the interview. At the same time. Terrific and appropriate."

He decided to stop there.

"Have you got any advice?" said Sophie. "Should I be flirty?"

"Now?"

"With Tom Sloan."

"Oh. Yes. I see what you mean. No, not flirty. And he's

very suspicious of people who he thinks are telling him what he wants to hear."

"Right-o. What happens if he says no? What do we do then?"

"We'll cross that bridge when we come to it."

"We're about to come to it."

The lift had arrived, but Sophie made no move to get into it. The doors closed and it was called elsewhere.

"Brian doesn't think he'll say yes."

"He'll love you."

"But what will we do if he doesn't?"

"I don't know," said Dennis. "We'd have to have a chat."

"Would you just make it without me?"

"The boys wouldn't like that. They're writing for you."

"So what could they do?"

"I've no idea."

"What are their choices?"

"It depends on how cross they are, I suppose."

"What about if they're very cross?"

"They could march off and show it to the other side, I suppose."

"They don't have *Comedy Playhouse*, do they?"

"No. They'd have to sketch out a series, but they've got lots of ideas. Anyway. It's not going to come to that."

"Would you go with us?"

"No. I'm a BBC employee. More's the pity. The money's much better over there. But please. It's all going to be fine."

The lift came back and this time Sophie got in it.

"Thank you," she said when the doors had closed.

"For what?"

"I've got something to come back with if he doesn't think I'm a good idea."

"No," said Dennis. "No. We don't want to mention any of that to Tom. He hates the other lot. He's losing all his best people."

"I can see why," said Sophie.

"He hasn't even done anything yet!" said Dennis.

He didn't want to get out of the lift when the doors opened upstairs, just as Sophie hadn't wanted to get into it downstairs. But Sophie had already gone, and he was obliged to chase after her.

So," said Tom Sloan, when they had been served tea and talked about Sophie's favorite BBC series. "I understand the boys are jigging the script around a bit for you."

"They're chucking the old one altogether."

"I rather liked it."

"Well," said Sophie, "there's no accounting for taste," and she laughed.

Dennis felt a sudden urge to go to the lavatory.

"What was wrong with it?"

"Ooh, it was awful," she said. "They were a right couple of drips."

"And there was me hoping it might become a series," he said, and laughed.

"Oh, no," said Sophie firmly. She was, Dennis could

see, trying very hard not to tell him what he wanted to hear.

"Well," said Sloan, "the thing is, as Head of Light Entertainment, if I want something to be a series, it usually happens."

"Was *Talk of the Devil* your idea?"

Dennis didn't know whether he could stay in the room. *Talk of the Devil* was a comedy series about the Devil. He had gone to all the trouble of adopting human form so that he could work in the Vehicle Registration Department of a provincial town hall. It hadn't gone down terribly well with either critics or audiences, and hadn't been commissioned for a second series. Nobody talked about *Talk of the Devil*, not out loud.

"Unfortunately it never quite found its feet," said Sloan. "I thought it had some very good things in it."

"It couldn't have found its feet if you'd cut them off and stuffed them into its mouth," said Sophie. "You don't want another one of those on your hands."

Tom Sloan had gone from enchantment to irritation and mild outrage.

"There are a lot of good actresses from the North who could play Barbara," said Sloan.

Sophie was amazed.

"Really? Comic actresses?"

"Yes."

"Like who?"

"Marcia Bell, for example. She's very good."

"I've never heard of her."

"That's a coincidence, because we've never heard of you," said Sloan.

"Marcia Bell, Dennis?"

They both turned to look at him.

"Well," he said, "she's one way we could go, certainly."

Sophie didn't draw a finger across her throat, because she was on her best behavior, but she managed to convey, with a little smile and her eyes, that Dennis was a dead man.

"How funny is she, Dennis?" said Sophie.

"On a scale of one to ten?" he said, and laughed.

"Yes," said Sophie.

"If you like," said Sloan.

"Well," he said, "on a good day . . ."

"What was her best day?"

Dennis stood up.

"Anyway," he said. "Thanks so much for finding the time to say hello."

"Oh, he doesn't mind," said Sophie. "He knows I'm right."

Dennis looked at Tom Sloan. It wasn't entirely clear that either of these assertions was correct. Dennis sat down again.

"The other thing is," said Sophie, "do you really want to lose us all to the other side?"

"Who am I losing?"

"Not Dennis," said Sophie. "He'll stay here, won't you, Dennis? He's a BBC man from his head to the holes in his socks."

Dennis smiled weakly. He presumed she wasn't being complimentary.

"But Bill, Tony, and I . . . The trouble is, the money is so much better over there."

"They don't even have a *Comedy Playhouse*," said Sloan. "You can't take a thirty-minute program to them and expect them to know what to do with it."

The commercial channel was Sloan's nemesis—he'd lost a lot of his star writers and performers over the last few years. Sophie had altered the power balance in the room simply by mentioning the other lot.

"We wouldn't be taking one program to them," said Sophie. "We'd be taking a whole series."

"Have they got enough material for a series?" Sloan said to Dennis.

"Easily," said Sophie. "This morning we were talking about the second series."

"The second series?"

Sloan had the look of a man who had arrived on the railway platform just as the train was leaving the station. To Dennis's amazement, he started chasing after it.

"Listen," he said. "Before you do anything too hasty, why don't we just see how the *Playhouse* goes?"

Sophie made a face suggesting that although this suggestion was not without its merits, it didn't meet all her expectations. She was extraordinary, thought Dennis. They had come up here hoping to persuade Tom Sloan to give an entirely unknown and inexperienced actress a starring role in the BBC's showcase comedy series. They had achieved this, against considerable odds, and now she was acting as though she'd been vaguely insulted.

She brightened, eventually. She was prepared, apparently, to give him a chance.

"Oh, all right, then," she said.

Dennis was too angry to speak to her on the way down. She didn't care.

"You'll thank me one day," she said.

"Why on earth will I ever thank you for the most excruciating fifteen minutes of my life?"

"Because the rewards will be greater than the pain."

"There isn't enough money in the world," said Dennis.

"It's not about money, is it?" said Sophie.

"Isn't it? So what is it about?"

"I don't know yet," she said. "And neither do you. Oh, and I haven't forgiven you yet either."

"Me?"

"Yes, you. You and bloody Marcia Bell."

"Are you always going to ask for this much?"

"You'd better hope so," she said.

5

ennis lived in a rented flat in Hammersmith with his wife, Edith, and a cat. That evening, neither Edith nor the cat showed the slightest interest in his return—the cat because she was asleep for most of it, and Edith because she was in the middle of an affair with a married man. Perhaps it wasn't the middle; perhaps it was the very beginning, but it wasn't anywhere near its end, Dennis could tell. Edith was elsewhere even when they were at home, visiting him only to convey disappointment and dissatisfaction.

The most excruciating time of his life had not been spent in Tom Sloan's office, despite what he'd told Sophie. The most excruciating time of his life had been spent reading and then rereading a letter he'd found between the pages of a manuscript she'd brought home from work. He'd put it back where he'd found it and hadn't said anything, and now he was just waiting, although he had no idea what he was waiting for. His anguish meant that he made a poor husband, silent and watchful and raw.

Edith was tall, dark, beautiful, and clever, and when she agreed to marry him his friends made the kinds of jokes that friends were supposed to make in those circumstances, all of them various articulations of disbelief along the lines of "How did you hook her, you lucky so-and-so?" They didn't seem so funny now, and he didn't seem so lucky. He shouldn't have hooked her. She wasn't the sort of catch one could take home and show off to people; she was the sort of catch that drags the angler off the end of the pier and pulls him out to sea before tearing him to pieces as he's drowning. He shouldn't have been fishing at all, not when he was so ill-equipped.

Why had she married him? He still wasn't sure. She must have thought that he was going places, but then he got the sense that he wasn't traveling as fast or as far as she'd been expecting. This was unfair, because despite the constant barbs he had to endure about Other Dennis, he was doing all right for himself. Tom Sloan liked him, up until but possibly not including recent incidents; he had good relationships with writers and actors, and the programs were good, mostly, with only the occasional misfire. (He had to take some of the blame, he knew, for *Talk of the Devil*.)

The problem was that Edith didn't really have a funny bone in her entire body and couldn't see that comedy was any sort of a job for a man with a university education.

She'd presumed that he'd trudge through a couple of years with people like Bill and Tony, and then move on to somewhere smarter, to News and Current Affairs, or to one of the arts programs. Dennis, however, loved his job, and wanted to work with funny writers and funny actors for the rest of his life.

Edith was an editor at Penguin Books and had met her lover at work. Vernon Whitfield was a poet and essayist, a frequent contributor to the Third Program, older than her and quite insufferably serious-minded. His last radio talk had been entitled "Sartre, Stockhausen, and the Death of the Soul." Even before Dennis had found the letter, he'd always turned the radio off when he heard the familiar drone. If he could have chosen any living person to represent everything he opposed, Whitfield would probably have been the man.

And now Edith was sleeping with him, and Dennis didn't know what to do about it. She would leave him in the end, he supposed, but he knew he wouldn't be able to leave her, not unless he awoke from this miserable dream and realized that a wife who chose to sleep with another man was unlikely to make him very happy anytime soon, and a wife who chose to so much as smile at Vernon Whitfield was in any case the least suitable life partner he could possibly have found. What a terrible thing an education was, he thought, if it produced the kind of mind that despised entertainment and the people who valued it.

Edith didn't want to stay at Penguin Books, of course. She hated being stuck in Harmondsworth, right out near London Airport, for a start, and anyway she wanted to move to Jonathan Cape or Chatto & Windus, proper publishers who happened to be based in proper parts of town. She wouldn't ever confess to disapproving of the Penguin principle, the idea of selling books to people who had never previously bought them; she was a socialist, and an intellectual, and in theory she was heartily in favor of creating more people like her. But there was something about it that made her feel queasy, Dennis could tell, and she'd been appalled by the sex-starved herd buying copies of *Lady Chatterley's Lover* in their millions. Dennis bought one himself, just to annoy her, and read it in bed, guffawing at all the silly dirty parts. That drove her mad, so he'd stopped. It wasn't doing him much good anyway, in any direction.

What was he doing with her? How on earth could he love her? But he did. Or, at least, she made him feel sick, sad, and distracted. Perhaps there was another way of describing that unique and useless combination of feelings, but "love" would have to do for now. He, like everybody else in the room, had been charmed by Sophie, by her laugh and her eyes and her sense of humor, and on the way home he'd tried to imagine what it might be like to take her out to dinner, take her to bed, marry her. But he'd failed. He was a Cambridge English graduate with a pipe and a beard, and he was doomed to be with someone like Edith.

E dith hadn't done any shopping, so there wasn't anything to eat.

"Do you want to go out for something?" he asked her.

"I don't think so," she said. "I have a lot to read. There are eggs, I think, if you're hungry. And some bread."

"How was your day?"

"Oh, bloody," she said.

"Bloody," he had learned, didn't mean what it might have meant to a soldier or a surgeon. It usually meant that a telephone call with a politics professor had gone on longer than she had wanted it to.

"Oh dear," he said. "Did you get out at all?"

She looked at him.

"Did you try calling me? I had to go into town for a meeting."

"No, I didn't call. But it was a lovely afternoon."

"Oh," she said. "Yes."

"That's all I meant."

It wasn't all he'd meant at all. But that was the sort of dangerous, poison-dart territory one could wander into, with just a casual observation about the weather.

"How about you?" She didn't often ask, and he took the feigned interest as a sign of guilt.

"Had a very tricky meeting," he said.

"What does 'tricky' mean?"

He imagined things, he knew he did, but he definitely heard a faint mocking superiority, a refusal to believe that anything connected with light entertainment could ever be onerous.

"It means exactly the same as it does in your job, I should think. I mean, there wasn't any blood, obviously. But there were very difficult moments involving very strong characters."

She sighed heavily and picked up a manuscript. He'd misjudged his tone, again. He always did. How on earth could she love him? But she didn't.

"I'm going to have a bath," he said. "Do you want scrambled eggs, if I make them later?"

"No thanks," she said. "And I think she's just gone in the bathroom."

"She" was Mrs. Posnanski, their Polish landlady, who lived on the top two floors of the house. Edith and Dennis had the whole of the ground floor, but the bathroom was on the half-landing. If Mrs. Posnanski had only just gone in, it meant that she wouldn't be out for hours.

"Do you mind awfully if I turn the radio on?"

"Then I'd have to read in the bedroom."

"I'll go for a walk, then."

It was intended as an expression of pique, but Edith didn't say anything, so Dennis went for a walk down to the river. On the way home, he stopped off at the Rose and Crown for a Scotch egg and a pint, and he watched a game of darts. If, during his engagement to Edith, someone had tried to explain how lonely marriage could be, he wouldn't have believed it.

There were four mornings of rehearsals, Tuesday to Friday, 10 a.m. to 1 p.m. On Saturday they met the director of the program, a pleasant, slightly dull man called Bert, who had done lots of episodes of *Comedy Playhouse*, and as a consequence didn't seem to have any new ideas for this one. The uninspiring conversation with Bert was followed by a technical run-through which took up the rest of the day; Tony and Bill watched helplessly as Bert told the actors where to stand, and in the process seemed to sap precious life out of their script. Sunday was the day it all happened—more technical rehearsals and a performance in front of an audience in the evening.

They didn't have a moment of doubt about Sophie, because she didn't leave them room for one. She learned lines, she improved them, she got laughs out of pleases and thank-yous and pauses. She took direction, and she charmed Clive into believing, temporarily at least, that the work was worth doing.

And the script, formerly a sickly, derivative, and occasionally embarrassing scrap of a thing, had become the piece of work that Tony and Bill were most proud of. Sophie had pushed them uphill, hard, until they had reached heights they had always hoped, but weren't sure, they were capable of. In the first draft of the second stab, Jim was meeting a friend in the pub where Barbara worked—a friend who was cut out of proceedings as Jim and Barbara's mutual attraction and sparky antagonism edged him aside.

They'd asked Warren Graham from *The Awkward Squad* to come in and read Bob, and he'd made a solid fist of it, but it was clear that every second that Jim and Barbara weren't talking to each other was an opportunity lost. So Bob was ditched, and Jim and Barbara meet because Jim has half an hour to kill. He intends to kill it with a pint and the evening papers; instead, he falls dramatically and dizzyingly in love.

The show was quicker than anything anyone involved could remember: Clive and Sophie burned through the lines. The final version of the script was forty pages, ten pages longer than the usual half-hour comedies, and when Bert the director first flicked through it, he told Bill and Tony to cut it down. They had to persuade him that it could work at this length, although he didn't believe them until the cast proved it to him. It was fast, funny, and real, and it said things about England that Tony and Bill had never heard on the BBC. And the relationship between the couple was something different too. They went from fighting to flirting and back again on the turn of a six-pence. Everyone came into work happy and excited and jabbering with contributions and improvements. If Sophie hadn't been told that her father was dangerously ill after a heart attack, everything would have been going swimmingly.

She found out on the Saturday morning, just before the technical rehearsal; he'd been ill for two days, but Sophie didn't have a phone, and her Sunday night trudge down to the phone box had become fortnightly in recent weeks, when she remembered at all, so Marie had written her a letter.

Sophie called her as soon as she read it.

"Oh, Barbara, love, thank heavens."

"How is he?"

"He's very poorly."

Sophie began to panic, and not all of the panic could be sourced to concern for her dad. Oh, please God, not today, she was thinking. Or tomorrow. Not today or tomorrow. Monday I'll do anything I have to do.

"What do the doctors say?"

"He's comfy at the moment, but they're worried he might have another one."

"Is he speaking?"

"No, he's been asleep for the last two days. I checked the trains, just because I had to do something. You can get one at midday and you'll be in the hospital in time for evening visiting."

"Right."

"Have you got enough money for a ticket?"

She thought for a moment. If she didn't have the fare, there wasn't an awful lot that Marie could have done about it, not on a Saturday.

"Yes," she said eventually.

"Good," said Marie. "I'll get Jack to pick you up from the station."

Perhaps there would be another chance. Perhaps they would forgive her for leaving them in the lurch, twenty-four hours before the recording; and they couldn't replace her, not now, so perhaps they'd reschedule. But perhaps not.

"I can't come home, Auntie Marie."

There was silence, broken only by the pips telling her to put in more money.

"Hello?"

"I'm still here," said Marie. "You can't come home?"

"No."

The panic had gone.

"Why not?"

"I can come on Monday. I'll tell you then."

"He might be dead by Monday."

This wasn't, in Sophie's view, the clinching argument Marie seemed to think it should have been. She didn't want her father to die. She would mourn him. She owed him . . . not everything, exactly, because there were lots of things she'd had to obtain for herself, but enough. If, however, the choice was between a brief good-bye and a new life, then it was no choice at all.

"I'd be letting a lot of people down."

"Derry and Toms isn't even open on Saturday afternoons, is it? You don't have to be at work until Monday."

"It's not that. I'm not working there anymore."

The pips were going again.

"Auntie Marie, I haven't got any more change. I'll see you in the hospital on Monday."

Marie managed to put the phone down on her just before she was cut off. The panic had been replaced by something else, something between nausea and an intense sadness. She'd always suspected that she was the sort of girl who wouldn't go home to see a sick father if she had a shot at a television series, but she'd rather hoped that the news would be revealed slowly, and not for a while yet.

Every day, it seemed, more and more people had become involved in the program. And there was something exciting about the idea being made real by props ladies and set designers, script editors and electricians, but there was something sad about it too, because it didn't belong to the five of them anymore. When Sophie arrived at Television Center, she had to dodge people she didn't know, people who hadn't been there at the beginning and probably didn't care about the program very much, and certainly not as much as she did. It was just another job to them, and every time she saw a wardrobe mistress roll her eyes or heard a carpenter swear, she wanted to go back to the church hall where they'd rehearsed and where she knew everybody. She didn't want this to be just a job, not to anybody. Sophie wanted to be on television, but now she wished they could rehearse for another two or three years.

Tony, Bill, and Dennis were in the corridor outside the dressing rooms, talking about the title.

"I'm afraid Tom's wedded to *Wedded Bliss*," said Dennis.

"Not *Wedded Bliss?*" said Tony.

"Yes," said Dennis. "That's what I just said."

"No," said Bill. "You said *Wedded Bliss*. You didn't say *Wedded Bliss Question Mark Ho Ho Ho*."

"You knew the question mark had gone," said Dennis. "You are a bugger."

"I think it's useful for you to be reminded on a regular basis of your past crimes," said Bill.

"How can it be *Wedded Bliss*," said Tony, "when they're not married for a single second in the episode? We know that if we get a series, they'll be married in the first episode. But in this one, he clocks her for the first time in a pub and then spends thirty minutes chatting her up. In the old one, they were already married."

"He's right," said Bill. "We can only call it *Wedded Bliss* if old Sloan guarantees the series before the *Comedy Playhouse* goes out. If it stays a one-off, then the title just seems potty."

"Here she is," said Tony. "Have you got a good title for us?"

"*Barbara*," said Sophie.

To Sophie's embarrassment, Dennis thought about it, or pretended to think about it, for a moment.

"Hmmm," he said. "It doesn't quite convey as much of the, the relationship side of things as we want it to."

"I think she was joking, Dennis," said Bill.

Dennis laughed at the joke, appreciatively, twenty seconds too late.

"Very good," he said.

Tony caught Bill's eye. Everyone loved Sophie, but Dennis loved her the most.

"Perhaps the names of both the characters?" said Dennis. "*Barbara and Jim?*"

"Have you put a bloody question mark back in there?" said Bill.

"I was asking a question," said Dennis.

"*Barbara and Jim*," said Tony. "*Barbara and Jim.*"

"Thrilling, isn't it?" said Bill. "Things you will never hear the Great British Public say—number one in an occasional series. 'Oh, I can't wait to find out who Barbara and Jim are.'"

"You know what we were talking about the other day?" said Dennis. "How this is Sophie's show?"

"Were you?" said Sophie.

"You weren't supposed to know about it, though," said Tony. He looked at Dennis meaningfully.

"Why is it my show?" said Sophie.

"Never you mind," said Bill.

"I wonder if we can convey that in some way," said Dennis.

"We're not talking about it, though," said Bill. "We're especially not talking about it in front of the cast."

"Why is it my show?" said Sophie.

"Oh, for Christ's sake," said Bill. "Because you're the pretty one and he's smitten, you get all the gags and he's the straight man."

"Oh," she said.

"You hadn't noticed?"

She'd certainly noticed that she'd got more laughs during the rehearsals, but she'd thought this was because she was winning, beating Clive at a game. It hadn't occurred to her that she'd simply been given more gags.

"Perhaps we should make it official," said Dennis. "And I know you'll laugh, but I have another punctuation idea."

"I'm not going to laugh," said Bill. "I promise."

"Brackets around the 'and Jim.' *Barbara (and Jim)*. Barbara open bracket and Jim close bracket."

Bill laughed.

"Funny?" said Dennis hopefully.

"Only because of what it will do to Clive's self-esteem," said Bill. "That makes it hilarious."

"Oh," said Dennis. "I hadn't thought of that."

"Then let's not tell him until after the recording."

"We can't do that," said Dennis.

"Put it another way," said Tony. "We definitely can't do it before. I know him. He won't show up."

"Can you do that?" said Sophie. "Just not show up?"

It had never occurred to her, and maybe it was something to consider.

"Of course," said Bill. "As long as you don't mind never working again."

Sophie stopped considering. She decided that her personal problems were of no relevance to her colleagues and went to get changed for the final rehearsals.

6

On the day of the recording, Clive discovered that from the dressing room you could hear the conversations of the audience members queuing outside. You couldn't not hear them, unless you hummed loudly to yourself at all times.

"At least the tickets are free," the loudest voice, a man, from the sound of it middle-aged, was saying.

"They had to be," said a woman. "Nobody would have paid for them. Have you heard of anybody?"

"The bloke rings a bell," said another man. "Clive somebody."

"What's he been in, then?"

"That's just it. I haven't a clue."

A fourth person joined the conversation, another woman.

"Did you listen to *The Awkward Squad*?"

"Oh, that was awful."

"Did you think so?"

"That daft captain, with his silly posh voice."

"Well, that was Clive Richardson."

"Oh, Gawd. Not him."

"I thought he was funny."

"Come off it."

"I did."

"That silly posh voice?"

"He was putting it on. For comic effect."

"I hope he leaves it off tonight. Still, it's only half an hour, isn't it?"

There was a knock on Clive's door.

"It's me," said Sophie. "Are you listening to all this?"

Clive let her in.

"I don't have much choice. Only the BBC would let the audience queue up outside the dressing rooms."

"I thought it was quite interesting."

"That's because they haven't been talking about you."

With exquisite timing, Clive's female fan brought up the subject of Sophie.

"She's supposed to be hopeless, though."

"I thought she was a newcomer."

"Oh, no. My daughter saw her in Clacton, in a summer show."

Clive looked at Sophie and Sophie shook her head.

"Thinks she's it, apparently. My daughter waited half an hour for an autograph and she just walked right past her. Mind you, what my daughter was going to do with her autograph I don't know."

"Might be worth keeping if this takes off," said one of the men.

"Yes, but it won't take off, will it?" said the woman. "Not with her in it."

"Or him."

"She'll be the problem."

"They both will."

"I don't mind him."

"I don't like either of them. Oh, well. What else are you going to do?"

"I've been to one before," said the woman. "It's nearer an hour, once they've got everyone settled and the warm-up man's told his jokes."

"What was the warm-up chap like? Last time?"

"Oh, you know. Not very good. Not as funny as he thinks he is."

"Oh, lumme," said the man. "I've half a mind to go home."

"Oh, don't," said the woman. "It might not be as bad as all that."

Sophie puffed out her cheeks.

"Shall we go and stand in the corridor?" she said.

"It's going to be great," said Clive.

"We've all been living in a bubble," said Sophie.

"What sort of bubble?"

"A lovely squishy pink bubble."

"I wouldn't knowingly live in a squishy pink bubble," said Clive.

"Any color you like, then. We all love the script. I do anyway. Tom Sloan loves Dennis. Dennis loves Tony and Bill. And now it's all gone pop. Suddenly."

"That's what bubbles do," said Clive. "That's why you shouldn't choose to live in them."

"People don't come to these things because they want to cheer you along, do they?" said Sophie. "They come because they're bored. Or because they want to see the inside of a TV studio."

"Or because they applied for tickets months ago in the hope of getting something good," said Clive. "And they got us instead."

"We're good."

"We think so. But they've never heard of us. So now they're cheesed off. I went along to one once because the producer had turned me down for a job. I went because I was hoping it would be awful."

"And was it?"

"Anything can be awful if you want it to be."

"Even good things?"

"Especially good things, sometimes. They make people jealous."

"I don't want it to go out in the world," said Sophie. "I want to stay like we were."

"It's a TV program," said Clive. "It belongs in the world."

"Oh, hell," said Sophie.

Dennis knocked on the door.

"Everyone all right?"

Sophie made a face.

"Oh, you'll be fine," said Dennis.

"How do you know?" she said.

"Because you're not normal," he said. "Nothing matters to you as much as this. You're not going to mess it up."

And she didn't. Clive had been in plenty of student productions in which the object of the exercise was to destroy one's friends, classmates, and contemporaries onstage, but he'd never experienced anything like this: the moment the red recording light came on, Sophie was at him, like a vicious dog that had been kept in a dark shed and then released into the light. All through the rehearsals she had been trying things out in an attempt to wring more out of the script than Tony and Bill had intended to provide: she made faces, held a line back for a couple of seconds longer than anyone was expecting, found intonations and emphases that could turn a simple "Thank you" into something that made people laugh, or at least watch her. So he shouldn't have been surprised by her energy or her relentlessness, but he was rocked back on his heels fighting her off: she was everywhere, in every gap, over and under every line, hers and his. Poor old Bert, Clive could see, was lost, which meant that some of her performance was too. Clive felt as though he'd gone three goals down in the first two minutes of a football match, and though he now suspected that even a draw was beyond him, he could at least make a better fist of things. He was always decent, in any part he was given, but nobody had ever pushed him to go further, and because he hadn't been pushed, he coasted. Sophie wasn't ever going to let him coast. Perhaps that was even a good thing, if you looked at it the right way. Now, though, he had to watch, listen, feel, during every single second of the performance, and respond to what she was actually doing, rather than what he'd presumed she was going to do. It was all rather exhausting.

At the end, the man with the APPLAUSE board didn't even have to lift it above his head. Clive ushered her forward so that she could take a bow, and the audience cheered, and he applauded too. He hadn't been left with a lot of choice.

Sophie was beside her father's hospital bed by lunchtime on Monday afternoon. He hadn't died, and he hadn't had any more heart attacks, and he was awake and talking. There was an argument to say that this was the worst of all possible outcomes, because now he could sit there, looking wounded. Marie was on the other side of the bed. She wasn't wounded. She was just sour and disappointed. Sophie gave her dad the grapes she'd bought in London, and a bottle of Lucozade, and a Commando War Stories book called *At Dawn You Die.*

"You must be made of money," he said, by way of thanks.

"Or made of guilt," said Marie.

Sophie took a deep breath.

"I'm sorry," she said.

"Yes, but what are you sorry for?" said Marie.

"I'm sorry I couldn't come."

"Not good enough," said Marie. "We talked about this. We decided you had to be sorry you didn't come. Not sorry you couldn't come."

She understood the difference. They wanted her to admit she'd made a mistake.

"I couldn't come," she said. "I wish I had been able to."

"So why couldn't you?" said her father. "What was so important?"

"I was in a BBC program."

"What do you mean, you were in it? In the audience?"

"I was in it. Acting in it. A *Comedy Playhouse*."

They both stared at her.

"*Comedy Playhouse*?"

"Yes."

"On the BBC?"

"Yes. That *Comedy Playhouse*. And we had to rehearse on Saturday and they recorded it on Sunday and if I'd come home I might have lost my chance. And it's a big chance. They want it to be a series, and it's about a couple, a man and a woman, and I'm the woman."

They stared at her some more, then stared at each other.

"Are you . . . are you sure?"

She laughed.

"I'm sure."

"And did it go all right?"

"It went well. Thank you. Anyway. Do you understand better?"

"You couldn't have come," said her father. "Not if you had a *Comedy Playhouse*."

"With the hope of a series," said Marie.

"You're going to be on telly!" said her father. "We'd be so proud of you!"

It had never occurred to Sophie that she would be forgiven so readily for her trespasses and she wasn't sure that she liked it. She had refused to visit her dangerously ill father in hospital because her career was more important to her, and the least he could do was judge her. You could get away with anything, it seemed, if you were on the telly.

THE FIRST
SERIES

7

Clive Richardson was an actor because being an actor was easily the best way of meeting pretty girls. He'd suspected as much before he got into the game, and he hadn't been disappointed: there were pretty girls everywhere he went. It started at LAMDA, his drama school, where he understood properly for the first time that actresses were better-looking than ordinary people; if he'd gone to teacher training college, or a school of medicine, then he'd have had to reject nineteen out of every twenty classmates. At LAMDA, he wanted all of them. And then he left, and went on to work at the BBC and in the repertory theaters, where there were hundreds more.

Out in the real world, he discovered that it wasn't just pretty actresses who were available to him. Pretty girls who worked in other professions loved actors. Sometimes they were looking for a way into the entertainment business—and as far as Clive was concerned, he was as good a way in as any—but mostly they just wanted the association. An actor has the pick of the pretty girls, so any pretty girl he looked at seemed to feel validated in some way: *he wants me!* It was beautiful. Being an actor was like having a system for the horses that actually worked.

Clive's chief objection to comedy was that he feared the system would stop working for him if all he did was make people laugh—especially if he made them laugh by being stupid. He wasn't at all sure pretty girls liked that. Richard Burton and Tom Courtenay and Peter O'Toole were movie stars, and that brought advantages of a different order entirely: Clive had not yet bagged an Elizabeth Taylor. But were they movie stars because they were born movie stars? Or were they movie stars because they refused to play Captain Smythe? The only comedian whose career gave him pause for thought was Peter Sellers: he had recently married Britt Ekland, and there had been rumors about his offscreen relationship with Sophia Loren. If Clive could be guaranteed women of Ekland/Loren quality, he'd speak in silly voices to whoever would listen, but Peter Sellers was doing his voices in *Dr. Strangelove*, on the big screen, not *The Awkward Squad* on the wireless. He suspected that Sophia Loren wouldn't be terribly interested in the man who played Captain Smythe. *Wedded Bliss* was a television program, at least, but his character showed very few signs of doing him any favors.

Sophie would be an interesting test case. She was more Sabrina than Sophia Loren—Sophia Loren was an Italian film star, not a Blackpool beauty queen—but she was magnificent, in her own way. He'd thought he detected a tiny spark of something, when they first met, but then she'd trampled all over him in the *Comedy Playhouse*, and that was before he heard about the change of title.

Clive had not yet had a telephone installed in his flat, and had not yet been persuaded of the benefits of doing so. His parents couldn't call, and neither could girls who had turned out not to be exactly what he was looking for. He lived off Warren Street, and if anyone wanted to reach him, they knew that they could leave a message at the Three Crowns on Tottenham Court Road with Davie behind the bar. Davie didn't mind. He thought that writing down phone messages for Clive, and very occasionally accepting scripts on his behalf, was the most glamorous part of his job. After a couple of months of regular patronage, Clive came to the conclusion that this was true. The Three Crowns was not a glamorous pub.

Davie, who had moved down from Glasgow at the end of the war in an attempt to break a cycle of crime and punishment, was particularly keen to see Clive in a Western series—he admired both *The Virginian* and *Rawhide* equally. Clive had long since given up trying to explain that very few actors from Hampshire, especially actors from Hampshire known mostly for their radio work, had had much luck landing a part in either. Davie remained undeterred. In his mind's eye, he said, he always saw Clive as a cowboy. Clive had always thought that Davie needed his mind's eye tested.

Clive dropped into the Three Crowns at lunchtime on the day after the *Comedy Playhouse* recording to find Davie in a state of high excitement.

"Monty called," he said. Monty was Clive's agent and it was true that he didn't call very often. "Do you think it's The One?"

"It could be, Davie."

"You can call him from here," said Davie, an offer indicating his level of excitement and his investment in Clive's career.

The saloon bar was empty, so Clive let himself behind the bar and Davie poured him a half of bitter while he dialed Monty's number.

"So what's the bad news?"

Monty had been an agent since the mid-1920s, and Clive never knew whether his best days were behind him or whether there had never been many good ones in the first place. He had approached Clive after a LAMDA performance of *The Long and the Short and the Tall* at Edinburgh, where Clive had made a pretty good fist of Private Smith, everybody said. Afterward people were swarming over the insufferable Laurence Harris, who'd grabbed Bamforth for himself while the rest of them had been looking the other way; any idiot could play Bamforth and get noticed. When Monty sidled up to Clive in the bar and asked if he needed representation, Clive asked him why he wasn't chasing Harris, like everyone else. What Clive wanted to hear from Monty was that he could see underneath the surface of performances, however flashy, to the true talent underneath. Instead, Monty said sadly that he was too old to chase after people, that he'd get trampled in the rush; he was, as he put it, "seeing what was left at the end." Clive should have known then that Monty wasn't someone with a lot of fire in his belly.

"You always think there's bad news," said Monty.

Clive didn't say anything. He had found that this was the easiest way to unnerve Monty.

"I can get the money up," he said eventually.

"So the money's no good."

"It's BBC money. But even they can do a bit better."

Clive stayed quiet again. If there was any bad news that didn't involve money, he couldn't imagine what it might be, but it was worth trying to flush it out.

"And obviously I'm trying to get rid of the brackets."

"What brackets?"

"In the title."

"I can't hear any bloody brackets."

"Oh. Sorry. *Barbara . . . and Jim.*"

"I'm still not hearing any brackets."

"Well, they're sort of around the '*and Jim.*'"

"The series is now called *Barbara* bracket *and Jim?*"

"Bracket."

"What?"

"After '*Jim.*' Close brackets."

"You're saying that my character is now parenthetical?"

"It's just a little joke. To show that she's the boss."

"Oh, well, that's all right, then," said Clive.

"They told me not to tell you. But I thought I should."

"When was I supposed to find out?"

"When you saw it in the *Radio Times*. You don't mind, do you?"

"Of course I bloody well mind."

"It's sixteen episodes."

"That makes it worse, not better."

Clive had never heard of a new series getting an order for sixteen episodes. It was usually six, sometimes twelve, but never sixteen. They loved Sophie, and they thought everyone in the country was going to love Sophie. And that's why there were brackets around his character's name.

"Tell them to shove their bloody brackets."

"What does that mean?"

"You know the brackets around Jim's name? I don't want them there."

"Oh, Gawd," said Monty. "I'm all right with money. I don't mind arguing with them about that. But I've got no experience with punctuation."

"Sort it out, there's a good chap."

The following day, Monty told Clive that the money had gone up but the brackets were staying put.

"Well, tell them thanks but no thanks, then."

"Are you serious, old chap? You're a semi-employed actor who's just been offered sixteen half-hours of television. It'll turn you into a household name."

"It'll turn *her* into a household name. Won't do much for me. I'll spend the rest of my life saying, I was 'and Jim.' In *Barbara (and Jim)*. Hold on . . . What's the episode of *Comedy Playhouse* called?"

"*Barbara (and Jim)*."

"What happened to *Wedded Bliss*?"

"You're not married now. It made no sense."

"Oh, for Christ's sake. The bastards. They're broadcasting it under that name without asking me?"

Monty chuckled.

"They put one over on you, I'm afraid."

"Right. That's it. I'm not doing it. Find me some work, Monty."

The day after that, Monty left a message to say that they'd offered the part of Jim to Clive's old nemesis Laurence Harris. Clive knew Laurence Harris wouldn't take it, not with the brackets. Unless the brackets were magically vanished, for someone like Harris. Of course, that's what would happen. "Oh, well, if Laurence Harris is interested . . ."

Damn and blast them all to hell.

As luck would have it, he had arranged to visit his parents in Eastleigh that weekend. It was never an enjoyable occasion, Sunday lunch with his parents, for two reasons. The first was his job. It wasn't so much that they disapproved of his choice of profession. His father was a dentist, but his wasn't the traditional middle-class straitlaced disapproval of bohemianism; Clive had tried that one and got nowhere. If Clive had been able to earn a decent living, his father wouldn't have given two hoots about what he got up to, what he wore, what he drank, or who he slept with. "You're just no bloody good at it," he said, loudly and often.

The second thing that made his visits home so miserable was the permanent and inexplicable presence of Clive's ex-fiancée, Cathy. They had got engaged when he was eighteen, after his first term at LAMDA, for reasons that Clive could no longer recall, but which almost certainly had something to do with sex. He had broken it off soon after, presumably once he had got what he wanted, but it didn't seem to have made much difference to her position in the family. As far as Clive could make out, she went to the parental home every Sunday. Cathy had somehow become a daughter-in-law while remaining unmarried. She was a sweet, dull girl, and Clive feared that he would be eating Sunday lunch with his mother's daughter-in-law once a month for the rest of his life.

He had made the mistake of telling his parents that he was to appear in an episode of *Comedy Playhouse*, and that this would almost certainly lead to a job in a series. His father asked him about it almost as soon as the fatty lamb and the wet cabbage appeared on the table.

"How did that BBC thing turn out?"

"Oh, that. Not as well as I'd hoped."

Cathy and his mother made sympathetic faces. His father chortled.

"I knew it," he said. "What happened?"

Clive briefly entertained the notion of telling his father the truth: that he'd turned down the chance to star in a television program because he didn't like the way the title was going to be punctuated.

"It wasn't really what I was looking for, so I said no."

"You mean it was work?"

"That's not fair," said his mother. "He's always looking for work."

"Hasn't he just found some? And turned it down?"

"It doesn't sound as though that's what happened," said his mother.

Sometimes, Clive didn't know which parent irritated him more. His mother's blind devotion could be every bit as dispiriting as his father's scorn; he was patronized either way. He decided, perversely, to turn on his mother.

"Were you even listening? That's exactly what happened. We made the *Comedy Playhouse*, it went all right, they offered me sixteen episodes, I didn't like the part."

"Believe that and you'll believe anything," said his father.

Clive groaned.

"I thought that's what you did believe? And you accused me of being work-shy? I was backing you up!"

"You hadn't told us the full story. The full story is not believable."

"Why not?"

"Nobody's going to offer you sixteen episodes on television."

"They just did!"

"And you turned it down. Now what?"

"I may end up going to the United States."

"Oh, Clive," said Cathy. "America?"

Clive's imaginary plans seemed to be driving a distressing hole through their imaginary relationship.

"Yes," said Clive.

His father put down his knife and fork and rubbed his hands.

"What?" said Clive.

"I'm going to enjoy this."

"Why?"

"Because whatever you're about to say will be both amusing and untrue."

"God, Dad. You're a monster."

He tried to think of a lie that wouldn't make his father laugh.

"I've been offered something in *The Virginian*."

"*The Virginian*," his father said flatly. "The Western serial."

"Yes," said Clive. "It's not much, but it might be rather fun."

"And do they know you cried when a horse came too close to you in Norfolk?"

"Yes. I told them. They wanted me anyway."

"*The Virginian*!" said his father. He was pretending to wipe tears of mirth away with his napkin. "So this might be the last time we see you for a while?"

"Oh, Clive," said Cathy.

"Unless I take the other thing," said Clive.

"What other thing?"

"The BBC comedy series."

"Oh, we're still pretending that exists?" said his father.

Clive was tempted to move to America and beg for the chance to play a cowboy, or even a cow, just to prove his father wrong. But then it occurred to him that there was an easier way of proving his father wrong, while at the same time earning a living at the only thing he was capable of doing.

He got Monty to phone Dennis the next day. The brackets were staying, the money had gone down, and Clive had a job.

Sophie's first-ever press interview was for a new magazine called *Crush*. The journalist had asked if she could do it in Sophie's home, but as she was still living with Marjorie, Brian didn't think it was a very good idea and told her to come to his office. She'd bought a new skirt for it, as short as she could find, and a new pair of shoes, and when Brian saw her, he shook his head and tutted, and reminded her that he was a very happily married man, as if she had made an improper suggestion.

When Diane from *Crush* arrived, Brian showed them into a spare room that had become a repository for broken furniture and old accounts, and they had to sit side by side on a dusty old brown sofa. For the first few minutes of the conversation, Sophie was distracted by a box file which was labeled "ARTHUR ASKEY 1935–7."

"Do they always make you come in here?" said Diane.

Diane looked like someone from a pop program on TV. She had long, dark hair, white boots, and no bust. She was as skinny as Sophie's twelve-year-old cousin.

"Why would they make me come in here?" said Sophie.

"For interviews."

"Oh. No. I've never done one before."

"Gosh," said Diane. "Well, it'll be painless. Have you seen *Crush*? It's for girls. We just want to know what you wear and who your boyfriend is and what you cook for him."

Diane crossed her eyes and made a face to indicate that *Crush* wasn't her favorite magazine. Sophie laughed.

"You don't like your job?"

"No, I do," said Diane. "It's fun. I get to meet pop stars and people off the telly. Like you. And people are always sending us gear. But it isn't what I want to do forever."

"What do you want to do forever?"

"I want to write, but not this stuff. I'd love to do Tony and Bill's job."

Sophie was surprised she even knew their names. Not many people cared about who wrote telly and radio programs.

"Do you think you could?" said Sophie.

"Will anyone let me? That's the question. There aren't many funny girl writers."

"You should just write something," said Sophie.

"Ah, well," said Diane. "When you put it like that . . . it sounds impossible. Anyway. Answer my wretched questions. Clothes, boyfriend, cooking."

"Oh," said Sophie. "Well, I don't have a boyfriend and I don't cook. I wear things, though."

"Why don't you have a boyfriend?" said Diane.

"I had one at home in Blackpool, but we broke up when I came here, and . . . well, I haven't met anyone."

"I wouldn't have thought you needed to meet anyone."

"I don't know how you get a boyfriend without meeting them first."

"I thought all the men would be phoning you up after they saw you on the telly," said Diane.

"I haven't got a telephone, so they'd have a job."

"You haven't got a telephone?"

Sophie realized that she didn't want to talk about Earl's Court bedsits or Marjorie, not to *Crush* magazine.

"I've just moved and they haven't come round to put it in yet."

"Oh, that's fabulous," said Diane. "It's all happened so fast for you. Where have you moved to?"

"Oh, that would be telling."

"Just the area. I won't put in your address."

"Kensington. Near Derry and Toms," said Sophie.

"That's where you used to work, isn't it?"

"How did you know that?"

"The BBC press officer told me. Cosmetics. I've got all that. Complete unknown walks in off the street, wows everyone at the audition, gets the job. It's a great story. Where do you like to go out?"

She was interviewing somebody else, Sophie thought, someone who had done something. Sophie had come to London, worked in a department store, listened to Marjorie snoring, and then been cast in a television series. She didn't watch television, though, because she didn't have one of those either.

"I like the Talk of the Town," she said.

There was really nothing left now. All her London experiences had been used up.

"Fabulous," said Diane. "Lovely. And are you excited about the series?"

"Really excited."

"Great," said Diane, and she stood up.

"Is that it?"

"That's plenty. No boyfriend, no phone, new flat, the Talk of the Town . . . Really, I just have to say that I met you. If you told me your favorite Beatle, my editor would explode with joy," said Diane joylessly.

Sophie laughed. She liked Diane.

"George."

"He'll read this and ask you out."

Sophie blushed.

"Oh, I don't know about that."

"He won't," said Diane. "I was pulling your leg."

"Can we do another interview one day?" said Sophie. "When . . . when something has happened to me?"

"We'll see how the show goes," said Diane.

She wasn't being unkind. She was just refusing to make promises. It hadn't occurred to Sophie that her first interview might also be her last. She wished she'd enjoyed it more, and she wished she'd found something to say.

Tony and Bill weren't writing in the coffee bar anymore. They had rented an office, a room above a shoe shop in Great Portland Street, around the corner from the Underground station. On the day they moved in, they had gone out shopping in Oxford Street together, and bought two desks, two armchairs, a lamp, a record player and some records, a kettle and some tea bags. In John Lewis, they had argued about buying an expensive sofa. Bill wanted to lie down during the day and stare at the ceiling. Tony thought that a sofa would lead to inactivity and sleep, and told Bill he wouldn't pay half for something that would produce only a reduced income. Bill said he would buy it himself, in which case Tony wasn't even allowed to sit on it. And Tony told Bill to be his guest, that his rear end would never touch the sofa. And then it turned out that there was a twelve-week delivery time, so Bill decided not to bother, but there was a residual irritation that took them a couple of days to shake off. They had never argued before, but everything had seemed more casual before. Now they had a sixteen-episode commission, an increase in fees, an office, a kettle . . . They were in deep.

And they weren't quite sure how they were going to fill eight hours of television time either. They weren't even sure how to fill the first thirty minutes. They sat in their new office, on their new armchairs, facing each other, with notepads on their knees, and they chewed their pencils.

"So," said Tony eventually, "Barbara and Jim are a couple."

That much they knew. Barbara and Jim became man and wife at some time between the *Comedy Playhouse* episode and the first episode of the brand-new series. Jim was going to carry Barbara over the threshold and drop her in the opening ten seconds.

"Shall I write that down?" said Bill.

"I just meant . . . We need some couply stuff. As well as all the brave, brilliant, witty, important stuff about class and England."

"Shall we go back to the Gambols? Hairdos and burned dinners?"

"No!"

"So what do couples do that's brave, brilliant, witty, and important? What do you and June do?"

"Why are you so interested in me and June?"

"Because you're a married couple, half of which is sitting opposite me."

"We're not the same as Barbara and Jim."

"Understood," said Bill, and laughed.

"It's not that," said Tony.

"Isn't it?" said Bill. "How interesting."

"I just meant, you know, we're not opposites. June works for the BBC, we like the same things, we . . . Anyway."

"But the other business is going all right?"

"It's none of your beeswax."

"Can't blame me for being nosy."

"I can and I do."

The other business, predictably, had been a disaster—two disasters, if one were keeping count, a few months apart. He had no idea what had happened, or how much. He had no idea whether he was still a virgin, or whether

June was still a virgin, or whether she had been when she married him. They didn't talk about any of it, even though June had wept after the second attempt.

"I wish Jim were queer," said Bill.

"I'm glad he isn't," said Tony. "Because if he was, we'd be out of a job."

"But it's such a great setup, the married homosexual."

"Bill," said Tony, "let's not waste time thinking up ideas that will get us banned from ever working again."

"People are interested in anything to do with, you know. Slightly off-kilter sex."

"You don't think people are interested in any kind of sex? They can't watch it, they can't listen to people talk about it . . ."

Bill's eyes lit up.

"Right, then!"

"Oh, Gawd," said Tony. "First episode?"

"That's the place to try," said Bill. "Before they've done anything."

"You don't think they've done anything?"

"Maybe not . . . All of it. They got married very quickly."

"Did they? How do we know that?"

Bill shrugged.

"*Comedy Playhouse* didn't go out long ago."

Tony laughed.

"All right, then. They got married quickly. So what?"

"What if nothing happens?"

"Ever?"

"For a couple of weeks. Or a month, or something. Someone's got troubles."

Tony wrinkled up his nose.

"What sort of troubles?"

"Nothing, you know, *medical*. Psychological."

"It should be Jim," said Tony.

"Why?"

"Because we've seen women who don't like sex too many times already."

"Maybe she does like it but she can't do it," said Bill.

"Why not?"

"There are conditions."

"You've gone medical already."

"Psychological ones. Where everything closes up. Like a bank vault at night."

"You seem to know an awful lot about it."

"I don't, really. But I'll bet there is something like that."

"Even if there is, I don't want to write about it. Do you?"

"No. So it's him."

"It's him. The usual."

"What variety of usual? There are at least two."

"Ah. Yes. Well, the easiest is the nothing-going-on one."

"In what sense the easiest?"

"The easiest to get past Tom Sloan. I'm not sure he'd be so keen on the other one. It's a bit messy."

"All right. Nothing going on. Good. Why?"

"He's terrified."

"Excellent. It all fits in terribly well with the brackets."

"Poor Clive," said Tony. Poor Tony, thought Tony.

Tony loved his wife, but ever since the disasters he dreaded going to bed with her. He always made sure he watched the TV right the way through to the National Anthem, in the hope that by then June would have fallen asleep reading a script, or a pile of short stories submitted for broadcast, and he could creep under the covers without disturbing her. They seemed to have reached the unspoken agreement that staggered bedtimes and changes of subject whenever necessary were the best way forward. June thought she understood the root cause of her husband's problems, and had made it clear that she was prepared to adapt to them in any way he saw fit; she would have been amazed to learn that it was even more perplexing than she knew, and that Tony's sexuality was a mystery to him as well. He was attracted to June, he knew he was, and in that way too. But he had no idea what to do about it.

He decided that he didn't want to talk about work at all. Work was suddenly very close to home.

"But is it going all right?" said June.

They were eating a bread-and-cheese supper in front of the television.

"Yes, I think so."

"You'll let me read it when you've got something you're happy with?"

June was his first and best reader. Everything that he and Bill wrote she made better; she challenged them when they were being lazy, understood what their characters would and wouldn't say and do, spotted illogicalities. He would have to be insane not to let her read something that might determine the success of his entire career.

"Oh, you don't want to end up reading everything we ever do. You've got your own scripts to work on."

"I love what you and Bill write. And you're my husband. And this is the first episode of your first television series. Just tell me what it's about."

"It's a terrible idea."

"Well, don't do it, then."

"Simple as that?"

"Are you saying it sounds like a terrible idea, but when I read it I'll see that in fact it's a work of great genius?"

"No."

"Then, yes, simple as that. Terrible ideas are never a good way of . . . Well, actually, they're never a good way of doing anything at all. Is it Bill's terrible idea?"

"Yes."

"Will you promise me you'll march in tomorrow and tell him he's an idiot?"

"No."

"Why not?"

He sighed.

"Because it's rather a good idea."

She put her plate down on the coffee table, walked over to the TV set, and turned it off.

"I don't understand anything you're saying."

"No," said Tony. "I can see why."

"Can you help me?"

He sighed.

"It's about sex."

"Really?"

"Yes."

"Their sex life?"

"Yes."

"That's a brilliant idea," said June.

"Yes," he said.

"If it's intelligent and funny, which it will be, everyone will watch it. And it will feel young and contemporary."

"Yes."

"You don't want to do it?"

"I do want to do it."

"So what on earth's the matter with you?"

"The marriage between Barbara and Jim hasn't been consummated, because Jim is having difficulties."

"Ah."

"Bill's idea."

"I can imagine."

"It's not supposed to be you and me," he said. "It just started to go that way, and I didn't feel I could stop it without giving too much away."

"Are they going to sort it all out in the end?"

"Yes."

"Then I will enjoy watching it," said June.

She stood up, kissed him on the head, and turned the television back on.

8

Dennis had been landed with Bert as his director. There had been no discussion, and there had certainly been no choice offered. Bert had just turned up in his office, waving a chit.

"I know you didn't think I did much of a job on the *Comedy Playhouse*," Bert said.

Dennis was hoping that Bert might follow up with a "but," indicating his willingness to learn, listen, or get it right, but there was nothing. Bert was probably hoping that Dennis would reassure him in some way, but Dennis didn't see why he should. He had been frustrated by Bert's apparent determination to make *Barbara (and Jim)* look like every other comedy program the BBC had ever broadcast. Dennis appreciated that there was only so much that could be done with a live recording in a studio, but Bert was plodding, uninterested in spontaneity, allergic to anything that might contain collaboration.

"I don't want *Barbara (and Jim)* to look like any other comedy series," said Dennis. "I want it to feel young and fresh."

Bert snorted.

"You've got the wrong bloke for that," he said. "Look at me."

Dennis did as instructed and saw a grumpy middle-aged man.

"As long as it's blocked out by Saturday evening," said Bert. "That's all I'm interested in."

"What about the show?" said Dennis. "Are you interested in that?"

"As long as it's blocked out by Saturday evening."

"So that's a yes. Blocking by Saturday evening creates an interest in the content on Sunday."

Bert blinked slowly, like a frog.

"I've been thinking about the theme music and the title sequence," said Dennis. "I want something different."

"Oh, Gawd," said Bert. "Here we go."

"Do you ever get involved in that?"

"No, thank you."

"So whatever I did would be fine by you?"

"No. Course not. Not if my name's going out on it."

"Right," said Dennis. "So what do we do about that?"

"You go off and get your theme music and your title sequence," said Bert. "And then I tell you I don't like them."

Dennis wanted the music to reflect the differences between the two characters, and he had commissioned something from Ron Grainer, who'd done *Maigret* and *Steptoe*.

"Well," said Grainer, when Dennis had told him what he wanted. "On your head be it."

"Really? I think it could sound rather good."

"It'll sound like a mess."

And when he played the results back to Dennis a week later, it sounded like a mess. Thirty seconds of a pop chorus, followed by thirty seconds of contemporary jazz, followed by thirty seconds of a pop chorus, and so on. It sounded like two cats fighting on a drum kit.

"I'm not sure it's a good idea to chop and change like that," said Grainer.

He was being polite, and Dennis was grateful. Grainer could have been forgiven for questioning his professional competence.

"Any suggestions?" said Dennis.

"I'd get either a pop group to play a jazz tune or a jazz saxophonist to do a song by the Beatles or something."

A couple of days later, he had his theme tune. Ron Grainer had asked a record producer called Shel Talmy at Decca Records to recommend a session guitarist, and Talmy had told him to use a young man called Jimmy Page. Under Grainer's supervision, Page played Miles Davis's "So What" in a sort of blues band style, and it sounded terrific, Dennis thought.

"Oh, hell," said Bill, when he heard it.

"What's wrong with it?"

"We haven't written that kind of script," said Tony.

"What kind of script have you written?" said Dennis.

"This is all moody and classy," said Bill. "We're not moody and classy. Get him to do 'Freddie Freeloader.'"

"What's that?"

"It's the next cut on the LP."

"How does it go?"

"Daaa, da . . . Daaa, da . . . Daaa, da . . . Daaa, da . . . Da da, da da, da da."

Dennis nodded his head thoughtfully along to the music. He could see what Bill meant.

"It's not funny," said Bill. "But at least it's cheerful."

Dennis got Jimmy Page to do "Freddie Freeloader" the next afternoon. He had now gone through fifty-eight pounds of the forty-pound budget he'd given himself for music. He'd wanted to get a proper photographer, David Bailey or Lewis Morley, to take a picture of Sophie, and a local wedding photographer to do Clive, but the overspend made that impossible. Instead, he spent an entire day collecting artifacts—lipsticks and pipes and book jackets and miniskirts—intended to represent the couple, and got an in-house chap to snap them all on a background of white chipboard. It looked better than he'd dared to hope. He held the pictures up while he played the theme song and suddenly felt a little thrill of possibility.

Bert hated everything, the music and the photographs.

"You just want everyone to turn off before the actual program starts?"

"I don't think they will," said Dennis.

"Oh, they will," said Bert. "I would."

"Of course you would," said Dennis. "That goes without saying."

"And my missus will," said Bert.

"You won't tell her to stick with it because you directed it?"

"I can try," said Bert. "But it won't do any good. Not with that racket."

"So it's the music you particularly object to?"

"And the pictures."

"Right. You and your missus would turn off because you don't like the photographs in the opening titles."

"No," Bert said patiently. "We'd turn off because of the music."

"So if the opening titles were to play silently—"

"We'd think the sound had gone."

"Bert," said Dennis. "What I'm trying to do here is locate the objection to the images. I understand you don't like the music—"

"It's horrible."

"—but what is the problem with the pictures?"

Bert shuffled through them again.

"I like it when a comedy starts with a little cartoon," he said.

"I thought we'd try something a bit more daring," said Dennis. "Something a bit different."

"Well," said Bert, "different has never worked before."

Later that day, after a conversation with Tom Sloan, Dennis became the producer and the director of *Barbara (and Jim)*. He went straight to see the set designer: he wanted the marital home to contain the youngest, most fashionable living room in television. And with every suggestion that the set designer made—white walls! Op art posters on the walls! Danish furniture!—Dennis felt that the ghost of Bert, and the ghosts of stale British light entertainment, were being banished to the Shepherd's Bush streets.

At the end of the read-through, Dennis made the Big Ben noises intended to indicate that the marriage between Jim and Barbara had been consummated, but nobody laughed or cheered. Bill and Tony were too busy trying to gauge the expressions on the faces of Sophie and Clive; Sophie and Clive, expressionless, were too busy flicking back through the pages of the script, trying to work out precisely what had been intimated about their characters' sex lives.

"When I say . . ." Sophie began.

"Yes?" Bill said.

"Oh. I see. Right."

"Which page?"

"Fifteen."

"Go on."

"Well. Does that mean what I think it means?"

"Yes."

"Are we allowed to say that?"

"We're not saying it."

```
1.   BARBARA:   Well.

2.   JIM:       'Well' isn't the answer I was looking
                for.

3.   BARBARA:   What was the answer you were looking
                for?

4.   JIM:       I suppose...more 'No' than 'Well'.

5.   BARBARA:   Ah.

6.   JIM:       Now we've had 'Well" and 'Ah'.

7.   BARBARA:   Yes.

8.   JIM:       And 'Yes. 'Well', 'Ah' and 'Yes'.
                Everything except 'No'.

9.   BARBARA:   Mmm.

10.  JIM:       And now...

11.  BARBARA:   Please don't put 'Mmm' in there.
                Otherwise we might as well start
                singing 'There Was An Old Lady Who
                Swallowed A Fly'.

12.  JIM:       Is it possible for you to say 'No'?

13.  BARBARA:   No.

Pause, while Jim tries to work out which question Barbara
is answering.

14.  JIM:       No it's not possible? Or yes it's
                possible and you just said it?

15.  BARBARA    What about you?

16.  JIM:       No.

17.  BARBARA:   Just...no? Crikey.
```

15

"Bill," Dennis said patiently. "I don't mind making that argument to the Powers That Be. But let's be fair to our cast. Yes, Sophie. We are saying—"

"Implying," said Bill.

"We are saying that Barbara is sexually experienced."

"Oh, bloody hell."

"We don't have to," said Dennis. "If you're not comfortable with it."

"Oh, don't we?" said Tony. "What else have you got, then, Dennis?"

"What don't you like about it, Sophie?" said Dennis.

"Oh, just stupid things, you know. My dad, and my auntie Marie, and . . ."

"But they know it's made up."

"Sort of. I'm never quite sure whether they've got the hang of it yet. You know, Barbara's from Blackpool and I'm from Blackpool. She's called Barbara and I'm called Barbara. It's confusing."

Suddenly she was aware of everybody looking at her.

"You're called Barbara?" said Clive.

"Oh," said Barbara. "Well, yes. I used to be."

"When?"

"Until the week before you met me."

"Why didn't you say anything when we decided to call her Barbara?"

"I didn't know what was allowed then. Please don't call me Barbara all the time now."

"You're seriously used to being called Sophie already?"

She thought about it and realized she was. A part of her felt she'd only really begun her life when she moved to London, which meant that she'd been called Sophie for most of her life.

"Yes," she said. "Barbara is a fictional character in the series we're making." And she left it at that.

"Can we talk about me now?" said Clive. "You're saying in this that I'm a . . . a virgin?"

"Oh, you're like my auntie Marie," said Sophie. "It's Jim who's the virgin. And he's not real."

"Yes, but . . . will people believe it?"

"Why wouldn't they believe it, Clive?" Sophie could see that they were all trying to suppress mirth, but Bill's poker face was so expert that he had been charged with the job of mickey-taking.

"I know Jim's fictional, but I'm . . ."

"Yes?"

Clive stopped and tried a different tack.

"Isn't it the other way around? Conventionally? The man has had sexual experience and the woman hasn't?"

Bill groaned and then stared at him pityingly.

"What?"

"It is, yes," said Tony. "That's sort of the point of the script. I don't know if you've noticed, but we're trying not to do the conventional thing."

"In which case," said Clive, "I will just have to not give a damn about appearing immodest and voice my other objection, which is this: nobody will believe it."

"Which part?" said Tony.

"I don't mean Barbara's experience . . . They'll be fine with that. No offense meant."

"A lot taken," said Sophie.

"It's Jim. Jim, to my mind, is not a virgin."

"I didn't think he would be, to your mind."

"I can act, you know, insecurity and donnishness and shyness and the rest of it. But I can't do anything about what I look like."

"I didn't think you'd have the nerve to go through with it," said Bill. "But you have."

"I make no apologies for frankness."

"I'm not sure I quite understand what he's being frank about," said Sophie.

"Clive thinks he's too good-looking to be a virgin," said Tony.

Sophie laughed. Clive looked pained.

"It's a serious point," said Clive. "I knew I'd be mocked for it, but that doesn't make it less valid."

"You don't have to wear specs and have acne to be a virgin," said Bill.

"I understand, but . . . don't you think it shows on my face?"

Bill wrinkled his nose up in disgust.

"What?"

"Experience."

Sophie looked at him, because he was inviting scrutiny, and decided that even though he had probably slept with loads of girls, there was an innocence that could be mistaken for sexual inexperience. He hadn't lived much, as far as she could see. He'd spent too much time waiting around for something to happen to him.

"And anyway," said Clive, "why can't I . . . Why am I a virgin until the end of the script?"

"What we're implying," said Tony, "is that you're, you know . . . hopeless."

"Meaning?"

"Well. There are various forms of hopelessness, obviously. The one we were thinking of was impotence."

Clive slumped into his chair. He couldn't speak for several moments.

"Where does it say that?"

"It doesn't."

"Oh, bloody hell. Where is it implied?"

"Page nine. Did you not understand a word you were saying just now?"

"I just read the lines. I don't think about them."

He scanned the page.

"Oh, Christ. 'Hydraulic failure'? What would happen if I marched straight round to see a solicitor the morning after the first episode has gone out?"

"A solicitor?"

"There's got to be something legal here. Slander. Libel. Something."

"You'd be suing a fictional character who you'd agreed to play. I'd go to every day of the trial, if it came to court."

"I should never have agreed to those brackets," said Clive. "I'll be saying that for the rest of my life."

"It might have been the brackets that made us think of it," said Tony. "They're sort of a *droopy* punctuation mark, aren't they?"

"Well," said Clive, "mark my words: nobody's going to believe it."

He was wrong. They believed it and loved it and carried on loving it. There was one kind of life for them before the first episode of the new series and another kind of life afterward, and the night the program was transmitted marked the end of the life before. They would all remember the transmission at some point or another in the years to come, and they never failed to be surprised by the memory: their new lives had already been born, but they watched television with people who belonged to the old. Sophie went home to watch with her father and Auntie Marie; her father was appalled and confused and proud, and tried to anticipate jokes and plot developments, and always got it wrong, and then tried to make a case for the superiority of his own version, which meant that half the lines, and all the subtleties of timing and delivery, were lost. Dennis watched with Edith, who didn't laugh once, and told him at the end that it was very good indeed, if that was the sort of thing one liked. Clive could not resist going home to Eastleigh, to watch with Cathy and his mother and his gratifyingly disbelieving father, who had recovered himself by the end of the episode. He enjoyed the brackets and the hydraulic failure more than Clive's performance, he said, and told Cathy that she was well off out of it. Tony watched with June, who wept tears of pride at the end; they had both invited Bill, but he went home to Barnet to watch with his parents, who, he felt, with absolutely no evidence, seemed relieved by the unambiguous heterosexuality of the program. After that night, they belonged to each other as much as they belonged to anyone else.

BARBARA (AND JIM)

You will probably remember Barbara, the pneumatic, kinetic Blackpool lass who leaped, thrillingly, through the screen and into our living rooms, from a recent and especially noteworthy episode of *Comedy Playhouse*; you may even remember Jim—or, as the title of the show cruelly has it, (Jim), who was lucky enough to pick her up in the West End pub where she was working. Jim is now her handsome but hapless Home Counties husband, and he works for Mr. Wilson at 10 Downing Street. But now Barbara (and indeed Jim) have been given their own BBC Television series, they will be as hard to forget as one's own immediate family.

We are, of course, talking about a comedy series here, and therefore one should hesitate before invoking the practitioners of other, greater, art forms. But the superb work of Tony Holmes and Bill Gardiner (who wrote the popular but generic radio show *The Awkward Squad*), with its careful attention to the cadences and rhythms of ordinary speech, and its affection for the sorts of people who, until the last few years, have been underrepresented in any form of drama or fiction, brings to mind the work of Messrs. Braine, Barstow, and Sillitoe; none of these writers, however, are famous for their jokes, as yet, so one must of course acknowledge the debt that Mr. Holmes and Mr. Gardiner owe to Ray Galton and Alan Simpson, and perhaps even to Kingsley Amis.

There is, as yet, no Galton and Simpson series that attempts to deal with the relationships between men and women, however, specifically the relationships between husbands and wives; nor have the creators of *Hancock's Half Hour* yet ventured north of Watford to find their characters. Mr. Holmes and Mr. Gardiner, both from London, have to these ears provided Sophie Straw, the young and hitherto unknown actress who plays Barbara, with strikingly authentic dialog; she must be thanking her lucky stars for their ears every single day she goes into work. But then, she has repaid them in heaped spades, because Miss Straw is the most extraordinarily gifted comic actress I have seen since the war. She could not shine as she does without the subtle, unshowy but nonetheless impressive work of Clive Richardson, another *Awkward Squad* alumnus, but Miss Straw is a revelation, and the soul of the series.

Last night's episode revealed, startlingly, that the marriage between Barbara and Jim had not yet been consummated—a sorry state of affairs that had clearly been remedied by the end of the program, when we were presented with the ecstatic and amusingly metaphorical bongs of Big Ben. Indeed, the revelation may be too startling for some, and one suspects that, as we speak, the Director-General of the BBC will be looking with some dismay at thousands of green-inked letters asking him to resign. He should on no account do so. The very existence of *Barbara (and Jim)* indicates the birth of a modern Britain, one prepared to acknowledge that its citizens are as sex-obsessed as our neighbors across the Channel, and that those who have not received the benefit of a public school or university education are just as likely to make clever, amusing observations as those who have—maybe more so, if poor old Jim is any guide. This marriage can, over time, come to contain everything we have only just begun to think about in Britain; perhaps we would have done so sooner, had not the war and the long years of austerity intervened. Barbara (and Jim) could not be better, funnier, or more congenial guides to a decade that seems, finally, to be shaking off the dead hand of its predecessor.

The Times, 11 December 1964

NICK HORNBY

9

The interview galvanized her, and anyway she hated the idea that she might get caught out in a lie, so she found a flat in the neighborhood she'd already described—to Diane and the readers of *Crush*—as home: in Kensington Church Street, just up the hill from Derry and Toms. Sophie could walk out of the front door and be buying cosmetics at her old counter within ten minutes, if she wanted to. And it was only a little bit further on to Biba in Abingdon Road. She walked there on the first morning she woke up in her own bed and bought herself a brown pinstripe dress.

Marjorie seemed to be under the impression that they would be moving together.

"Oh," said Sophie. "No."

"Why not?"

"Well," said Sophie. "It's only got one bedroom."

"This place has only got one bedroom."

"Yes," said Sophie. "But I didn't think either of us liked it that way."

"I don't," said Marjorie. "I wish you were moving into a place with two bedrooms."

Sophie hadn't really thought of Marjorie as a dependent, someone she'd be carting around until Marjorie got married, or got promoted, or got her own television series.

"We never talked about staying together," said Sophie.

"I didn't think we needed to," said Marjorie. "I thought it was just one of those things."

"No," said Sophie. "It's not."

That degree of firmness felt uncomfortable, and Marjorie could tell.

"You are lucky," said Marjorie.

"I know."

"I don't think you do."

"I do."

"It's all looks," said Marjorie. "Honestly, I'd cut your face and bust off and put them on me if I thought it would make any difference. I don't know what I'd do about your waist. You can't steal waists, more's the pity."

Oh dear, thought Sophie. Not this again. She couldn't share a flat with Marjorie any longer, not with all the sharp implements around.

"You can't steal busts and faces either, is the truth of it," said Sophie.

"No, but at least they're actual things. A nice waist is sort of the absence of something, isn't it?"

"Anyway," said Sophie, who felt they were drifting away from the subject at hand, "I know how lucky I've been."

"But you don't want to share the luck."

"We're flatmates, Marjorie. I don't know how much I owe you."

"A lot, I think."

"I can tell."

"I took you in when you had nowhere to go."

"You were looking for someone to share the rent."

"There's always two ways of looking at everything."

There was nothing to be done about good fortune, if that's what she'd been given. Sophie could see that as long as it lasted, people would want some of it.

"You'll get someone else in," she said. "It's a nice flat."

"It's not."

"It's handy for work."

"So this is it, then?" said Marjorie. "You're just . . . off?"

"I think so," said Sophie. "I'll pay rent for another month, though."

"Ooh, the last of the big spenders."

She couldn't get her stuff out quick enough.

Her home in Blackpool had dark furniture and wallpaper and paintings of horses on the wall. The dark furniture had been inherited from her grandparents, and couldn't have been worth anything; the paintings of horses had been bought from Woolworths. But every home she went in was the same, even if the people she was visiting had a bit of money—the same fustiness, the same feeling that the good things in this country, the things that people valued, had all happened a long time ago, way before she was born. Before she'd moved to London, she'd loved looking at magazine photos of famous people at home, young people, fashion designers and singers and film stars, and she was dazzled by the white walls and the bright colors. Was it really only young people who wanted to paint over the misery of the last quarter of a century? The first thing she did when she moved in was strip off the brown wallpaper, and then she paid a man to paint the place white. As soon as she had the money and the time, she'd find things to hang on the walls. She didn't care what these things were, as long as they were yellow and red and green and there were no sailing ships or castles and there was nothing with four legs anywhere.

She bought herself two Le Corbusier–style chairs and Afghan rugs and a bed and two beanbags and even some pasta jars, though she hadn't ever bought or cooked pasta, from Habitat in the Fulham Road. The first people to visit were Brian and his wife; they came for drinks and then took her out to supper. The first person to stay the night was Clive.

The day after the first episode, with its ruinous insinuations, had aired, Clive took the view that he needed to mount a desperate public relations campaign that would entail sleeping with as many girls as possible, the less discreet the better. By the time he got to Bev, a lovely little thing he'd picked up at a party to launch a new cabaret club in Glasshouse Street, the naked female form was beginning to appear a little odd to him, and he didn't enjoy the occasion as much as he might have done. He didn't think Bev had noticed. He was, after all, a good actor, and, unlike Jim, he was never afflicted by any bizarre psychological and/or physiological problems. He was almost uncannily reliable, but as he rarely slept with the same girl for more than a couple of weeks, he didn't receive as many admiring comments as he thought he deserved. It was, he supposed, a good argument for marriage, perhaps the best he'd come across. If he were to sleep with the same woman all the time, then that woman would know just how extraordinarily dependable and responsive he was.

"Can I say I cured you?" said Bev afterward.

"Cured me?" he said, as if he didn't know what she was going to say next.

"In the first episode of *Barbara (and Jim)* . . ."

"Oh," he said. "Yes. I see what you mean. I'd forgotten all about that."

There had been two episodes since, neither of which, thankfully, made any reference to his marital inadequacies; he had urged Bill and Tony to include references to his subsequent marital adequacies, just to help the audience develop a fuller picture of the marriage, but they hadn't shown any interest in his notes so far.

"The thing is, I was cured by the end of the episode,"

said Clive. "Don't you remember? The chimes of Big Ben and all that?"

"I didn't really understand that bit," said Bev. "I thought it was New Year's Eve, suddenly."

"No," said Clive. "The bongs represented satisfactory sexual congress."

"Lost on me," said Bev. "But I do love the program. I never go out on Thursdays now."

Bev was not alone. They had started off with ten million viewers, and so far they had added another million a week.

"What's she like?" said Bev.

"Sophie? Yes, she's very nice."

"You should be with her," said Bev.

There was no wistfulness in her voice. She seemed to be speaking as a television fan, rather than as a lover.

"Do you think?"

"Yes. Can you imagine?"

"Imagine what?"

"You'd be like the Burton and Taylor of the BBC. Everyone would go mad."

"Do you think so?"

"Well, I'd love it, and I'm lying in bed with you."

It was quite a persuasive observation.

Clive took Sophie to the Trattoo, just down the road from Sophie's new flat, on a Saturday night, after the technical rehearsal for the fourth episode. He told her that Spike

Milligan and Peter Sellers ate there all the time, but there was no sign of either of them. And in the absence of any proper celebrities, heads turned when they walked into the restaurant and people started whispering. And because the sight of the other diners whispering was so startling, Clive and Sophie started whispering too.

"Are they whispering because we walked in?" said Sophie.

"I think so," said Clive.

"Bloody hell," said Sophie.

"I know," said Clive.

"Has that ever happened to you before?"

"Because of my radio work on *The Awkward Squad*, you mean?"

"This is so odd. What do we do?"

A lady on the table behind Clive's shoulder smiled at her. Sophie smiled back.

"Give them something to talk about."

He took Sophie's hands in his and looked into her eyes. The whispering in the room didn't get louder, because the people were all very well dressed and well behaved, but it got faster: the *s*'s all got squished up together until the room sounded like the African bush, and Sophie had a giggling fit. Clive looked hurt.

"I'm sorry," she said. "Did you mean that?"

"Well," he said. "I did, rather."

And that was how their relationship began. There was more to it than that, of course. There was wine, and delicious food, and Sophie deciding that Clive was actually very handsome indeed. After dinner, they walked up the road hand in hand, and she invited him in, and they drank some more, and then they went into her bedroom and he made love to her. There were no difficulties whatsoever, so Clive didn't mind Sophie referring jokily to Jim's first-episode nerves afterward. But it didn't seem quite the same, when they were on their own. It was rather as if the point of them had been lost. They couldn't give the people what they wanted, if there were no people around to receive the gift.

Toward the end of the series, Tony and Bill found themselves running out of inspiration and straying back dangerously close to Gambols territory. All they had for the last episode was an idea about a new secretary starting in Jim's office at Number Ten.

"Let me guess," said Clive when he saw the title page of the script. "Jim employs a new secretary and Barbara gets jealous."

Tony and Bill didn't say anything.

"Oh, Christ," said Clive.

"Line by line it's funny," said Bill.

Clive closed his eyes and opened a page at random.

"Don't do that, you bastard," said Tony.

"If it's funny line by line . . ."

"Yes, but you'll read it out in a way that destroys it."

"Is that what I normally do, then? Thanks a lot."

He read one of his lines out anyway.

"'I haven't even noticed whether she's a man or a woman.'"

There was a silence round the table.

"Shall I try it again? 'I haven't even noticed whether she's a man or a woman.' Give me a little help here," said Clive. "Tell me how to wring maximum mirth out of that particular gag."

"Don't be daft, Clive. You know that's not how it works."

"It's just a boring situation," said Clive. "The new secretary has been done to death."

"You haven't read it. How do you know we haven't found something new in it?"

Tony groaned.

"What did you say that for?" he said to Bill. "You know we haven't."

"I hadn't seen this script until just now," said Clive. "But let me tell you what's in it."

He was given no encouragement, but he went ahead anyway.

"Jim hires a new secretary. Barbara gets it into her head that this secretary has the looks of Marilyn Monroe and the morals of Fanny Hill. She makes an excuse to visit Jim at the office. It turns out that the new secretary is a fat Sunday School teacher with a harelip and three-inch-thick specs."

This time there was a long, long silence.

"You won't be happy until we've hung ourselves, will you?" said Tony.

"It's a lot of cock," said Clive. "You've gone back to the

Gambols. George Gambol seems to get a new secretary every third week."

The Gambols were becoming a disease, like the measles or the mumps. The moment Barbara started feeling jealous, or Jim started spending too long tinkering with his car, Tony and Bill knew that their script wasn't feeling very well.

"All right," said Bill. "Let's not do what Clive expects. Let's say Barbara's got something to worry about."

"That's more like it," said Clive. "Dennis can get some gorgeous dolly bird in to play the secretary, and—"

"Who?" said Dennis.

"I don't know," said Clive. "There are a million of them out there."

"Name one," said Dennis.

"Anne Richards is very pretty."

Anne Richards was the old LAMDA friend Clive had lunched recently. She'd be grateful for the work.

"We don't want pretty," said Dennis. "We want someone who's a complete knockout."

"Why? Pretty would do the trick."

"Barbara isn't going to be scared of pretty," said Dennis. "We have a twenty-one-year-old blonde bombshell as our leading character . . ."

Tony and Bill winced. Sophie winced once she'd worked out what Dennis had done wrong.

"Leading character?" said Clive.

"Leading female character, I should have said . . ."

NICK HORNBY

160

"Except you didn't," said Clive. "I should never have agreed to those bloody brackets. They were a terrible mistake."

"Here we go again," said Tony.

"You know what's going to be on my gravestone?" said Clive. Nobody showed any interest in the question. "'Here Lies the Unknown Actor. He Should Never Have Agreed to the Brackets.'"

"Oh, you won't live for another year," said Tony. "I'll murder you before then."

"We have a twenty-one-year-old blonde bombshell as our leading *female* character," said Dennis. "Jim's already out of his league. And he works in Whitehall, which, let's face it . . . Well, it's not known for, for . . ."

"The quality of its skirt," said Clive helpfully.

"Barbara is young, gorgeous, childless, fashionable . . . Even if Jim were to fall hook, line, and sinker for the new secretary, the audience would find it hard to believe that she represented any kind of a threat."

"Especially if Clive's trying to find employment for one of his raddled ex-girlfriends from LAMDA," said Bill.

"I resent that," said Clive.

"Which part?"

Clive thought for a moment too long, provoking cruel laughter from the writers.

"I suspect," said Dennis, "that the old new secretary story line is for a more established marriage and a more . . . careworn woman."

"Young women can get jealous," said Sophie.

"But nobody would understand why, is the thing," said Dennis.

One of the things he loved about rehearsals was that he could sometimes sneak in a compliment and nobody noticed.

Tony and Bill looked glum.

"Looks like we've got the rest of the day off," said Clive. "Hurrah for the hackneyed imaginations of our writers."

He stood up and stretched.

"You haven't forgotten about tonight?" said Dennis.

He and Edith were throwing a drinks party. None of them wanted to go: they were all afraid of Edith and her friends, and they hated the way she talked to her husband.

"We haven't even got a script," said Tony.

"You have to come," said Dennis.

He knew he sounded panicky, but if none of his BBC friends came, then it was only Them, the Vernon Whitfields of the world, the critics and editors and Third Program horrors.

"It's not going to be all that lot, is it?" said Clive.

"What lot?"

"All those critics and poets and editors?"

"No," said Dennis. "I've insisted that only jolly people come."

Nobody believed him, he could tell.

"We'll be there," said Sophie. "I'm not scared."

She looked threateningly at the others, and they all caved in. Dennis was grateful to them. It wasn't every night that his wife's lover came to his home—not with his knowledge anyway.

Clive and Sophie went to the party together.

"There are a lot of rumors about Edith and Vernon Whitfield," he said to her on the way there. "Just so you know."

"That sounds spicy. What happens in Vernon Whitfield?"

Clive snorted.

"It's not a place. It's a man. He's a critic, and a broadcaster, and a novelist, and so on and on."

"How do you know that?" she asked him.

"I don't. Not for sure. It's a rumor. But it makes perfect sense."

"No, I mean . . . How do you know that Vernon Whitfield is a critic and a broadcaster and a so-on?"

"Ah. That's not a rumor. That's more what you might call a fact."

"But why do you know this fact and I don't?"

"You're not very interested in critics and broadcasters, are you?"

"Is he on the Third?"

"The Third and the Home."

"I listen to the Home sometimes, but only the comedy."

"He's very much not a comedian. He's the opposite of a comedian. He's the least funny person who ever lived."

"So what do I do?"

"To find out who Vernon Whitfield is? Well, I suppose you start listening to the Third and the unfunny bits of the Home. And reading the weeklies. I really wouldn't bother."

"But when I'm talking to clever people like you, I might start talking about picnics in Vernon Whitfield."

"Oh, he's no picnic, I can tell you."

"You know what I mean."

"Have you seen the TV series *Barbara (and Jim)*?" He drew the brackets in the air. He always did that. "You'd enjoy it. The girl in that is very intellectually insecure."

"Why didn't you go to university?"

"I went to drama school instead. Why didn't you?"

"You know I couldn't have gone. I was working behind a cosmetics counter when I was fifteen."

"And look at you now."

"Anyway," said Sophie, "poor Dennis."

"I don't know. He may get shot of her."

"I'd never be able to have an affair with Vernon Whitfield," said Sophie wistfully.

This made Clive laugh a lot.

"What have I said now?"

"I think you'll find that if you were to offer Vernon Whitfield a roll in the hay, he'd be a very, very happy essayist and broadcaster."

"I don't want that sort of affair."

"I'm not sure how many varieties of affair there are."

"I'll bet the kind Vernon Whitfield is having with Edith isn't the kind he'd have with me."

"You'd be surprised."

"I might try," she said artfully. "Just to see."

"Be my guest," he said, and laughed.

She didn't understand the laughter until they got to Dennis's flat: Vernon Whitfield was not a traditionally handsome man. He was short, bespectacled, and nervous-looking. Sophie had never met anyone who broadcast on the Third Program before, but she could see why he'd been given the job. The strange thing was that Edith was actually quite attractive. She wasn't sexy in the least (too thin, too cold), but she was tall, much taller than Vernon, and she was elegant, and she had a very long neck that Sophie rather envied.

She glided over to Sophie and asked her whether she wanted a top-up. Everyone else Sophie knew had temporarily deserted her for an *Awkward Squad* reunion.

"Red wine," said Sophie, holding out the glass.

"Was it the Beaujolais?" said Edith.

That was all it took for Sophie to begin to feel that she shouldn't have come to the party, shouldn't know Dennis, shouldn't be working for the BBC. It was so stupid. Maybe Beaujolais was a red wine and maybe it wasn't: who cared? She could have just nodded and smiled and said thank you and drunk whatever Edith brought her. Instead, she just froze.

"Beaujolais is a red wine, dear," said Edith. "We're not trying to poison you."

And she could have just walked over to the *Awkward*

people and the others would have introduced her to the actors she didn't know and they would have said things like, "Pleased to meet you," and "Congratulations!" and "We love your program!" and "We love you!" But Edith had gone to get her a drink, so she wasn't allowed to move.

"Salut," said Edith, and chinked Sophie's glass.

Sophie smiled. Vernon Whitfield wandered over to join them.

"Do you know Vernon Whitfield?" said Edith.

"I've heard of you, of course," said Sophie.

Vernon Whitfield nodded, as if this was inevitable and also a bit boring.

"Sophie's the star of Dennis's TV program," said Edith.

"Ah," said Vernon Whitfield.

He was the star, in his head, in this room; he was the one who delivered lectures on the Third. Sophie's variety of stardom—seventeen million viewers now, and on the cover of the *Radio Times* (with Jim)—didn't really register.

"Everyone has a television now," he went on, with obvious disapproval.

"I don't," said Edith.

"Good for you," said Vernon Whitfield.

"Isn't that a television?" said Sophie, nodding toward the corner of the living room.

"It's not mine," said Edith.

She snorted at the very suggestion that it might have been, so Vernon Whitfield snorted too. Was it really possible that these two were having an affair? Sophie could imagine them having a good snort together, but that was about all. She had no idea what Dennis was like in bed, and she didn't want to think about it too deeply, but she could imagine his enthusiasm and kindness. And also, he looked nothing like a frog.

"It's funny that you've got a television and I haven't," said Sophie. It was true. The Radio Rentals people still hadn't delivered hers.

"First, it's not my television," said Edith. "And secondly, why is it funny?"

"What's funny," said Vernon Whitfield, "is that because Suzy has no television, she has managed to find the time to read the latest Margaret Drabble and we haven't."

This, it turned out, was even funnier than the idea that the television in Edith's house belonged to her. It was obvious that Margaret Drabble was an author; obvious too that she was an author Sophie was not expected to have read. She wasn't dim. But these people made her dim. They made her afraid, and the fear resulted in mental paralysis.

"I haven't read Margaret Drabble," said Sophie.

This was the sentence she'd been instructing herself not to say a couple of minutes before. It popped out anyway. Vernon and Edith got a fit of the giggles then.

"The New Colleague," formerly "The New Secretary," was ready by the following lunchtime. Everyone, including Dennis, had pitched in, during a long, boozy, loud session in a pub on Hammersmith Grove, round the corner from Dennis's house. Dennis had left his own party, and later that night, when he got home, he left his own marriage. He told Edith he knew about the affair, he didn't love her anymore, and he wanted her to leave. She was shocked, and embarrassed, and upset, but she left. He had been drunk when he made the speech, but in Dennis's opinion it didn't diminish its magnificence or his pride in it.

"The New Colleague" was conceived as an act of revenge—on Edith, for her crimes against Dennis and Sophie, and on the British middle classes, for their crimes (unspecified) against Tony and Bill. Jim invites Edwina, the eponymous addition to the staff at Number Ten, to dinner at the house; Edwina turns out to be a bluestocking socialist who is both amused and appalled by Barbara, tries to patronize her, and clearly regards her marriage to Jim as temporary. (There is a suggestion that she sees herself as filling the vacancy.) Over the course of the thirty minutes, Barbara runs rings around Edwina—to Jim's initial discomfort and, later, great delight. Just about any position Edwina tries to adopt—on politics, or the arts, or religion—Barbara rips apart with her teeth. She doesn't know as much as Edwina, of course, but Edwina is revealed to have a plodding intelligence and her blue stockings are full of unexamined assumptions, as well as long, bony legs. (Dennis cast the tallest, poshest girl he could find.) Edwina hands in her resignation the next day and goes off to work for the Conservatives—much to Tory-voting Barbara's confusion and dismay. It was a show that polarized critics, but the critics who didn't like it didn't believe in Barbara's speed of thought, which rather proved the point.

After Sophie had scraped the last of the makeup off her face, she was aware of the first sharp pangs of something that felt like homesickness. They'd already been told that the BBC wanted another series, but that was months away; and anyway, the last episode of the first series made her realize that one day there would be a last episode, and she didn't know whether she'd be able to bear it. And it didn't help, telling herself that when it was time for the last episode, she'd have had enough, because she couldn't bear that either. She wanted to stay like this forever. She changed her wish quickly: not like this, not exactly . . . she wanted it to be the Monday just gone, with a whole week of rehearsals to look forward to, and then a recording. That's where she would like to stop. She was already afraid that she'd never be happier than now—then—and it was already over. She went to look for Clive, and she took him home and made him something to eat and he made love to her. But it wasn't work.

THE SECOND
SERIES

If Sophie had asked Brian to custom-design a miserable few months intended to make her grateful for *Barbara (and Jim)* and all who sailed in her, he couldn't have done a better job. People from Hollywood wanted her to be in movies, he said, and when she didn't believe him, he sent her a script called *Chemin de Fer*. She read it, and didn't really understand it, and called him on her phone. She never got tired of picking up her phone and dialing a number and not putting a coin in a slot.

"First of all," she said, "what does *Chemin de Fer* mean?"

"It's the same thing as baccarat."

"You're going to have to say something else it's the same thing as."

"Shimmy."

"No. Try again."

"It's a card game they play in casinos."

"Nobody knows about casinos."

"Of course they do, sweetheart. They're even legal now. You're being naive."

"I've never been in a casino."

"Of course you haven't."

"I'll bet Tony and Bill have never been in casinos."

"Why do we care what Tony and Bill have never done? They're BBC writers. They've never done anything."

Tony and Bill would never have written *Chemin de Fer*. They cared too much about things being real, and about how one scene led to the next. This script was like a dish made from things you'd found in your larder and had to use up before they went off: a Welsh mountain, a casino, a blonde with a big bust.

"They could have gone to a casino. They're on good money," said Sophie.

"They're not on commercial television money."

"I mean, compared to everyone else in Britain. People who work in shops and live in the North."

"Oh, well," said Brian, "I don't know how much we can worry about them."

"You don't want them to see the film? If it's only for people who play chemin de fer, it isn't going to do very well."

"Nonsense," said Brian. "Crockford's was packed on Friday."

She gave up.

"Anyway, what did you think of it?" Brian asked.

"It's terrible."

"They know it's terrible. They're getting John Osborne

to rewrite it. And he's putting in a lot of jokes for your character."

"Is he going to explain why they end up shooting people in Wales?"

"They're up a mountain, Sophie. There are no mountains in Paris or London or wherever you want them to be shooting people. Honestly. What are you looking for?"

Sophie could see that it wasn't a script one could spend any time arguing about. You either did it or you turned it down. She had nothing else to do, and the money was extraordinary, and Brian was very excited. If she insisted on being an actress, then this was exactly the sort of thing she should be acting in, he thought. She was only one or two moves away from the gold spray paint and the bikinis, and then the world was hers. Clive, on the other hand, didn't seem to care one way or the other whether she disappeared off to Wales.

"I'll say no if you want me to."

"Why on earth would I want you to say no?"

"Because you'd miss me too much."

"I'll come to Wales and see you."

"Will you?"

"Of course."

"And can I ask you a favor?"

"Anything."

"Will you feed Brando?"

She had been sent a Siamese cat by a proud Blackpool

pet shop. It had been delivered to the BBC in a van and the van driver wouldn't take it back again.

"That would be lovely. I'll feel connected to you when you're gone."

He didn't come to Wales. (He didn't feed the cat either. When she got back, Brando had gone.)

John Osborne, it turned out, was not available for the rewrite of *Chemin de Fer*. (Sophie suggested Tony and Bill, but the American producers weren't interested.) A man who'd written something for a Dean Martin film did it instead. He put in three jokes for her character, two of which were removed before the shoot and one of which didn't survive the edit. She hated the director.

She liked the leading man, a French pop singer named Johnny Solo, presumably by his manager rather than by Monsieur and Madame Solo. He was charming and extraordinarily handsome, and after he'd chased her around the hotel they were staying in, she could no longer remember why she was running away, so she stopped. It wasn't as if she had a boyfriend, as far as she could tell. Johnny was a terrible actor, though, and in any case he couldn't speak English. Most days Sophie had to ask the cameras to stop rolling, because she could only listen to the French pop star's American accent with a straight face for very short periods of time. They had a bad script, an awful director, and a terrible leading man; it was all so hopeless that she didn't even have to consider her own performance, luckily.

Clive didn't call her until a few days before they were supposed to start rehearsing again.

"Where've you been?" she said.

"Where have I been? Nowhere. You, meanwhile, have been lounging around in your underwear in Wales, while Johnny Foreigner ogles."

"You could have ogled, if you'd come to Wales."

"Who goes all the way to Wales for an ogle? Especially a secondhand ogle."

She didn't want to have a conversation about second-hand ogling, and she certainly didn't want a conversation about Johnny Foreigner.

"What did you do instead, then?"

"Oh, you know," he said airily. "Thinking. Reading. Taking stock."

She wished he'd chosen any three other activities—space exploration, say, and needlework and coal mining. He wasn't a thinker or a reader or a stock-taker.

"Seeing girls?"

"Oh, for God's sake."

"'For God's sake' is different from 'no.'"

She couldn't seem to stop herself. And what right did she have to say anything, when she'd stopped running from Johnny Foreigner? If Clive had come to Wales, though, she wouldn't have stopped running. She'd have run and run.

"I was actually phoning to ask you out to dinner," he said eventually. There was to be no further discussion about the precise meaning of the expression "For God's sake," apparently.

She shrugged down the phone, but he couldn't see her, so in the end she had to say yes.

They had another argument in the Trattoo, a nasty one. He accused her of being bourgeois, whatever that was—it seemed to involve engagement rings and babies and all sorts of things she wasn't interested in. He got so heated about them that for a moment she thought he might actually be proposing, in an angry, cack-handed fashion. She asked him about other girls, and he was cagey, and she said she didn't mind; he asked her about Johnny Foreigner, and she was cagey, and he didn't speak to her all the way home. He didn't stay the night.

Tony booked a table in the Positano Room at the Trattoria Terrazza for his wedding anniversary, mostly because Bill told him to.

"The place in Romilly Street? I'll never get in there. Isn't that where they all go? Michael Caine and Jean Shrimpton and everyone?"

"'We.' Not 'they,'" said Bill.

"Who's 'we'?"

"You and me and Michael Caine and Jean Shrimpton."

"Oh, get out of it," said Tony.

"People know who we are."

"People in the contracts department of the BBC. And a couple of reviewers. Let's not get above ourselves. We're writers."

"That'll be enough to get you a table."

"I'm not going to call them and tell them I'm a famous television writer and they have to let me in."

"Get Hazel to do it."

Hazel was their new secretary. The phone in the office had been ringing a lot since *Barbara*, mostly with offers of work, and they'd employed Hazel to answer it. This occupied perhaps half an hour of her working day, and they didn't know what to do with her the rest of the time. And they couldn't work with her in the one-room office, so for the moment they'd gone back to the coffee bar.

"How is that going to help?"

"She'll tell them you're a famous television writer and they have to let you in."

"But then I'll get there and I'll just be me and it will be embarrassing."

"What night do you want to go?" said Bill.

"Our anniversary's next Tuesday. I was going to take her out Saturday."

"Oh."

"What?"

"You're not Saturday-night famous. Take her out on Tuesday night and you'll be all right."

There were famous people in the Positano Room, even on a Tuesday night. As Tony and June were waiting to be seated, Terence Stamp looked straight at them, and Tony momentarily lost his nerve.

"Shall we go somewhere else?"

June looked at him, baffled.

"Why?"

"Terence Stamp just looked at me."

"Where is he supposed to look?"

"You can see what he's thinking. He's thinking, Who let them in? They're not beautiful or famous."

"Thanks."

But she laughed. Tony never had to worry about her sulking, or looking for offense and then taking it. It was a miracle that they had stayed married for one hundred weeks, given everything, and June's view was that they had enough trouble, without looking for it. She seemed determined to find the unintended insults and the accidental ironies funny, whenever she could.

An impressively Italian waiter in a stripy matelot T-shirt that showed off his beautiful dark skin took them to a table on the edge of the room. Their nearest neighbors were two debby girls who were apparently too pretty to talk to each other, or even to eat. Their meals were untouched, and they were both smoking long, thin cigarettes. June was trying not to stare at their long, thin legs and their short skirts.

"We're supposed to order the osso buco," said Tony as they looked at their menus.

"Who said?"

"Bill."

"Who did he come here with?"

"I don't know."

Why hadn't he asked? He might have learned something about Bill's life outside the office and the rehearsal hall and the studio.

"Is he happy, do you think?"

June knew as much about Bill's private life as Tony did.

"He seems happy, yes."

"Why don't you ever ask him about things like that?"

"Men don't."

"What do you ask him about, then?"

Tony thought. He couldn't really remember asking Bill about anything that wasn't related to the script they were working on. Bill asked him about June all the time, but Tony didn't ask him anything in return. He was afraid of what Bill might tell him.

"Oh, you know. Whether he's got a girlfriend, and things like that."

June made a face.

"What?"

"I'm not that naive. Of course he hasn't got a girlfriend."

"You knew that?"

"Yes. I mean, not straightaway. He's not a queen. Neither of you is."

"I'm not one at all."

"You're a married man, you mean?"

The waiter with the beautiful dark skin came, and they ordered melon and the osso buco, as instructed. Tony asked him for a wine recommendation too. He wanted to ask him about his aftershave, but decided that this was an inquiry that June would misinterpret.

"There's something we have in common," said June when he'd gone.

"What?"

"Him."

"The waiter? Really?"

"Not half. But I think I'd be making the same mistake again."

"It isn't . . . It wouldn't be the same mistake. Well, it might be. I'd have to know more about him."

"Oh, that old story."

She laughed. Tony was becoming excruciated.

"I don't know what I am."

June looked at him.

"Really?"

"Yes. I thought I did. And then I met you, and now I don't."

"Gosh. So . . . Right. OK. Golly. I had no idea."

"You thought I was just . . ."

"Not at first. Obviously. But then . . . Well, yes. To cut a long story short."

There was an awkward pause.

"Can I ask you questions?"

"Oh, Gawd."

He got a laugh, but he couldn't deflect her.

"Do . . . Well, did you ever do anything about the other thing?"

"No," he said too quickly. And then, because he wanted to give due weight to the Aldershot incident, "Not really."

"What does 'Not really' mean?"

"I went looking once. During National Service. It all ended badly, and nothing happened."

"Oh. And . . . is that how you want to spend the rest of your life?"

He had tried very hard not to think about the rest of his life. He saw flashes of it sometimes, and these flashes made him uncomfortable, because he saw the possibility for pain and drama, and he didn't want that.

"I don't know. I hope . . . What I hope is that nothing keeps happening. On that side. And something starts happening on this side."

"Thank you," June said.

"For what?"

"For even saying that much. It helps."

"Thank you," he said.

"For what?"

"You're so patient, and kind, and loving, and I don't know why."

"I love you," she said with a shrug and a little smile—not a sad smile, exactly, but a smile conveying complications.

"I love you too."

They had said the things you were supposed to say at an anniversary dinner, but they hadn't said them glibly. They chinked glasses.

"It's funny, sex," she said. "It's a little thing like a glass of water is a little thing. Or something that falls off a car and only costs a couple of bob to replace. It's only a little thing, but nothing works without it."

The nice-smelling dark-skinned waiter in the white T-shirt arrived with their melon.

"What do we use?" said Tony. "A spoon?"

"I think so."

"I've never had this before," said Tony. "Terrible, isn't it?"

"Why is it so terrible?"

"I dunno. Seems like I haven't done anything I should have."

"I haven't had it either."

"Well, there's a reason for that."

June laughed.

"This is like the eating scene in *Tom Jones*," she said. "Do you remember? With Albert Finney and Susannah York?"

"It wasn't Susannah York in the eating scene. It was Joyce thingy."

"Joyce Redman," said June.

"Joyce Redman," said Tony.

A nice life wasn't so far away, if they could somehow get hold of the little thing that makes the engine work. He could remember that it was Joyce someone, not Susannah

York, and she could remember Joyce's second name, and in forty years' time they would make a great couple.

"When's Barbara and Jim's anniversary?" said June.

And that was another thing: the series was always somewhere near the front of her mind. How could he not love that?

"I've got no idea."

"Maybe you should pick a date."

"Oh," he said. "I see what you mean."

"And they haven't talked about starting a family yet either."

"Christ." He laughed. "We hadn't even thought about that. I could kiss you."

"Men normally say that to people they don't want to kiss," she said. "The old secretary, when she does something clever. The cleaner, when she finds a pair of spectacles." She laughed, but he could have kicked himself.

"All right, then, I will kiss you," he said.

And when they got home they had another drink, and, after a lot of encouragement and some laughter and a little imagination, they managed something. It probably wasn't quite enough to prevent other conversations in the future, unless Tony had somehow stumbled upon some alchemical admixture of alcohol, ardor, dissociation, and competence that he could bottle, but it wasn't nothing. After June had gone to sleep, he realized that they had never talked about starting a family either. It had never occurred to him that he'd be able to.

One afternoon in July, Dennis phoned Tony and Bill up at the office to tell them to watch that night's *Comedy Playhouse*.

"What is it?" said Bill.

"It's called *Till Death Us Do Part*."

"Bugger," said Bill.

"What?"

"It's a clever title. Why didn't we think of it?"

"The program is really rather good," said Dennis. "I went to the recording. It's one of Other Dennis's. He invited me. He's very proud of it."

"Will it depress us?" said Bill. "Because I don't want to watch anything that's depressing."

"It's very funny," said Dennis.

"That's exactly what I'm talking about," said Bill. "Very funny is depressing."

"Our show is very funny," said Dennis. "This one's funny in a different way."

"A better way or a worse way?" said Bill.

"Different," said Dennis firmly. "Anyway. They may not even make a series out of it. Sloan hates it, apparently."

"Why?"

"Too subversive."

Bill knew beyond any doubt that *Till Death Us Do Part* was going to be very depressing indeed.

Tony and Bill watched the show together, at Tony's house. June cooked sausages and mash and they all sat

down with trays on their laps. The Ramseys, the family at the center of the program, were working-class East Enders; docker Alf was a Conservative, as foulmouthed as the BBC would allow, prejudiced (blacks, Jews, anyone who wasn't white and British, as Alf saw it), a Churchill-lover, a fervent monarchist. Nobody had ever seen anything like him on television. When Alf's Scouser son-in-law first appeared, Bill howled in outrage.

"They've nicked our idea!"

"Because he's from the North?" said Tony.

"They seem to be very different people, him and Barbara," said June.

"And they come from a different place," said Tony.

"It's the same thing!" said Bill. "We thought of that!"

"Yes," said Tony. "We're brilliant. We had the brain wave of a character who came from somewhere else."

"You didn't, actually," said June. "Sophie did. She came up with it by actually coming from somewhere else."

"Can we all shut up?" said Bill. "I want to listen."

Till Death Us Do Part was brilliant, savage, fresh, real, and unlike anything they had ever seen. Tony and June enjoyed it a lot, but by the closing credits Bill was sunk in a gloom so deep that he could hardly talk.

"We're finished," he said eventually.

"Why are we finished?"

"They're ahead of the game. We were something when we started. We're nothing now."

June laughed.

"It's not even a series yet. It might never be a series. You're miles ahead of them. And people adore *Barbara (and Jim).*"

"Oh, *people,*" said Bill. "I'm not talking about *people.*"

"Who are we talking about, then?" said Tony. "Critics?"

"While there are still people, you're not finished," said June. "That's what it's all about."

"Why didn't we set ours in an ordinary working-class home? We lived in ordinary working-class homes."

"Yeah, and they were horrible," said Tony. "I wouldn't want to look at them once a week, let alone write about them every day."

"And the whole point of *Barbara (and Jim)* is that they come from different classes," said June. "That was the joke."

"Why did she end up in his, though?" said Bill. "Why couldn't he have gone to live in hers?"

"Because why would he?" said Tony. "Why would she, more to the point? Why would anyone, if they had the choice? People want to get out of those places, Bill. They're all being knocked down."

"And hers was in Blackpool," said June. "I don't know how someone who works at Number Ten goes up and down to Blackpool every day."

"Yeah, well, we shouldn't have had him working at Number Ten, should we?"

"So you're saying we wrote the wrong program altogether," said Tony.

"Yes."

"The series that just about everyone in Britain watches every week . . ."

"The show that made a star out of Sophie . . ." said June.

"The series that pays you a decent wage because it's done so well for us . . . No bloody good?"

"Tom Sloan hates *Till Death Us Do Part*, according to Dennis," Bill said. "Why doesn't he hate anything we write?"

"Is that what you'd prefer? That our boss hated what we do?"

"Yes," said Bill. "Of course."

Tony was beginning to realize that he and Bill might want different things. It had never occurred to him before.

S o," said Dennis when they reconvened for the second series. "What have we all been up to?"

He was genuinely happy to see them all. He'd been

lonely, and he didn't like any of the other programs he'd been working on, and he'd missed Sophie, who had achieved mythical status in her absence, a cross between Helen and Aphrodite. When he saw her again, he realized that he'd been selling her short.

"Well," said Clive, "Sophie's been sleeping with French pop stars."

"And Clive has been sleeping with anyone he bumps into."

And they both gave thin-lipped smiles.

"Oh, Christ," said Bill.

"What?" said Dennis.

He was bewildered, and appalled. He didn't want Sophie to sleep with anyone, let alone French pop stars.

"You had to go and bitch it all up, didn't you?" Bill said to Clive.

"Me?" said Clive, outraged. "How have I bitched it up?"

"Oh, bloody hell," said Tony.

Dennis now understood only that he was the one person in the room who didn't understand.

"Am I missing something?" he said.

"It's obvious," said Bill, in the manner of a detective in the last scene of an Agatha Christie play. "These two"—he gestured at Clive and Sophie—"have been at it. Except Clive can never be at it with one person at a time, so it's all gone wrong. And we have to deal with the consequences."

Of course, Dennis thought. Of course these two would end up sleeping together. He was a fool to think any different. He took a deep breath and tried to concentrate on the issues at hand. He was a producer, not a spurned lover.

"Do you want to tell them about Johnny Foreigner, or shall I?" said Clive to Sophie.

"Is he the French pop star?" said Bill. "You mentioned him a minute ago."

"There won't be any consequences," said Sophie. "We're professional people."

Clive didn't say anything.

"Clive?" said Dennis. "Are you a professional person?"

"Yes, of course I am," said Clive sulkily.

"Right," said Dennis. "Shall we start?"

"Before we read, can I say something?" said Sophie. "About the script?"

Bill made a be-our-guest gesture.

"Right. Well. I don't want to talk about having a family."

"We're not asking you to," said Bill. "We're asking Barbara to. You can talk about what you want."

"It's too much of a commitment," said Sophie.

"I agree," said Clive.

"I know we've told you before, but it's worth repeating," said Bill. "These are fictional characters. In the program, they're married. In real life, you're not. We're not asking you to have an actual baby."

"We're not even asking the characters to have a bloody baby," said Tony. "We're asking them to *talk* about it. They've been married for a year and neither of them has shown the slightest bit of interest in raising a family."

"I didn't sign up to be a father," said Clive. "That's a different thing entirely."

"I know we've told you before, but it's worth repeating," said Bill. "These are fictional characters. In the—"

"If I become a fictional father, I have a real commitment to my fictional children," said Clive.

"Ah," said Tony. "That might be where we're going wrong. I don't know who told you that, but it's not true. An actor has no legal responsibilities to any dependants named in a television comedy script."

"I know you think I'm an idiot," said Clive. "But it isn't me that gets confused. It's that lot out there. The viewers. People already say things. If Jim becomes a father, they'll say more things."

"What sort of things?"

"They . . ." He glanced at Sophie nervously. "They think I should be at home with Barbara."

"When?"

"When I'm not."

The others looked at him, fascinated.

"What do they say?"

"Oh, you know. 'I'll tell Barbara.' Things like that. They've been saying it all the time we've been off the air."

"What are you doing when they say it?" Sophie asked.

"Nothing! Having dinner with a colleague."

"Aren't we your colleagues?"

"Colleagues in the acting industry."

"I don't understand," said Sophie. "You're in a pub—"

"For example," said Clive.

"—having a pint with another chap . . ."

She left a pause, but Clive decided not to fill it.

". . . and people say that they'll tell Barbara? Why would they do that?"

"And what does it matter what they say?" said Tony.

"I don't like it," said Clive. "And it's embarrassing for my, my colleagues."

"These fellas, just standing there drinking their pints."

"I wonder," said Bill, scratching his chin thoughtfully, "whether it gets even more confusing because you've been having sex with the actress who plays Barbara?"

"They don't know that."

"They probably will by now," said Sophie. "That's all anyone seems to talk about these days, my sex life."

"Confusing for you, I meant," said Bill. "You probably wouldn't mind them saying that they'll tell Barbara if you didn't care whether Barbara knew."

"There's nothing for Barbara to know," said Clive.

"There's nothing you want to tell her, anyway."

"All I'm saying is that it's a right palaver, being on a successful TV show," said Clive. "And I don't want to make it worse. What if I wanted to leave?"

"Are you talking as Jim or Clive?"

"Clive, you idiot."

"If you left, we would no longer have a show entitled *Barbara (and Jim)*," said Bill.

"That's the nicest thing you've ever said to me."

"It would just be called *Barbara*," said Sophie. She never tired of that joke.

"But that's what worries me," said Clive. "If I walked out on Barbara and the kids, I wouldn't be able to go out anywhere. I'd be attacked in the street."

"What about you, Sophie?" said Dennis. "Why don't you want kids?"

"I do," said Sophie. "I just don't want them with him."

"You should have thought of that before you married him," said Clive.

Dennis suddenly understood that Bill's joke didn't work anymore: Barbara and Jim were not fictional characters. Their popularity, the public's investment in them, made them real, and they needed care and guidance. He was prepared to do it, because he had nobody at home to worry about. He hoped the others felt the same way.

The majority of the episodes had been two-handers, and writers, cast, and critics seemed to prefer them that way. "The Anniversary" was mostly set in a smart restaurant, however, and Tony and Bill had written parts for another, elderly couple at a nearby table, who end up bellowing out their marital grievances and disappointments, much to the consternation of Barbara and Jim—Jim is eventually obliged to separate the pair when the wife starts raining blows upon the husband's head.

When Dennis arrived for work on Wednesday morning, the two actors he'd booked were sitting outside the rehearsal room looking perplexed. The man was wearing a bow tie and the woman was wearing a hat that she might have borrowed from Mary Pickford. They both looked desperate, and they'd both lied about their age—Dennis had specifically asked casting for a couple in their sixties, the man just retired, the well-preserved woman active in the Women's Institute, that sort of thing. These two, however, looked like they'd been let out of an old people's home for the day. If the violence went ahead as scripted, there would be deaths.

"*Barbara (and Jim)*?" said the man hopefully.

He had a loud, posh voice. If bow ties could talk, Dennis thought, that was exactly what they'd sound like.

"That's us," said Dennis. "Me anyway. I don't know where everyone else has got to."

They walked into the rehearsal room and Dennis put the kettle on while Dulcie and Alfred fussed around with coats and hats and scripts. Their clothes and even their names smelled of mothballs and Edwardian defeat.

"We loved it," said Dulcie.

"We read our scenes aloud to each other in bed last night," said Alfred.

Dennis was momentarily startled.

"Ah," he said. "You're married?"

The question clearly disappointed them.

"People forget," said Dulcie to Alfred sadly.

"This young man might not even have known in the first place," said Alfred. "It's been nearly fifty years."

"How old are you, dear?" said Dulcie.

"I'm twenty-nine."

"There you are, then," she said to Alfred.

"Ask your mother," said Alfred.

"I will," said Dennis. He could see that it wouldn't be wise to ask for help with the exact form of the question.

"Will the writers be in?" said Dulcie. "Because we do have a few suggestions."

"Good," said Dennis. "I'm sure they'd love to hear them."

It would serve them right for being late.

It was an hour before Bill and Tony arrived with a new version of the script, an hour that reminded Dennis of a wet summer that he'd once had to spend with his grandparents in Norfolk during the war.

"Who have we got here, then?" said Tony.

"It's Dulcie and Alfred," said Dulcie with a big smile.

"You come as a pair, do you?"

Dulcie's smile vanished.

"Well, yes," said Alfred. He left it for as long as he could, but it became clear that elucidation was required. "We're married."

"Good for you," said Bill.

Dulcie gave her husband's hand a consoling squeeze.

"Never mind."

"Television people," said Alfred darkly.

Tony gave Dennis a mystified look, but Dennis could think of no wordless way of explaining that Dulcie and Alfred may have been famous around the time of the Great

War, and that their union had possibly been a cause for national celebration.

"We've got a few notes for you," said Alfred to Tony and Bill. "Nothing major."

"Just think of them as observations," said Dulcie.

"Do you mind if we don't think of them at all?" said Bill pleasantly.

Dulcie gasped and clapped her hand to her mouth.

Sophie and Clive were last in.

"We're not unprofessional," said Sophie to Dulcie and Alfred. "We knew the script was going to be late."

"We're great admirers of yours," said Alfred.

He stared at Sophie hopefully and smiled. She thanked him and smiled back. She was clearly supposed to say something else, but she couldn't think what, and this failure to reciprocate, to tell Alfred and Dulcie how much they had meant to her over the years, caused another collapse in morale, another bout of hand-squeezing.

"We're still working, that's the thing," said Dulcie.

"And we're still together," said Alfred.

"So we see," said Clive. "Lovely."

Clive looked at the others, to work out whether they wanted to hang themselves too. The longevity of both the relationship and the career felt like a terrible lesson to them all.

"Shall we push on?" said Dennis.

They read the script out loud, and it sang, beautifully, as it usually did once it had cleared its throat, and despite

Alfred's tuneless, tone-deaf bellow. Dulcie turned out to be surprisingly good. She was understated and intelligent, and Bill and Tony ended up writing her a little bit more.

And suddenly Barbara and Jim became the only people that mattered in the world, and the only marriage that counted, and everything else fell away. Clive became clever and kind and steady, Sophie swam in the confidence and security that come from being loved. Dennis enjoyed the company, Tony the simplicity and the straightforwardness of the attraction, Dulcie and Alfred the youth and the promise. It was such a joyful world that Tony worried for a moment whether he and Bill had gone soft, but these characters had real problems, and they spoke in real sentences, so it wasn't that. It was the form itself, with its promise of next week, another episode, another series; it couldn't help but offer hope, to its characters and to everyone who identified with them. Tony didn't think he would ever want to write anything apart from half-hour comedies. They contained the key to health, wealth, and happiness.

"We should do an anniversary episode every year," said Dennis.

"For the next fifty years," said Sophie.

Dulcie and Alfred smiled sadly.

"Oh," said Sophie. "Sorry."

"Barbara and Jim probably wouldn't have sat next to the same couple in the same restaurant every year anyway," said Clive.

After the recording, and after Dulcie and Alfred had

been helped into their taxi, they sat in the BBC Club drinking wine and talking about getting old.

"It was sort of pathetic, wasn't it?" said Clive.

"What else are they going to do?" said Sophie.

"The crossword. Gardening. Jigsaw puzzles. Anything but acting."

"Yes," said Dennis. "All those waiting-to-die things. They should just accept that they're filling in time with good grace."

"I'm going to be like her," said Sophie. "People are going to have to throw me out."

"They will," said Clive. "That's what happens."

11

The week before work began on the second series, Dennis was cornered in the canteen by Barry Banister, the producer of *Pipe Smoke*. Dennis hated *Pipe Smoke*, even though he watched it every night. It was a program in which men with beards and spectacles (but no pipes, which had recently been banned because the fug was making life difficult for the cameraman) talked with an annoying certainty about God and the H-bomb and theater and classical music. Dennis had a beard and spectacles, and he smoked a pipe, but he hoped that he wasn't as insufferable as Banister's terrible windbags. *Pipe Smoke* was the last program in the schedule before the 11:20 closedown, and Dennis sometimes wondered whether its dullness was deliberate, an attempt by the BBC to persuade the workers of Britain that they needed more sleep than they were getting.

"Do you know Vernon Whitfield?" Banister asked him.

Dennis hopped into the nearest available rabbit hole,

which led down into a whole labyrinth of interconnected tunnels. These all brought him to rooms full of pain and humiliation: letters tucked inside books, chilly bedtimes, lies, tears, and (toward the end) a long poem about loss that Edith had read out to him, naked, with no explanation for the poem or the nudity, while she wept. Time passed, and all he did was smile at Barry blankly. This sort of thing had been happening a lot since Edith had gone. Entire minutes could go by, in shops and pubs and work meetings, in which he seemed to lose track of himself. When he came back again, he frequently found that people had given up on him. Conversations had moved on, shopkeepers were serving somebody else. He was, he supposed, glad that his marriage was finally over, but he hadn't managed to prepare himself for the shock of it, the sheer exhaustion.

"Hello?" said Barry Banister. "Are you receiving me?"

"Sorry," said Dennis. "Late night."

"Vernon Whitfield?"

"Know *of* him, of course. Don't know him."

"Well, he wants to come on *Pipe Smoke* and attack your program when it comes back again."

"Why on earth would he want to do that?"

"It's nothing personal," said Banister, and Dennis resisted the temptation to apprise him of all the relevant information. "He just thinks that the BBC should be aiming higher than fatuous comedies about uneducated young women. His words, not mine."

"And what do you want me to do about it?"

"I wondered whether you'd come on and defend yourself."

"Why me? Why not Tony and Bill? Or one of the actors?"

"Because . . . Well, you're the producer and the director. And you're more of a *Pipe Smoke* man, aren't you? Cambridge, articulate, well-spoken. I'm not saying we're against people who aren't—"

"That's very tolerant of you."

"—but what's interesting from our point of view is that you've chosen to go and bat for the opposition, as it were."

"Who are the opposition?"

"Light Entertainment."

"You think of Light Entertainment as 'the opposition'?"

"I don't personally. But I suppose the guests we usually have on the program might. And quite a few of our viewers too."

It was true, then, Dennis thought. He'd always suspected it, but nobody had ever come out and said it. Some of the cross-looking men he saw beetling around in the dingier corridors of the BBC believed that comedy was the enemy. They actually wanted people not to laugh, ever.

"So what would someone like Vernon Whitfield want, then?"

"How do you mean?"

"Well, if we're the opposition . . . how does he win? Does he get us taken off the air?"

"Oh, I don't think he'd want that. He'd just prefer it if

you were on the commercial channel. I can't speak for him, but I suppose he'd argue that the taxpayer shouldn't be paying Sophie Straw's salary."

Dennis hated Vernon Whitfield for personal reasons, and he hated people like Vernon Whitfield for philosophical, political, and cultural reasons. More and more frequently, Dennis found himself in the middle of a fantasy in which he turned someone like Vernon Whitfield, but usually Vernon Whitfield himself, into a big sobbing red-faced baby, and here was Barry Banister giving him the chance to make his dreams come true. Was he clever enough, though?

"Oh, I'll give it a go," he said.

Dennis didn't know whether it was possible to train for a debate with an intellectual on television in the way that boxers would train for a fight with Cassius Clay, but he tried. The night before the recording, he lay in bed imagining every punch Vernon Whitfield might throw at him, while trying to prepare a convincing attack of his own. What could Whitfield say? What was there to object to, in *Barbara (and Jim)* or any decent popular comedy program? Did Whitfield think it was lowbrow? What was lowbrow about cleverly observed comedy? Could Dennis think of any examples of clever observation? No, he could not. Or rather, he could, but Vernon Whitfield could simply say that they weren't clever at all, and Dennis would then have to say, Yes they are, and Whitfield would say, No they're not.

What if Whitfield argued that taxpayers' money should only be used for things that ordinary people didn't enjoy? What would Dennis say then? He would ask who Whitfield was to tell ordinary people that they should only eat intellectual roughage, that's what he would do. Ah, but what if Whitfield asked him why he thought that ordinary people didn't like intellectual roughage? Who was patronizing whom? Well, then he, Dennis, would tell Whitfield that he shouldn't sleep with other men's wives, and then they would have a wrestling match, and Dennis would sit on his head, and Whitfield would beg for mercy. Dennis realized at that point that lying awake worrying was leading him to some unhelpful places, but he couldn't sleep. As a consequence, he awoke the next morning exhausted and fearful.

Barry Banister introduced them in the greenroom, and they shook hands and pretended that it was a perfectly run-of-the-mill meeting between bearded late-night BBC intellectuals. But once Barry had left, there was a long, embarrassed silence. I'm buggered if I'm going to say anything, thought Dennis.

"Thanks for not making this awkward," said Whitfield eventually. "Very decent of you."

"How do you mean?" said Dennis pleasantly, suddenly seeing a way of making things more awkward than anything Whitfield could have imagined, and as awkward as anything in Dennis's numerous vengeful fantasies.

Whitfield stared at him, clearly trying to decide whether it was possible that Dennis didn't know.

"Oh," said Dennis. "Sorry. It's fine, really."

"Well. You're a gentleman, I'll say that much for you," said Whitfield with the air of a man who wouldn't say any more than that much.

"We can't all like the same things, can we?"

"That's very true," said Whitfield uncertainly. "So . . . we don't?"

"Sorry?"

"Like the same things?"

"I don't think so," said Dennis. "We can't, is my point."

"Yes."

"I'm sorry, though."

"I'm sorry," said Whitfield.

"Oh, bless you for apologizing," said Dennis.

He felt sick, and he had to force himself to make eye contact, and he was closer to angry tears than he had been since his twelfth birthday. But he had the advantage, and he wanted to keep it, and that meant not vomiting and not weeping.

"I don't suppose we did any better this week?" said Dennis.

"This week?"

"*Barbara (and Jim)*?"

"The program?"

"Yes. What did you think I was talking about?"

Whitfield thought, for a long time, and then said, finally, "I thought you might have wanted to talk about Edith."

"Oh," said Dennis. "No. God. Just the program."

"You know I don't like the program," said Whitfield.

"We can't all like the same things, can we?" said Dennis. He was worried that he'd given up too much by clearing up the confusion, but he could tell that he had irritated Whitfield by keeping it going for so long.

"I'd seen it before, of course. But this week was really pretty poor stuff, I thought."

The episode, "The Speech," hadn't been one of the best, to Dennis's regret. It had been a good idea: Jim is asked to deliver a lecture at his old Oxford college. Barbara listens to the speech, chimes in with a few improvements, and then decides to accompany him. When she gets there she antagonizes and then charms Jim's old tutor. Dennis hadn't directed it well, he didn't think. There was no fluidity, the college room was unconvincing, and the tutor had been miscast. But that wasn't the point. Vernon Whitfield would have hated the best episodes.

"The studio audience were in stitches."

"Yes, well," said Whitfield. "I don't know where they find the people who turn up for those things."

"We don't have to find them," said Dennis. "They apply for tickets. They come from all over the country, in coaches."

"I'm sure they do," said Whitfield.

"They're ordinary people."

"I'm sure you're right," said Whitfield. "That's what troubles me."

Finally, Dennis felt a hunger for the fight that he'd been invited to have. They *were* normal, the people who dragged themselves out to see *Barbara (and Jim)* every Sunday night; or rather, they were, as far as he could tell, reasonably representative of the millions of people who watched it on television. Sometimes Dennis sat at the end of a row and listened to the conversations around him. He heard talk about the journey, about work, about the desperation for a cup of tea or a smoke. And sometimes he heard lines—sometimes misremembered but always quoted with enthusiasm—or synopses of past episodes, offered to viewers who had often already seen them but who nodded enthusiastically anyway, and chipped in with plot snippets of their own. These people were always excited, no matter how far they had traveled. They couldn't believe that they were about to see the real Barbara and the real Jim. Dennis didn't know what any of them did for a living, although he was pretty sure that there wasn't a broadcaster from the Third or a critic from the *Times Literary Supplement* among them. And of course he was bound to love them, because they loved the program, but he was sure of one thing: they weren't fools.

"Do you not like ordinary people?" said Dennis.

"I love ordinary people individually," said Whitfield. "It's ordinary people en masse that trouble me. They seem to lose the ability to think. And I'm sorry that the BBC of all organizations feels the need to talk down to them."

"I don't think we're talking down to them."

"Well, of course this is what we should be discussing on

air. But . . . where are we going with all this? The BBC is full of horse-racing and variety shows and pop groups who look and sound like cavemen. What will it look like in ten years' time? Fifty? You're already making jokes about lavatories and God knows what. How long before you people decide it's all right to show people taking a shit, so long as some hyena in the audience thinks it's hysterical?"

"I don't think anyone wants to see anyone taking a shit," said Dennis.

"Not yet," said Whitfield. "But the day will come, mark my words. You can sense it. And while I have breath in my body, I will fight it."

"But to sum up, you think *Barbara (and Jim)* is hastening the arrival of a program called *Thirty Minutes on the Crapper*?"

"I know so, dear boy."

Dennis wondered whether he might actually be mad, and then whether he and Edith would end up killing each other, or killing themselves, perhaps while living in a nudists' colony in Sweden.

Barry Banister came to lead them round to the back of the set.

"The other guests are just finishing off their review of the week," said Banister. "They'll sit and listen to you do your bit. Robert will ask you a couple of questions, but mostly he's there as a facilitator. We want you to talk to each other."

Robert Mitchell, the host of *Pipe Smoke*, was a man with

a beard and spectacles who wrote for the weeklies and broadcast on the Third. He and two other men were talking about the death of poetry.

"OK," whispered Barry. "They're nearly finished. He'll turn to you in a sec. On you go. And remember it's live, so try and spit it out first time, eh?"

They followed him through the gap in the enormous curtain.

"I do wish you hadn't been sleeping with Edith," Dennis whispered, and they stepped into the momentarily blinding light and sat down.

"Good evening," said Whitfield loudly, while Robert Mitchell was still talking, and while the camera was trained elsewhere.

The tiniest flicker of irritation crossed Mitchell's face, and Whitfield started blinking and sweating furiously. He was wearing too many clothes—a shirt and a tie and a cardigan and a jacket—and suddenly Dennis realized, with a slight pang of disappointment, that Whitfield was going to be completely hopeless on television.

He kicked off with an attack on the emptiness of light entertainment, mostly routine Third Program stuff that Dennis had anticipated. The blinking, however, had now been replaced by a wild-eyed stare, and the perspiration was beginning to turn his white shirt translucent.

"I wonder," said Dennis carefully, "whether there's a different way of looking at intelligence."

Whitfield smiled patronizingly.

"I'm sure there is, these days," he said. "I'm sure people who work in comedy have found a way of redrawing the boundaries so that they include themselves."

"You don't think comedy can be intelligent?"

"Some of it can, of course. The new satirical shows are very clever."

"But then, they're written and performed by Cambridge graduates," said Dennis.

"Exactly," said Whitfield. "Bright chaps."

"And what about Shakespeare?" said Dennis. "*Much Ado About Nothing* and *All's Well That Ends Well* and so on?"

"Ah, I see," said Whitfield. "*Jim and Barbara* is Shakespeare, is it? Jolly good."

"Shakespeare made ordinary people laugh."

"'Ordinary people,'" said Whitfield. "The last refuge of the scoundrel."

"But what's the difference?"

"*Much Ado About Nothing*," said Vernon Whitfield, with all the relish of a man who'd lured his opponent into a fatal trap, "had its roots in the Italian Renaissance."

"*Barbara (and Jim)* has its roots in the golden age of BBC radio comedy."

"I'll presume you're being facetious and ignore that," said Whitfield.

"I'm just pointing out that everything has roots," said Dennis.

"Not in the Italian Renaissance," said Whitfield.

"Well, no," said Dennis. "But you can trace a great deal of pornography back to the Italian Renaissance too."

He had no idea whether this was true, but it sounded true, and that was good enough. Anyway, it produced a lot of blinking and sweating.

"And, in any case, *Much Ado About Nothing* has Shakespeare's glorious language."

"You've got me there," said Dennis. "Let's hear some of it."

Whitfield stared at him with panic in his eyes, like a dying Nazi in a war film. Dennis smiled politely. There were long moments of silence.

"I wonder whether people laughed, not because of the glorious language, but because of Shakespeare's technical skill," said Dennis. "The plays are extremely well constructed. And that's where the intelligence of my writers goes. Into the construction, and the characterization, and—"

"'Sigh no more, ladies, sigh no more'!" Vernon Whitfield said suddenly. "'Men were always deceitful'!"

"Marvelous stuff," said Dennis. "They didn't call him the Bard for nothing, did they?"

Robert Mitchell laughed.

"'Deceivers ever'!" said Whitfield. "Not 'always deceitful.'"

"That's better," said Dennis.

"That's not a very good bit," said Vernon Whitfield.

"Perhaps we should move on," said Robert Mitchell, fearful of Whitfield's long, sweat-drenched silences.

Dennis knew it was over.

"I think you might have been on a show like this four-hundred-odd years ago," said Dennis, "complaining about the morons laughing at Shakespeare."

"On television?" scoffed Whitfield.

Dennis rolled his eyes, and Whitfield became red-faced with rage.

"Don't roll your eyes at me!"

"What worries me," said Dennis, "is that Vernon Whitfield and his type don't really like people enjoying themselves very much. I don't think he likes people at all, in fact. It won't be long before Vernon Whitfield starts banging on about eugenics."

"Oh, for God's sake," said Whitfield.

Robert Mitchell didn't help Whitfield's cause at that point by offering him a glass of water, as if he were an old lady overcome by the heat of a sunny summer's day.

"He sounds very reasonable and intelligent and so on, but earlier on you described the audience for *Barbara (and Jim)* as a bunch of laughing hyenas."

"That's not at all what I said. You're distorting and coarsening what was, actually, a private conversation."

"I'm sorry. It seemed relevant. After all, you did use the words 'laughing hyenas' to describe the typical audience for a BBC comedy show."

"Hyena, singular."

"So sorry to misquote. It made you sound a little condescending, that's all."

"What I actually said—"

"Please, I do want to get this right," said Dennis pleasantly.

"—was that you people would show someone taking a *shit* if you thought some hyena would laugh at it."

Dennis had only wanted Whitfield to make a twerp of himself. He hadn't intended to goad him into the first use of a four-letter word on British television. Now that it had happened, however, Dennis could hardly pretend that it hadn't. He was duty-bound to stop talking and look toward Robert Mitchell for guidance.

"Well," said Robert Mitchell, "I do apologize to our viewers for, for the industrial language that was inadvertently used during what became a very heated discussion. Let's end tonight a couple of minutes early, and we can all put the kettle on and calm down."

(Robert Mitchell was also forced to apologize a couple of nights later. The Trades Unions Congress had written to the BBC to point out that it was an Oxbridge intellectual who was responsible for the only four-letter word ever heard on television, not a representative of the British working class.)

"I'm so sorry," whispered Whitfield.

"Good night," said Robert Mitchell.

Three weeks later, another critic used an even worse word on another program and Vernon Whitfield's crime was forgotten, but he never appeared on television again. Later, Dennis regretted the inarguably lowbrow tactics he had used. Now he would never know whether he could have won a fair fight.

12

S ophie had finally run out of excuses, so her father and her auntie Marie came to London for the first time to see her, and her flat, and a recording of the show. They stripped away some of the fun and pride, of course: Sophie sent them the money for first-class train tickets, but they insisted on coming by coach; she booked them two rooms in the Royal Garden Hotel at the end of her road, but when they found out that the rooms cost nine guineas a night, they moved into a smaller, family-run bed-and-breakfast nearby.

"That hotel had a twenty-four-hour coffee shop," George Parker said, outraged eyebrows hoisted as high as they would go.

He was in her flat, drinking tea and shifting uncomfortably in her Habitat chair. Marie had gone shopping.

"Yes," said Sophie. "The Maze. I've been there."

"And the restaurant is on the roof."

"Yes. I've been there too. The Royal Roof. It overlooks

Kensington Palace. Where Meg and Tony live. I thought you'd like it."

"Meg and Tony?"

"That's what people call them."

"No, 'people' don't."

It was a recurring theme of the visit: people versus people. The people versus her people. London versus the North. Show business versus the world. She had, she could see, become used to a lot of things that she once would have imagined to be a permanent source of wonder.

"Well, we didn't want meals on the roof, or all-night coffee."

"You didn't have to have it," said Sophie. "But other people might enjoy it."

"That's what we didn't like," George said.

"Why on earth not?"

"Because if there are people staying in that hotel who want to drink coffee at four o'clock in the morning, then it's the wrong hotel for us."

There was no arguing with them, and she let them stay where they wanted, at a considerable saving of six guineas per person per night, cooked breakfast included.

They wanted to meet Clive, and when she made the mistake of telling him they were coming, Clive said that he wanted to meet them. She told him that he would meet them, at the recording, but Clive felt that he deserved more.

"I'm sparing you," she said.

"I don't want to be spared. I belong in a different category to Dennis and Brian and whoever else is knocking around."

"Why do you?"

"Because I'm your on-screen husband, and your off-screen . . ."

"What? You can't finish that sentence in a way they'd understand."

"I'm going to buy you all dinner. Saturday night. I can't just shake hands after the recording and then disappear."

"Well, don't. Stay around for a drink."

"They feel like my in-laws."

She knew he meant it. He would drive her mad. Sometimes they slept together and sometimes they didn't, and she never knew where she stood, and she found herself getting jealous even though she knew that jealousy was utterly pointless, and in any case belonged to the kind of relationship she didn't want with him.

"They'll get the wrong end of the stick."

"So let them. Where's the harm? A stick is a stick. Doesn't matter which end they pick up."

"I'd never hear the last of it."

"I can't be a friend?"

"They don't understand friends. Not on a Saturday night. They understand husbands and wives and courting couples and that's it."

"I'll book at Sheekey's. They'll like it there."

"You know them so well."

He was right. They loved Sheekey's, not least because it

closed at 8:30 and he had guessed, correctly, that they preferred to have their tea at six o'clock. If Sophie had been paying, they'd have walked out when they saw the prices on the menu, but they just kept asking Clive if he was sure, and telling him that he was very kind.

"Are you courting, Clive?" Marie asked him more or less as soon as they'd sat down.

"Still window-shopping," said Clive.

"You're young yet," said Marie.

"Our Barbara is still available," said George.

"Sophie," said Sophie. "And I'm not 'available.'"

"Are you not?" said George.

"Tell us all," said Clive.

"I mean, I want to get on in my career before I start thinking about all that."

"Clive can wait, can't you, Clive?" said George.

"Of course I can," said Clive.

"And it wouldn't stop you courting anyway, would it?"

"Of course it wouldn't. Courting doesn't get in the way of anything."

"There we are, then," said George.

"Oh, for God's sake," said Sophie.

"What have we said now?" said George, and rolled his eyes at Clive to indicate that there was always something.

"Can we change the subject?" said Sophie. "How's work, Dad?"

But they hadn't come all the way to London to talk about Blackpool. They wanted to know about the program, and other television and film stars Clive and Sophie had worked with, and whether they had ever met the Beatles. (Clive had just missed Paul at a party, he told them, an anecdote greeted with much head-shaking and marveling.) And then the magician and comedian Maurice "Mr. Magic" Beck sat down on the next table, on his own, and Clive's near-miss was forgotten.

"Good grief," said George. "Is that who I think it is?"

If this remark was intended for anyone, it was for Mr. Magic, who smiled, and then did a big stagy double take when he saw Sophie and Clive.

"Good grief," he said. "Is that who I think it is?"

Sophie's father roared with laughter and delight, and Sophie remembered how embarrassing he'd been when he realized that the local paper had sent their top photographer to take her picture.

A few moments later, the waiters were rearranging the tables so that the five of them could sit together, and a few moments after that, Mr. Magic began the Mr. Magic show. He was in the middle of last-minute rehearsals for a variety performance at the Palladium, so he gave them a preview of some of the smaller-scale, table-friendly bits of business while they ate. (Plaice and chips for George, smoked haddock with a poached egg for Marie.) He told jokes while making things disappear, watches and spoons and napkins, and Sophie was worried that her father was going to have another heart attack, such was the volume of his laughter and the intensity of his amazement.

Sophie found herself watching Maurice Beck's face as much as she watched his hands. To her surprise, he was, in odd moments of repose, passably handsome. She had seen him on television, back in the days when she watched at home on a Saturday night, and he made so many odd faces—intended to indicate bafflement, mirth, disaster— that she would never have thought of him as being attractive. In the restaurant, however, he was only putting on half a show, and in any case Sophie could tell that he was aware of her attention. He allowed his face to sit still, most of the time, and she could therefore see that he had sharp cheekbones and deep brown eyes. He was younger than she'd realized too, maybe not even forty. He wasn't as good-looking as Clive, but Clive was too vain ever to forget that women liked him. Or maybe he simply thought that his looks, and not his talents as an actor, were his prize possession, the gift that needed the most protection and attention, so he couldn't afford the sort of animation that Maurice allowed. Sophie suddenly realized that Clive was never going to make it, not in the way he wanted to. He was a leading man or he was nothing, and he wasn't a leading man.

"Can I ask you two something?" said Maurice. "Your show . . . is it just a show?"

"How do you mean?" said Sophie.

"I don't want to tread on anyone's toes, that's all. If the show isn't just a show."

"Oh, I see where he's going," said Marie.

"Where's he going?" said George.

"Don't you see?" said Marie.

"No," said George.

"He already said he can't see," said Sophie. "And neither can I."

"Can you not? He wants to know if you two are courting in real life. And if you're not—"

"Marie!" said Sophie. "He might not be saying that at all!"

"That's exactly what I'm saying," said Maurice. "You're very astute, Marie."

Marie looked delighted.

"It's just . . . I've always said to myself, Maurice, if that girl's not been taken already—"

"It could be," said Sophie, "that the show is just a show, but I've got a boyfriend anyway."

"You just told us you weren't courting," said George.

"He didn't know that."

Clive was desperately looking for a way into the conversation. He felt as though he was at the Yalta Conference, and Europe was being carved up into pieces while he watched helplessly.

"He does now," said George triumphantly. "She's not courting, Maurice. She's free as a bird."

"She might like it that way," said Clive.

"You've had your chance," said George. "You didn't take it."

"I'm sorry this is all so public," said Maurice, "but could I have your telephone number?"

He dug around in his wallet, found a receipt and a pen, and thrust them toward her. She didn't know what to say. She was going to upset someone whatever she did.

"What are you waiting for?" said her father. "Maurice Beck has just asked for your phone number! You can't just stand there gawping like a fish!"

She wrote her number down, just because it seemed like the quickest way of ending the embarrassment. For a moment she was afraid that Marie and her father were going to applaud when he picked the piece of paper up and tucked it back in his wallet, but they just nudged each other.

"Let's not get carried away," said Sophie. "It's early days."

When the bill arrived, Clive and Maurice fought over it, and Maurice won.

"When I get home, nobody will believe that Mr. Magic bought me dinner," said George.

"They won't believe he asked for your daughter's phone number either," said Marie.

"Thanks," said Sophie.

They said their good-byes to Maurice outside the restaurant. He kissed Marie on the cheek and Sophie on the hand, and her father laughed in disbelief throughout. Maurice then pretended that he was going to kiss George, which took hilarity to unprecedented heights. Clive was largely forgotten, and Sophie felt bad for him: she suspected that Marie and George didn't think of him as a star because she knew him and worked with him and therefore he didn't count. And in any case they'd been watching Maurice Beck for years and years. They had a preexisting relationship with him. Clive disappeared off into the night before they'd even hailed their taxis.

Mr. Magic dug out his receipt and called Sophie's number while she was drinking tea with Diane, the journalist from *Crush*. She had come to do a piece on Sophie's flat. Diane's editor had liked the story of the TV star with no telephone and no boyfriend, and *Barbara (and Jim)* was the most popular comedy series on television. The girls who read the magazine, all of whom wanted to be Sophie, would enjoy regular updates, the editor said. So Diane sat and listened while Sophie made monosyllabic plans for Saturday night, with as much mystery and obfuscation as politeness and her ingenuity would allow.

She put the receiver down, smiled, and tried to continue the conversation about the Habitat furniture and the poster she had just bought, of a big red sun setting over a deep blue sea.

"Out with it," said Diane.

"I'm not telling you my plans for Saturday night."

"You don't have to tell *Crush* readers. You just have to tell me."

"It's nobody you know."

"I know it wasn't Clive."

"How do you know it wasn't Clive?"

"Because you said, 'Hello, Maurice.'"

Sophie opened her mouth, shrugged, laughed.

"It was Maurice," she said.

"There was some gossip about you and Clive. People keep seeing you out and about."

"If I was with Clive, I wouldn't be going out with Maurice, would I?"

"I don't know."

"Well, I wouldn't."

"The only Maurice I know is Mr. Magic from *Sunday Night at the London Palladium*."

Sophie blushed, and she saw Diane's eyes widen. She wouldn't just surrender the information, though. She would plow on.

"What do you mean, the only Maurice you know? You were never at school with anyone called Maurice? You haven't got a relative called Maurice? Why does it have to be a famous Maurice?"

"You didn't want me to know. You kept saying yes and no and thank you. And also, my uncle Maurice is happily married to my auntie Janet and living in Redcar."

"That's what you think."

"He's not your sort. You're going out on Saturday night with Maurice Beck!"

"Oh, bloody hell," said Sophie. "Why did he have to call when you were here?"

"He's probably tried a thousand times when you were out."

"If you say anything to anyone I'll kill you. We haven't been on a date before."

"Mr. Magic!"

"Do you think I'm mad?"

"No," said Diane thoughtfully. "He's younger than he looks. And he's better-looking than you think."

"Better-looking than I think?" And Sophie groaned in mock despair.

"Where are you going to go?"

"I don't know. He's picking me up. He said he wanted to go somewhere fun."

"Go to a discotheque."

"Ooh, I'd love to go somewhere like that," said Sophie. "Do you know any?"

"I like the Scotch," said Diane.

"I don't know what that is," said Sophie.

"The Scotch of St. James. It's quite classy."

"Not too with it?"

"Not for you. And he's famous. People forgive you a lot if you're famous."

Sophie used the same groan.

"Will you call me afterward? I'll be dying to know how it goes."

Sophie told her that she would, and she meant it too. It hadn't really occurred to her before that, while she had a lot of things she hadn't ever anticipated getting her hands on, she didn't have any friends.

At first they were told that Maurice—or Sophie, she supposed, but the man on the door was working on the presumption that this was the gentleman's business—had to pay three guineas for a temporary membership of the Scotch of St. James, but then a couple of girls queuing up behind them asked for their autographs and suddenly they were both made honorary members. This immediate recognition made them both nervous, but once they were inside they were ignored. There was something almost studiedly self-conscious about this lack of attention, Sophie felt, as if they were being told that they weren't famous enough, or were famous for the wrong kind of thing. All the girls looked like Diane, skinny and dark, short skirts, panda eye makeup, and all the men looked like guitarists or maybe even singers in a pop group. Sophie had dressed up, but Maurice, bless him, was wearing a suit and tie. Sophie couldn't shake the feeling that she was dating Diane's uncle Maurice from Redcar, although it was a very nice suit that Maurice was wearing.

There was dancing downstairs and a bar upstairs, and smoke, noise, and tartan everywhere. The tartan seemed to explain the name of the club, or the name of the club seemed to explain the tartan, but neither explanation was very satisfactory. They went upstairs, because not even Sophie could walk straight in off the street and begin dancing. She sat down at a table in the corner, and after they'd waited a few minutes for someone to take their drinks order, Maurice went up to the bar.

A handsome young man with very long hair and wearing a loud striped blazer replaced Maurice in seconds.

"Hello," he said. "I'm Keith."

Sophie smiled at him, but didn't introduce herself.

"We're friends, am I right?"

"I don't think so," said Sophie.

"Oh. But . . . We're not, you know. Not friends."

"I don't think we're not-friends," said Sophie. "I just think that we don't know each other."

"Good. That's a relief to me."

"How would we be not-friends?"

"I'll tell you the truth," said Keith. "Sometimes it turns out I've met a bird before and one thing has led to another and then because of my busy lifestyle I've not really seen her again."

"Not *really*? What does 'really' mean?"

Keith laughed.

"You're right. 'Really' means 'never.'"

"I think I get the gist anyway," said Sophie.

"Don't let it put you off," said Keith.

"Oh, no," said Sophie. "You sound like a dream date."

Keith stared at her again.

"But we are friends, aren't we?"

"No," said Sophie. "But I don't think we're not-friends."

"I just got déjà vu," said Keith. "I feel like I've stood in this exact spot having this exact conversation. Have you ever had that?"

"I got it just now. Just this second."

"My mum and dad," said Keith suddenly.

"I beg your pardon?"

"My mum and dad like you, but I don't know how they know you. Or how I know they know you. And like you."

He seemed genuinely perplexed. Sophie understood what her relationship with Keith's parents consisted of, but saw no reason why she had to go into it.

"I don't blame them, by the way. You're gorgeous."

"Thank you."

Maurice came back with their drinks, but Keith didn't move.

"My friend has come back now," said Sophie gently. "It was nice talking to you."

Keith looked up at Maurice.

"Him?" he said to Sophie. "Really?" He stood up and peered into Maurice's face as if it were a mirror and he was looking for pimples. "How old is he?"

"Do you mind?" said Maurice.

Sophie managed to suppress the temptation to laugh. It would have been disloyal and unfair. And though Maurice was at least ten years older than Keith, it wasn't the age difference Keith was referring to, she didn't think; it was something else. Maurice seemed to belong to another time altogether. He looked like a magician who appeared in variety shows, while everyone else in the club looked as though they lived in a world that had just been specially invented for them. She didn't want to sound like her father, who'd spent his entire visit shaking his head at just about everybody under the age of twenty-five, but Keith and all the other faces in the Scotch of St. James were a little like Clive's face: unmarked by life somehow. She'd wanted to live in a city that felt young, but now she was beginning to wonder whether there wasn't something rather shifty about these people, as if they'd got away with something.

"I think you should clear off now, Sunny Jim," said Maurice.

"Mr. Magic!" said Keith. "Fuck me! Show us some magic, Mr. Magic!"

Maurice looked confused and a little frightened, Sophie thought.

"I can't do tricks in a discotheque," he said eventually.

"Why not?" said Keith.

"Did you come with anyone, Keith?" said Sophie. "Because perhaps you should go and look for them. They'll be worried about you."

But she'd said too much. The sound of her voice sparked something in the recesses of Keith's memory.

"You're the missus! In that program! That's why I know you. My dad's in love with you! I went round there for my dinner and I wasn't allowed to speak! They had to watch. They never miss it. What's it called? I don't believe this. Mr. Magic and the bird my dad loves off the telly! I'm Keith from the Yardbirds. Pleased to meet you."

He offered his hand to Maurice, who had to put the drinks down on the table to take it. Sophie gave him a little wave.

"Well," said Keith. "I don't watch either of you myself, but God bless the pair of you for keeping the oldsters happy. Anyway."

"Anyway," it turned out, meant "good-bye." Keith walked away.

"Who are the Yardbirds?" said Maurice when Keith had gone.

"They're a pop group," said Sophie, but she had never

heard of them. She just wanted to feel that she knew more than Maurice about that sort of thing. Neither of them confessed to discomfort, but they finished their drinks quickly, and went on to a restaurant where it was quiet and they could talk and eat and sit down and not be afraid. It wasn't as if Sophie felt old—she didn't. She felt young and alive and successful, full of hope and ambition. But she was an entertainer, and even though she suspected that Maurice Beck was not the right man and this was not the right life for her, she was on his side. Sophie went out for dinner three more times with Maurice over the next few weeks. After the second dinner date she invited him in for coffee and kissed him, just to see if a kiss made any difference, but long before their lips touched, she was alerted to old-fashioned bad breath, the sort of thing she associated with schooldays and in particular a girl called Janice Stringer, who, legend had it, didn't own a toothbrush. Sophie didn't want to be thinking about Janice Stringer when she was kissing someone. The kiss was followed by some unfortunate and undignified wrestling, of the sort that Marjorie had warned her about but that Maurice seemed to think was all part of the fun. She knew then that she'd have to tell him that their relationship had run its course, but she couldn't do it ten seconds after he'd kissed her, so there would have to be another dinner, another evening spent listening to stories about the Magic Circle and the Bournemouth Winter Gardens, and a difficult conversation afterward.

Unfortunately, her willingness to see him again after the bad-breath kiss was misinterpreted and he asked her to marry him. He took her to Sheekey's, because it was the closest place they had to a Site of Romantic and Historical Significance; he made the ring appear in a glass of champagne while the staff applauded. When she didn't say anything immediately they found jobs to do in one of the other rooms. It was the wrestling, she realized, that had persuaded him to buy a ring. He must have thought that she was fending him off because she was an old-fashioned girl, but it wasn't that at all. It was simply because she didn't want to go to bed with him.

"This has all gone wrong, hasn't it?" said Maurice when their table was no longer surrounded by onlookers.

"No," she said. "It was a very good trick. And it was romantic, with all the waiters watching."

"I can hear a 'but' coming . . ."

"We don't really know each other," she said.

"I think you know me," he said. "But then, I have been on TV longer than you. And also, you're an actress."

"What does that mean?"

"When you're on TV, you're not you. You're playing a part. But when I'm on TV, I'm me. I'm Maurice."

This part was true, unfortunately. The private Maurice was very similar to the Maurice that the public knew. He never seemed to go anywhere without makeup, for a start, and that toothy, insincere smile flashed on and off, randomly, like a faulty car headlight.

"I'm sure there's a lot more to you than that," said Sophie.

"No," he said. "There really isn't. What you see is what you get with me. And I'm not ashamed of that. You could be married to me for a thousand years, and I'd still be the person you see on *Sunday Night at the London Palladium*."

Sophie was tempted to thank him for the evenings out by advising him that he should never say that again, to any woman, unless he wanted his date to kill herself for some reason.

"I'm sure," said Sophie.

"So what you're saying," said Maurice, "is . . . I should just give it time. And we should keep going out. And we must kiss and cuddle a lot."

That was one of the things wrong with him: he used expressions like "kiss and cuddle." It was the sort of thing her grandparents said. There was probably an old music-hall song called "We Must Kiss and Cuddle a Lot"; there would never be a Rolling Stones song with the same title. Or a Yardbirds song, she imagined, although she still didn't know what the Yardbirds sounded like. And also, what kind of a job was comic magician? She didn't think she could bear to be married to a comic magician, even if his breath was sweeter than Parma violets and his kisses were like atom bombs. Comic magicians belonged on seaside piers. Comic magicians were what she had come to London to escape, not to find, and certainly not to marry.

"I don't think I am saying that really," she said eventually.

"Oh."

"I think what I'm saying is that giving it time won't make any difference."

"Why not?"

He was looking at her earnestly. He really wanted to understand.

"I don't think I'm right for you."

"You are. Definitely. I know that."

"Ah. Well. I think it must be the other way around, then."

"I'm still not following you."

She didn't think she'd ever shown enough gratitude for the quick wits of the people she worked with, and if the evening ever ended, which it showed no signs of doing, she would rectify that. She would buy them all flowers or whisky and write a card thanking them for being so clever. There were a thousand reasons why she would never have this conversation with Dennis. He would never have made an engagement ring appear in her champagne glass, of course, but once he'd realized that she was never going to put it on, he wouldn't have asked her why not. She didn't want to be a dim comedy magician's wife, and she didn't have to be, but she also saw that it wouldn't amaze people if that was the choice she made.

She explained, as clearly as she could, and broke Maurice's heart, and then she went home on her own.

13

When Bill had become used to the idea, and was no longer quite so dismissive of the first and depressed by the second, he liked to joke that Tony was responsible for two pregnancies in the same month. Tony didn't spoil the joke by pointing out that the paternity of the other child was in doubt: Tom Sloan was a suspect, and Dennis, too. And Bill himself could hardly be considered blameless. But yes, fatherhood. There was suddenly a lot more of it in Tony's life than he could ever have predicted.

He and Bill had moved into a bigger office now, one which could accommodate Hazel while allowing them to work in the room at the back. When June came to see him to tell him the news, she didn't walk straight through, as she usually did when she dropped in; she stood by Hazel's desk and waited while Hazel came through to tell him she was there. He knew what it was about as soon as he saw her.

He took her outside onto the street, away from curious eyes, and hugged her tightly.

"Can you believe it? You've knocked me up," she said, and Tony laughed at the implication of violence, or at least vigor, in the phrase. He hadn't knocked her up. There had been a lot of patience, coaxing, maybe-tomorrows, never-minds, and I-think-sos. Just recently, there were signs that it was getting better, or at least less complicated.

"We'll have to move," said Tony. "A house with a garden."

"Hold your horses," said June. "We'll be all right for a bit."

They lived in a flat in Camden Town, and June loved the shops, the cinemas, and the market.

"Somewhere leafy and quiet. Pinner or somewhere."

"Really? Oh dear. Anyway, there are other things to worry about before that."

"What have we got to worry about?"

"Childbirth, for a start. I'm terrified."

"Sorry. Yes."

"And whether I'll be a good mum."

"You'll be a wonderful mum."

"You'll be a wonderful dad."

"Oh, God," said Tony. "And here's me worrying about gardens."

"How do you feel?"

"I feel great."

And he carried on feeling great, until he told Bill.

Perhaps it was healthy, and great things would come of it, but he and Bill were in the process of becoming two different people. At the end of a working day Tony ached, in the way that he'd ached after all those stupid training exercises he'd endured during his National Service. Up until now it was as if they shared a brain, or at least had created a new one that hovered between them, and they filled it with stuff, lines and stories and characters, like two taps might fill a bath. Sometimes one was working better than the other, and sometimes the bath needed more hot than cold, but the process of adjustment was self-evident, obvious. They just talked and then wrote.

During this series, however, the shared brain was becoming harder to find. Now they were two men yoked together by talent and circumstance, trying to speak with a single voice, and suddenly every single line and every narrative choice had to be debated, attacked, defended; both Tony and Bill won small triumphs and endured small defeats. Maybe this was how every writing partnership worked, but they'd never had to do it like this before, and it was hard.

Tony tried to think of how to break his news to Bill in a way that somehow wouldn't invite sarcasm and scorn. Bill liked June, and they seemed to enjoy each other's company when they met. Maybe it was Tony's paranoia, but he couldn't help thinking Bill looked on the marriage as bogus, an indication of cowardice and a desire to conform. Tony and Bill used to be two different shades of chalk. Now Tony was turning into a variety of cheese. It wasn't a strong cheese, admittedly—he was probably closer in flavor to a cheese spread than to a seeping blue French thing riddled with maggots. But he was a mild married man, and even before June got pregnant, the two of them had stayed in, night after night, watching television, listening to the radio, talking about what they'd seen and heard, analyzing scripts. Once or twice a week, they went to the pictures, and dissected the films they saw on the way home. Tony could listen to June talking about scripts all night. She couldn't write them—she'd tried, although she would never show Tony or anyone else the results—but she always knew where they'd gone wrong, what they were lacking, where they'd turned right when they should have turned left, why scenes were lifeless when they should have fizzed and crackled. He was beginning to wonder whether June's facility, and their shared interest, might serve them better in the long run than a passionate sexual relationship that would eventually die on them.

Bill, however, went to clubs and bars that nobody else knew about, and drank a lot, and met wild, dangerous people who constantly ran the risk of imprisonment for their sexual preferences but who didn't seem to care. And he was starting to look at a world beyond light entertainment, a world that Tony didn't really understand. He went to the theater—he had discovered Harold Pinter and N. F.

Simpson and Joe Orton—and he knew Peter Cook and Dudley Moore and the people at *Private Eye*. He'd submitted a couple of clever, angry sketches to Ned Sherrin's new satirical show, *Not So Much a Program, More a Way of Life*—he'd even written something called "The Two-Thousand-Year-Old Homosexual Virgin," satirizing the time it was taking to do anything about the recommendations in the Wolfenden Report. It had been turned down, but he was proud of it, and Tony got the impression that he was writing something longer which allowed him to visit the places that *Barbara (and Jim)* could never go. Tony admired all of it, and he wished he could be more like him, but he knew he wasn't, and probably wouldn't ever be.

"Oh, fucking hell," said Bill when Tony told him.

His swearing was more ostentatious these days too. He'd tried to avoid bad language when they'd started out, because he didn't want people to think that he was some uneducated oik from Barnet. Now half the actors and writers he knew wanted to sound like uneducated oiks from Barnet, so he effed and blinded with the best of them.

"How did that happen?"

Tony smiled sheepishly. "The normal way. More or less."

"Mr. Normal," said Bill. "Mr. fucking Average."

"That's me," said Tony.

"You are, though, aren't you?"

"I don't know, Bill. I'm a TV writer who left school at fifteen and once got arrested in an Aldershot toilet. And I've just found out I'm about to become a father after making love to my wife a dozen times over the entire duration of our marriage with a success rate of less than 50 percent. Is that average?"

"Probably better than average, that last bit."

Tony laughed, and remembered his mother's savage digs at his father's expense.

"But you're ironing all the kinks out," said Bill. "You want to be respectable."

"It just happened. I haven't tried to do any of it. And it suits me."

"Yeah, well. I suppose it's good one of us is like that."

"Why?"

"That's what we're trying to do, isn't it? Write about Mr. and Mrs. Average?"

"Yeah, she looks like Sabrina and he works for Harold Wilson."

"Well, we're writing *for* Mr. and Mrs. Average anyway."

"First of all, I don't believe anyone's average. And second . . . what if we were? What's wrong with that? We wrote about whatever we wanted, and we ended up with eighteen million people watching us. That's the thing about television comedy, isn't it? It makes us all a part of something. That's what I love about it. You laugh at the same thing as your boss and your mum and your next-door neighbor and the television critic of *The Times* and the Queen for all I know. It's brilliant."

Bill sighed. "Anyway," he said. "Congratulations."

t was just bad luck that Dennis was called to Tom Sloan's office the following day, and Sloan told him about ITV's plans to launch a new quiz show on the same evening as the last episode of the second series.

"The same time?"

"No, they're not that mad. But they think *Up Your Alley* is weak."

Unfortunately, *Up Your Alley*, a drama series about life in the workhouse of a Yorkshire mill town during the Depression, was weak, in the sense that nobody wanted to watch it.

"How can I help?" said Dennis, although he didn't know whether he meant that. The offer would almost certainly lead to trouble.

"What have you got planned for the last episode? We need something that everyone will want to see. And then we're hoping they can't be bothered to get up and switch over afterward."

"Oh, it's rather good," said Dennis. "You remember that in the first episode Barbara mentioned that she'd come down to London to be a singer? Well, she goes for an audition at . . ."

"No singing."

"You wouldn't hear her sing, even though Sophie's actually got a very good voice. It's about Barbara wanting to do something and be someone in her own right, rather than . . ."

"Let me stop you there. We don't want politics in the last show of the series."

"Is it politics, really? To find an ambition for a bored young woman?"

"Sounds political to me."

"We could look at that, certainly," said Dennis.

Dennis had encouraged Tony and Bill to find something for Barbara to do, and they had responded imaginatively, and now he feared that he was going to have to tell them to find something else.

"Why isn't she pregnant yet? Is there a reason? Can't they have children?"

Dennis didn't want to have to explain that Clive and Sophie were reluctant to commit themselves to a fictional family.

"They haven't been married for that long, and Jim . . ."

"So no reason. Right. Get her in the family way. That'll bring them in."

"Right-o," said Dennis.

Oh, fucking hell," said Bill when Dennis told him.

Tony laughed.

"What's so funny?" said Bill.

"You say that every time you hear someone's going to have a baby," said Tony.

"Why does he do that?" said Dennis.

"I don't know. You'd have to ask him."

"It's the logic of bloody couples," said Bill. "Doesn't

matter who they are: a man and a woman meet, get married, set up house, have kids. It's like . . . food. It might all look different on the plate, but there's only one way it can go down and it all comes out the other end looking and smelling the same. And who wants to write about that?"

Dennis looked at Tony, perplexed, and Tony shrugged.

"I don't know what to do with him," said Tony.

"Can she have a miscarriage before the next series?" said Bill. "Or an abortion? Are abortions funny?"

"Ask a woman who's died of septicemia after having knitting needles stuck into her," said Dennis.

"She wouldn't hear me," said Bill.

"You are a bastard sometimes, though," said Dennis. "Why can't the poor woman get pregnant?"

"She can," said Bill. "But am I right in thinking that she would then have a baby to look after? And if so, what the bloody hell are we supposed to do with it for sixteen episodes?"

"Babies can be funny," said Dennis.

"Tell us your best baby joke."

It was a rhetorical question, of course, but Dennis made the mistake of taking it seriously, in an attempt to allay Bill's fears.

"All right. When my niece was three months old . . ."

"Oh, Lord, spare us," said Bill.

"You don't even want to listen," said Dennis.

"A baby," said Bill, "will scupper everything."

"Thanks," said Tony. "I'm going to be a father, Dennis."

"That's wonderful news," said Dennis.

"Try telling him that."

"I don't care what other people do in their spare time," said Bill. "But . . ."

"That's not true," said Tony.

"Let's stick to Jim and Barbara," said Dennis. "What can we do to make it more palatable to you?"

"How long does she have to be pregnant for?" said Bill. And then, when Tony and Dennis were about to provide different versions of the same joke, "Yes, yes, very funny. How long in screen time?"

"Off the top of my head?" said Dennis.

"Is there an actual formula you can check later?" said Bill. "Official TV Pregnancy Durations?"

"First episode of the next series to warm us up, and she can pop it out in the second."

"Christ on a bike," said Bill.

"It's not as bad as you think," said Tony. "There are things to say."

"Give me a for-example."

"The christening. Jim's an atheist, I'd imagine. So he objects. We can have a whole episode poking some fun at some soppy Church of England vicar."

"We might need to talk that one through first," said Dennis. "Tom's a Presbyterian."

Bill gave him a look of such contempt that Dennis decided he'd rather face Tom Sloan's Presbyterian wrath.

"Point taken, Bill, but Tony's right. Just because they're

going to become a family doesn't mean you have to stop doing what you've been doing. You just have to be ingenious about it."

"And some weeks not mention the little sod at all."

"If it makes you feel better."

"It does."

Never, thought Tony, has a beautiful girl been impregnated with such irritation and reluctance.

In the end it was Bill's idea, the scene in which Barbara tells Jim and the people of Britain that he is going to be a father. It was a good one too—so unexpected and clever that it felt to Tony as though Bill's professionalism, imagination, and talent would always trump his reluctance and hostility. In "The Surprise," Barbara simply forgets to say anything to Jim, on the grounds that it's such a cataclysmic piece of news that he's bound to know already. Jim wanders into the living room while Barbara is on the phone to her mother, and comprehension, which is signaled by the slow lowering of the newspaper, dawns on him at exactly the same time as it dawns on the studio audience, just as Tony and Bill had hoped. Clive's expression, when it was finally revealed, was perfect, a moment that ended up representing everything people loved about the show. Tom Sloan came to the recording, for the first time, and was so pleased with what he saw that he caused two bottles of champagne to arrive backstage. And the champagne, in turn, helped Clive and Sophie to find their way back into Sophie's bed.

Sophie was beginning to realize that there was nothing to be done about actors: they would always end up sleeping with one another. They had always done so, and they probably always would. Actors were more attractive, by and large, than ordinary people. That was one of the gifts with which they had been blessed—perhaps the only one that counted. In a lot of cases, there weren't any others at all. And these attractive people spent a lot of time together, and other, less attractive people dressed them, put makeup on them, lit them in ways that accentuated their beauty, told them they were wonderful. They were often penned up together in glamorous locations a long way from home. They were frequently given adjoining bedrooms in nice hotels, and everything in their lives encouraged a late-night knock on the door. Clive and Sophie were a permanent irritant to each other, a constant itch that had to be scratched. They slept together, then vowed not to do it again, and then did it again, and they always enjoyed it very much when it happened. There was no harm in it that Sophie could see, but neither was there much future in it, usually; Clive wasn't someone who could see beyond the next morning's breakfast. The thing about "The Surprise" was that it provided them with the excuse to romanticize a sort of substitute future.

"I don't mind having a baby with you," said Sophie afterward. "In the show, I mean. I'm sorry I said what I said before."

"I know what you mean," said Clive. "I feel the same way. And I'm sorry too."

"I think we'll make very nice screen parents," said Sophie.

"Maybe this will be good practice for me," said Clive. "I can poke my toe in the water, sort of thing."

"I suppose so."

She liked his sense of responsibility, and she didn't want to discourage it, but she felt obliged to keep the conversation grounded.

"You know it will be a plastic doll, most of the time?"

"Yes, of course, but it's symbolic."

"D'you think?"

"Absolutely. I'll have to become a different person. Someone I've never been before. Some people would say, "Yes, but you're an actor, that's your job." It's not just that, though. Jim's got to change, and I've got to change with him."

"I'd say . . . Jim's got to change less than you have. No offense."

"None taken. Why d'you think that?"

"Well, he's a devoted husband, really, isn't he? He's besotted with her. And he has a proper job, and—"

"What's a proper job?"

"I don't know. One where you have to put a suit on and do important things."

"Yes, but I've been playing him rather well, if I do say so myself. So it can't be that much of a stretch."

"I'm just saying. Jim's ready to be a father, but you're not."

"Should I be insulted?"

She was trying to insult him, she supposed.

"No, of course not. I just mean . . . Can you imagine being a real father?"

"God, no."

"Really? Never?"

"Oh, I'm sure I'll be one, one day. But I can't imagine it. Just . . . don't have the imagination. That's another reason I'm pleased about Barbara's baby."

"And yours."

"Yes, you're right. That's how I should think of it. Anyway. If Tony and Bill write it for me, I'll be able to see it all more clearly."

She kissed him on the shoulder. He was very sweet, and funny, and hopeless.

THE THIRD
SERIES

14

Tony and Bill had forgotten what it was like to have the luxury of time—time to plan, time to talk, time to write and rewrite. Time was money, a beautiful crisp, new ten-pound note, and they weren't going to break into it. They were going to save it up and spend it on sixteen new episodes, each one funnier and richer and more truthful than anything they'd written before. They were going to find clever and elegant ways of dealing with the Baby Problem so that they could eventually forget about the little sod entirely.

They needed a break, of course. They were exhausted, and they both felt sure that the writing would come more easily if they had a couple of weeks away in the sun, eating and drinking and sleeping and thinking and not staring at each other in the sickly fluorescent glare of an office. Bill went to Tangier with an actor friend, and Tony and June booked a hotel by the sea in Nice, for their first and last holiday as a childless couple. None of them had been abroad before, not even during National Service; none of their parents had so much as held a passport. So they were all staggered to learn that abroad was an astonishingly beautiful place. They'd been told, several times, by colleagues, actors and writers and agents, that the sea was warmer over there, and the skies bluer, and the food was like nothing you could buy in London no matter how much you spent. But none of these colleagues had done what Tony wanted to do when he got back: grab people by the lapels and shout at them, wild-eyed, until they agreed to book tickets. Most people in England, he thought, had no idea that within a few hours they could be somewhere that would make them begrudge every single second they'd ever spent in Hastings or Skegness or the Lake District. Perhaps it was better that way.

The trips left them with a little bit less time than they'd accounted for, because it proved impossible to coordinate holidays—Bill's actor friend had a repertory season starting in August, at precisely the moment June had booked her annual leave. Still. No matter. What was the difference between four months and three?

They weren't worried about the time they had been asked to spend translating the best episodes of *The Awkward Squad* into the language of television. They were sure that most of the changes required would be grammatical rather than structural, and that therefore their secretary, Hazel, could do a lot of the work. Television wasn't so different from radio, just as Spanish wasn't so different from Italian, a joke was a joke in any language, and so on.

What they hadn't anticipated was that *The Awkward Squad* had been written, not in Italian, but in Latin. Its jokes were creaky and tired and overfamiliar, probably even at the time they had written them, and guiltily they began to remember how much they had borrowed from shows and comedians they admired back then. The few women they had bothered with were shrewish or stupid, and the men were unattractive, leering buffoons who, as far as they could remember, were intended to be likable. The world had moved on, and if *The Awkward Squad* was ever to appear on television, it would need to be reconceived. They didn't even know if they wanted to think about National Service anymore, or if anyone else did either. It made them feel old. The Beatles had missed the army altogether. That was another country, all that. They spent a desultory couple of weeks working on a pilot episode, but to their fury and their relief, it never did get made. They suddenly found themselves with less than three weeks left to spend on *Barbara (and Jim)*, the only thing they cared about.

This panic explained but did not excuse the first episode of the third series, their attempt to portray Barbara and Jim preparing their nest for the new arrival. Tony, who was preparing his nest for his own new arrival, had recently attempted to install a sink at home, after watching a do-it-yourself program, and comical pandemonium had ensued—June had laughed like a drain when the waste pipe simply dropped off the first time the taps were turned on. In "The New Bathroom" Jim decides to do without the services of a plumber after watching a do-it-yourself program on television, although he tries to do not just it but everything himself. Tony was working on the mathematically dubious basis that a sink *plus* a bath *plus* a lavatory would produce sufficient comical pandemonium to entertain the entire population of Britain, rather than just a very pregnant and slightly hysterical June. It turned out, though, that the more porcelain a script contained, the less amusing it became, a discovery that might one day be helpful to future generations of comedy writers but was of no use whatsoever to Tony and Bill. It was too late. They had spent the entire tenner, frittered it away, and they had nothing else.

"You can say it was my idea," said Tony before the first rehearsal.

"I will, because it was your idea," said Bill.

"You know what I mean," said Tony.

"It's going out with my name on it, so I'll defend it."

"Do you want to take your name off it?"

"Of course not!" Bill said quickly. "No." The "no" was delivered with much less conviction.

"What does that mean?"

"What do you think it means?"

"Tell me."

"It means, 'We've never done that before.'"

Tony laughed.

"I knew it meant something. Do you want to see how it goes down with the others?"

"No."

"What does that mean?"

"It means no. Definitely. That's a terrible idea."

"Why?"

"You're saying that if they all think it's a load of rubbish I can take my name off? But if they think it's all right I take half the credit?"

"I suppose so."

"That's a recipe for disaster. We can't run a partnership like that. But maybe it's something to think about in the future."

"Why wouldn't it be a recipe for disaster, then?"

"We just agree in advance. Before a word's been written. 'I just fancy doing this one on my own.' Or, you know, 'The baby's teething, will you take over this week?' Maybe the break would do us good."

"I see what you mean."

It made perfect sense to Tony, and it scared him half to death.

It needs a bit of work," said Tony after the read-through. "And a lot of it will be funnier once the special effects are in."

The script hadn't got a single laugh. Even Dennis, who usually tried to help them out with a sticky first draft, seemed nonplussed.

"Special effects?" said Clive. "It's a leaky tap, not *The Ten Commandments*."

"Did you even understand what you were reading?" said Bill. "It's a flood. The bath, the WC, the sink . . ."

"Hilarious," said Clive. "The WC overflows. Do you really want to begin this series with lavatory humor?"

"It's not lavatory humor," said Tony. "It's humor about a lavatory. And a sink, and a bath. That's different."

"But it's that physical unfunny stuff."

"Like Laurel and Hardy, you mean?" said Bill. "Or Harold Lloyd?"

"Exactly," said Clive, slightly mystified as to why Bill would make his argument for him.

Bill rolled his eyes.

"You don't think Laurel and Hardy are funny, Clive?" said Dennis.

Clive simply laughed.

"I'll tell you what it reminds me of," said Clive. "An old Lucille Ball episode. I mean that in a bad way, Sophie, before you get excited."

But it was too late.

"Give me something to do," she said to Bill and Tony. "I just stand about shrieking."

"I don't know what else you can do when your toilet is flushing straight through the ceiling," said Tony.

"Why can't Barbara watch the do-it-yourself program?"

"Why would Jim think of having a go? If Barbara's the one who's watched the program?" said Clive.

"I think what Sophie is suggesting," said Dennis, "is that she have a go at plumbing the bathroom."

Clive snorted.

"What's so funny?" said Sophie.

"Hopefully, the idea of Barbara plumbing a bathroom," said Dennis.

"Yes, the idea of it," said Clive. "But not the, the *reality*."

"What wouldn't be funny about the reality?" said Dennis.

"And are we talking about me, or Barbara?" said Sophie.

"And are you just snorting at the idea of a woman doing the plumbing?" said Tony.

Clive was looking hounded, but Tony's question offered him an escape.

"Well, I presume she's going to make a right mess of it," he said. "Otherwise there's no show."

"She will make a mess of it, yes," said Tony. "But the idea of a woman plumbing a bathroom isn't funny per se."

"I disagree," said Clive.

The conversation, Tony thought later, neatly captured all the maddening contradictions of the show. Jim plumbing the bathroom was boring and obvious; Barbara making a mess of it was funny and fresh and then entirely predictable. Maybe that was how television—and, he supposed, life—always worked.

One member of the audience was physically sick during the recording. Laughter took hold of her body and shook it and shook it until she was forced to vomit all over the back of the seat in front of her. The business with the flood—and admittedly Tony and Bill had rebuilt and polished and tinkered until the script was a gleaming, ugly, loud machine, an American motorcycle of an episode— had to be rerecorded because the delight of the audience drowned out the dialog. Sophie plumbed and flooded with such artful dizziness that finally she earned comparisons with Lucille Ball, in the popular press anyway. The scene in which Jim comes in to find Barbara standing on the toilet cistern, whereupon she pretends that nothing has happened, was shown in the BBC's Christmas highlights program four years in a row, and came to define *Barbara (and Jim)*. And Bill, in a spirit of desperation, began to take his novel seriously.

ennis had been invited to more dinner parties since Edith's departure than he had during his entire marriage, even if he discounted the ones that his mother had been throwing with humiliating regularity. He seemed to have become an official Eligible Bachelor. He had been introduced to single women who were terrifyingly similar to Edith and single women who were clearly intended to be the opposite. The Ediths were tall and skinny and intellectual; the opposites were short and stout and intellectual. Dennis's Cambridge degree, which was apparently as cramping and defining as a devout religious belief, meant that the cleverness was an unalterable given, but he found it hard to convince himself that short, stout intellectuals were his type. This was, he was sure, due to his shallowness, but there didn't seem to be anything he could do about it.

Edith's true opposite was a quick-witted, unpretentious, high-spirited, funny, curvy, clever, beautiful blonde.

Dennis had been in love with Sophie for far longer than he would ever admit, but it had only occurred to him relatively recently, probably because of this plague of anti-Ediths that was being visited upon him, that every single one of the qualities that he worshipped in Sophie was absent in his former wife. Maybe he was being unfair and she'd changed since he'd last seen her, but he doubted it. It was hard to imagine that Vernon Whitfield had brought out Edith's previously buried fun-loving side.

He wasn't, as far as he could tell, Sophie's type. Both Clive and Maurice were what one might call conventionally good-looking, if you were prepared to overlook Clive's rugger nose and Maurice's deranged smile. They were also famous, and though Sophie would be horrified by the implication of the observation, he knew to his cost that it made a difference. Maybe Edith had gone off with Vernon Whitfield because of his mind, but if that mind had been buried deep in some dusty varsity history department, then she might have decided that it was best enjoyed in the pages of the *Times Literary Supplement* rather than in bed.

Dennis had been working on the assumption that it was best to suffer in silence. A declaration of love would almost certainly be met by embarrassment and, if he was lucky, a little speech about how lovely he was, how much she valued his friendship and professional support. And anyway, what kind of producer would risk damaging his relationship with his leading lady and possibly, if Sophie were indiscreet, his leading man, by confessing a devotion that might well be a direct result of recent psychological trauma anyway?

He was finding it increasingly hard to keep it bottled up, however. That wasn't the point of love, in his opinion. Love meant being brave, otherwise you had already lost your own argument: the man who couldn't tell a woman he loved her was, by definition, not worthy of her. He had finally decided that he had to say something when Clive and Sophie announced their engagement.

They told everyone on the first day of rehearsals for "The Arrival," right at the end of the read-through. The last couple of pages of the script, written by Tony in anticipation of his own emotional state, were serious, shot through with love and tenderness, and clearly the happy couple had been so overcome that they could no longer keep the news to themselves. The audience for the announcement included Sandra, the rather difficult and unlikable actress that Dennis had cast as the midwife. Sandra was the first to speak; Tony, Bill, and Dennis merely gaped in disbelief and, in Dennis's case, misery.

"That's marvelous news," said Sandra. "I'm so happy I was here for it."

"We didn't know you were going to be here for it, to be honest."

"No, but you saw me and went ahead anyway," said Sandra. "I'm honored."

"You shouldn't be," said Clive. "In an ideal world, you wouldn't—"

"Stop it now, Clive," said Sophie.

"Are you actually going to get married?" said Bill.

"Why else would we get engaged?" said Clive.

"People like you are always getting engaged," said Bill. "And half the time there's nothing at the end of it. It's like a phantom pregnancy. Or wind."

"I take it all back," said Clive. "It's just as well Sandra's here to wish us well. We've got Bill comparing our engagement to a fart and nobody else saying anything."

"Sorry," said Tony. "We're all very pleased for you."

They looked at Dennis, who still hadn't spoken.

"Yes," said Dennis. "I'm still trying to process it."

"In your own time," said Bill. "We'll just wait here."

"The thing is, I was going to ask Sophie myself," and he gave a nervous little laugh.

Tony hoped that he was the only person in the room who understood that Dennis was serious.

"I see what you're doing," said Tony.

"What's he doing?" said Clive.

"Very good. OK."

Tony stood up.

"I am Spartacus."

Bill laughed and stood up with him.

"I am Spartacus."

"I haven't seen *Spartacus*," said Clive.

"If we all ask Sophie to marry us, she won't know how to choose, and she'll be spared a fate worse than death."

"Ah!" said Dennis. "Very good."

He stood up.

"You don't have to do it, Dennis," said Tony.

"Oh."

"You started it. You can't do it twice."

"I didn't say, 'I am Spartacus,' though. I just said I was going to ask Sophie to marry me."

"That was you saying, 'I am Spartacus.'"

"Right-o," said Dennis. "I see."

Tony could see that he was sweating now—an indication that the strange bubble of insanity had floated right across the brain and out into the room. They could get on.

"Congratulations," said Dennis.

"Thank you," said Sophie.

She was still looking at Dennis when everyone else had gone back to the script.

Diane wanted to interview the happy couple for *Crush*, quickly, but Clive was nowhere to be found, so the two girls ended up going out for dinner, Diane's treat, to celebrate.

"How did he propose?"

"He took me to the Tratt, bought champagne, got the pianist to play 'And I Love Her,' produced a ring, and got down on one knee."

"Oh, my God."

"Oh, my God, good, or oh, my God, bad?"

"Oh, bad. Terrible. Embarrassing. Cheesy."

"I'm glad you think so."

"What did you do?"

"I told him not to be so bloody stupid. I told him that if the question were actually popped, I'd leave the restaurant."

"And then he popped it and you said yes."

Sophie laughed and sighed at the same time.

"Yes. Sort of. A lot later on. He kept on about it, and I said yes to shut him up, really."

"Beautiful. A fairy tale come true. I'll have to be a bit more upbeat for *Crush* readers, or they'll end up sticking their heads in their gas ovens. Anyway. A bit of the Diane gloss on it and you'll make people very happy."

"Them again," said Sophie.

"Who?"

"'People.' Will it make me very happy, that's the question? I'm a person."

"So why on earth did you say yes?"

"Because . . . Well, because it would make people very happy. It's hard to resist, when everyone goes on about it all the time."

It wasn't true, really. When they went out together, people smiled, asked for autographs, made jokes. Nobody ever said, "Please get married." A wedding would make newspapers and magazines happy, she knew that, but the overwhelming pressure to give the people what they wanted came from within. One very small step sideways and she could make everything fit together, Jim and Barbara and Sophie and Clive, and perhaps there would be a baby to match the baby that she was about to give birth to on television. There was a part of her that wished she was married already, pregnant already, because then everything would double back on itself and give her more pleasure than any ordinary woman or any fictional character would ever know. But she knew that the pleasure wouldn't last long, because there was nothing real at the center of it, and then she found herself longing for something else.

"Do you love him?"

"Oh, come off it, Diane. Perhaps it is time you left *Crush*," she said.

She knew immediately she'd been too sharp with her. It wasn't the silliest question to ask a girl who had just become engaged.

"Can I say, 'I couldn't bear to let another girl steal my Jim'?" said Diane.

"Yes," said Sophie. "That will do."

The *Daily Express* found out about the engagement before *Crush* came out, and a couple of other newspapers printed the story too. Another newspaper claimed to have found out that Barbara was having a boy. The return of the series felt, to them at least, as though they were the only thing happening in the whole wide world.

t was an exciting week. On Thursday, Dennis got a message saying that Tom Sloan had called and wanted him to phone back straightaway.

Dennis stood up.

"Sit down," said Bill. "He can at least wait until the end of the scene."

Dennis sat down. He knew that Bill and Tony regarded him as a Corporation lickspittle, and every now and then he liked to make a small gesture that might help to convince them that he was his own man, even if, as in this case, someone had told him to do it.

"Where were we?"

"I was just wondering whether the midwife would say a little more at this point?" said Sandra the midwife. She spent a lot of the rehearsal time wondering whether the midwife should be saying a little more; to Sandra, a midwife was a combination of medical professional, counselor, priest, third parent, and Greek chorus.

"No," said Bill.

"I'm not sure I agree," said Sandra.

Dennis stood up again.

"Sit down," said Clive.

Dennis decided that he couldn't sit down again just because someone had told him to, and in any case he couldn't concentrate, so he went to call Tom.

"Well," he said when he came back.

"Good or bad?" said Clive.

"I'll let you be the judge."

"Oh, God," said Bill.

"What?"

"If it's a matter of judgment, it can't be good. It can't be a raise, for example."

"I don't think Tom Sloan suddenly decides to give everyone more money. We've signed contracts."

"What does he decide, then?" said Sophie.

"Well," said Dennis. "Ultimately, he's responsible for all the Light Entertainment output on—"

"Oh, for Christ's sake," said Clive. "She didn't mean that. She meant, What did he phone you about?"

"Ah," said Dennis. "Well."

"That's what you said when you came in two hours ago," said Tony. "And we're still none the wiser."

"I've just spoken to Marcia Williams."

"You never have!" said Bill. "What did she want?"

"We don't know who Marcia Williams is," said Sophie.

"Yes, we do," said Bill. "Why d'you think I said, 'You never have'?"

"I thought you were being sarcastic. Who is she, then?"

"She's the Prime Minister's secretary. You know what they say about her, don't you?"

"Be very careful," said Dennis. "We're on BBC premises."

"Oh, don't be such an ass, Dennis," said Bill. And then, just to be perverse, he started shouting, "THEY SAY THEY'RE AT IT!"

"Who?"

"WILSON AND MARCIA!"

"It depresses me that I am attempting to wring a sophisticated comedy series out of such childish minds," said Dennis.

"Go and boil your head," said Bill.

"Is that true?" said Sophie, wide-eyed.

"Supposed to be," said Clive.

"'Supposed to be,'" said Dennis scornfully. "If there was ever a phrase that encapsulated the futility of gossip, that's it. 'Supposed to be true' . . . Dear God."

"Well, we don't know for sure," said Clive.

"No. If we knew for sure it would be a fact."

"But that's what people say?" said Sophie.

"Yes," said Dennis. "It's gossip."

"Ignore him," said Bill. "He's not human. He's a robot."

Dennis looked wounded. "Just because I don't have the same level of prurient interest in other people's affairs doesn't make me a robot," he said. "It just makes me . . . decent."

"What a lot of cock you talk," said Clive.

"Shall I tell you what Marcia and I spoke about?" said Dennis. "Is anyone interested?"

"Get him," said Sophie. "'Marcia and I.'"

"She wanted us to know how much they all enjoyed the program. Harold and Mary never miss it, apparently."

"At least Mary knows he's not at it at eight o'clock on a Thursday," said Sophie.

"With anyone else, anyway," said Bill. "Maybe that's their Big Night In."

"Oh, don't be so vulgar," said Sophie.

"I'm just going to ignore you all and plow on," said Dennis. "Marcia said—"

"Get him," said Sophie. "'Marcia said.'"

"Marcia said the Prime Minister wished he had someone as clever as Jim working for him in real life. And then she asked if we'd like to go to Number Ten and have a look round."

"We're going to meet Marcia?" said Sophie.

"I think we might be going to meet the Prime Minister," said Dennis.

Sandra the midwife clapped her hands together in excitement.

"I can't believe it," she said. "We're going to Number Ten?"

"Ah," said Dennis. "That's the thing."

"Oh, don't tell me," said Sandra the midwife. "Not after everything I've done this week."

This, they could only presume, was a reference to her relative punctuality and her willingness in rehearsal to read the lines as they were written.

"I'm afraid so," said Dennis.

"They specifically said I couldn't come?"

"No, but . . . they don't actually know you exist."

"But if they watch every week, they'll see me next week, and—"

"They invited 'the team,'" said Dennis. "Would you say you're part of 'the team'?"

"Yes," said Sandra. "You've all made me feel very welcome."

Dennis looked at Sophie helplessly. None of the others would be any use to him.

"If there is a spare place," said Sophie, "it should probably go to Betty Pertwee."

Betty Pertwee, who played Barbara's mother, had appeared in the show three times so far, and Tony and Bill were planning to use her again in the christening episode.

"But I don't think even Betty is going to be able to come," said Dennis.

"But she's your mother!" said Sandra.

"I know," said Sophie glumly. "It's awful, isn't it?"

And thus Sandra was mollified, and a crisis in morale averted. And it was all Sophie's doing. She was so clever, Dennis thought, and so kind, and he found the familiar gloom descend upon him.

That night, Sophie called her father, who wasn't as impressed as she'd hoped he might be.

"My dad says we should refuse to go," she said at work the next day.

"I'm not going to listen to your dad," said Bill. "I'm bloody going."

"So am I," said Tony.

"Good," said Clive. "As long as Harold can get his photo taken with the writers he'll be happy."

"Very funny," said Bill.

"May we ask what objections your father has?" said Dennis.

"He thinks the country's going to the dogs," said Sophie, "and we shouldn't prop him up."

"And in which direction are these dogs going?" said Bill. "Where are the kennels?"

"Are you asking what he's unhappy about?"

"I think he was, in his own ponderous and pretentious way," said Clive.

"He doesn't like the balance of payments," said Sophie.

"None of us do," said Clive. "But I'm sure the nation can still run to a pot of tea and a few biscuits."

"And he's worried about the coloreds."

"Are they causing him a lot of trouble in Blackpool?" said Bill.

"A colored man whistled at me last week," said Sandra. "A window cleaner."

"Disgraceful," said Bill. "Send him back. No white man has ever whistled at a woman in the entire history of window cleaning."

"No white man has ever whistled at me before," said Sandra.

There was a respectful silence.

"And he thinks Harold should have offered more support to Mr. Smith in Rhodesia."

"Oh," said Bill. "That explains everything."

"Does it?" said Sophie hopefully.

"Yes. Your old man is an imperialist buffoon. I'll bet he reads the bloody *Daily Express*."

"How did you know that?"

"Do you think these things?" said Bill. "Or is it just your dad?"

"I don't know," said Sophie. "I've never really thought about them before."

"You've never thought about what you think?"

"Sounds funny when you put it like that."

"You're a clever girl," said Clive. "Why do you trot out that poisonous rubbish?"

"Do you think it's rubbish?" said Sophie. "And poisonous?"

"Of course I do," said Clive.

"Everyone does," said Bill.

Sophie looked round the table. There was no sign of dissent, unless one was to count Sandra's sudden hunt for a cough sweet in her handbag.

"Oh," she said. "I had no idea."

It took her a month. She listened to *Any Questions?* and she talked to anyone who showed the slightest bit of interest in what was going on in the world. She bought the *New Statesman* and the *Listener*, because Bill told her to, and made herself read three articles a week. She didn't understand everything, but she came to understand that Bill was right: everyone thought that her father's views were poisonous rubbish. Feeling sorry for Ian Smith, or complaining about the colored problem, was like saying you preferred "How Much Is That Doggie in the Window" to "Twist and Shout." And, in the end, that was all the education she needed. She wasn't sure that the people she worked with and listened to and admired were right about everything, and as she got older it only became more confusing. But she had learned that, to her friends and colleagues, all the things her father believed were as musty and unattractive as a trouser suit in a department store sale. You could refuse to care about fashion if you wanted to, but if you were going to spend all your time in the company of with-it people, you needed to know when they were laughing at you.

Bill had cared a lot about viewing figures, once upon a time. But after "The New Bathroom," he began to crave the approval of people who would never be caught dead watching a popular BBC comedy program. He wanted to be respected by the people he saw at the fringe theater shows, and by the producers of the satirical shows who were turning down his sketches. He wanted to impress the clever young homosexuals he picked up in the arts clubs, and even the television critics who had loved the show once but who hadn't bothered writing about it since the first series. He and Tony had had all that once upon a time, and they'd lost it, and hadn't worried about the loss very much. They needed love, then, as much as they could shovel in, and love came from an enormous popular audience. Now they had grown fat on love, and Bill found himself looking enviously at the social realists and the surrealists and the experimentalists and the satirists who would always be scrawny and pale. It was all to do with money, he supposed. He had it now and he didn't need quite so much of it as he did, and anyway he had the means to make more whenever he wanted. So of course he'd set his sights on something else entirely.

But the things he wanted weren't going to come with *Barbara (and Jim)*, and "The Arrival" made matters worse. He wasn't particularly proud of the work, although it had done a job: labor pains, Jim lost in a meeting, a catastrophically nervous taxi driver, a midwife—played by Sandra with surprising charm and spirit—who wanted Barbara to join her in estimating the royal family's grocery needs, and then a baby, and love. Out of the corner of his eye, Bill noticed that Tony was weeping during the recording, although he managed not to let anyone else see him at it. Bill felt only a slight sense of self-disgust. They got their highest viewing figures to date; as it turned out, they got the highest viewing figures they would ever get. Before the recording, someone in the press office borrowed a baby, a real one, from a girl in Contracts, so that Sophie could pose for pictures with her newborn. (He was indeed a boy—Timothy, to be known as Timmy.) Most of the popular papers carried the pictures before the broadcast. And, as Bill had feared, Timmy the baby made everything harder. The christening episode was good: they invented a vicar who had lost his faith, but who was too lazy, elderly, and unqualified to do anything else. And "The Soirée" had some good things in it too. Jim invites an old college friend and his wife round for dinner, and decides that he has to take over the cooking after Barbara tells him what she has planned. Jim doesn't say as much, but he's clearly worried that Barbara's menu is too plain, too old-fashioned, too English. The first half of the episode, Bill thought, was sharp and fresh, and poked fun both at Barbara's working-class insularity and Jim's middle-class aspirations. But then they lost their nerve and went back to the safety of "The

New Bathroom"; in the second half, the front two rows of the audience had to be provided with waterproof mackintoshes as a protection against flying béchamel sauce, much to their giddy excitement. Dennis told them afterward that his superiors had loved the cooking part and hated all the chat beforehand: the headline note from on high was "More Béchamel Sauce, Less Elizabeth David."

"Nobody else I know is doing this stuff," he said to Tony. "They're all trying to upset their parents, not entertain them."

"By doing what?"

"They're having sex onstage at the Royal Court. Or they're making underground films about decadent Romantic poets."

"Nobody's stopping you," said Tony. "You can go off and earn three bob in your spare time whenever you want. And during the day you can write the most popular comedy series in Britain."

"It isn't the most popular comedy series in Britain with everyone."

"No. Half the country isn't watching us. I can live with that."

"Except the other half contains all the smart people. They've given up on us."

"Who are the smart people?"

"The people having sex onstage at the Royal Court."

"They're out on Thursday nights," said Tony. "We don't have to worry about them."

The only time Bill felt anything like the old spark was when Barbara and Jim argued, which, presumably as a consequence, they seemed to be doing with more frequency. Otherwise, he had to turn to his hobby for absorption, and the feeling that what he wrote was who he was.

He'd started on *Soho Boy* in the mornings, early, before he met Tony at the office. He'd never written prose before, and at first it didn't come easily: he began with the belief that if he wanted reviews, then every sentence had to contain a minimum of five subclauses. And he was dishing out the adverbs as if there was no tomorrow, possibly because neither Barbara nor Jim had any use for them. They never said anything witheringly or walked gingerly or smiled icily. They just walked and smiled and said things. But after "The New Bathroom," when he knew that he needed something else to keep him sane, he started thinking about the book more seriously, analyzing what it was he didn't like. And as a result, he started to allow his character—a young homosexual who'd walked out on his life in the West Midlands and come to London—to speak conversationally. *Soho Boy* became *Diary of a Soho Boy*, and suddenly he felt like someone who might at least finish a book. He set himself a target of twenty single-spaced pages a week, and some weeks he managed more than that. Before they'd finished writing the third series, he had a sheaf of papers by his typewriter which could, if looked at from the right angle, be described as a manuscript.

16

Sophie met Lucille Ball and Harold Wilson within a ten-day period, and the near-collision, which would have seemed like something from a rather desperate school English essay just a few years before, wasn't even a wild coincidence. She met famous people almost routinely. She didn't know them well, but she was frequently in the same room, and she was frequently asked to say hello—to George Best, who was gorgeous and wanted her phone number, to Tommy Cooper, to Marianne Faithfull, even to Reggie Kray. Famous people were two a penny. And in any case, Lucy wasn't as famous as she had been. She no longer meant very much to Sophie's generation. But when Diane called to say that Lucy was in London making a television special, Sophie knew that she had to at least make an effort to thank her for everything.

"Will she speak to me, though?" she said to Diane.

"She'd be silly not to. You're Sophie Straw, now. She's Lucille Ball, then. It will do her more good than it'll do you."

"Don't say that."

"It's true."

"What would I say to her?"

Sophie could already feel the panic in her stomach. She would let herself down, probably in a Lucy-like way—by falling over, or getting her name wrong, or taking Lucy's handbag by mistake and getting arrested by the police, although she would manage to do it in a way that wasn't the slightest bit funny.

"Just say how much you love her show, and how she was an inspiration, and all that."

"And then what?"

"Well, she'll probably ask you a question, and you'll be away."

"What sort of thing will she ask me?"

"It won't be anything you don't know the answer to. She won't ask you what the square of the hypotenuse is."

"Give me a for-instance."

"Sophie, how long have you been acting for?"

"Oh, God. Then I'll have to tell her this is my first show and she'll ask me how come I started as the lead in a series and—will you go with me?"

"I'd like to write about it for the magazine. 'Sophie meets Lucy.'"

"'Lucy meets Sophie,' more like."

"Oh, she's got all cocky all of a sudden."

"Oh, I didn't mean that. I thought you had it the cocky way round."

"No."

"That's why I changed it, do you see?"

"Yes. I know you're not cocky."

"Oh, I don't think I'd better go. You're making me nervous enough, and you're just the one telling me about it."

"They're filming outside Buckingham Palace on Monday, apparently."

"Oh, hell. I'm not working on Monday."

"I know. I remember. That's why I found out where they'd be then."

"She won't have heard of me."

"No. But I'm sure she'll be very polite. Someone will tell her what a big star you are here."

"Do they have to?"

"If they don't, she'll probably wonder why she's having her picture taken with you."

"She's so beautiful, though."

"Sophie, she's in her mid-fifties. She's got a lot more to be afraid of than you have."

Lucy was older than her father? How had that happened? This made her feel even queasier. She was afraid that she would see the Ghost of Sophie Future.

Lucy didn't look older than her father. She was wearing what appeared to be a Foale and Tuffin dress, a moddy white thing with a big orange 3-D letter on the side, and she had the figure and the legs for it, still. She looked old, though, in the way that a ghost looks old. Her makeup was so thick that her face was white and blank, those big eyes lost in the middle of it, the only features capable of expression. That's where Sophie could see Lucy, in the eyes, but

they looked trapped, the eyes of a frightened animal buried in snow. And she was too old to be prancing around outside a sentry box with a bunch of young dancers wearing busbies, while a pop group that Diane said was the Dave Clark Five mimed on a makeshift stage to the side of them. (They cut the scene, in the end. *Lucy in London* turned out to be terrible, but even a terrible show had no room for the dancing guardsmen in the busbies.)

"Do you think this was *written*?" said Diane.

"Everything's written," said Sophie.

"Gosh," said Diane. "I really do have a chance, don't I?"

Sophie was staring intently at Lucy.

"She looks different," she whispered.

"She's had something done to her face," said Diane. She wasn't whispering, and Sophie shooshed her.

"What do you mean? Why would anyone do anything to their face?"

"They have operations," said Diane. "To make them look younger. Face-lifts and so on. I think she's had her eyes tucked."

"Tucked?"

"They stretch the skin, to get rid of the wrinkles. Can you see? That's where the makeup is heaviest, around the eyes. She can't make her faces. Look. It's so sad. Promise me you'll never do that."

Sophie didn't answer. She understood that one day she'd have to choose, as Lucy had had to choose. You could have all sorts of operations that left you unable to act; or you could let your eyes and your bust and your chin go where they wanted to go. And if you did that, then nobody would give you a show called *Lucy in London*, or *Sophie in Holly-wood*. She wished Lucy wasn't making a spectacle of her-self outside Buckingham Palace. It was undignified. But was it any more dignified to sit at home waiting for the phone to ring, like Dulcie, who'd appeared in the first-anniversary episode of *Barbara (and Jim)*? Or to give up entirely, and get fat, and spend the last twenty-five years of your life thinking about the time when you were young and pretty and famous? She wished she didn't spend so much time worrying about the end of it all, but she couldn't help it. Being at the top of your career was like being at the top of a Ferris wheel: you knew that you had to keep moving, and you knew which way you were going. You had no choice.

Lucy and the dancing guardsmen got to the end of their routine, and they took a break, and a young man came over to usher Sophie toward Lucy. Sophie suddenly realized that Lucy was going to look at her, that those eyes would meet hers, and she thought her knees might buckle.

"Hello, dear," said Lucy.

"Hello," said Sophie. "I like your dress."

"Isn't it darling? Congratulations on your show."

"Have you seen it? Did you like it?" said Sophie.

She couldn't stop herself. It was a mistake, of course. She knew it was a mistake because she saw a door close in Lucy's head, the door that led from her brain to those eyes. Those eyes were still looking at her, but they may as well have been behind a television screen. Lucy had gone.

"Oh, it's all right," Sophie said then, except she was squeaking now, not speaking. "You wouldn't have. Sorry."

"Thank you so much for coming all this way to say hello, dear," said Lucy, and then she was led away. Nobody took a photograph.

"Oh," said Diane. "Oh, well. What an old bag."

"No," said Sophie. "No. I did it all wrong."

"What did you do wrong?"

"I shouldn't have asked that."

"Why on earth not?"

"I overstepped the mark."

"How are you supposed to know where the mark is?"

But she had known. It was very faint, and nobody else would have known it was there, apart from the two of them, her and Lucy. (The two of them! Her and Lucy! Even that distinction, between them and the rest of the world, seemed presumptuous.) Sophie had seen it and she had ignored it, because she'd been greedy. She had asked Lucy for proof that she existed, and Lucy wasn't able to provide it, because Sophie didn't exist, not yet, and maybe not ever, not in the way that Lucy existed. She began to fear that she would always be greedy, all the time. Nothing ever seemed to fill her up. Nothing ever seemed to touch the sides.

They took two taxis to Downing Street, even though the five of them could have fitted into one. Clive said that it would look undignified, bumping heads and extricating limbs while policemen and assistants watched. Sophie wanted to be with Clive, but he said he didn't want the stars to be in one cab and the nobodies in another.

"I wouldn't have thought of that," said Sophie.

"You know why not?" said Bill. "Because you don't think in terms of stars and nobodies."

"You know what I mean," said Clive. "You're not a nobody to me. You're just a nobody to the rest of the world."

They had to knock on the door, as if Number Ten was a house, and a secretary showed them into a reception area before leading them upstairs. On the wall over the staircase

there was an ascending line of pictures, paintings and then photographs of every prime minister in the history of Britain, and Sophie silently chastised herself for recognizing so few of the names.

Marcia Williams was waiting for them in a sitting room upstairs. She was excited to see them, or pretended to be, and when she shook Sophie's hand she gave her arm a little squeeze at the same time. She seemed nice, Sophie thought, but it was hard to think of her as the Prime Minister's mistress. It was hard to think of her as anyone's mistress. She was obviously very brainy, and her teeth were too big for her mouth. She wondered whether it was a case of needs must. Harold probably didn't meet thousands of glamorous women in an average year, what with all the TUC meetings and the visits to the Soviet Union. Marcia might have been the closest Harold could get to Raquel Welch. But

Sophie suddenly felt self-conscious, and wished she'd worn a longer skirt. She didn't want to make Harold unsatisfied with his lot, if it was true that Marcia was his lot, or some of his lot. And she didn't want to have to rebuff the Prime Minister, if he liked what he saw. That would be embarrassing.

They sat down, and Marcia ordered coffee and biscuits, and offered them cigarettes from a lacquered case on the coffee table. They talked about Number Ten, the odd shape of it, its deceptive size, how there was another entrance in another street entirely. Marcia's answers were so smooth that they'd been worn away to almost nothing, and Sophie suspected that none of them had asked a question she hadn't heard a thousand times that week.

"Harold's just on his way," said Marcia. "But I thought it would be nice to have a little chat first."

"Lovely," said Sophie.

"Ever since I started watching *Barbara (and Jim)*," said Marcia, "I've been brewing up plans."

"Oh," said Dennis. "What sort of plans?"

"Well, it seems silly that whenever you've shown Jim at work, his office is in a BBC studio. But he works here, at Number Ten. So what I was wondering was, would you like to film somewhere in here?"

"Gosh," said Dennis.

"I don't mean every week," said Marcia. "Worse luck. I'd like it, but Harold would probably start grumbling."

They laughed politely.

"But I'm sure we could manage something as a one-off."

"Golly," said Clive.

"And we'd like to do it quite soon," said Marcia.

"Oh," said Dennis.

"The thing is, everyone says this election is really boring, and Harold's going to win easily, and we're desperately trying to think of ways to pep it up a bit," said Marcia. "Otherwise it's all a terrible grind, and the turnout goes down, and if we do win, it'll start off with a bit of a whimper, rather than a bang."

There was a lot of smiling and nodding, but still nobody said anything.

"We wouldn't ask you to take sides, of course," said Marcia. "The BBC wouldn't have that. But an amusing debate about the issues between Barbara and Jim would do so much more than party political broadcasts. People love the program so much."

"That's very kind of you to say so," said Bill.

Sophie wondered whether everyone else had gone mad except her. The Prime Minister's secretary was asking them whether they wanted to film in Number Ten and all anyone said was "gosh" and "golly."

"We'd love to," said Sophie.

"Good," said Marcia, and she beamed at them all.

Dennis, Tony, and Bill looked at Sophie as if she had spoken out of turn.

"But I'm not sure that . . ." said Dennis.

"Here's Harold," said Marcia, and there he was, the

Prime Minister, sucking on a pipe as if nobody would recognize him without it.

They stood up and introduced themselves, except before Sophie could speak he stopped her.

"And you must be Barbara," he said, and everyone laughed politely.

"Yes," said Sophie. "Sophie."

He looked perplexed for a moment.

"I'm Barbara in the program," she said.

"Of course you are," said Harold. "I've seen it. Very good."

They had been led to believe that at eight o'clock every Thursday night, Harold shucked off the awful responsibilities of his position, lit his pipe, sat down with his wife, and chuckled away for thirty minutes. Now he was telling them that he was not unfamiliar with the show. Perhaps her perception was being warped by professional oversensitivity, but it seemed to her that there was a difference.

"And where do you come from? I'm detecting a scent of red rose."

"That's right. I'm from Blackpool, Mr. Wilson."

"Oh-ho. I'll bet you're keeping that from the BBC, aren't you? They never usually give northerners much of a look-in over there. Still too many Home Counties public-school boys for my liking."

There were a lot of looks flying around under the Prime Minister's radar now. Tony and Bill both caught Sophie's eye, and Marcia caught Tony and Bill looking at Sophie. Dennis was still laughing politely, as Home Counties public-school boys were wont to do, but the laugh was now all form and no content.

"You are daft, Harold," said Marcia, and the moment she said it, Sophie knew what was going on between them. Marcia's not-quite-affectionate exasperation was that of a daughter talking to her father. There was no affair, she was sure of it. "You know very well that Barbara's from Blackpool."

Harold looked confused again.

"I thought she was Sophie?"

"Oh, for God's sake," said Marcia, and shook her head. "Barbara in the show is from Blackpool," said Marcia. "As well."

"Of course she is," said Harold. He didn't seem at all concerned that he'd inadvertently owned up to never having seen five minutes of the series. Perhaps he had other things to worry about. "What do you think of Marcia's idea, anyway?" the Prime Minister said. "Would you like to set an episode inside Number Ten?"

"I told Dennis here how you wished you had someone as clever as Jim working for you in real life," said Marcia.

"I've not got a bad lot," said Harold. "But there's always room for a clever young man."

"I'll tell Jim if I see him," said Clive.

Marcia laughed.

"Thank you," said Harold uncertainly.

A photographer came in and took a few snaps of Clive and Sophie chatting to the Prime Minister, and then he said his good-byes and disappeared.

They shared a taxi on the way back, because they were excited and indignant and giggly, and they couldn't bear to miss a word of anything anybody had to say. To begin with, all that was said was an endless reformulation of the same outraged complaint: "He didn't know us from Adam!" "He's never watched a second!" "It was all a public relations stunt!"

And then Dennis managed to change the tone, from one kind of disbelief to another. "We've just been to Number Ten!" he said, and so then everyone had a go at rewriting that line: "We've just met Harold!" "We've had a cup of coffee with the Prime Minister!" "Bloody hell!" "Harold and Marcia!" The third wave of chatter was about Marcia. Nobody was very interested in Sophie's certainty that nothing was going on, and she understood. They already knew that they would be telling people about the morning for a long time to come, maybe for the rest of their lives, and the taxi ride was the first attempt at a first draft of a story that would have to satisfy parents, siblings, children, and grandchildren. If they could somehow convey the impression that they'd been given a privileged glimpse of the Prime Minister's unconventional personal life, then they were duty-bound to do so. Eventually, somewhere in Paddington, the interjections and exclamations and exhalations gave way to a contemplative silence.

"How many Beatles records do you think he'd heard before he gave them MBEs?" said Bill.

"Oh, he thinks we're the Beatles now," said Tony.

"Do you think we're getting an MBE?" said Sophie. "Because I wouldn't mind."

"Bill's right," said Dennis. "If there's something going on, then Harold wants a bit of it, because it's going on under a Labor government. It's reflected glory. Even if he doesn't know the first thing about it."

"I'm sorry to go on about this," said Sophie, "but nobody answered my question. Do you think we'll be getting MBEs?"

"We might if we do what he wants us to do," said Tony.

"And you won't be getting anything anyway," said Clive gleefully. "It'll only be me and Sophie. Nobody cares about the writers."

"Or the producer," said Dennis.

"Can we do it, then?" said Sophie.

"No," said Tony, Bill, and Dennis at the same time.

"I told her we would," said Sophie.

"Yes," said Dennis. "We noticed."

She didn't care. She didn't care that they weren't going to film at Number Ten, she didn't care that she wasn't going to get an MBE, not this year anyway. She didn't even care that Harold Wilson had never seen the program. If he had, then wanting to meet them all would have been merely a personal quirk, something just for him and Mary. But Marcia's invitation was official acknowledgment that they mattered. Dennis was right. Harold had wanted a bit of reflected glory. Well, that meant that they were the glory.

They didn't film in Number Ten; they weren't even allowed to put out a show in the week of the general election. The Director-General apparently thought that *Barbara (and Jim)* was too nakedly political, and would damage the BBC's commitment to neutrality and impartiality.

"What a lot of cock," said Bill. "We're not taking that lying down, I hope."

"No," said Dennis. "I'm going to march into the DG's office and tell him that we're taking over the Crystal Palace transmitter."

"Seriously, though," said Bill, "what are we going to do about it?"

"I think what Dennis is saying," said Tony, "is that we're not doing anything about it."

"And that's all right with you, is it?"

"I don't mind a week off. We've got plenty to do."

They had begun work on a new series called *Reds Under the Bed*, about a cell of hapless Soviet spies becalmed in Cricklewood, and Anthony Newley had asked them to write a screenplay. Hazel turned down other offers most days of most weeks.

"We've been recommissioned, though, if that's any consolation," said Dennis.

"If they won't put out a show in general election week, you can tell them where to stick their new series," said Bill.

"Oh, tommyrot," said Dennis.

"I'm not having them cancel a show whenever they feel like it," said Bill.

"It's not whenever they feel like it," said Dennis. "It's whenever there's a general election. They may stop you from banging on about the iniquities of the class system during the next one too. Factor in a week off some time in the spring of 1971."

"So what's the bloody point?" said Bill. "Seriously? If they gag you the moment it counts?"

"Just a gentle reminder that you're supposed to be writing a situation comedy about a married couple," said Dennis. "Not the Labor Party Manifesto."

"Of course, it would be a gentle reminder," said Bill. "A gentle reminder about a gentle comedy. Everything's so bloody gentle and polite. Especially you."

"Steady on, Bill," said Tony.

"I've been called worse," said Dennis.

"Why aren't you more worked up about it anyway?" Bill said to Tony. "Trust you to lie on the ground with your belly up and your paws in the air."

Every story contains a moment you can point at and say, "Look, there, that's where it all unraveled," and maybe this was such a moment. That was what Dennis would say, in years to come: "It was never the same after that election-week row." But Tony was a storyteller, and he knew that if you looked at any narrative closely enough you could trace the unraveling back and back and back—right to the very beginning, if the story was good enough.

The strange thing was that the argument seemed synthetic to Tony. Could anyone really care that much about being paid not to work? The anger was clearly real, though. It was in there, sloshing around, looking for the nearest hole to escape through.

"Are you really going to tell them where to stick their new series?" said Tony later. "Because I'm not."

"You'd do it without me?"

"No," said Tony. "Of course not. But I've got to do something. I've got a wife and a kid on the way."

"Oh, have you, Tony? I didn't know. You should have mentioned that before."

"That's a bit unfair."

"I'm sorry," said Bill, without meaning it.

Tony caught a glimpse of something. Was that what it was all about? Perhaps it was. The nuclear family always represented something to a man, especially a single man, especially a single man with an anarchic streak, especially a single man with an anarchic streak who found himself having to write about a nuclear family to earn his living. And Tony's nuclear family meant a lot more to Bill than most nuclear families, for obvious reasons. Tony didn't want June and his unborn child to be a sort of Vietnam, and he didn't want to be on the wrong side. But he was starting to fear that it was too late and that the battle lines had been drawn up a long time ago.

THE FOURTH
SERIES

17

oger Nicholas Holmes was born in the Bushey Maternity Hospital, three weeks after the last episode of the third series had been broadcast. It was a relatively short labor, five hours, but it seemed like an eternity to Tony. He had started off in the corridor outside the maternity ward, smoking and attempting to do the *Times* crossword, but the terrible noises and the occasionally urgent dashes of the midwives and nurses upset him too much, so in the end he went to the pub, and came back on the hour every hour until eventually he was presented with a thirty-five-minute-old son.

He'd been worried that he wouldn't feel enough. He'd wept when Barbara had had her baby in the series, which he'd hoped at the time was an indication of normal human emotions, but afterward he wondered whether the tears had come because of his investment in the program, or because he always found it easy to cry at things that weren't real. He'd been in a right mess at the end of *The Sound of*

Music, for example. But when he held his son for the first time, he was beset immediately by spasmodic and uncontrollable sobs that seemed to start right deep in his stomach. He needn't have worried. Everyone loved their own children, it turned out. Tony wished there was a way that homosexual men could be given this moment. He'd like Bill to feel what he was feeling.

"You OK?" said June.

"Yes," he said. "Very. Thank you."

"That's all right."

"I meant, thank you for everything, not thank you for asking. Thank you for sticking with it. Thank you for him."

It was an inappropriate thought, but the baby wasn't so much like a love child, the effortless product of the blissful or even oblivious union of two people. He was a different sort of miracle, the effortful product of a tricky collaboration between unlikely partners. He was their version of a television program.

June and Tony spent a contented few weeks walking and sitting in parks eating ice creams while their newborn slept, and then, after the phony war, the job of being a husband and a father started properly. It turned out to be a difficult job too. The baby had made everything seem solid and frightening, and Tony was finding it much harder to breathe, all of a sudden. If being part of a family was a job like any other, then Tony would have been counting the days until Christmas, and the other holidays to come, but there was no respite, and there never would be. He didn't even enjoy the return to the office, because he had a living to earn—a proper, serious living, enough for three people. Everything was down to him, now that June had given up work. He had to turn the contents of his head into prams and rusks and reins and mortgage payments, and suddenly there seemed to be less in there than he'd hoped. Each listless hour spent shooting paper clips at the light fixtures with a rubber band, or listening to music on the record player they kept in the office, seemed ominous, rather than an indulgent part of the routine. Could he seriously keep this going forever? Was it really possible to come up with enough ideas—for lines, jokes, characters, plots, episodes—to feed and clothe and educate a child?

He was relying on Bill, and Bill had disappeared. He came to the office every day, but he wasn't there, and didn't even seem to want to be there. He spent most of the time playing the Beatles' *Revolver* LP over and over and over again, until Tony started to dislike it.

"Do you remember when they were all 'I love you yeah yeah yeah'?" said Bill.

"'She loves you,' I think," said Tony.

"Same difference."

"What about it anyway?"

"They've gone from that to this in whatever it is . . . three years. Where have we gone?"

"Where do you want to go? Where should we be going?"

"Moving."

"Moving where?"

"I can't think of a single new permutation of domestic life. The in-laws to stay. Going to stay with the in-laws. Anniversaries. Embarrassing dinner parties at home. Embarrassing dinner parties out. Babies. Bathrooms. Nannies. New carpets."

"Moving!" said Tony. "That's brilliant! 'The New House.'"

Bill shrugged.

"Might as well. We haven't got anything else."

"You don't seem very excited about it."

"It's not a seam we're going to be mining in five years' time, is it? If we're still banging on about it in episode two we'll be stretching it thin."

"What's brought this on?"

"I dunno."

"*Till Death Us Do Part*?"

The series was showing now, and everybody was talking about it, and nobody was talking about *Barbara (and Jim)* anymore because nobody ever talked about two television programs at once, especially when one of them was old hat. Alf Ramsey had turned into Alf Garnett—Alf Ramsey had just won the World Cup for England, and nobody, least of all the BBC, wanted his newly hallowed name besmirched by the fictional character's bigotry and belligerence. But otherwise Alf was the same character, and, somewhat alarmingly, the people of Britain loved him, in ways that his creator might not have intended.

"I don't care about that lot," said Bill, in a way that conveyed both hurt and irritation. "I do care about us being stuck. It's one marriage, between two people. Have you got any more to say about it? You're the one with the family. Where are the gags? Where are the stories? Come on. You're the expert. Although I have to say, you haven't looked like a man with the keys to the comedy bank vault since you became a father."

"I'm bloody knackered, that's why. Knackered and a bit frightened."

"Ah, bless him. What are you frightened of?"

"You and your movement."

"Don't you want to move?"

"No. I don't want to go anywhere."

"That's not true."

"It is! I'm happy! I just want to fill up pages!"

What he meant was that it was a job he enjoyed, loved even, and a job he could do, and a job he was well paid for. All of this seemed like a miracle to him. He had been given more luck than he could have predicted for himself. So, yes, he wanted to fill up the pages, with jokes and observations and situations that Dennis, the BBC, and the audience wanted. If he did that, then he'd be allowed to do it over and over again. He didn't think about anything else. He didn't think about what else he had to say, or whether he was frustrated by the confines of their chosen medium. He just wanted to keep page thirty of the script well away from page one, like a mechanic wanted to fix a car, like a doctor wanted to make people better. He couldn't imagine mechanics getting frustrated because engines were too simple. Presumably every engine presented a different problem, just as every episode offered a new challenge. And if you were up to it, then why not keep going?

"What an ambition."

"There are worse things to aim at than making people happy."

"I feel like we keep coming back to the same place," said Bill.

"We must be going somewhere, then. Even if it's round and round."

"You can honestly see yourself doing this forever?"

"If we can keep it good, why not?"

"You wouldn't get bored?"

"We're beginning to sound like a problem in a women's magazine," said Tony. "'Dear Evelyn, Our marital life is becoming humdrum and I worry he'll go elsewhere. What should I do?'"

"She'd tell you to put on lacy underwear."

"I will, if it will help."

"She'd tell you to do something different anyway. What she wouldn't say is, 'Just keep doing the same old thing and eventually he'll become so old and uninterested that he'll forget all about it.'"

"I thought your novel might be enough."

"The trouble is, I like doing it too much. Makes me realize what I'm missing."

Tony sighed. "It's hard, isn't it?" he said.

"What?"

"I dunno what you'd call it. This. You and me. Our marriage. You start off thinking someone's exactly the same, and as the years go by you realize they're not."

"I knew we weren't the same after the army," said Bill. "When you chickened out."

"Of what?"

"You know."

"You think I chickened out?"

"What would you call it, then?"

"You think I married June because I was scared?"

"So why did you?"

"I . . . Well, I fell in love with her."

"So you're ambidextrous?"

"Both or neither, I don't know. At the time it felt like I was completely . . . 'armless."

"Very good," said Bill, without actually registering amusement on his face.

"Thank you."

"It was very convenient that June was the one you fell for, then, wasn't it?"

"Why was it convenient?"

"Because that was the easier option. And here you are, in a nice little house in Pinner with a wife and a baby."

Tony could only give a helpless shrug.

"Yes. And it suits me. I'm happy. I couldn't do what you do."

"You have no idea what I do."

"You break the law any time you do anything."

"The law's an ass."

"I know that. I'm just saying. If you can go both ways or neither, why go the way that's going to get you banged up?"

"I didn't have any choice."

"I know that. But I did. And that doesn't mean I'm always going to make the boring, safe choice."

"I'm sure that's what it feels like to you," said Bill.

He was being kind, not confrontational, Tony knew that, and Tony suddenly understood what he meant: one thing led to another. The years since they'd started writing *Barbara (and Jim)* would have been entirely different for Bill if he hadn't been queer. He'd met different people, of course. But he'd read different books, seen different plays and films, heard different music, wandered into a world a long way from Tony's little house in Pinner.

"We need more than an agony aunt," said Tony. "We need the Marriage Guidance Council."

And Bill's eyes suddenly brightened, for the first time in weeks.

don't understand," said Dennis when they told him the idea. "What's wrong with them?"

"What's wrong with them," said Bill, "is that they're the opposite."

"But they've always been the opposite," said Dennis. "That's what the show is about."

"Yes, and now it's coming to its logical conclusion. They're struggling to make their marriage work, because they're too different. They need help."

"Just checking," said Dennis. "You're keeping it as a comedy, are you? Or is it a *Wednesday Play*? Perhaps he could strangle her at the end."

"Why can't marriage guidance be funny?" said Bill.

"How many couples who go to marriage guidance are laughing?" said Dennis.

"How many of them want to be?" said Tony.

"There's a divorce epidemic," said Bill.

"You don't need to tell me that," said Dennis.

"Sorry," said Bill. "Forgot."

"But that's just it," said Dennis. "You can't go round apologizing to everybody." He looked at Bill searchingly. "Is this all because of bloody *Till Death Us Do Part*?"

Bill refused to make eye contact.

"It's really put your nose out of joint, hasn't it?"

"I just want to write something about the real world," said Bill. "And in the real world, a couple like Barbara and Jim would need help."

Dennis sighed. He liked working with talented, thoughtful people, but sometimes he wished he could have the same level of success with unimaginative hacks.

"And are they going to survive it?" he said eventually. "Because I want this marriage to work."

"Let's get them through to the end of the series and worry about the rest later," said Bill.

Nancy Lawson, the actress Dennis found to play Marguerite, was the poshest person that any of them had ever met. She was posher than Edith, even, the previous world record holder; Edith's father was a doctor, but Nancy's father was some sort of lord. He had a little castle somewhere in Northumberland and Nancy had gone to an expensive boarding school, before being expelled—for smoking during sex, she claimed. It was a line that she'd clearly used before, many times, but it still worked: not only did it get a laugh, but Tony noticed that Clive immediately started to fiddle with his packet of cigarettes. He didn't offer Nancy one for a couple of minutes, though, in the hope that Sophie wouldn't make the connection. (She did.)

Sophie was pinup sexy, all legs and bosoms and blonde hair, but Nancy, who must have been ten years older, seemed to promise something darker and more dangerous. She also had a strange collection of filthy aphorisms, a parody of the kind of thing you might find in etiquette books: "A gentleman always lets a lady use the flannel first," for example. Or "A lady never uses her hands to put on a French letter." She wouldn't have made a very good marriage guidance counselor in real life, unless you went to her with a very specific set of marital problems. She was an excellent comic actress, though—Dennis had noticed her in a couple of the Brian Rix farces—and once they had made her do up a few buttons and tuck her artfully long, wavy dark hair up into a bun, she managed to convey the necessary gravitas. It was those rounded vowels they were after. Tony and Bill had, unusually for them, done a little research, and as far as they could tell, the ladies who worked for the Marriage Guidance Council were the bored private-school-educated wives of bishops, surgeons, and captains of industry, and Marguerite would almost certainly go home every night to a nice house in Hampstead or Primrose Hill. Nancy was cut from a different cloth. Yes, one could imagine that she might have married a captain of industry once upon a time, but she would either have left him or, more likely, killed him within weeks of the wedding.

Tony and Bill rewrote their script when they understood how good Nancy was. In the first draft it took fifteen minutes to get Barbara and Jim into Marguerite's office. They spent the first half of the script shouting and crying, before coming to the conclusion that they needed help. The misery was cut down to a couple of pages, and the show now started in the middle of a row which, it was suggested, had been going on for months—so that they could get to Nancy sooner.

And she brought the house down at the recording. She had the advantage of surprise, of course—nobody had come along expecting to see a three-hander. But the interplay between the characters seemed to give the show and the cast a whole new energy, and the theme attracted a lot of attention in the press. "No comedy show has ever attempted to deal with the subject of marital crisis, as far as this critic can recall," said *The Times*. "And with the shocking increase in the number of divorces since the turn of the decade, *Barbara (and Jim)* has become both timely and brave, while retaining its characteristic wit and charm. This is no mean feat."

Tony found himself hoping that Marguerite was good at her job: the future welfare of his family was depending on her. Unfortunately, Marguerite could have been the best counselor in the world, but she still wouldn't have known what to do with Nancy.

C live was rapidly coming to the conclusion that being engaged to somebody meant that he spent an awful lot of time not doing things he wanted to do. That, as far as he could tell, was the difference between having a fiancée and not having a fiancée. Curiously, he didn't seem to spend very much time doing things he didn't want to do. Sophie didn't want to prepare for their wedding or introduce him to her friends and family. She didn't have any friends that he didn't already know and she tried to avoid all members of her family whenever possible. It was the not-doing that he felt restricted by. The silly thing was that if he'd sat down and tried to explain it to Sophie, she would have been sympathetic and practical: she was neither naive nor censorious. She would, however, have pointed out that this indicated a certain unpreparedness for married life, and she may well have suggested that they call off the engagement. Looked at from one angle, he could see this made sense. He enjoyed being engaged to Sophie, though. People seemed to like him more. As a consequence, he was keeping extracurricular activity down to the very bare minimum. To all intents and purposes, he had been entirely monogamous.

Nancy, however, his new colleague, was an entirely different, unambiguous, and frequent proposition. He knew he had only himself to blame, but it was more or less entirely her fault: why was she trying so hard to seduce him? Why did she keep making those off-color jokes in front of him? (Yes, she made them in front of the others too, but he couldn't help feeling that they were aimed at him.) Why did she constantly make references to deviant sex and her familiarity therewith?

The first time he slept with the woman who was supposed to rescue his fictional marriage to the character played by his actual fiancée, it was to settle a bet with himself: he was convinced that Nancy was all talk, probably frigid, possibly even a virgin. Unfortunately, none of this proved to be the case. There was no talk, Nancy was molten rather than frigid, and if she was a virgin, then there was no sign of the nervousness or modesty that frequently accompanied first nights, in his experience. He had yet to meet a virgin who had asked, loudly and repeatedly, to . . . Anyway. The long and the short of it was that the sort of temptation Nancy had placed in his way could only be resisted with the sort of fortitude and heroism that he knew he did not possess. Her relentless lewdness, her dependency on alcohol and pills, and her repellent name-dropping were all bad news, of course, and she was possibly mad—once or twice, Clive had found himself wondering whether he could count on her to be as discreet as he needed her to be. But, like all bad news, you could put your hands over your eyes and ignore it easily enough if there was good news on the very next page.

18

Dennis's heart sank when he saw the middle-aged woman looking imploringly at Sophie outside the stage door, on her own, away from the people waving autograph books. If he was lucky, he was going to get fifteen or twenty minutes alone with Sophie: the cab ride to Ming's in Bayswater, the only restaurant they'd found in west London that was open on a Sunday night, and then however long it took Bill, Nancy, and Clive to finish their drinks in the bar and join them. Sophie didn't like hanging around after recordings much. She liked it even less now that Nancy was part of the team, with her low-cut dresses and her loud voice and her off-color jokes that made Clive roar with laughter. For the previous two or three weeks, Dennis had been the one to lead her away.

It wasn't as if he even knew what to do with the time he got with her. If *Barbara (and Jim)* lasted for another twenty or thirty series, then perhaps the accumulated professional chitchat during cab rides and the silent perusals of Chinese restaurant menus might add up to something. Sophie would eventually realize that he'd been constant and patient and sensitive to her quiet post-recording introspection and tell him that she loved him. And by that time the engagement with Clive would surely be over. If he were a betting man, he'd put ten bob on it being ended by Sophie hurling the ring at him before they got as far as the church; a marriage and a divorce would be the safe each-way punt.

He would be in his sixties when the thirtieth series started, and the twentieth century would be nearly over, but if he ate his greens and went on lots of long walks and gave up his pipe, he might be fit enough to consummate the marriage. And actually, he wouldn't care if he couldn't. He wouldn't care about it in thirty years' time, and he was pretty sure he didn't care about it now. It wasn't essential to his vision of their relationship anyway. Could he tell her that, perhaps? Just to break the ice? Could he tell her that he was prepared to share a bed with her for the rest of his life without ever straying over to her side? Or would she find that odd? He could sleep in the spare bedroom, if they had one. As long as he could eat breakfast with her every morning, he'd be happy.

But he was almost certain that the middle-aged woman was Sophie's mother, the mother who'd walked out on her when she was only a child. She looked like Sophie, a little, around the eyes and the mouth. And she looked so nervous and so forlorn that it was hard to imagine any other circumstance or any other explanation. It was only her plainness that gave any room for doubt. You had to be glamorous, surely, to run off with a married man? And it went without saying that you had to be glamorous to be Sophie's mother. Fifteen years was a long time in the life of a woman, though, when those fifteen years had been disappointing.

Ever since Sophie had told him the story of her childhood, he'd been waiting for this moment: that's what happened to famous people. Long-lost parents turned up, looking for the reflected glory that they thought they deserved, and usually for money too. And how long was it all going to take, the apologies and the self-justification, the anger and the accusations? Dennis couldn't see how they'd get through it in under ten minutes. His blissful, sacrosanct Sophie-time was under threat.

"Hello," said Sophie. "I was wondering when you'd turn up."

"I'm sorry," her mother said. "I know this must be a shock. You don't have to talk to me. I just wanted to see you."

"Weren't you watching the show?"

"Yes. I applied for tickets over and over again, but I haven't been very lucky."

"Well, you saw me in there, then, didn't you?"

"I wanted to look at you and have you look back at me. That's all."

"Shall I see you there, Sophie?" said Dennis. "Give you some time?"

"No, just hold on a sec," said Sophie.

"Well," said Dennis gently, "I'm no expert in these things, but I'm not sure a sec is going to do the job."

"Hello," said Sophie's mother. "I'm Barbara's mother."

"Yes," said Dennis. "I'd rather guessed as much. I'm Dennis. I produce and direct *Barbara (and Jim)*."

He shook her hand.

"It's nice to meet you, Mrs. Parker."

"I don't suppose she is Mrs. Parker, is she?" said Sophie.

Dennis could feel her anger from feet away. He could have warmed his hands on it.

"I think you'd be better off asking her," he said. "While she's here."

Sophie's mother smiled gratefully at him.

"I'm Mrs. Balderstone," said Gloria.

"You can't be Mrs. Balderstone," said Sophie. "You can be Mrs. whatever-his-name-is, or Mrs. Parker if you didn't marry him, but you can't stick Mrs. in front of your maiden name."

"Well, that's what I've done," said Gloria. "You can call me whatever you like."

There was no aggression or even indifference in her voice. These were the words of a penitent, someone who had made a mess of several lives and was aware of it. Sophie felt the first pang of sympathy, but she squashed it.

"You can't call me whatever you like," she said. "I'm Sophie, and that's that."

"I'm sorry," said Gloria. "Even though I keep reading about Sophie this and Sophie that, I always think, Oh, there's our Barbara again. Sophie will probably take me a while to get used to."

"You haven't got a while," said Sophie.

"We're going to a Chinese restaurant in Bayswater to meet Clive and a couple of the others," said Dennis. "Ming's. You don't have to have Chinese food. They do steak and chips. Or omelet and chips. Maybe . . ."

"You can recite the whole bloody menu and it wouldn't make any difference," said Sophie. "She's not coming with us."

Sophie marched toward the waiting taxi without looking back. Dennis made an apologetic face.

"I'm sorry," he said.

"I had to try," said Gloria.

"See you again, I hope," said Dennis, and he started to walk away. Almost immediately, however, he turned back. He was the last link between one world and another, and he had a duty to keep the two worlds connected for as long as possible. "Are you staying in London tonight, Gloria?"

"Yes."

"Could you tell me where?"

"Oh. Yes. Of course. I'm staying at the Russell Square Guest House. It's not in Russell Square, by the way."

"Ah." And then, when no further information was forthcoming, "Where is it, exactly?"

"Oh. You're very kind. Farringdon Road. I'm going home in the morning. I'll be leaving at around 10:30."

"Right-o."

Dennis realized that a home address might be useful too. Sophie's rage was unlikely to have subsided by the morning.

"And actually, where do you live? Will you write it all down?"

As she fumbled in her bag for a piece of paper, Sophie's taxi drove away.

"I'm sorry," said Gloria. "She's gone without you."

"Don't worry about that."

"Tell her that I don't want anything," said Gloria.

"I will."

It was sincerely meant, but Dennis knew it couldn't possibly be true.

He hailed a cab, and when he arrived at the restaurant he found Sophie sitting on her own. There was a God after all.

"What were you talking to her about?" she said.

"Can I get a drink first?"

They stopped serving alcohol at ten o'clock on a Sunday and he wanted to get a couple of drinks down as quickly as possible. He'd been rattled by Gloria's appearance, and the show had not gone very well. The cast had tried their best, and Nancy had tried too hard, but since Barbara and Jim had begun using the services of a marriage guidance counselor, the jokes seemed to have been pushed out to the edge of the script. He ordered a bottle of beer and a glass of wine, and drank the beer before answering Sophie's question.

"I asked her where she lived."

"What did you do that for?"

"In case it came in handy."

"Where does she live?"

"She lives in Morecambe."

"Why?"

"Maybe you should ask her yourself. I didn't know that living in Morecambe required an explanation."

"After all that fuss, she's a few miles up the coast."

Dennis was about to point out, flippantly, that Morecambe's proximity to Blackpool seemed like an odd detail to get snagged on, but he stopped himself just in time when he worked out why it had seemed remarkable. Clearly, Dennis had never thought about it much before, but on the whole mothers tended not to dump their children and disappear off with colleagues, never to be seen again. Sophie must have spent a lot of her younger life in a perpetual state of shame and humiliation. Gloria should be living somewhere a long, long way away, somewhere unimaginable, Patagonia or Tasmania.

"What's she doing in London anyway?"

"I'm presuming that she came to see you."

"Well, I'm not going all the way to bloody Morecambe," said Sophie.

"You don't have to," said Dennis. "I know where she's staying."

"Oh, hell," said Sophie. "What should I do?"

"Do what you want."

"You think I should go. Otherwise you wouldn't have gone back."

"No, that's not what I think. I wanted you to have the

choice. I didn't want you sitting here all agonized because you'd made a mistake."

"That was it," said Sophie.

"That was what?"

"I've just realized. That was it, and I missed it, because I was too angry. That was what it was all about, right from the beginning. I wanted to make myself so famous that my mother would read about me in the paper or see me on the telly and come and find me."

"And then what?"

"I'd tell her to bugger off."

"There you are. You've done it all."

"But I missed it. Because I was too angry. I didn't notice it was happening."

"Well, I suppose that was always likely to happen, in the circumstances."

"So now what?"

"It all depends on whether you have any use for a clearly rather pathetic and very remorseful middle-aged lady who used to be your mother."

"I don't, really."

"Do you want an apology? Because she seemed to me like a woman who wanted to offer one."

"Oh, bugger," Sophie said. "I do, I think." And then, "Thank you."

Clive, Nancy, and Bill turned up, tipsy and loud and stupid. Nancy immediately launched into a story about a friend of hers who had performed a sexual act on a former government minister in a box at the Royal Opera House.

She seemed to have a suspiciously large number of friends who got up to that kind of thing, Dennis had noticed, and yet the stories always seemed to contain detail that friends would never have provided. Clive also seemed to have taken the view that they were all thinly disguised autobiography, and as a consequence he always listened with rapt, gleeful attention, like a small boy sat cross-legged in front of the family radiogram during *Dick Barton*.

"Could you take me home?" Sophie said to Dennis quietly, amidst the gasps of shock and the roars of laughter.

Not only was there a God, but He was fair and just and wise: Dennis's dealings with Gloria had somehow earned him another fifteen-minute cab ride.

Sophie took her mother for coffee at the Ritz, in a taxi, simply because she could, and simply because she knew it would make her mother uncomfortable.

"Will I still be able to get the eleven-thirty train?" her mother asked when it became obvious to her that the Ritz wasn't just around the corner, as Sophie had airily promised.

"Do you have to?"

"If I miss that one, I'd have to wait two hours for the next."

"I suppose it depends how much you miss it by, doesn't it? If you get there at one twenty-five you'll only have to wait five minutes. You never know, there may be a lot to say."

This was Gloria's cue to stare out of the window silently until they got to the hotel. As they walked in, the doorman greeted Sophie by name, and told her to keep a careful eye on Jim, and Sophie laughed and said she would. She'd been to the Ritz before and something similar had happened; that was one of the reasons she wanted to take her mother there.

They sat down on one of the sofas in the big lounge and ordered coffee and biscuits.

"Is this what it's like, then?" said Gloria. "The Ritz, and so on?"

"If I want it to be." And then, because that sounded too haughty, "But most of the time I'm at work. Or at home. I work hard."

"Oh. This is a very comfy settee, isn't it? But it's hard to sit up straight in."

Sophie waited and waited for something, some further flicker of interest in the last fifteen years of her daughter's life, but Gloria seemed lost in the soft furnishings and the admittedly mystifying residents of the hotel.

"Is that all you can say?" said Sophie. "That the settee is comfy?"

She'd promised herself that she would try to stay calm, but it was impossible.

"I don't know what to say, to tell the truth," said Gloria.

"So why did you come down?"

Her mother shrugged.

"I had to."

"Have you been in Morecambe all this time?"

"No, we moved around a bit. He got a job in Bolton when . . . when we moved. And then another one in Lancaster. And then we'd just moved to where I am now when he went."

"Where did he go?"

"I don't know. I think he might be back in Blackpool."

"Did you marry him?"

"No. He was happy as we were. He could have his cake and eat it."

Nobody walking past them in the Ritz would ever have described her mother as cake. She was bread and butter, Sophie could see that now. She'd always thought of her as cake, though. She'd grown up listening to her father talk about running off and fancy men, and so she'd dressed her up, put makeup and stockings on her, given her a cream and jam filling, and slathered her in icing. But she was just a woman clutching a mackintosh and a shabby old-fashioned handbag that Sophie wanted to snatch from her and dump in the nearest bin.

"I've got nothing to say, Barbara. Sophie. Really. Nothing. Nothing interesting, no secrets. I've just got a long boring story about nothing."

"So what was the point of all that, then? What were you hoping for?"

"Only something better. I didn't get it, if that's any consolation."

"It isn't really."

It was, though. She understood the need for something better. Sophie hadn't hurt anyone when she'd come to London, but she would have done, if she'd had to. And she could argue that she had talent, and if she'd let it swell and fester, then it would have killed her. But she hadn't known for sure it was real, and she hadn't known for sure it would save her. Her mother's escape route struck her as something that was a part of the old days. Gloria would never have dreamed of moving to London and finding out what she was capable of, how far she could go. Her way out was to latch on to a man and move with him to Bolton. It had never occurred to Sophie before, but the worst thing about being Miss Blackpool was the title. Taking your husband's name when you became his wife was one thing. Taking your town's name when you became its beauty queen was something else again.

"You know I'm sorry, don't you?" Gloria said.

"No. How would I know that? You've never told me. You never even tried to get in touch."

"Oh, of course I did. But your father wouldn't have it, and I felt so guilty anyway . . . He said it was for the best if I kept away. He told me you hated me."

Sophie didn't say anything. It was true: she'd hated her. This hatred had been a child's hate, untrustworthy, carefully nurtured by her father, and therefore immature, but it was hatred nevertheless. She thought again about what she'd confessed to Dennis the previous evening, that she'd long dreamed of her mother turning up so that she could ignore her. The dream could never have been realized if Gloria had been a better, more determined, more desperate mother. They would have had a handful of unhappy meetings, and nobody would have felt the benefit, and there would have been no rage, no fire, no move to London. She would have become Miss Blackpool, and her mother would have been on a deck chair, clapping and crying. She would have married someone with a car showroom. And why stop there? What if Gloria had stayed married to her father? Where would she be now? In Blackpool, for sure. In R. H. O. Hills, probably.

She owed her mother everything and nothing, all at the same time. For a couple of hours, she wanted to celebrate the everything, so she took her mother shopping. Finally, once they were no longer looking at each other, they began to talk. It was much easier to fill in gaps and ask questions while they were going through racks of coats and rejecting handbags. Jobs, Marie, cousins, London, Bolton, back and back and back through cosmetics counters until they reached school. They didn't talk about the day Gloria left, though. Sophie couldn't imagine that she'd ever want to talk about that.

"I told your Dennis I wasn't after anything," said Gloria as they were walking into Selfridges. "And it'll be much more expensive here than at home."

"Who told you he was my Dennis?" said Sophie.

"Isn't he?"

"No," she said. "I'm engaged to Clive."

"You're engaged?"

"Yes."

"And you're going to get married?"

Why did everyone insist on treating her engagement and her future marriage as two separate, independent events? It was as if one was a kiss and the other a pregnancy: one could lead to the other, but only if a lot of other things happened in between. And yes, she sometimes thought that the chances of her and Clive becoming man and wife were slim, but when other people took the same view, she felt patronized.

"Yes. We're going to get married."

"Really?"

"You didn't see me with Clive. You didn't meet him."

"No, but I saw you with Dennis . . . He looks after you."

"That's his job."

"He's supposed to run after long-lost mothers and get their address?"

"That was him poking his nose into where he doesn't belong."

"He's soft on you, though, isn't he?"

Sophie felt a sudden catch in her throat.

"Well, he's very nice."

"You didn't know anything about me and Clive?"

"What would I know?"

"Oh, there have been a couple of magazine articles and so on."

There had been hundreds, or so it seemed to her. The agency sent her cuttings, and something came in the post every other day.

"I haven't seen any," said Gloria.

"What do you see?"

"I don't get a paper. I watch the news."

Her relationship with Clive had not been on the news.

"Doesn't anyone ever tear something out and give it to you?"

"No," said Gloria. "Nobody knows you're my daughter."

Gloria's secrecy, her willingness to forgo the pleasures of pride in order to atone for the sins of her past, could have been winning, if Sophie had been paying attention, but she was momentarily distracted by her mother's ignorance. It had stung her. People like her mother should know that she was engaged to Clive. They were celebrities, and they were together, and their togetherness was a part of it all. Before she said good-bye, Sophie bought her mother a whole pile of magazines from the kiosk outside the station. There was bound to be something in one of them.

L ater that week she called Diane, who came to the flat with a photographer, and the photographer snapped away while she made Clive pork medallions in Madeira sauce. After they'd finished the meal (more photos, toasting the camera with a glass of wine), they sat down on beanbags and pretended to examine her LPs (more photos, pretending to argue about the Beatles and the Rolling Stones by pointing angry fingers at each other and smiling), while they talked to Diane about the future. Diane wrote two pieces, one for *Crush* and one for the *Express*. And yet when the articles appeared, Sophie was left wondering whether she'd missed the point of her conversation with her mother somehow.

19

ill didn't know what you were supposed to do with books you'd written yourself. He didn't know any publishers. He didn't know any literary agents. And he didn't know whether you could just heave a four-hundred-page manuscript at friends and colleagues and ask them to lug it home and then provide a kind but honest—but, above all, kind—assessment of your worth as a novelist and therefore as a human being since this book was the closest he'd ever come to pure self-expression. There weren't that many friends and colleagues he could ask. *Diary of a Soho Boy* wasn't for the faint of heart, he could see that: he'd written the kind of book he wanted to read, and he'd told what he knew to be the truth about men like him. He hadn't described what went where, but neither had he made it all so opaque that nobody would be able to tell what was going on. He didn't even know whether it was publishable. The kind of love he had described was still illegal, so did that make the descriptions illegal too?

In the end he decided to tell Tony he'd finished, just to see what happened next.

"Can I read it?"

"What do you want to read it for?"

"Because I want to read everything you write, you twerp."

"You don't have to."

"I know that."

"What if you hate it?"

"I wouldn't tell you."

"So what's the point of reading it?"

"What's the point of reading anything? I wouldn't tell Graham Greene I didn't like his last book either."

"But presumably you don't write comedy scripts with Graham Greene."

"All the more reason not to tell you if I don't like it."

"So you're just going to tell me I'm a genius?"

"That's about the size of it."

"Can we start again, then?"

"How d'you mean?"

"Tony, will you read my book? And tell me what you think of it?"

"What's the difference?"

"Before, you asked me. Now I'm asking you. As a favor."

"I'm not Vernon Whitfield. I couldn't tell you what's wrong with it. Not that there will be anything wrong with it."

"I don't want Vernon Whitfield stuff. Just tell me it reads like a book. Whether there are boring bits. Whether

I should put it in the bin or show it to someone else. Whether I'll get arrested."

"I'm not a legal person either."

"All right, whether I'll get fired from the BBC. Thrown out of pubs. That sort of thing."

"Gotcha."

"And . . ."

"I'll just read it," said Tony.

"How long will it take you, do you think?"

"How long is a piece of string?"

"Do you mean how long is my book?"

"I suppose I do, yes."

"Four hundred pages. Double-spaced."

"And how boring is it?"

"Fuck off."

Tony read it twice in the next three days, while telling Bill that he hadn't had time to start it yet. He read it so quickly the first time that he could think of nothing to say, except that he had taken himself off to the bedroom after the baby had gone to sleep, and was still there when June switched the TV off and came in to get undressed.

"What's it like?" she said.

"It's . . . Well. Blimey. I dunno."

"If I may state the obvious, you're finding it impossible to put down."

"Yeah, but he's my best friend."

"I've read lots of scripts by best friends. I've put a lot of them down. And scripts are short."

"OK, then. It's good. But blimey."

"What's the blimey bit?"

"It's . . . Well. Bloody hell."

"Whatever job you decide to do when you get older, make sure it doesn't involve the English language."

"It's . . . I haven't read anything like it before."

"Is it well written?"

"I dunno. It's just . . . him."

"So he has a voice."

"Well, if that's a voice, everyone's got one."

"No, not everyone's got one. Most people can't get it out onto the page. I had a go once and I sounded like an A-level literature student being strangled while writing an essay about Jane Austen. So he's more than halfway there. I want to know about the blimeys and the bloody hells."

"The, you know. All that. It's pretty steamy stuff. D'you know what? I don't think I do go both ways."

"So it's a handbook as well."

"I don't know about the hand bit. It didn't do much for me."

June rolled her eyes.

"Sorry," said Tony. "It isn't half going to cause a fuss, though, if he can find someone to publish it."

"It's that . . . honest?"

"It's not like *Lady Chatterley* or *Fanny Hill*. But it's still blokes kissing blokes."

"So what are you going to tell him?"

"I'm going to tell him what I told him I was going to tell him: it's a work of genius."

F uck off," said Bill.
"I mean it."

"A work of genius like who? Dickens? Tolstoy?"

"It's different from them."

"Have you ever read Tolstoy?"

"No, but I'm guessing he didn't go in for the homosexual passion bit. I don't know, Bill. I don't read a lot of books. All I can say is that it wasn't boring in the least, you have a voice, and I can't imagine there's anything else out there like it."

They talked about characters for a little bit—it was, Bill said, supposed to be a picaresque novel, although he had to explain the word, and it was stuffed full of memorable, hilarious rogues, Soho chancers, down-on-their-luck artists, the kind of people you could find in the Colony Room, according to Bill. And they talked about a section in the middle, a long description of the narrator's childhood, that Tony thought was the only place where he'd started to feel as though he were reading a book.

"It is a bloody book."

"It never felt like that. I never felt I was reading. And that bit was, you know, 'Oh. Here I am, plowing through an Important Novel of Today.'"

"I hate that bit," said Bill eventually. "It took me fucking forever, and it didn't come naturally. I just didn't want to cut it because of all the work."

"What are you going to do with it now?"

"I'm going to give it to Hazel."

Hazel was now their agent as well as their secretary. Every year, when Dennis phoned to make an offer for a new series, Tony and Bill made Hazel talk to him about money, because she could be bolshie on the subject and Dennis was scared of her, so they'd started to give her 10 percent instead of a salary. She was gentle with Dennis, which Bill and Tony wanted her to be. But she was ferocious with anyone they didn't know, the ITV producers who had commissioned *Reds Under the Bed*, and the film producer who wanted them to write the Anthony Newley script. Bill and Tony couldn't bear to be in the same room when she talked to them.

"Will she have to read it?"

"I suppose so. I just want her advice. Her sister works in publishing."

"Right," said Tony doubtfully.

"She's made of stern stuff," said Bill. "And it's not like I keep things a secret."

"No," said Tony. "But you don't shout them from the rooftops either."

"She'll be fine," said Bill. "She'll know what to do with it."

Give it to Michael Braun of Braun and Braun," said Hazel the following morning.

She didn't make eye contact with him as she handed him the bag containing the manuscript.

"Right," said Bill. "Michael Braun."

Hazel sat down at her desk and picked up the telephone receiver, ready to start her day's work.

"Is that . . . it?" said Bill.

"Yes," said Hazel.

"Thanks," said Bill. He started to walk toward the back office and then stopped. "What did you think?"

"Braun and Braun," said Hazel.

"If they're interested, will you represent me?"

"No," said Hazel.

"Thanks for reading it."

"I didn't read it. Not all of it. Just enough to know that you should give it to Michael Braun."

Bill gave it to Michael Braun, and never mentioned the book to Hazel again.

There was only one Braun. Michael Braun didn't think Braun sounded like a proper publisher, so he simply made up another one. "Who's the other Braun?" people would ask him sooner or later. "Oh, they're both me," he would reply airily.

He was ten years older than Bill, handsome, loud, almost certainly a drunk, certainly queer, and he took great interest and pride in books that upset people, including but by no means limited to Hazel. He published French novels about incest, and American novels about drug addicts, and he very much wanted to publish an English novel about homosexuality. He spent a lot of his time preventing his books from being seized by various authorities, customs officers, the police, and the Lord Chamberlain's Office, but he didn't seem to mind much. Indeed, he seemed to regard legal battles as the quintessence of a publisher's job. As far as he was concerned, publishing a book that caused no offense to anyone was a waste of his time and energy. "That's what everyone else does," he said.

He took Bill to a Pall Mall club that served steak and kidney pudding and treacle tart; he seemed permanently amused by the incongruity.

"Half the members here are lawyers who spend their time trying to close me down," he said. "Except none of them know it's me."

Bill doubted whether that was true. He hadn't known Braun for very long, but it was obvious that he had no talent for discretion, or even for talking at a volume level that could be described as conversational. He seemed to enjoy emphasizing the words likely to offend, so anecdotes involving, say, buggery and a young Catholic priest could be shared, albeit piecemeal, by the furthest corners of the dining room.

"I think your novel is remarkable," he said after the claret had been poured and appreciated. "Where have you come from? Why don't I know about you? What do you do all day?"

"I'm a scriptwriter," said Bill.

"How glamorous. Anything I would have heard of?"

"Television, mostly. Have you seen *Barbara (and Jim)*?"

"Good Lord, no," said Braun. "Why on earth would I

have seen something called *Barbara (and Jim)*? And why do you ask?"

Bill was flustered. He thought that there was an obvious link between the two halves of his reply, but Braun hadn't spotted it.

"Well, that's what I do."

"What?"

"I write *Barbara (and Jim)*."

"Presumably they only let you do the Jim bits," said Braun, and laughed at his own joke.

Bill managed a smile. He was, he realized, disconcerted by the recognition of his sexual preferences in a professional context. He'd spent so long hiding them in meetings about work that he wondered whether he preferred it that way.

"And has it gone well for you?"

"Yes," said Bill. "It's very popular."

"People watch it?"

"Yes."

"Lots of people?"

"Yes."

"How many?"

"It's gone off a bit recently."

They were getting lots of nice notices for this series, but they were losing viewers every week. The British public were apparently unsure about the comic potential of marital discord and the BBC Audience Research department had spoken to several people who were very concerned about the welfare of baby Timmy.

"I just want to know what popular means," said Braun.

"Well. The highest we got was eighteen million. We're down to about thirteen at the moment."

Braun looked at him and laughed.

"You know there are only fifty million people in the country, don't you?"

"Yes."

"So . . . You're being serious?"

"Yes."

"Dear God. Have you ever heard of Jean-François Durand?"

"Yes. *The Python's Mustache.*"

"Read it?"

"Bought it."

"Lovely reviews—'The best book to have been published anywhere in Europe this year,' the *TLS* said, an interview with the author in the *Listener*—7,229 copies sold. Unless someone's bought one this morning."

"Right."

Bill knew that publishing was different. He had no idea that it was a virtually uninhabited country, like Australia.

"We'll do better with yours," said Braun. "It will be a *succès de scandale*. Do you want your own name on it?"

"Yes."

It was his book. He wanted to see his name on the cover.

"Are you prepared for that? With the BBC, and your family and so on?"

"I need to have a little chat with a few people."

"I'm hoping by the time the book is published we won't be breaking the law every time we pick somebody up."

There had been a debate about the new Sexual Offenses Bill in Parliament, finally; there would be a change in the law, and homosexuals would no longer need to fear imprisonment. Roy Jenkins had said that "those who suffer from this disability carry a great weight of shame all their lives." Bill supposed he'd meant it kindly, but it hadn't made anyone feel much better about themselves.

"When will you publish?"

"As soon as possible. Now is the time."

Bill suddenly felt weak with relief. He had had enough of trying to guess the thoughts and feelings of eighteen million people he didn't know. He wanted to talk to the few thousand that he did.

He had to have a little chat with one of his colleagues the very next morning: Sophie had come into rehearsals with a plan.

"Are you doing anything tonight?" she said to him during the first tea break.

"Nothing in particular. What are you offering?"

"Will you come out for dinner with me and Clive?"

"Is he buying?"

"I am."

"Lovely."

"I want you to meet a friend of mine."

"Excellent."

"Diane."

Bill froze.

"She's a bit younger than you," said Sophie, and then, apparently off Bill's look of panic, "but not that much younger. And she's very pretty, and clever, and I can't understand why she hasn't got a boyfriend. Just like I can't understand why you haven't got a girlfriend."

He had known Sophie for three years, and he had spent all of them hiding himself from her, while at the same time presuming that she had worked him out. He now saw that he'd been asking a lot of her.

"Ah," he said.

"Don't tell me I'm too late," said Sophie.

"Well," he said. "You are a bit, yes."

He took her outside for a walk and a smoke. She was shocked, then apologetic and self-flagellatory, and Bill became aware of how much he loved her.

"Has it been hard, writing about a man and a woman and a baby, then?" she said. "Are you sick of us?"

He just smiled. He felt at peace with the world.

I t all fell apart very quickly in the end.

Tony and Bill discussed the possibility of Barbara and
Jim separating one Tuesday evening, a couple of weeks
before the end of the fourth series. They were in the pub
after work, trying to come up with an idea for the last episode, something that would address the hemorrhaging of
audience figures, and they were tired.

"I haven't got the energy to fight for this marriage,"
said Bill.

"One last push," said Tony.

"And then what?"

"A holiday. The Anthony Newley script. *Reds Under the
Bed*. Can't wait."

"And then what?"

"And then what? I dunno. We retire to Bexhill and
we die."

"Before then?"

"Another pint and a packet of potato crisps."

"I think they should knock it on the head," said Bill.

"Who?"

"Barbara and Jim. I don't know how to dig them out of this. And I don't even know if I want to."

They had been delighted by the logic of the marriage guidance idea, and it had seemed even better when Nancy turned up, with her posh voice and her comic timing. She had helped the fourth series settle into a predictable, slightly lazy rhythm. The episodes always began in the Marriage Guidance Council office, grievances were aired, jokes were made, Marguerite gave Barbara and Jim homework—exercises to do, problems to solve. And by the end of the thirty minutes, a new, previously unanticipated problem had emerged, directly as a result of Marguerite's suggestion. They had gone into marriage guidance with several bones of contention, all dug up from the soil of the original idea: he was from the South, she was from the North, he was Labor, she was a Tory, he was timid and thoughtful, she was quick-tempered and instinctive, he was Oxbridge, she had left school at fifteen. (Cynics might have pointed out that it was such an unlikely marriage that it could never have existed outside of a television scriptwriter's imagination in the first place.) But such were the demands of television that Tony and Bill had chewed all the marrow out of the old problems and had added a whole new set—sex, friends, parenting, in-laws, tastes. They now had a whole magnificent skeleton of contention, instead of the original bones, a skeleton as complicated and as intimidating as the diplodocus in the Natural History Museum.

"Right," said Tony. "Christ."

"I'm not saying, you know, that's that. Talk me out of it."

"Can you do that? Just . . . knock the series on the head? Without my say-so?"

Just for a moment, Tony had a flash of something awful, lawyers and arguments about ownership.

"No. Course not. If you want to keep it going, that's up to you."

"But you're out."

"I never said that either. I'm just . . . holding an idea up to the light and having a look at it."

"OK. So where do we go from here?"

"I dunno," Bill said. He took a long pull on his pint. "I'm out."

"You just said you were having a look."

"I had a look. I didn't like what I saw."

"When did you have a look?"

Tony knew he sounded panicky. He tried to breathe deeply without Bill noticing.

"Just now."

"When you were drinking your beer?"

"I'm not drunk. I knocked back a quarter of a pint, that's all."

"I know. But . . . was that when it happened? When you made your mind up?"

"I made my mind up weeks ago. But I didn't want to march into work and say it with no preamble. I was look-ing for an opportunity."

"You want to pack in *Barbara (and Jim)*?"

"Isn't that what we've been talking about?"

"I'm just checking."

"I can't see that they've got anywhere left to go," said Bill. "If you want to keep it open so that you can write the next series, I'll help you. But I think she should ask him to leave."

"Bloody hell."

Tony felt a little sick, as if he were breaking up with June.

"You all right?" said Bill.

"Yes. Course. It's not like they're real people."

They were real people. They were going to get a divorce. It was sad. Also, Tony needed them to be happy and together so that he could look after his own family. He had been foolish to agree to marriage guidance. It had put them in danger, made the unthinkable possible.

"Anyway," he said, "I'm going to carry on. If they'll let me."

"They'll let you," said Bill. "Dennis knows you don't need me."

"You won't think less of me?" said Tony.

"Why would I think less of you?"

"Because I know I'm going to have to more or less pretend this series didn't happen. They'll start off next year all happy and shiny and repaired, and I'll have to piss around with new bathrooms a lot."

"It's hard to make a living in this game," said Bill. "You've got to do what you've got to do."

"Thank you."

Nancy came in after lunch the worse for wear and immediately the atmosphere, sleepy and good-natured but focused in the morning, changed. Sophie became irritable and Clive looked like a man who was walking as carefully as he could through a minefield but knew he was going to lose a leg anyway.

Barbara and Jim were receiving advice from Marguerite about the corrosive effects of jealousy.

"They're quite . . . square, aren't they?" said Nancy when Dennis had finished talking about the long marriage guidance scene.

"Who?" said Dennis.

Clive started to walk briskly toward the door.

"Need some air," he said.

"Ha-ha," said Nancy as she watched him go. "So are you, I see."

Clive ignored her. Sophie was mystified.

"Why does that make him square?"

"He's squeamish," said Nancy. "Thank heavens women have more sense."

"I don't understand, I'm afraid," said Sophie.

"Jealousy," said Nancy. "I don't get jealous."

"Good for you," said Sophie.

Tony stopped scribbling in the margins of the next scene and looked over at the girls. There was an atmosphere in the room, although he couldn't have described it.

"I think we perform different functions, don't we?"

"In the script?" said Sophie.

"In life," said Nancy.

"I expect so," said Sophie.

She wasn't interested, and her lack of interest only made Nancy more determined to attract her full attention.

"You do the homely stuff, and you're marvelous at it. And I do the exotic stuff. You'd have to ask Clive whether I'm marvelous at that."

"I'd stop there," said Bill pleasantly.

"Stop where?" said Sophie.

"He doesn't want me to talk about my sexual relationship with Clive," said Nancy. "He thinks it will pollute the working environment."

"I know it will," said Bill.

Sophie finally understood.

"You're saying you've been sleeping with my fiancé?"

"'My fiancé,'" said Nancy. "Gosh. It's 1959 and I'm in rep at Chichester."

"I won't be working this afternoon," said Sophie.

"Understood," said Dennis.

They all watched her leave.

"And, Nancy, I don't think Barbara and Jim will be requiring marriage guidance anymore."

"As from . . . ?"

"Well. Now, really."

"I'm contracted for another two episodes," said Nancy.

In the end, Dennis had to escort her from the premises.

"Perhaps we should tell Dennis what we were talking about last night," said Tony when Dennis came back.

"That?"

"Yes. That."

"I didn't think you wanted to talk about that," said Bill.

"I don't think we've got any choice," said Tony. "We're supposed to be writing a comedy series, not *The Perils of Pauline*. There's no rescuing them."

And so, with appropriate solemnity and regret, Tony and Bill started to talk about divorce.

Sophie found Clive sitting on a bench up the road, smoking. She sat down next to him, took one of his cigarettes, listened to his apologies. He was distraught, of course: he was just the kind of idiot who could only understand what things meant by doing them first. He apologized, and vowed everything there was to vow, and called himself every name under the sun, and very soon Sophie found that her rage had evaporated. She gave him his ring back, but she didn't hurl it at him.

"I have to admit, I thought you'd be crosser than this," said Clive. "I thought there'd be violence."

"I don't think I ever really believed you were serious," she said. "So somewhere in the back of my mind I thought there might be a day something like this one."

"Were you serious?"

"I'd have gone through with it."

"Why?"

She almost laughed, and stopped herself. Why? It was a fair question. She had, in theory, agreed to spend the rest of her life with someone, and yet she couldn't immediately remember what had made her think it was a good idea. She was hopeless at taking care of herself. She forgot to eat, for example, and suddenly found herself picking at stale bread or peeling a blackened banana. She wondered whether Clive fulfilled a similar function. He wasn't stale or beginning to go moldy. But there must have been something inside her, some dimly recognized need, making her reach for him. She was beginning to wonder whether she was lonely.

"Can we carry on working together?" said Clive.

"I'm not going to let the chaps down," she said. "I can put up with you until the end of the series. So long as everybody agrees that we don't need marriage guidance."

"That seems fair."

"Can I ask you something? What is the 'exotic stuff,' and why is it so important?"

"I'm sorry?"

"Nancy said that you needed her for the exotic stuff."

"Oh, hell."

"What does that mean?"

"Nothing."

Clive lit another cigarette, puffed on it furiously, played with the engagement ring.

"All right, I know what it means. But why is it so important to you?"

"It's not. Now."

"Why was it?"

"Because . . ."

She gave him as long as her patience allowed.

"I thought we were all right," she said. "I mean, you know."

"Yes," said Clive quickly. "We were."

"More than all right. Good."

"Yes, good. Lovely."

"So I don't understand."

"Do you remember what it used to be like?"

"We haven't been at it that long."

"No, I mean . . . here. In this country."

"Are we still talking about the same thing?" said Sophie.

"Yes."

"Well, no, I don't remember. I didn't do anything until I came down to London."

"I don't mean you personally." Another cigarette, more furious puffing. "I mean . . . Well, here."

"In this country."

"Exactly!" he said, relieved to be finally understood.

"You just said that and I didn't understand it then."

"Oh."

"Try again."

"Everything hidden away. Everybody scared. Nothing ever mentioned. A woman like Nancy . . ."

"They existed, I believe," said Sophie darkly.

"Exactly! But now . . . you just meet them! It's amazing! And you can read about it, and you can go to the cinema and see it, and you can probably listen to recordings of it, I don't know. And I didn't want to miss out. When my children ask me what I was doing when everyone else was helping themselves to free love, I don't want to say, you know . . ."

"'I was sleeping with a famous actress,'" Sophie offered helpfully.

"I've always slept with actresses," he said helplessly.

"And Nancy is another one."

"Yes, but she seemed . . . modern. The sort of thing all those French tourists come to Carnaby Street for."

"They come here to see tarty actresses who are pushing forty and make off-color jokes? I thought they came because we're all young and groovy and we've got the Beatles."

"I knew you wouldn't understand," said Clive sulkily.

Her fear was that she was still Miss Blackpool—that, despite all the things that had happened to her since then, she was stuck back there, somehow, a big fish in a small pond, a beautiful girl surrounded by pudgy dignitaries and dark mackintoshes and elderly people with no teeth. She didn't want to be like that in bed. She didn't want to regard herself as a prize, to be given up only grudgingly to hardly anybody. But Clive wasn't talking about that. He was talking about the times they all suddenly lived in, and how hard it was not to be a small boy in a sweet shop with no cash register. None of that was anything to do with her.

The last show went out on 16 November 1967. The word "divorce" was never mentioned, but Jim was shown leaving the family home, despite Clive's protestations.

"I told you this would happen if we had a child," he said after the first read-through. "Old ladies will beat me about the head with umbrellas in the street for the rest of my life. Why can't she leave, if she's so bloody unhappy?"

"Women don't leave their children," said Dennis, and then, remembering too late that Sophie's mother had left her, "not as a rule."

Clive still managed to negotiate an offscreen divorce settlement, though, as compensation for his forthcoming shame: he got Tony and Bill to write an unambiguous speech for Barbara in which she stressed that none of it was Jim's fault, and he got himself a guaranteed part, at a preferential fee, in the next script that Tony and Bill saw through to production.

The last rehearsal nearly ended with Clive saying, "Is that it, then? Do you mind if I slope off?" but Sophie felt as though she had to recognize the occasion.

"Thank you," she said. "All of you."

"That's all right," said Clive, and he walked toward the door.

"Sit down, you unfeeling bastard," said Bill. "Sophie's going to make a speech."

Clive sat down, reluctantly.

"No, I'm not," said Sophie. "I just . . . I didn't want it all to end without someone noticing."

"We all noticed," said Clive. "But we were trying to end it with dignity."

He stood up.

"These have been the best years of my life," said Sophie

suddenly, and Clive sighed and sat down again. "I think they've been the best years of your lives too."

"Steady on," said Bill.

"What were your best years, then?" said Tony. "The army? Writing jokes for Albert Bridges?"

"Writing jokes for Albert Bridges," said Bill, and he got a laugh, but then he felt bad, so he said, "Only joking," and he got another one.

"I've never been happy in the way that I've been happy in this room, and in the studios," said Sophie. "I've never laughed so much, or learned so much, and everything I know about my job is because of the people here. Even you, Clive. And I'm worried that I'll spend the rest of my working life looking for an experience like this one, where everything clicks and everyone pushes you to do the best you can, better than anything you think you're capable of."

There was a thoughtful, respectful silence.

"Is that it, then?" said Clive. "Mind if I slope off?"

And this time they let him go.

The last script required both Barbara and Jim to cry; Clive was horrified by the stage direction when he first read it, but he seemed to have an easy access to tears. Nobody teased him about it afterward. The last words of the last script were "Take care, love," delivered by Barbara in a broad Lancashire accent that hadn't been heard since the beginning of the first series. She was holding Jim as she delivered the line, and she had to hold him for a long time, because they wanted to run the closing credits over the embrace. Sophie found herself weeping properly then,

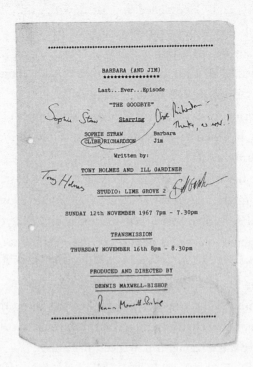

BARBARA (AND JIM)
****

Last...Ever...Episode

"THE GOODBYE"

Sophie Straw   Starring   *Clive Richardson - Thanks, as ever!*

SOPHIE STRAW   Barbara
~~CLIVE~~ RICHARDSON   Jim

Written by:

TONY HOLMES AND ~~ILL~~ GARDINER   *Tony Holmes*

STUDIO: LIME GROVE 2   *B.M.Gardner*

SUNDAY 12th NOVEMBER 1967 7pm - 7.30pm

TRANSMISSION

THURSDAY NOVEMBER 16th 8pm - 8.30pm

PRODUCED AND DIRECTED BY

DENNIS MAXWELL-BISHOP

Dennis Maxwell-Bishop

and she had to bury her face in Clive's jacket. She tried to convince herself that she was upset about breaking up with Clive, but it wasn't that. It was always about the work. She'd never been in love with Clive, but she'd been in love with the show since the very first day.

When the audience had left, Sophie went back to the studio and sat down on the sofa in Barbara's lounge, while the crew were striking the set. She felt self-conscious, as if she were playing the part of an actress whose popular TV show is ending and wants to do something sentimental to demonstrate that the show has meant something to her. She had to do something different, though. She couldn't simply have changed, removed her makeup, and gone to the Chinese restaurant.

Dennis came to find her.

"Are you ready for something to eat?"

"Yes. In a sec. Sit down for a moment."

There wasn't much left of the set apart from the sofa, and she could see that Dennis was being made uneasy by the trouble they were causing, but she felt the crew could give her this much. She'd never caused any trouble before.

"I can't help feeling we let Barbara down," said Dennis.

"How?"

"She wasn't asking for much, was she? And we took it away from her. The divorce is a failure for the whole country."

"Steady on, Dennis," said Sophie, and laughed, but he didn't seem to be joking.

TELEVISION REVIEW
BARBARA (AND JIM)

You may have stopped watching *Barbara (and Jim)* a year or two back, despite the likability of its two central performances and the sharpness of its scripts; freshness is, regrettably, not a quality that can be retained, by definition. What was once both pertinent and laudably impertinent became familiar and sometimes even a little polite compared to the very best of contemporary television comedy—there are only so many overflowing baths one can watch before one ends up feeling that the show has gone a little soggy. *Till Death Us Do Part* in particular, so far ahead of the field when it comes to daring, rawness, and confrontation, has made all its competitors seem a little staid.

And yet last night, its swan song, *Barbara (and Jim)* reminded us of why we fell in love with it in the first place—ironically, given the subject matter of the final program. Barbara and Jim are no more; sadly, they decided to go their separate ways. They did so in a mature, touching, and responsible way, by simply agreeing that they no longer loved each other and that they should part, rather than stay together for the good of their child. There was, as you can imagine, very little room for humor, and though the studio audience laughed gamely at the couple of bones they were thrown, this was not a comedy program. It was, however, a thoughtful and surprisingly touching portrait of a modern relationship gone wrong. The Church and certain fuddy-duddy politicians may huff and puff about how this sad turn of events will do nothing for the catastrophic divorce rate: an amicable parting, after all, simply makes separation appear attractive. But the writers are to be commended for addressing the problem head-on, and suggesting solutions that many couples will, regrettably, need to consider at some point in the future.

We will miss Barbara and Jim. We will especially miss Barbara, played by the delightful and—despite the ruinous effects of motherhood—still shapely Sophie Straw. Let us hope a television producer somewhere knows what to do with her. In the meantime, we should raise a glass to the series. Like most of us when we are having fun, it slightly outstayed its welcome. But the BBC, and the country, would have been poorer without it. For a little while, it had something to say about the way we live now. And last night, as its candle was being snuffed out, it found its voice again.

The Times, 17 November 1967

EVERYONE

LOVES

SOPHIE

And still it was not the end of the divorces and the separations.

The week after the last-ever *Barbara (and Jim)* had been aired, Dennis asked Tony and Bill to call in and see him at the BBC. They sat down in his office and made small talk about the good old days, and they had just been served coffee when Sophie came in, flustered and apologetic.

"I'm sorry I'm late. It's not because I'm not keen," she said. "I am keen. Really keen."

"I haven't said anything yet," said Dennis.

"Oh," said Sophie. "Well. I'll just sit down and shut up."

Dennis smiled at her indulgently.

"*Just Barbara*," said Dennis, and looked at them expectantly.

They didn't know what he was talking about, so they stared back.

"I don't think they understand," said Sophie.

"I'm not sure it's a failure of comprehension," said Bill. "I think it's more a failure of communication. Dennis has provided us with the name of a character in an old comedy series and put the word 'just' in front of it. I don't think Bertrand Russell would have understood."

"Sorry," said Dennis. "Sophie and I would like you to write a new series entitled *Just Barbara*, which follows our girl as she deals with life as a divorcée."

"Oh," said Tony. "That's interesting."

"Do you really think so?" said Bill.

"Yes," said Tony.

He thought any offer of work was interesting. They were struggling with *Reds Under the Bed*, and the Anthony Newley thing was going nowhere fast: they had recently been told that he wanted to turn it into an X-rated musical. And Bill turned down new offers every week, apparently without even a moment's consideration for Tony's situation.

"What are the problems, Bill, as you see them?" said Dennis. "Let's kick them around. I'm sure we can sort it out."

"Well," said Bill. "The first one is, it's a terrible idea."

"Oh," said Dennis. "We were rather pleased with it. What's wrong with it?"

"Doesn't go anywhere."

"It can go anywhere you want it to go."

"It's got no legs. Or wheels. You won't get it out of the garage."

"Why not?"

"There's the bloody baby, for a start. Every bloody episode you've got to explain where it is."

"Perhaps he could be with Jim. He said he was going to help out."

"He meant take it for a walk sometimes, not invite it to stay for the weekend. And is she going to work? Or is she knocking round the house all day? And how many boyfriends can a divorced mother of one have in a television comedy before someone calls the police on her? No. It's not for me."

"Just no?"

"Just no," said Bill, and that appeared to be that.

Thanks, mate," said Tony when they got outside. He was angry.

"Do you really want to write a series called *Just Barbara*?" said Bill.

"I just want to write," said Tony. "I'm a writer. It's my living."

"'*Just Barbara*,'" said Bill, in a whiny, simpering voice.

"One woman who can't do this and can't do that because we've visited every corner of her personality fifteen times over the last few years. Is that what you want to spend your life doing?" said Bill. "Really? You don't want to do something fresh and different and interesting?"

"Yes, but . . ."

"There aren't any buts," said Bill. "That's the whole

point of being a writer, isn't it? If I wanted buts, I'd go and work in a fucking but factory."

"Bully for you. In my life there are fucking buts everywhere."

"You're living the wrong life, then."

"Oh, I'll just change it, shall I?"

It was the wrong response. He didn't want to change his life. His buts were June and baby Roger, and he was happy with both of them.

"This is all because of that bleeding book, isn't it?" said Tony.

It still hadn't been published, but it had already changed Bill's life. Braun and Braun had asked him for another one, and the literary editors were asking for reviews and columns and anything they could think of to get him into their pages.

"Yes," said Bill. "Of course it is. It turns out I can do something else. I don't have to write for grannies in bloody Melton Mowbray."

"You've become one of that lot," said Tony.

"Which 'lot'?"

"One of the Vernon Whitfields of this world. You think you have to write a book to be clever."

"Oh," said Bill. "Now he finds the fire in his belly. Where was all your revolutionary fervor when you came up with 'The New Bathroom'?"

They had reached the tube station.

"Do you want a drink?" said Bill.

"June's going out," said Tony. "I've got to look after the

baby. And when I wake up tomorrow I've got to work out a way of supporting both of them."

Bill fished around in his pocket for some change and seemed to be trying to remember something.

"'. . . the writers are to be commended for addressing the problem head-on, and suggesting solutions that many couples will, regrettably, need to consider at some point in the future,'" he said eventually.

"That rings a bell," said Tony. "Oh, it's the *Times* review. We're the writers."

"Yes. Ironic, isn't it?"

"Why?"

"There we are, commendably suggesting ways that couples can separate without fighting. And here we are fighting."

"Oh, Christ on a bike," said Tony.

Tony's peculiar romantic history meant that he had never broken up with a girl or a boy. He had never given anyone the push, and he'd never received it either. But he imagined it felt exactly like this: the sudden lurch in the stomach, the acute awareness of time and place and temperature, the terrible realization that this was it, there were to be no second chances or mind-changing or persuasion.

"You coming?" said Bill.

"I'm just going to buy a paper," said Tony.

"I'll wait for you."

"Nah, don't worry."

He didn't want to have to make small talk with his oldest friend on the train while his world collapsed around him.

Tony went back to see Dennis the next afternoon.

"I'm sorry about yesterday," he said. "You know what he's like."

"I hope you've come to tell me he's changed his mind."

"I'm afraid not," said Tony.

"Oh dear," said Dennis.

The feeble, insecure part of Tony—the writing part, as he often thought of it—didn't like the sound of that.

"I've come to ask if you'd give me a crack at it on my own," he said.

"Oh," said Dennis. "Oh. I see."

"We're going to do different things for a while. Bill's got his book coming out, and he wants to write another one, and . . ."

Tony began to feel hot. Dennis's hesitation was killing him. It hadn't occurred to him that there would be anything less than immediate and grateful enthusiasm, even though Dennis had no idea who did what in the partnership. Tony wasn't sure that he knew either. Bill was the clever one, but was cleverness important, or did it get in the way? And maybe it wasn't true anyway that Bill was his intellectual superior; maybe those were the roles they'd somehow fallen into over the years. Bill read more than Tony did, that was true. But then, Tony didn't read as much because he was always watching TV with June. Surely that had to count for something, his obsession with the medium, his conviction that you could say anything you liked in situation comedy, as long as you remembered to include gags and characters, and wrote in ways that grannies in Melton Mowbray could understand?

"Gosh," said Dennis. "That's headline news."

But he still wasn't offering him a job.

"I could find somebody else to write with, if that's any help," said Tony. This had just popped out, without him even thinking about it. "If you think I'm better, you know, with someone."

"Ah," said Dennis. "That might be interesting."

Tony felt a little stab of self-pity, and another little stab of betrayal. His pride was wounded too, presumably by a third stab.

"I'm pretty sure I could have a go at it on my own, though," said Tony. "I'd like to, in fact."

"What happened to finding someone else to write with?" said Dennis. "Because that was an idea you had quite recently."

"That was before I realized you thought I wasn't up to it."

"It's not that," said Dennis. "It's not that at all."

"What is it, then?"

"Sophie and I think that a woman should be involved."

"Oh," said Tony gloomily. "A woman. Well, there's not much I can do about that."

"There's not much you can do about being one," said Dennis. "But you could work with one, couldn't you?"

"Do you know anybody? There aren't many of them. Or any that I've ever come across."

"Sophie has someone in mind. A girl called Diane."

"What's she done?"

"Nothing that's actually been on the telly or the radio. She works for a magazine at the moment and she's desperate to get out. But she's been writing scripts and showing them to me. They're different from yours, but I think she could be good."

What Tony thought was that he was too long in the tooth, too set in his ways, too recently bereaved by the death of his first partner, too weighed down by anxiety to coach someone who didn't have a clue about scriptwriting. But—but!—he kept these thoughts to himself.

Diane was dressed in the latest gear, pretty, friendly, puppyishly keen to learn.

They met in the office, which Bill didn't need anymore, because he could write on his own at home. Through Diane's eyes it must have looked as though Tony and Bill had constructed a thriving scriptwriting corporation: there was Hazel, and the sofas, and the desk, and the record player, and all the telephones . . . Bill had even bought an espresso machine, imported from Italy, exactly the same make as the one in Bar Italia in Soho. The office, Tony suddenly saw, was the product of highly successful adult labor.

Diane stared at it all, intimidated.

"Do I have to pay for it?" she said.

"Not until you see your name on the credits every Thursday night," said Tony.

"Is that what will happen?" said Diane.

"It better," said Tony. "Or I won't be able to pay the rent on this place either."

They spent the morning talking. Dennis wanted *Just Barbara* to get as far away from *Barbara (and Jim)* as it was possible to go; he wanted a cast of characters rather than a two-hander, he wanted Swinging London reflected in the locations and the stories, he wanted Barbara out of her flat and into the world, he wanted youth and fun and glamour. Tony knew nothing about any of that, whereas Diane knew everything about where girls shopped, ate, drank coffee, danced, met boys. If Tony had somehow persuaded Dennis to let him have a go on his own, he'd have been fired approximately halfway through the first page.

Tony knew more about other things, though. He knew a lot about budgets, structure, and timing, so he was able to tell Diane that they couldn't set a scene there, or there, or even there. He knew everything there was to know about Barbara, so he was able to tell Diane that she wouldn't think this or say that. And he knew about babies, so he could point out that Barbara would be unable to do just about anything at all. In other words, he was perfectly equipped to prevent *Just Barbara* from being written. Bill, it turned out, was right. It was a hopeless idea.

"Does she have to have a baby?" said Diane.

"She's already had it, is the problem."

"No, I mean . . . can't we just forget about it?"

"The good people of Britain never forget anything. But . . ."

There was something here. He felt a familiar little prickle of excitement.

"Go on. But . . . ?"

"But what if she's not Barbara?" said Tony.

"If she's not Barbara, we can't call it *Just Barbara*, can we?"

"No. We'd definitely have to change the name of the show. But what if she was *Just* somebody else? *Just Sophie*, say? No divorce, no Jim, no baby Timmy. Just a young girl making her way in the big city. And going out in the evenings."

"Can we do that?"

"We're writers," said Tony. "We can do anything we want."

He had learned that much, at least.

22

Diary of
a Soho
Boy

Bill Gardiner

T he party for Bill's book was in the upstairs bar of a
Soho pub that, for various reasons, Tony had always
been too afraid to enter. He went with June, and once
they were there they huddled in a corner and watched
everyone. The book, it seemed, was going to be a great

success, or as much of a success as it was possible to be when half the bookshops in London wouldn't stock it and most of the newspapers wouldn't review it. The literary editor of the *Daily Express*, for example, had phoned Michael Braun to tell him that the *Express* would ignore not only this book, but all other books that Braun might publish in the future. But the *New Statesman* had called Bill "a towering, fiery, obscene talent," and even the *Spectator* had said "the broad-minded reader would find much to admire." Tony felt close to the novel and far away from it all at the same time; and he felt guilty too, for wasting Bill's time with overflowing baths and the like. It was as if he'd made Arthur Miller write lines for pet-food advertisements.

"How do you feel?" said June.

"I'm pleased for him," said Tony, as Bill received a kiss on the lips from a young man who appeared to be wearing eye makeup and who was definitely wearing a feather boa.

"Are you?"

"Yes. Of course."

"Lots of people hate their friends doing well."

"Not me."

"Good for you," said June. "But you don't mind all this?"

"All what?"

June gestured at the men in the room.

"I don't suppose any of these chaps have a mother-in-law in Pinner babysitting for them."

"I don't mind that."

"Really?"

"No. None of it. Not the Pinner bit, or the mother-in-law bit, or the babysitting bit. And I'm sorry if I've ever given the impression that I do."

"I think perhaps I feel guilty."

"For what?"

"I'm worried that life is passing you by."

"I'm a writer. Life is supposed to pass me by, while I watch it."

"Doesn't that mean you at least have to be sitting somewhere interesting?"

"This isn't life."

A bald woman wearing a kaftan came into the room, sought out Bill, and kissed him on the lips. Tony didn't know whether she proved or disproved the statement he'd just made.

Bill finally came over to see them, and they shook hands warmly. They'd met for lunch a few times, and Tony had told him about his troubles with Diane and the new series. Bill had been mildly sympathetic but uninterested; he'd gone to a better place. He had nearly finished a second novel, and he'd been commissioned to write a play for the Royal Court.

He kissed them both on the cheek. Tony tried to pretend that he was bohemian enough to carry it off without self-consciousness, but he was acutely aware of his jacket, his tie, and his wife.

"Thank you both for coming to this den of iniquity," Bill said.

"The Pinner Mothers' Union will be agog when I tell them," said June.

"She's not actually a member of the Pinner Mothers' Union," Tony said, completely unnecessarily.

June and Bill both laughed, but at him, not with him.

"You can't have it all ways," said Bill, and then Michael Braun pulled him away to introduce him to someone else.

Tony's eyes wandered around the room and then came to rest on a beautiful young colored woman wearing a beautiful shimmering silver chemise and a dramatically tied head scarf. Why didn't he know any young colored women? Why didn't he know people who tied their head scarves in a dramatic way? He didn't care about Bill's success, he thought. He liked it. It was great. And he didn't worry about whether he was missing out on life. What Tony really wanted was to walk into a room somewhere and feel he was at home in it.

Years later, Tony would discover that writers never felt they belonged anywhere. That was one of the reasons they became writers. It was strange, however, failing to belong even at a party full of outsiders.

t's not working," he said to June suddenly, on the way back to Pinner.

"What?" She looked alarmed, and he squeezed her hand.

"Oh. Sorry. I meant work. Diane. All that. It's hopeless. I'm writing with a kid who thinks that wearing the wrong heels to a discotheque is the stuff of life."

"I don't see why it couldn't be the stuff of a joke," June said.

"A joke she wants to turn into thirty minutes of peak-viewing television."

"Well, stop her," said June. "You're the senior writer in the partnership."

"I have stopped her," said Tony. "But I don't know what to replace it with. I don't know anything about young women or fashion magazines or boyfriends."

"So turn it into something else."

"What, a searing indictment of race relations in Britain?" He was still thinking about the colored girl at the party and feeling resentful. "How come Bill knows colored girls?"

"Wasn't she beautiful!"

"But how did he meet her?"

"I'll tell you how," said June.

"You actually know?"

"I can guess."

"Go on, then."

"He was at a party, and this beautiful girl came in, and he went over and said, 'Hello, I'm Bill.'"

"But how do you get invited to parties like that?"

"Are you serious?" said June.

"Yes," said Tony.

"You do know you were invited to a party exactly like that."

"Tonight, you mean?"

"Yes. Tonight."

He tried to think of a reason why tonight didn't count, but there wasn't one.

D ennis told Sophie, Tony, and Diane that he wanted to do things differently this time. *Comedy Playhouse* was still on the BBC, still showing half-hour comedies that were all desperate to become grown-up series, but he explained that, in his view, they could afford to be more ambitious. Sophie was a known quantity, a much-loved TV star, and he didn't want her grubbing around for a commission like the rest of them. He paid for twelve scripts, and when everyone was happy with them, he was going to dump them on Tom Sloan's desk, the whole lot of them. And if Sloan didn't want them, he'd have to go through them page by page and explain what was wrong with them. He was aware that there was a different version of the future, one in which Tom turned them all down without really reading them and Dennis apologized for wasting his time, but at least Dennis's fantasy indicated the strength of his determination and enthusiasm.

He was aware that the path he had chosen was the longest and least direct available to him, but there was method in his procrastination. He had chosen that path because he could meander along it with Sophie. There would be endless excuses for coffee, lunch, maybe even dinner. The *Comedy Playhouse* route offered intensive contact time over the course of a week, and was therefore not without its attractions; but if there was no further interest, he would run the risk of Sophie embarking on a professional life that didn't involve him, and he wasn't sure he could bear that. Slow and steady, he told Tony and Diane, wins the race. He didn't convey the same message to Sophie. He felt that he had enough self-promotional problems as it was, without introducing the notion of tortoises.

The weeks of waiting for Tony and Diane passed slowly. Dennis was producing two other comedy programs for the BBC, neither of which was making him happy. *Heirs and Graces* was about an impoverished aristocratic couple who had lost their stately home and were now attempting to run a seaside boarding house. Dennis Price and Phyllis Calvert had already turned the script down, with great firmness and speed, and now Dennis was avoiding telephone calls from the writer, who thought that Laurence Olivier would be ideal for the role of Lord Alfred. He could hardly bear to think about *Slings and Marrows*, a *Comedy Playhouse* episode about the ruthless behind-the-scenes politics of a village fete. There were people at the BBC who thought that *Slings and Marrows* had enormous potential, but Dennis had already decided that if it went to series he would retire to Norfolk and grow prizewinning vegetables. Work was going nowhere, and he was worried that Sophie was beginning to look at other scripts, other producers, other potential husbands. And then, just as he was beginning to wonder whether he should plod off toward one of his mother's stout bluestockings, there were three significant advances.

The first was an invitation to the theater: Sophie had been given tickets to the first night of the musical *Hair* at the Shaftesbury and she needed someone to go with.

"When is it?" said Dennis.

It didn't matter when it was, because even if he was busy, which he wasn't, he would have canceled. But as Sophie had telephoned him, she couldn't see that he hadn't even bothered looking for his empty diary.

"Tonight," said Sophie.

"Ah," said Dennis. "You've been let down."

If tortoises could speak, they'd have sounded like him, he thought, mournful and elderly.

"No," said Sophie. "I knew you'd say that."

Dennis winced. His tortoise tendencies had been noted already.

"I've just been offered them," said Sophie. "This second. You were the first person I called. They didn't even know the show was opening until that business yesterday."

"What business?"

"I thought if I said 'that business,' you'd know, and I wouldn't have to say any more. I don't really know what business."

Luckily Dennis remembered what the business was: the Theaters Act, passed the previous day. The people of Britain were now allowed to see nipples and pubic hair in a West End theater, if that was what they wanted to do.

"I knew you'd know," said Sophie. "That's why I love you."

This was the second significant advance, coming so swiftly after the first that there was nearly a collision. It was some time before Dennis could bring himself to speak again. He knew that it had not been intended as a serious declaration, and she had only said it because he had ploddingly retrieved a fragment of knowledge about government legislation from the dusty recesses of his fusty Cambridge brain. But if he had recorded the telephone call and edited the tape carefully, he could listen to Sophie Straw telling him that she loved him all day.

"Ha-ha!" he said eventually, but the laughter seemed merely to confuse her, so he moved on. "In for a penny, in for a pound," he said. The expression was as inappropriate as the laugh, seeing as there was nothing in the conversation to date that could be given either of those metaphorical values.

"There's nudity," said Sophie.

"Yes," said Dennis.

"Are we happy with nudity?" said Sophie.

Had one of his scriptwriters tried to fob him off with something containing that line, he would have had the culprit escorted from the premises and shot. Now he could see that it wasn't just a cheap gag. On the contrary, it was priceless, and contained considerable subtlety, charm, and truth. A beautiful woman combining the prospect of happiness and nakedness in the same spoken sentence could achieve the power of the greatest lyric poetry.

"I'm happy if you're happy," said Dennis.

———————

The audience for *Hair* was a surprisingly typical first-night crowd: lots of men in suits and their nervous-looking wives. Dennis was both disappointed and relieved. He would have enjoyed telling his mother that he'd spent the evening sitting amidst long-haired, bare-chested men and kohl-eyed, bare-breasted women, but many of the men looked as though they'd come straight from the City, and their wives straight off the 5:20 from Godalming. The men had a gleam in their eyes that might not have been there if they were about to sit through three hours of *The Cherry Orchard*, and there was a loud, and somewhat self-congratulatory, hum of anticipation before the curtain came up. But—and here was the relief—Dennis didn't look out of place. He would go so far as to say that he looked rather young and bohemian compared to a lot of the people there—he'd decided, at the last moment and as a concession to the winds of change, to wear an open-necked shirt and a striped blazer. Sophie looked extraordinary in a canary-yellow minidress and white boots, and the photographers in the foyer surrounded her. She tried to involve Dennis in the pictures, a gesture he might have regarded as a significant advance had it not been for the immediate downward drop of the cameras the moment he went to stand by her side.

They had aisle seats, dead center, fifteen or so rows from the front, and within seconds of sitting down, Dennis found himself wishing that they were in the back row of

the Royal Circle. Members of the cast were roaming the theater, looking for accessible targets on whom to rain flowers and kisses. Sophie was not only accessible, but famous and attractive, so she was visited by several intimidatingly good-looking young men whose kisses were a rather more enthusiastic expression of the new age of peace, love, and understanding than Dennis thought appropriate.

"Steady on," he said to the third visitor, who apparently wanted to whet Sophie's anticipation by inserting his tongue into her mouth.

The young man skipped away, apparently amused by the antiquity of the admonition, but he was immediately replaced by a young woman who leaned across Sophie to push a sunflower into Dennis's hair. Finally, though, the lights went down, the show began and, despite occasional forays into the audience from the stage, Dennis and Sophie managed to avoid further trouble by studying their feet.

And, to Dennis's surprise, he loved the play. It was a mess, in parts, but it was also chaotic, funny, and gloriously tuneful, and the energy of the young actors was electrifying. Dennis spent as much time looking at the audience as he did at the stage, and more or less everywhere he looked there was genuine delight. The one exception was a scowling face a dozen or so seats to his left: it was Vernon Whitfield, who would go home and bash out a humorless, hostile, and laughably prissy review for the *Listener*. It failed to mention, inevitably, that everyone around him was having the time of their lives.

The nudity was confined to one scene immediately before the interval, and Dennis tried not to find it difficult, but failed. What kind of idiot would go and see *Hair* on a first date? He was a pipe-smoking, beer-drinking comedy producer on the cusp of middle age; why had he thought it would be a good idea to sit down next to the most beautiful woman he had ever met, a woman several years his junior, while she examined the naked bodies of young male actors and singers? The seconds seemed like hours, and he tried to pass the time by attempting to find actors whose penises were beyond any shadow of a doubt roughly the same size as his own; he found two, neither of them belonging to the leading characters. They had been hidden away, presumably to avoid audience scorn and disappointment. Sophie tried to make eye contact during the scene, as if she'd sensed his tension and wanted to defuse it, but

Dennis kept his eyes firmly on the stage. Afterward, she tried to tease him about his goggle-eyed appreciation of the female form; he made a face suggesting that she'd caught him bang to rights. Better that way, he thought, than the confession that, such was his nervousness and self-doubt, he'd forgotten to look at any of the breasts and bottoms on display.

Hair ended tumultuously, with members of the audience joining the cast to dance onstage. Sophie was dragged up there by the young man with the tongue. She reached behind her for Dennis's hand and he pretended he hadn't noticed, but as she ran down the aisle he realized that he might never have another evening with her, and she might be whisked straight from the stage to somewhere else, a party or a discotheque or a young man's flat, and it would be entirely due to his cowardice and awkwardness and embarrassment. So he followed her, caught up with her, and they climbed the steps to the stage together.

He wasn't the worst dancer up there, and he made sure that he positioned himself just behind the person who was, a portly man in a pin-striped suit for whom the Age of Aquarius had clearly dawned: he was throwing himself around with the air of someone who was never going back to his merchant bank ever again. He was throwing his arms and legs around as if they were not his, and he was singing along at the top of his voice to a song whose words he didn't know. Dennis took the view that he couldn't compete even if he'd wanted to, and that understatement was the key.

Sophie had been pulled to the front of the stage, where the audience could see her, but she managed to edge back toward him, and she took his hand and shouted into his ear.

"Well," she said. "What a thing."

"Thank you for asking me. I'll try and think of somewhere as exciting to take you."

"I'd like that."

He kept moving to the music, just in case she thought he didn't want to be up there. To his surprise, he did—but then, he wanted to be anywhere Sophie was, no matter how much embarrassment might ensue. And anyway, proximity to Sophie meant that embarrassment was no longer the terrifying ogre he had always believed it to be. Perhaps he would wake up the next morning realizing that he'd made an utter ass of himself, but there were worse animals than the ass. And in London you saw asses wandering around everywhere. Nobody seemed to mind, much. Dennis had spent an awful lot of time not making an ass of himself, and he didn't have anything to show for it.

The third significant advance came immediately on top of the other two: they spent the night together. That is to say, Dennis went to sleep in Sophie's bed, alongside Sophie, and woke up with her the next morning. This was obviously of greater significance than the other advances; if anything had happened between the sleeping and the waking, he'd have described the third advance as being of greater significance than all the other advances in human history combined. Nothing did happen, however, and it didn't happen for the reasons that most great advances don't happen: failure of nerve, incompetence, muddled thinking, idiocy.

They had left the theater on a high and went to a party that Sophie had been invited to while she was up on the stage dancing. She was unable to say who it was who'd invited her, or who was throwing the party, but whoever it was had taken over Sybilla's in Piccadilly Circus, just around the corner from the theater. There was a queue to get in, and a terrifying scrum at the bar, and there were strip lights around the dance floor that pointed artfully upward, so that everyone wearing a miniskirt ended up providing a free show to those lucky enough to have obtained a drink and a table. Dennis would have left immediately, but he didn't want to be the tortoise, so he stuck it out until she made a face and gestured toward the exit with her thumb.

"Take me home and come in for scrambled eggs and a drink," said Sophie, so they found a taxi and went to Kensington Church Street.

Dennis wasn't, of course, expecting to sleep in Sophie's bed. Even when she kissed him, in the hallway of the flat, as soon as he'd closed the front door behind him, he didn't dare to presume that it indicated anything in particular. The last girl he'd kissed in earnest had been Edith, some years before. (Kissing was not always an earnest activity, but nothing he did with Edith had ever been much fun.) An awful lot seemed to have changed in the world since then: there was, it seemed to him, simply more sex around. Only that very evening they had been to see what his mother might describe, might already have described, as a nude musical, and there had been no such thing as a nude musical, not in a respectable theater anyway, before or during his marriage. What did he know about sex or women these days? Not very much, he suspected, and perhaps all evenings out ended like this these days, with the woman pinning the man back against a door. He hesitated for a moment before kissing her back, not because he was suddenly, after all the years of pining, confused about how he felt, but because he wanted to make sure that he wasn't misinterpreting or overreacting in some way. Maybe she would suddenly break off the embrace and then ask him politely whether she could take his coat, and they would never mention it again. Maybe that's what happened after you'd been to see a nude musical.

She pulled away and looked at him.

"Gosh," he said.

"I'm sorry."

"Please don't be sorry."

"Are you sure?"

"I'm sure."

"Would you mind if I made you scrambled eggs in the morning?"

"No. Not at all. Of course not. Shall I . . . Shall I go home and come back?"

He was almost sure he understood what she was suggesting, but almost wasn't good enough, not for him. He would always be someone who assumed the worst. He would always be the person who made the safest, dullest, and most literal interpretation of an ambiguous situation. He would very likely stay single for the rest of his life.

"Oh. You have to go?"

"No. Not at all."

"That was the first time I've ever tried a sexy line, and you ruined it."

"I don't know that any line that mentions scrambled eggs can be as sexy as all that."

She laughed, and kissed him again. He had survived, just about. A couple of hours later, he wished that he'd insisted on leaving and coming back again.

How could Sophie not have fallen in love with Dennis, eventually? He was kind, he was single, he was vulnerable, he made her laugh (not always intentionally, true, but often enough). Every time she saw him, he seemed to have become a little more handsome. He was clever in the sense that he knew a lot about a lot, but he was clever in a way she valued more: he understood people and recognized what they might have to offer. It had taken a while, but she ached to have access to that kind of wisdom at all times, not just in script meetings. And he made no attempt to hide his adoration and admiration of her. She'd been aware of it for a long time, and it wasn't as though she'd been worn down by it, exactly; that would suggest that she'd been exhausted by his persistence, when the opposite was true: she was energized by it. It gave her confidence, made her feel as though she was both talented and beautiful, and she craved the affirmation. Her self-doubt was like water. It found the tiniest gaps and flooded in. The girl who had decided that she was too good to be a beauty queen was long gone; so too was the girl who had never done a day's acting in her life and turned up for auditions hoping for a job.

The last four years had brought her fame and money, but confusion too. Was she any good at anything? Had she just been lucky? If she had walked into any other rehearsal room in the world, one of the many rooms where there was no Bill and Tony, no Clive, no Dennis, would anything have happened, or would she still be selling perfumes to married men with wandering eyes? Or would the eyes have stopped wandering by now? Everywhere she went she saw younger, prettier, and shapelier girls (girls who were, unlike Sophie, still girls), girls who probably couldn't understand why brainy, witty people were trying to write a show named after her. Dennis's devotion was a fixed point, like the North Star, something that helped her find her way back whenever she became lost in her deep, dark forest of anxiety.

She'd been watching him carefully, half expecting his beautiful solidity to melt away with *Barbara (and Jim)*, but the end of the show hadn't changed him; if anything, it had enabled him to prove to her that she was all that really mattered. Maybe there were women who'd have been able to resist this month after month, but if so they were a lot tougher than Sophie. She'd found the right person at the right time, the man who made her feel good, the man who had banished her loneliness, and if that wasn't love, then she didn't know what was.

She had decided, though, that if she wanted anything to happen, she would have to make the first move. He was too nice, too respectful, and much too damaged by his marriage to that awful woman ever to do anything, and she was sure he'd have offered a pair of ears and a shoulder forever, through any number of divorces and professional disasters. Ears and shoulders, she decided, were all very well, but she'd need more than that if they were going to move along. She maneuvered him into the bedroom and they kissed some more on the bed. She was almost sure that he was beginning to see the big picture, so she didn't think that a description of it would alarm him much. And in any case, she wanted to tell him an awful truth.

"I've just realized," she said. "You'll be the first person I've ever slept with properly who wasn't an actor. Isn't that terrible?"

"Yes," he said, with greater conviction than she'd been expecting.

"Oh," she said. "I was only joking."

"So you've slept with people who weren't actors?"

"No," she said. "I was joking about it being terrible."

"So it wasn't terrible?"

"I didn't mean that either."

"I don't really understand the joke," said Dennis.

"I just meant . . . I should have slept with people from other professions by now."

"Which other professions?"

He was visibly alarmed by this time, and she could see that they had set off down the wrong path.

"I didn't have any professions in mind," she said. "Producers. I haven't slept with enough producers."

This didn't help either.

Suddenly, Dennis knew what he had to say. He wasn't happy that logic had led him to this point. He would much rather have been able to find another way of looking at things, but there wasn't one. He didn't know an awful lot about existentialism, but his decision felt as though it had come to him as a product of the existentialist process: a long train of gloomy thoughts, all of which led to the same bleak conclusion. And if he ignored it, who would he be? Nobody. Nothing.

"I'm not going to sleep with you," he said.

"Why on earth not?"

"I have my reasons."

"Could you tell me some of them?"

"It wouldn't help."

"I think you owe me that much. I took you to the theater, I've offered scrambled eggs . . . The very least a girl can expect is sex."

Dennis sighed heavily.

"I don't know how many actors you've slept with . . ."

It was four—Johnny Foreigner, Clive, and two very disappointing flings, and she wasn't even sure about one of those. He'd said he was an actor, but she didn't recognize him and he was very vague about what work he'd done. She decided to leave him out altogether.

"Three."

"All right, three. But I'm not an actor."

"Thank God."

"Well, I don't want to be compared to one."

"Why on earth would I compare you to an actor?"

"Because actors are all you have to go by."

"Don't you want to sleep with me?"

"That's not the issue. It's not about wanting."

"*Sex* isn't? Gosh. What is it about, then?"

Dennis didn't say anything, and then she got it.

"Oh, Dennis."

"What?"

"Listen. First of all, I think you're a very good-looking man. And all right, you're not handsome in a boring actory way, but I'm sick of that. You have beautiful, sexy eyes, and I get quite wobbly when you look at me. Did you know that?"

Dennis shook his head, astounded, and Sophie laughed. Of course he didn't know that.

"And anyway. Just because a man is good-looking in a boring actory way, it doesn't mean he's good at anything else."

"You're very kind," he said. "But I would prefer my function in your life to be, I don't know . . . something else."

"It didn't feel like that was what you would prefer. Just now."

"I cannot be held responsible for the conduct of an independent organ."

He was, as far as she could tell, serious, so she had to laugh.

"I didn't mean to sound pompous," he said. "But I'm not usually called to account in that way."

"Has there been anybody since Edith?"

"No," he said. And then, "Not really."

"What does that mean? If you don't mind my asking?"

"I said 'not really' because I thought it might make me sound more interesting."

"So . . . Maybe all this is because it's been a while?"

"No. It's because everybody finds you attractive."

"Even if that were true, you're the only one here."

"Can we just go to sleep?"

"If that's what you want."

They arranged themselves on the bed and she nestled herself into him. She could do it, she thought, despite the frustration. It was late and she'd been drinking champagne. And the next thing she knew, it was five o'clock in the morning, and she desperately needed a pee. It was clear to her that Dennis hadn't even closed his eyes.

"This is no good," she said when she came back from the bathroom.

"It probably won't happen again," said Dennis. "Friends don't often spend the night in the same bed."

"What if I wanted to marry you?"

"Separate bedrooms."

He was beginning to wonder whether he had strayed from the existentialist path.

"So there's nothing I could do that might convince you?"

Was it only yesterday that Sophie had asked him whether he was happy with nudity and his heart had nearly burst with joy? And yet that question had referred only to a night in the theater. He wouldn't even have been able to imagine the circumstances in which she might have posed the most recent question, and he certainly wouldn't have been able to explain his answer.

"I don't think so."

Oh, this was ridiculous. Whatever else existentialists might be, they never struck him as particularly cheerful coves, and he was beginning to see why.

"I suppose there might be something," he said.

Sophie hadn't pulled the curtains in the bedroom, and their faces were occasionally lit by the headlights of the passing traffic. He could see that there was an expression of mild alarm on her face.

"It's nothing . . . out of the ordinary," he said. "I want to know that if it happens, it will happen again. And not just once, but a few times. I don't want to be judged on a . . . an isolated incident."

Sophie laughed, and Dennis looked hurt.

"I'm sorry," she said. "It just sounded funny."

"Why?"

"Because . . . Well, how many goes were you thinking of?"

"I don't know. Three? Fifty? It's difficult, isn't it?"

"Do you think you'd need fifty goes?"

"Are you saying you wouldn't want to guarantee fifty goes?"

"I'd rather not . . . put a limit on it," said Sophie.

That was all the reassurance Dennis needed. And—

somewhat to her surprise, given the tentative start to their sexual relationship—Sophie discovered that he was in no need of a second attempt at anything, let alone a fiftieth.

'd never noticed before," Sophie said later, "but you're much more like Jim than Clive ever was."

"Is that a good thing?"

"Perhaps we can learn from their mistakes."

"Their biggest mistake was that they made themselves characters in a TV series," said Dennis. "Nobody ever told them that they were going to get fifty goes. They always had to make a big song and dance about everything, in case people stopped watching them."

"You don't have to be a fictional character to do that," said Sophie.

She was thinking about Clive. He always wanted to make a big song and dance about everything. He was terrified of not being watched, and she always had to worry about whether there was a prettier, younger thing in the room.

"I suppose not," said Dennis.

He was thinking about Edith. She was constantly on the verge of canceling their marriage. She would only commission a few shows at a time, reluctantly, and if he had listened properly, she'd always been telling him that it would all end one day.

"I'll make as many series as you want," Sophie said, and

when she saw how happy she could make him, she felt a little thrill of pleasure.

She suddenly remembered something.

"Was it . . . Did I . . ." She didn't even know how to phrase the question. "Was anything missing?"

"What sort of anything?" said Dennis, alarmed. "Should I have noticed?"

Sophie laughed.

"No, no, not an actual physical piece. I just meant . . . I don't know."

She shouldn't have started down this road, but she'd never forgotten her conversation with Clive about Nancy's appeal.

"Was there . . . anything else you wanted?"

"Good grief. Like what? Is there anything else I should have wanted?"

"No, no, it's just . . ."

And they went back and forth for some time, increasingly agonized, before each could convince the other that everything had been present and correct, and served in ample proportions.

They dozed off for a little while, and then Sophie made them scrambled eggs. They were both perfectly happy, and perfectly calm, and they wanted to stay that way for as long as they possibly could.

23

Sophie Simmonds (known as Simmonds to everyone involved with the program, in order to avoid confusion with Real Sophie) worked at *Peach*, a girls' magazine; the staff of *Crush*, the girls' magazine where Diane had worked until she became convinced that she could write comedy, would probably note certain similarities between their office and the one portrayed in the series. Simmonds interviewed pop stars, tried the new shades of lipstick before everyone else, spent all her money on the latest gear, and got into all kinds of messes with boyfriends. Or rather, she got into a certain kind of mess with boyfriends, the kind of mess that might amuse a BBC audience of all ages and classes. She didn't worry about getting pregnant, she didn't sleep with anyone's husband, there was no sexual dysfunction or perversion, she wasn't ever unfaithful. In the first episode she had inadvertently arranged two dates for the same evening, and in the time-honored way of situation comedy, she tried to oblige both parties, even though they were waiting a bus-ride away from each other. In the second, she had agreed, over the telephone, to go on a date with a speccy, spotty brainbox called Nigel because she was under the erroneous impression that Nigel was the dishy lead singer for the smash-hit pop group the Young Idea.

The first episode had taken them a few days to write and the second a couple of weeks. They had been talking about the third for longer than Tony wanted to calculate, but hadn't found a story, or even a fragment of a story, and they hadn't written a single line. Diane was convinced that Simmonds's love life, the details of which seemed to have been borrowed wholesale from her own, was a comedy gold mine. Tony, on the other hand, was beginning to feel the urge to hang himself.

"What's her problem?" said Tony after a day in which they'd produced a half-page about Simmonds's cat, a sudden, new, and desperate invention.

The half-page was now lying crumpled on the floor, just next to the wastepaper basket.

"How do you mean?" said Diane.

"In all these series, everyone has a problem," said Tony. "The Steptoes hate each other, and they're poor, and Harold thinks he should be living a different kind of life altogether. Alf Garnett in *Till Death*, he's a man out of time. The world's moving on without him. Barbara and Jim were different in every way, but they loved each other, and they wanted to make their marriage work . . ."

"Yeah, but they're all so depressing, those programs," said Diane. "None of my friends want to watch them."

Tony stared at her.

"Depressing?"

"What's funny about rag-and-bone men? Or a horrible old man and his ugly wife going on and on about Winston Churchill and the Queen? And Barbara and Jim . . . No offense, but they spent four years arguing about books and politics and then they got divorced! Nobody watches them because they're such a drag."

"What are you talking about, nobody watches them? Everybody watches them!"

"Yes," said Diane. "My mum and dad. My granny. My cousins in Devon. People like that. But nobody I actually want to spend any time with."

Tony suddenly felt old. For years, he and Bill and all the other writers of their generation had fought for the right to say things about the world they lived in, and then, suddenly, they'd broken through and there was this new England, full of books and films and music and television programs that said real things about real people. And all this stuff had made the country seem brighter, sharper, funnier, younger. Now Diane was saying to him, as far as he could make out, that she was only interested in the brightness and the youth that these things had brought into being, the clothes and the fashion and the money.

"So what's her problem?" said Tony.

He hoped he didn't sound as tired to Diane as he sounded to himself, but he suspected she wouldn't notice.

"She hasn't got any problems," said Diane. "That's what's so great about her. Everyone loves Sophie."

"Well," said Tony. "There's the title, anyway. Now all we need is the rest of it."

Diane began the next working morning with a passionate plea for the restoration of Simmonds's cat.

"It can be someone for her to talk to," said Diane.

"Do you have a cat?" said Tony, just to make conversation.

"Ringo's more of a kitten, really," said Diane.

"And do you talk to Ringo?"

"That's what I'm saying," said Diane.

Tony had suspected as much.

"And what do you say to him?"

"Oh, just . . . I don't know, really. I ask him whether he's hungry, and I tell him off if he's been naughty."

"Right," said Tony.

"And I practice interviews on him."

"Does that work?"

"He doesn't say much back. But it helps me work out whether the questions are interesting."

"Cat body language?"

Diane looked at him as if he were the mad one.

"No. He's a cat. He doesn't understand a word I'm saying. But when I say them out loud I can tell whether they're daft or not."

"Oh. Right you are."

"My flatmate used to think I was potty. It was probably why she moved out."

Tony had the urge to beat his head against the desk. He should never have been employed as a writer by anybody, that much was clear, but he was beginning to wonder whether he was mentally capable of any kind of work.

"You had a flatmate?"

"Yes. Mandy. We didn't get on terribly well, though."

"Well, I think Simmonds should have a flatmate."

"Instead of a cat?"

"Yes. Instead of a cat."

Somewhere in Tony's brain, a heavy, rusting piece of machinery began to turn. He was surprised that Diane couldn't hear the awful wheezing and clanking.

"And I think she should be colored."

"Colored?"

"Yes."

"Do you know any colored people?"

"One or two. Through Bill, to tell you the truth, but still."

"But . . . How do we get an actress to play a colored person?"

"I think what we do is find a colored actress."

"Oh. Gosh. Yes. Of course."

"What do you think?"

"Won't it be too depressing?"

"Why does it have to be depressing?"

"It's a serious problem."

"It is, but she doesn't have to be. She could just be a person."

"And nobody ever mentions it?"

"They'd mention it sometimes. But it's still a show about Simmonds. It just gives us something extra to work with. Let's talk to Dennis and Sophie."

He knew how the conversation would go; he knew that they'd be intrigued, stimulated, encouraging. He was more interested in the chat he'd have with Bill over lunch one day, in which he'd just happen to mention that he knew colored girls, was working with one, even. Perhaps he could be proud of this job after all.

Sophie met the odd TV company for coffee and the occasional theater producer for lunch, but she spent a lot of time shopping, and lying in bed with Dennis in the evenings, watching TV and talking about *Everyone Loves Sophie*. They wanted to work together as a couple, they loved the new idea that Tony and Diane had talked about, they couldn't wait until the new show was given the go-ahead. They never spoke about it, but they both wanted 1965 back. The peak that they had reached back then was only a short distance away, just up there, and how hard could it possibly be to climb those few feet? The difficult part, surely, had been scrambling up the slope underneath them, miles and miles of it.

Sophie put off going to see the doctor because she didn't want to know what he would tell her. It was as simple as that. She hid everything from Dennis, and managed to delay the retching by staying in bed with her eyes closed. This seemed to work until Dennis had left the house. Once she was vertical, the nausea would overcome her and she'd spend the next hour jumping out of a hot bath to kneel beside the toilet.

And then, finally, she knew she could ignore it no longer. She was not, of course, surprised by the news the doctor eventually gave her, after forty-eight hours in which she hardly spoke to Dennis at all. She tried to quell the feeling of dread, because she knew that there were millions of women who prayed for exactly this terrible thing to happen.

"What if Sophie Simmonds were pregnant?" she said when Dennis got home that evening.

He laughed.

"That would be very funny," he said, and for a moment she thought he meant that there were comic possibilities in the idea, that the show could accommodate such a calamity.

"We create a completely new show because we don't like her being a mother and she gets pregnant anyway."

She burst into tears then.

"She is pregnant," said Sophie eventually, and Dennis was just about to argue with her when he understood.

She could see that he was excited by the news but was trying to look somber and anxious, for her benefit, and this broke her heart in a different way.

"You shouldn't have to be sad," she said. "It's a good thing."

"I'm sorry," he said. "But I love you, I've loved you since the moment I met you, and I want to have a child with you. And I know it's bad timing, but I can make you happy. We can make you happy. The baby and I. I know it."

She hugged him.

"And we can still do the show," he said. "Just . . . not yet, that's all."

There was nothing to think about, but she thought about it anyway, and when she couldn't think about it any longer, she got on a train to talk to her mother.

Gloria took the day off work and they met in Blackpool, in the restaurant of R. H. O. Hills. It was much harder to get to Morecambe on the train, and when Gloria suggested the meeting place, Sophie felt a little thrill of something that she couldn't quite describe. R. H. O. Hills suddenly seemed like the only place in the world where she could understand the length of the journey she had taken. It was the other end, after all. It was only when she sat down and breathed in the familiar department store smell of pipe smoke, perfume, leather, and tea that she wondered whether she was thinking about how far she'd come because she knew she'd stopped. Gloria hadn't arrived, so she ordered the afternoon tea—sandwiches and anything you wanted from the cake trolley—and looked around, trying to see if there was anyone she recognized. She'd worn a head scarf to cover up her blonde hair, but after a little while she decided that she'd like it if somebody recognized her, so she took the scarf off. The couple at the next table stared, and by the time her mother arrived she was signing autographs.

Gloria smiled proudly, and sat down, but fifteen minutes

later they hadn't managed more than a couple of minutes of an unbroken conversation. It was a Tuesday afternoon, so it wasn't as if there was a queue. But those who did come to say hello were in no hurry to leave. One woman took a great deal of pleasure and a lot of time explaining that her sister had been upstairs in Toys when Sophie was downstairs in Cosmetics; the next woman was adamant that Sophie had been in her daughter's class at school, although Sophie didn't recognize the name.

"Cynthia Johnstone?"

"She's Cynthia Perkins now," said the woman. "But that probably won't help."

Sophie screwed up her face, as if to suggest that happy memories of Cynthia Johnstone were only seconds away from returning.

"Well," said the woman. "It must be hard, when you're having tea with the Prime Minister and all that."

Sophie could still chant the register, Anderson to Young, from her class, and there was no Johnstone. It went from Harvey to Jones. Cynthia's mother was quite wrong: it wasn't hard to remember. Sophie hadn't met many people before she moved to London. There were school friends and her colleagues in the shop and a couple of boyfriends and that was it. It was everyone she'd met since that confused her, an endless stream of faces looming in front of her, all of them saying that they'd met her before, at a party or a meeting or a recording.

"Oh," said Gloria. "Cynthia Johnstone. Pretty girl. Good at needlework."

A doubtful look crossed the woman's face and then vanished when she realized she was being offered a way out.

"That's her," she said.

"Of course it is," said Sophie. "Remember me to her, won't you?"

"I will," said the woman, but of course the whole point of the conversation was that Cynthia Johnstone had never forgotten her in the first place.

They finished their tea quickly and left, before anyone else could take Cynthia's mother's place.

"Thank you," said Sophie on the way out. She'd put her head scarf back on.

"She wasn't going to leave until we'd given in," said Gloria. "But I suppose it's not much to ask."

If she hadn't come home, Sophie wouldn't have understood why anyone was entitled to ask for anything at all, but now she could see that whatever it was she'd achieved had to be shared.

They went for a walk down to the South Pier and past the baths, the scene of Sophie's first triumph. It was sunny but very windy, and she remembered the gooseflesh on her arms that day.

"I won Miss Blackpool," she said to her mother. "In 1964."

"You never did."

"I did. And I told them I didn't want to do it."

It sounded preposterous now, the story of a fantasist, and she was glad she'd done something since.

"Why?"

"Because I didn't want to stay here for a year. I thought I'd get stuck."

"I'd have been so proud, if I'd seen that," said Gloria.

"That's what I'm saying. There was nothing to see. I didn't even stand on the podium to get my tiara."

"That's what I would have been proud of," said her mother. "I didn't want you to stay here, looking after George. I wanted you out."

The conversation, with its intimations of disappointment and imprisonment, reminded her of why she'd come home and why she'd chosen her mother of all people to talk to.

"Mum, I'm going to have a baby."

"Oh, Sophie. You're not even wed."

She'd forgotten that bit. She'd forgotten it would mean anything to her mother anyway.

"That's not the important part."

"It will be to a lot of people. It will be to your father. Are you going to tell him today too?"

"I'm not going to see him. I just wanted to talk to you."

"Am I allowed to know who the father is?"

"You can probably guess. You saw it before I did."

"That nice Dennis?"

"Yes," said Sophie, and she smiled in anticipation of her mother's pleasure.

"He's not as nice as he looks, then."

"He's wonderful," said Sophie.

"Will he marry you?"

"Yes, he'll marry me, but will you forget about that side of things?"

"What do you want me to say, then?"

"I don't know. I thought you'd understand."

"Understand what?"

"Did you want to have me? Or did you panic when you found out?"

"Panic? Why would I panic? We'd been trying for two years."

"Because you couldn't stick it."

"I couldn't stick him. He was killing me. And then I fell in love with someone. I didn't have what you've got."

"What have I got?"

And her mother laughed—not bitterly, but with genuine disbelief.

She hadn't seen Brian for ages. She hadn't needed an agent, because her career had been taking care of itself. He was at his desk, leafing through a huge pile of eight by tens, all of them featuring young, pretty, hopeful girls.

"She's nice," said Sophie, pointing at the photo he had just discarded.

"I'm a happily married man," he said defensively.

"I know," said Sophie. "I was just saying. She could make you some money."

He picked it up again, examined it, and wrinkled up his nose.

"What's wrong with her?"

"She looks clever."

Sophie laughed. It was impossible to be offended by an agent who made no attempt to disguise his self-interest, she found. He didn't like clever girls because they didn't want gold paint sprayed all over them. They wanted to act, and acting was a risky business.

"Talking of clever," he said.

"Meaning what?"

"How's your series? Have they finished writing it yet?"

"I don't know," she said. "I'm pregnant."

"Ah," said Brian. "Well, you've come to the right place."

"Have I?"

"Can you imagine how many girls have come in here saying that? Nothing to do with me, by the way. Any of them."

"You don't have to tell me," said Sophie. "You're a happily married man."

"Ask Patsy, if you don't believe me."

"I believe you. Anyway, what do you say to them, when they come in here and tell you they're up the spout?"

"I recommend a very nice doctor in Harley Street. He's not cheap, but he's safe and he's very discreet."

"Oh," said Sophie. "No. I'm not going to do that."

"Well," he said. "I'm not a medical man, but I don't think there's any other alternative."

"Apart from the obvious."

Brian looked puzzled.

"It's not obvious to me," he said.

"Some people, when they're pregnant, they have a baby," she said.

"Who?"

"People. Everybody."

"Oh, I see what you mean. But I'm presuming we're not in that category."

"I think we might be."

He put down the pictures he was holding and gave her his full attention.

"Start again," he said. "I'm lost."

"I'm going to have a baby."

Telling Brian she was going to have a baby was different, she could now see, from telling him that she was pregnant. The latter was a kind of temporary affliction; the former went some way toward helping him imagine a future in which Sophie was the mother of a small human being.

"What about the series?"

He wasn't interested in the father or her marital state, she noted. Together, Brian and her mother would form a whole, rounded person.

"They'll wait," she said.

"Do you think?" said Brian, apparently amused.

"It's called *Everyone Loves Sophie*. I'm Sophie."

He picked a photograph out of the middle of the pile.

"What about if they called it *Everyone Loves Freda*? She's Freda."

"Freda's a terrible name."

"We'll change it. *Everyone Loves Suzy*. How does that sound?"

It sounded both frightening and plausible, and for a moment she found herself thinking, Well, he's won the argument. But then she realized the argument wasn't real. She wasn't going to go and see a discreet doctor in Harley Street. She understood that she could: the option was real, even if the argument wasn't. The doctor could take the baby away, make it vanish, just as Barbara's baby had vanished. And Tony and Diane need know nothing about it, and she could appear as childless, carefree, girl-about-town Sophie in a series called *Everyone Loves Sophie*. But how much fun would it be to play the part of a childless, carefree girl-about-town immediately after an abortion? How would she feel, having an abortion so that she could become a carefree, childless fictional character? How much delight would Dennis, the father of the aborted child, take in producing the show? How funny would he find carefree Sophie's predicaments and pickles?

To her mother, it must have looked as though she could do anything she wanted to do. She could move from one end of the country to another, change her name, live on her own, sleep with whoever she wanted to without marrying them, drink tea at the Ritz, make babies disappear overnight, probably bringing them back again, if she felt like it. And it was true, she could. But it seemed to her that to take advantage of all of these opportunities, she had to turn something off inside her. She had to pretend that nothing mattered, as long as she got the life she thought she wanted. For some reason, she started thinking about how *Everyone Loves Sophie* or *Everyone Loves Suzy* would end, six months or five years into the future: Sophie or Suzy would meet someone, and want to have a baby with him, and Tony and Diane would run out of things to say. That was how half the stories in the world ended. She wasn't sure it was the best ending, but it was the only one people seemed to be able to think of for girls like her. And Sophie had met someone, in real life, and she was pregnant by him, and he made her happy. You couldn't keep asking to have the pages crumpled up and thrown in the bin, especially if they made sense.

"Well," said Brian, after he'd finally understood. "I'll still be here when you're ready to come back."

"Thank you," said Sophie.

Brian couldn't interest Dennis in Freda, or Suzy, or any of the girls who had sent him photographs, but one evening he saw *Caviar and Chips*, an ITV show about a working-class family that wins the football pools, and he had a bright idea: he approached the girl who played the family's teenage daughter, a pretty young actress called Jackie Chamberlain, and told her that he had a series for her. Then he talked to ITV, and then he talked to Tony and Diane, and a few months later *Everyone Loves Jackie*, a series about a young, carefree, single girl with a cat and boyfriend troubles, was given a Thursday night slot. It didn't last long, but then, that was the trouble with young people, Brian found: they would insist on getting older.

FROM THIS DAY FORWARD

BIOGRAPHIES

BILL GARDINER, who cowrote *Barbara (and Jim)* with Tony Holmes, is the author of the novels *Diary of a Soho Boy*, *The Gospel According to Nigel*, and *The Closet*. He is working on a film adaptation of *Diary of a Soho Boy*. His stage adaptation was put on at the Royal Court in 1969.

TONY HOLMES has written more than twenty series for radio and television. After *Barbara (and Jim)* he wrote (with Diane Stafford) *Everyone Loves Jackie*, before going on to create *Salt and Vinegar*; *The Green, Green Grass of Home*; and *Would Like to Have Met* for ITV. He is a frequent contributor to the radio series *I'm Sorry, I Haven't a Clue*, and *Just a Minute*.

CLIVE RICHARDSON has had a long career in television in both the U.K. and the U.S. He was Dr. Nigel Fisher in *ER*, and for many years played Chief Inspector Richard Jury in the successful and popular *Jury*, adapted from the books of Martha Grimes. He lives with his third wife, the American actress Carrie Courtenay, in Hollywood.

SOPHIE STRAW has been a much-loved star of British stage and screen ever since she introduced herself to the British viewing public in *Barbara (and Jim)*. Her TV series include *His and Hearse*; *Salt and Vinegar*; *The Green, Green Grass of Home*; *Would Like to Have Met*; and *Minnie Cab*. She is now probably best remembered for her work in the long-running soap opera *Chatterton Avenue*, in which she played Liz Smallwood from 1982 to 1996. Her stage work includes touring productions of *The Importance of Being Earnest*, *A Taste of Honey*, and several of the plays of Alan Ayckbourn, including *A Chorus of Disapproval* and *The Norman Conquests*. She was married to the producer and director of *Barbara (and Jim)*, Dennis Maxwell-Bishop, until his death in 2011. She has two children. Her daughter, Georgia Maxwell-Bishop, received a BAFTA nomination for her performance as Adela Quested in the BBC's adaptation of *A Passage to India*.

FROM THE PROGRAM NOTES TO THE BAFTA TRIBUTE
Barbara (and Jim): The Golden Wedding Anniversary,
OCTOBER 2014

24

Sophie tried to remember whether she had ever seen herself projected onto a big screen, and decided that she hadn't. Except she'd had a small part in that peculiar thing with Ewan McGregor four or five years ago, playing the mother of his deranged ex-wife, and she was almost certain that she'd been to the premiere, and been coaxed onto the stage with everyone else, Ewan and Ros and Jim Broadbent. Had she not even stayed to watch the film? She thought she had. She could remember huge chunks of *Barbara (and Jim)*, could have chanted along with the lines as she watched, yet half the time she couldn't remember what she'd eaten for supper the previous evening. She didn't care very often, because not many of the suppers were worth remembering, but her memory was annoying at times like this, when she wanted to remember.

And then she realized what it was: she'd never seen this version of herself cinema-sized, the twenty-one-year-old version. She'd only ever seen her ancient self up there, and shuddered, and looked away, and actively tried to forget the lines on her face and the lumpy shapelessness afterward. She hadn't bothered with the premiere of *Chemin de Fer*, the awful film she'd made with the French pop singer in Wales. (She had caught as much as she could bear to watch on TV one night, a few years ago, on one of the hundreds of obscure channels to which Dennis had insisted on subscribing. Without him, she would never be able to find any of them again.) And this was the first time that *Barbara (and Jim)* had been shown in a cinema, as far as she knew.

It wasn't something she would do again in a hurry, that was for sure. She had hoped that the tribute evening would be a happy experience, that it would be nice to see everyone and talk about the past and bask in all the praise and love. She had thought that she was even getting to a stage where she could listen to people talking about Dennis without feeling as though her guts were being pulled out through her throat. She hadn't, however, prepared herself for a different, less admirable grief. Maybe it was better to have been beautiful once than never to have been beautiful at all, but the advantages of beauty were now long gone. And she couldn't help but feel that she was depressing everybody else too—everybody up on the stage with her, everybody in the audience, even the young people who believed that there would be a cure for old age any day now. Look, everybody! Age has withered me. And also custom has staled my infinite variety!

After they'd shown the episodes and the house lights were turned on, the questions from the audience came in an apparently unstoppable torrent. "Just how wet did you get in 'The New Bathroom'?" "If you had your time all over again, Jim, would you have stayed with Barbara?" "Can you tell us something about your writing process, Tony?" "I'd like to ask all of you to name your favorite episode." "Which modern comediennes do you admire?" "Why isn't there anything as funny as *Barbara (and Jim)* on TV anymore?" (Applause.) "When did you know you were appearing in a classic sitcom?" Did people really want to know the answers to these things, or did they just want someone from the team to look at them?

The people who'd been laughing uproariously—ostentatiously, if you wanted to be unkind—weren't all as old as her. There were some who must have watched the show as kids, and there were some who were young—women, mostly. Young women often seemed to want to tell her that she had been an inspiration to them, that their careers in comedy would not have been possible without her. But when she tried to watch them, or listen to their recordings, or read their stories and scripts, Sophie couldn't understand what she'd had to do with any of it. If she was somehow responsible for all these jokes about anal sex and vaginal hygiene, she felt she owed the people of Britain an apology.

The audience had seen the pilot and "The New Bathroom," because they were two of the only surviving shows: the BBC had recorded over the tapes. And of course Sophie regretted that so much of her best work was gone, but she understood the impulse. They were only comedy programs, made fifty years ago to entertain people who were now all old or dead. And anyway, hadn't those tapes been recycled, at a time when nobody used the word, and nobody worried about the planet drowning in a sea of plastic rubbish? But a dozen episodes out of the original sixty or so had survived, or in some cases been found: every now and again, an engineer or an editor came across something in an attic or a shed. It wasn't much, but it was probably enough.

"One more question," said the compère, an earnest young man from the British Film Institute who looked as though he'd never laughed in his life, and certainly not at an English situation comedy.

Another young man who needed a shave thrust his hand up in the air, and the compère pointed at him, and everyone had to wait while the microphone was passed along the row.

"Would you consider reviving the characters?" he said. "If someone came along with the right script and the right idea?"

Sophie laughed. She always knew the kind of noise she wanted to make, but it always came out wrong, croaky, phlegmy, cracked. The terrible thing was that one always thought everything was temporary—the croak, the creaks, the pains, the insomnia. All those things used to be temporary. They cleared up. Not anymore.

"What do you think, Clive?" she said.

That was another thing she was suddenly self-conscious of this evening: her accent. There was no trace of Barbara from Blackpool. She sounded like a theatrical grande dame, she thought. Fifty years of *Barbara (and Jim)* meant fifty years of London. She had only lived in the North for a third of her life, after all that.

Clive was not awake, so she turned back to the audience.

"Do people really want to watch old people moaning on?"

There was laughter, and some shouts of "Yes!" and "We do!" and applause.

"You don't have to moan on," said the young man with the stubble.

"You're quite right," said Sophie. "I should remember that. In life, I mean."

"There's quite a market for things starring old people," said the young man. "There was that film about the old folks' home for opera singers, and *The Best Exotic Marigold Hotel* . . . The gray pound is really worth something."

"Well," said Sophie, "nobody's asked us, as far as I know."

"Sorry," said Clive. "Did you ask me something?"

Sophie raised her eyebrows despairingly, and got a laugh.

"I'm asking you now," said the young man with the stubble. "I'm a producer, and I have investors who . . ."

"Ah," said the BFI compère, "I now see that this is more of a sales pitch than a question. Perhaps you could have a word with Sophie privately afterward?"

He thanked everyone for coming, and they got a standing ovation, and afterward there was a long queue of people who wanted autographs on their DVD collections, and old eight by tens, and the first-day-cover series of Great British Sitcoms that the Post Office had issued at what young people called the turn of the century. (When Sophie had first heard that, she wanted to weep at her own confusion. That's when you know you're old, when you start to get your turns of the century muddled up.) She thought she'd be exhausted, but the more she signed, the younger she felt.

The young man with the stubble waited at the back of the line. Sophie—he'd focused on her—hadn't been able to get rid of him, so in the end they'd asked him into the greenroom for a drink. Sophie wasn't even sure that she'd wanted to get rid of him. Sometimes people asked her to do something, appear on a documentary about the 1960s or read a short story on Radio 4 about a grandmother forcing herself not to interfere in her daughter's parenting mistakes. (She had read three of those.) But Max, the young man with the stubble, was talking about a starring role in a play.

"I'm not going to tell you it'll take the West End by storm," he said. "It doesn't work like that."

"It works like that for some people," said Tony.

"Young people," said Bill.

"What can I tell you?" said Max, his arms spread in defeat. "You ain't young people. But you never know. If we got the story right, and it made people laugh, I can see you doing well in the regional theaters. Places like Bexhill and Eastbourne, anywhere, you know . . ."

"Anywhere people go to die," said Clive.

He was awake now. He'd flown from California for the tribute, so he could be forgiven his erratic participation in the evening. It did mean, however, that his long journey had been a complete waste of time. He'd slept through the episodes, woken briefly when the lights came up, and nodded off again during the Q&A.

"That's exactly not what I'm thinking of," said Max passionately. "I've got a title. *From This Day Forward*. From the marriage vows. Old people want to be offered hope. Don't you think? It's not all doom and gloom."

"It really is," said Bill.

"Well, your job is to find something that isn't," said Max.

"You'd love that," said June, who had been in the audience with Roger and his wife.

"It's not really a job, though, is it?" said Tony. "A job is when someone pays you to do something."

"Oh, I'll get the money to pay you for a script," said Max. "I wouldn't ask you to write for free."

"I'm in," said Bill.

Tony looked at him.

"What?" Bill said. "I'm fucking skint."

The last time they had all been in the same room was after Dennis's funeral, but it had hardly been a reunion, not with everyone else there. Sophie and Dennis had been together for a long time after *Barbara (and Jim)*, and the wake had been full of children, and grandchildren, and friends, and godchildren, and colleagues from all the shows that had come after. The program she always thought of as their show took up only a tiny little corner of their sitting room. There had been a moment when she'd looked over and seen Clive, Tony, and Bill talking and laughing, and she had longed for everyone else, even her children, to leave, just for thirty minutes, so that she could talk about Dennis to the people who'd watched her fall in love with him. But she knew that nobody else would have understood, and she wasn't sure she could explain the impulse even to herself, so the night had ended, as it should have, with Georgia and Christian and a Balthazar of champagne that Dennis had been saving for a special occasion. Either he had left it too long or he knew what he was doing, depending on how you looked at it.

If she were to bet on whose funeral they'd be attending next, then her money would have to go on Bill, but the odds wouldn't be very good: he looked awful. The long, yellowy-white beard was regrettable, and the walking stick that only just enabled mobility put years on him, but beards and sticks weren't going to kill him; the drinking and the smoking would do that. Except, of course, that they hadn't, and he was older than Sophie, and if he dropped dead tomorrow, nobody would talk about a life cut tragically short by his addictions. He'd lived his life. They all had. Any years remaining to them were a gift, if that was the right word. Oh, of course it was the right word. She wished she and her friends could stop speaking like that. She was almost certain that they made those bitter jokes just to disguise their pathetic, doomed hunger to live longer.

"How much are you going to pay us?" Bill said.

"You really want to talk about that now?" said Max. "In front of everyone?"

"He's going to pay you a tenner, Bill," said Clive. "Now what?"

"Oh, it'll be more than a tenner," said Max, at a volume and with a conviction that suggested fifteen would be closer to the mark.

"I think Clive's point was that it's a buyer's market," said Tony. "It doesn't matter what you pay us. We haven't got any other work."

"Tony, you don't want to think about shutting up, do you?" said Bill. "You're costing us money."

"I'll just have a chat to your agent about all that, shall I?" said Max.

"You do that," said Bill. "We'll lend you a Ouija board."

"Ah," said Max.

"I've still got an agent," said Tony. "You can speak to her."

"Do you just do this sort of thing at random?" said Clive. "Are you a regular ambusher of old duffers?"

"No," said Max. "It was you I wanted."

"I'll bet you say that to all the girls," said Sophie.

"I'm actually a bit obsessive about *Barbara (and Jim)*."

"I'll bet you say that to all the sitcom couples," said Clive.

"It's true," said Max. "I can prove it."

"In a way that doesn't involve you providing a synopsis of every single episode?" said Bill. "Because we had a lot of that tonight."

"There were sixty-four made, right?" said Max.

"And twelve have survived," said June.

"Well, I've got twenty-two," said Max.

He had their full attention.

"How?"

"Oh, you don't want to know. But they've cost me a few quid."

Bill hit him with his stick, hard. He'd clearly intended to crack him over the head, but Max thrust his arm up just in time and took the blow on his elbow.

"What the FUCK?" said Max.

June, it turned out, had done a first-aid course in preparation for a holiday with the grandchildren, and for a moment she was concerned that a bone had been broken. But after Max had walked around the room for a couple of minutes, stretching his arm and swearing, June decided that a hospital visit would not be required.

"What did you do that for?" said Max.

"That's our money," said Bill. "Ten episodes are two whole DVDs."

"Nobody's buying DVDs anymore."

"Repeat fees," said Bill. "Downloads. All that malarkey. You owe us thousands of pounds."

"We'll do all that when we put the stage show on," said Max. "If I decide I do want to work with a fucking lunatic."

"Excuse my friend," said Tony. "He's been down on his luck."

"Thousands of pounds," said Bill again.

"You'd only have pissed it up the wall," said Clive.

"My prerogative," said Bill.

Something had just happened, Sophie thought. It didn't really matter what it was, or that at its root was a pitiable desperation; tomorrow morning she would be able to call Georgia and tell her that Bill had walloped a young man with his walking stick, and Georgia would laugh, and express disbelief. Usually she had to listen to stories—about Georgia's work, or her useless ex-husband, or the children. If she ever had anything to offer in return, it was something from the library, an illustrative anecdote about Christian in Majorca in 1975, or *Chatterton Avenue* in 1987, and Georgia had usually heard it many times before. (Georgia would never pretend that the story was fresh. She wasn't that sort of daughter.) Sophie never had anything new. Already, Max's play was worth more than the money she could earn from it. She wanted to do it more than she had wanted anything for years, apart from all the obvious, impossible things.

25

Tony and Bill met in a Polish café around the corner from Bill's little house in Kentish Town. Bill couldn't travel very far, and he clearly didn't want Tony coming to his home. The cleaning lady was sick and hadn't been for a couple of weeks, Bill told him. If it had been any other friend, Tony would have told him that he was being daft and that they could put up with a bit of mess, but it had been many, many years since Bill was in a position to pay a cleaning lady. Tony imagined cobwebs, booze bottles, mounds of old newspapers, takeaway cartons.

They ordered coffees, and in an awkward moment's silence, Tony got his laptop out of his briefcase and put it on the table.

"Really?" said Bill.

"I haven't used a typewriter for years."

"I wasn't asking you to bring a fucking great Corona with you. Pen! Paper! The coffee bar is longhand, isn't it?"

"It was. All those years ago. Does that mean it still is?" said Tony.

"Nothing still is," said Bill. "It's all gone."

"Bloody hell, Bill."

"It's true, though, isn't it?"

"We've got to stop thinking like that, if we want to come up with anything anyone wants to go and see. Max is right."

"How can he be right about anything?"

"He wanted to employ us."

"And you take that as a good sign?"

"Let's not bother, then," said Tony. "I'll go home and watch *Millionaire Matchmaker* and have my lunch."

For a long time, Bill and Tony had met up every other month or so, but it had been harder over the last decade. Tony would try to steer a steady path between the perils that always threatened to capsize their fragile, leaky little boat: he didn't talk about work (because Bill didn't have any), or June (because Bill's life-partner, a younger man called Christopher, turned out to be no such thing and left him), or more or less anything that indicated happiness and fulfillment. Tony didn't mind long, brooding conversations about the state of the BBC and the dismal savagery of modern comedy; he too was confused by it. But in the end the discourse became so repetitive that when Bill stopped calling, Tony didn't chase him.

It wasn't the pursuit of art that had impoverished Bill; he just didn't work hard enough, and when he did write, he wrote the wrong things. *Diary of a Soho Boy* had done well, but he'd taken too long to write his second book, and his second book, when it finally appeared, was almost identical to its predecessor. He'd survived on his royalties, for a while, and the film option he sold, and the money he'd been given to write the screenplay, but he'd never finished it, as far as Tony knew, and it had saddened him to see it mentioned in the BAFTA program as a work in progress. There was nothing going on there, and nobody was ever going to make a film of it. *Diary of a Soho Boy* was old hat now. It was still in print, but only students of gay history wanted to read it these days. Twenty-first-century homosexuals in Britain had their own literature, different lives, new problems. Fear of imprisonment wasn't one of them. It had gone the way of polio and rickets.

Christopher had paid for everything in the last fifteen years of their relationship. Tony hadn't known him well, but he knew him to be a kind man, and he'd almost certainly tired of the relationship, and Bill's hopeless dependency, long before he actually left. Tony had "loaned" Bill money in the past, and he could see that if they were going to have another stab at working together, he wouldn't be able to avoid another request.

The coffee arrived, and Bill picked up his cup with two hands and trembling fingers.

"Be nice to put a drop of something in here," said Bill.

Tony ignored him.

"Just to get us going."

Tony put the laptop back in his briefcase and found a notebook and a ballpoint pen.

"We don't drink," said Tony. "Not during the day."

Clive and Sophie met in an Italian restaurant in Kensington Church Street, a few doors down from where the Tratt used to be. It had been Clive's suggestion, and the sentimentality made Sophie feel a little queasy; one of the many difficulties of aging, she found, was that people wanted to rekindle friendships the cheap and easy way, by pressing buttons—old jobs, old friends, old restaurants—without doing any of the work. But Clive didn't know London very well anymore and she couldn't think of anywhere better.

"May I begin by telling you how beautiful you're looking?" he said. "I won't say that you don't look a day older, but you have aged in a most charming way."

"It wouldn't kill you to say I don't look a day older," said Sophie. "You last saw me at Dennis's funeral three years ago. And I was a wreck."

"I was thinking about the other night. The BAFTA thing."

"I've only aged four days since then."

"You know what I mean."

"I've now lost track of the compliment," said Sophie.

"You look well."

"Oh. Is that what it boils down to?" She pouted to indicate disappointment, and Clive laughed.

"Did you enjoy seeing the shows again?"

"It was complicated. You?"

"You know, I don't really want to spend the whole lunch talking about the past," said Clive.

"What an annoying thing to say."

"Why?"

"Because nobody was asking you to. Because you just asked me about the other night, so out of politeness I asked you the same question. Because we wouldn't even be sitting here if it wasn't for the past, and for people wanting to talk about the past."

"If it's any consolation to you, I regret everything," said Clive. "And I always have."

"When you say you regret everything . . ."

"Related to *Barbara (and Jim)*, and my part in its downfall."

"I'm going to shove a breadstick up your nose in a minute," said Sophie.

"What have I done now?"

"Why on earth would your regret be a consolation to me?" said Sophie.

"I just thought you'd like to know."

"No."

"It doesn't give you any satisfaction?"

"No."

"You weren't annoyed with me?"

"No."

"Now I know you're not telling the truth. You were extremely annoyed with me at the time."

"I thought we were talking about the show. That's what I was talking about anyway. I wasn't annoyed with you about that. I was cross about you sleeping with that deranged woman when you were supposed to be engaged to me."

She could see why she had found him attractive, even now. He had aged well too. If men of his age still wore mustaches, he could have looked like John Mills, or David Niven, or one of the other twinkly old actors she used to see on the chat shows when the children were young and she and Dennis watched television every night. (Later, she looked David Niven up on Wikipedia and found that he'd been younger than Clive when he died, and nearly ten years younger than both of them when he used to sit on Michael Parkinson's sofa at the beginning of the 1970s, telling all those stories about Sam Goldwyn. The discovery made her feel shaky and breathless.)

"But that was why it all went wrong."

She was about to correct him on tiny, detailed points of chronology—to remind him about Bill and Tony and their decision to separate, and about the plotting in the series—and then she realized that she didn't want that kind of argument at all.

"Nothing went wrong," she said.

She could tell that he didn't believe her.

"Nothing went wrong," she said again. "I married Dennis. He was the best husband I could possibly have hoped for. We had two wonderful children."

"You're right," said Clive. "That's the most important thing."

"No, it isn't, and I haven't finished," said Sophie. "Nothing went wrong professionally either. I've enjoyed every second of my career, and I've worked whenever I wanted to."

Clive put up his hands in a gesture of surrender.

"All right. Everything's been marvelous."

"I never thought any of those things would happen to me."

"Yes, you did," said Clive gently. "You knew it would happen to you. You were the most confident young woman I'd ever met. You knew you were going to be a television star."

"Oh dear," said Sophie. "Was I one of those?"

"I'm afraid you were, rather."

"Yes, well. You live and you learn."

"But everything's been marvelous."

"What do you want me to say, Clive? What's the actual point of this conversation? You seem to want me to tell you that ever since *Barbara (and Jim)* it's all been a terrible disappointment. And I'm not going to do that. Has it all been a terrible disappointment for you? Is that it?"

A bottle of champagne appeared, just in time.

"I can't drink at lunchtime," said Sophie. "It makes me feel wretched."

"Oh, come on," said Clive. "Don't be so feeble."

She shook her head at the waiter and put her hand over the glass. The waiter, infuriatingly, looked at Clive for further instructions.

"Give her the tiniest taste," said Clive. "Just so that we can toast each other."

The tiniest taste wouldn't make her feel wretched, but if she took one now, it would make her feel irritated and resentful. She let the waiter pour a splash and then she drowned it in mineral water.

"Oh, that's a terrible thing to do," said Clive.

"Cheers," said Sophie, and chinked his glass.

"You never break that rule? For anyone?"

"It's about knowing your limitations. Which is what we were talking about."

"Were we?"

"I'd just asked you if it had all been a terrible disappointment for you."

"Which bit? Work? Marriage? Life?"

"Whichever you choose."

"I don't know if they were a disappointment. I just messed them all up. That's different, isn't it?"

After Sophie had told Clive that she didn't want to marry him, he had, inexplicably, gone back to Hampshire and proposed to his first fiancée, Cathy, and had made things even worse by marrying her. He'd stuck it out for about a year, just long enough for Cathy to get pregnant. He didn't get married again for a while after that, but when he did, in the early 1980s, the outcome was similar: one year, one child, this time in California. He'd been with Carrie, his third wife, for the last decade, although Sophie wasn't sure where she was, or why she hadn't traveled with him.

"I can see that the marriages might not have been ideal. Present wife excepted, of course."

"Oh, you don't need to make any exceptions for her," said Clive. "Ghastly woman."

"I'm sorry to hear that," said Sophie.

"Oh, it's not *news*," said Clive. "She's always been ghastly."

Sophie had some obvious questions about this assertion,

but decided not to ask them. And then she changed her mind.

"Why do you keep marrying ghastly women?"

"I've only married two ghastlies," said Clive. "Cathy was all right. Boring and pointless, yes, but she wasn't a horror."

"Why did you marry two ghastly women?"

"I'm weak. We know that about me."

"But when people say they're weak, they're talking about drink or drugs or sex or things that give them pleasure. Marrying horrors doesn't look like much fun from any angle."

"I suppose fun was involved, at some point."

"Let's draw a veil over that."

"Probably for the best. Anyway. I mess my marriages up, and my relationships with my children are as a consequence poor, and I messed work up too."

"How did you do that?"

"The same way as you, I suppose. We should have been famous, Sophie."

We are famous, she wanted to say, and then couldn't see any earthly reason why she shouldn't.

"We are famous."

"Oh, famous for soap operas and TV detective shows and so on. We should be more famous than that."

"Really? That's what we deserve?"

He looked at her, and for a moment she thought he'd detected the sarcasm, but he plowed on anyway.

"Look at my contemporaries. McKellen, Gambon, Ben

Kingsley . . . They're doing all right. They probably don't even think about being old, they're getting so many scripts thrown at them. I know you took time out to have babies and so on, but still. We just sort of . . . dribbled out."

Oh, but there was so much here she wanted to argue with him about; there was so much that made her want to grab him by his tie—yes, he was wearing a tie—and rock his head back and forth, and perhaps smash it on the table once or twice. What did they deserve? Certainly not what they'd got, she could see that much now, although it had taken her a while. They should be down on their knees every day, thanking God for what they'd been given in return for not very much. Sophie had been pretty, and she was able to make people laugh, and later, during middle age, she had been able to convince people—convince her employers anyway—that she was a middle-aged woman who had suffered bereavement, or who had taken over her imprisoned husband's minicab firm. These, it seemed to her, were marginal talents. And yet she could have raised a family with them, if she'd needed to, bought more than one home, sent her children to private schools. She'd been given awards, and space in magazines, and love. And after, or nearly after, all that, she'd been given money to write a book about her life, this life that had already been charmed, overfeted, too well rewarded. And this book, *Barbara (and Me)*, had sold so well that she'd been given even more money for it. And she hadn't even written it herself! Her friend Diane had done it for her! She wanted to say all this to Clive, loudly and scornfully, but he hadn't been asked to write a book, and he hadn't been given awards, and as far as she knew nobody took photographs of him at home and put them in women's magazines. He was disappointed about something else, she thought; he was disappointed that he'd never quite added up to as much as the results of his own calculations. The trouble was that he'd got his sums all wrong, but she didn't want to be the one to tell him that.

"Anyway," he said. "It's nice to be given this chance to get back on track."

"Which chance?"

She must have missed something.

"The play."

"Oh, Clive. Nobody will notice the play."

He looked at her, apparently trying to work out if this was some kind of cruel joke at his expense.

"So why is this Max person bothering?"

"He thinks he can make money out of old people in Eastbourne and he wants to give us some of it."

"That's it?"

"I think so."

"Do you need the money, then?"

"No. Do you?"

"I'll be all right, I suppose, if there isn't any more. So why do you want to do it?"

"I like working. And I like working with people I know even more."

"That's the thing," said Clive. "There's nobody I like in America."

"Out of two hundred million people?"

"Nobody I like who wants to work with me anyway."

"Ah."

She couldn't help thinking that he'd just told her he hated all food, before going on to explain that he was referring to a half-eaten sandwich in the fridge.

"The thing is, I want to come home."

"Who's stopping you?"

"It's a funny place, L.A. The thing is, it . . ."

"You're not going to tell me about the weather, are you? Or how it doesn't have a center?"

"I thought you might be interested," he said, a little huffily.

"It was interesting the first time someone I knew came back from California, in 1968 or so. But it hasn't been interesting since then."

"Suit yourself."

"And that's not why you want to come back anyway. Nobody wants to come back from a place where the sun shines all day. They say they do. But somehow it doesn't happen."

"So why do I want to come back, then?"

"I have no idea. Has Carrie actually left you?"

"I don't know."

"There's a good way of telling: is she living in your house?"

"No."

"Right."

"But she quite often disappears off on jobs and things."

"Has she disappeared off on a job? Have you called her agent?"

"Yes. He says not. It was quite an embarrassing conversation actually."

"I think we should work on the basis that she's left you, then."

"I was beginning to come to the same conclusion. Anyway. I don't want to be old and unemployed and friendless there."

"You'd rather all that happened here."

He looked at her, hurt, and she had to make a face to show she was joking. She was sure he would have laughed, in the old days, and she couldn't decide whether it was age or Hollywood that had sanded down his sharpness. She blamed Hollywood.

"Do you have enough friends?" he said. "I'm sorry if that sounds pitiful. But I have to say, you'd be central in the . . . in the construction of a new life."

"I'd be a plank," she said.

"Are you offering or clarifying?"

"I was clarifying."

"Oh."

"I suppose we'd better see how we get on during rehearsals," said Sophie. "But all being well, I'm sure I can turn clarification into a firm offer."

"I'm trying to think of an off-color joke that would work."

"Because of 'firm offer'?"

"I suppose so."

"I think you might be better off going down the clarification route."

"Something to do with butter?"

"If you must."

"There used to be loads of them, didn't there, during the *Last Tango in Paris* era?"

"You're right. It was the golden age of smutty butter jokes," said Sophie.

"Well, it was, wasn't it?"

It was absurd that they were getting old, thought Sophie—absurd and wrong. Old people had black-and-white memories of wars, music halls, wretched diseases, candlelight. Her memories were in color, and they involved loud music and discos, Biba and Habitat, Marlon Brando and butter. She and Dennis had gone to see a nude musical on their first date, and they'd been married for over forty years, and he had died—not of old age, quite, but of a disease that kills the elderly more than anyone else. She picked up her glass and drank down the champagne-flavored mineral water.

"Could I have a glass of champagne, please?"

She was going to get drunk, just to see whether it was as bad as she remembered.

26

ony and Bill wrote the script in three weeks. It came in at ninety minutes, the equivalent of three episodes. Max had told them that older people didn't want to sit in a theater for hours, which suited them, because they didn't want to sit in the Polish café for months. Max had even provided them with the two tent poles over which he wanted them to drape the play: a pair of weddings. Barbara and Jim—both single again after bereavement—start talking at their son's wedding, and in the process rekindle something; in the second act, they are preparing to remarry.

"They can't both have lost their spouses, can they?" said Tony on the second day, when they had talked about everything else they could think of, and could no longer postpone work. "Nobody dies now. Not before they're eighty."

There was a subtext to the observation, but Tony didn't

want to brush the soil off it and expose it to scrutiny. The truth was, however, that if Bill could live as long as he had, with all his years of drinking and unsafe sex and drug abuse, then humans were indeed a lot more durable than they ever had been. ("Abuse?" Bill had repeated scornfully a couple of decades ago, when Tony had expressed concern. "How am I abusing them? That's what they were made for.")

"Dennis died," said Bill. "He wasn't eighty."

"He was unlucky," said Tony.

Dennis was killed by an infection he'd picked up in the hospital, after a routine hip operation.

"One divorce and one bereavement?"

"Go on, then," said Tony, as if he'd been offered another cake.

"Which one's which?"

"We can't make Sophie play a widow, can we? Not when she is one."

"You can't make an actor play a character she knows something about?"

"But won't it upset her?"

"Heaven forbid we get a performance out of her."

"And Jim's divorced," said Tony.

"I suppose so," said Bill. "But that does mean he's got two broken marriages behind him. He never seemed like the type, to me."

"What about if he never remarried?" said Tony.

"And he's been pining for her all this time?"

"Why the sarcasm?"

"Do people really pine for that long?"

"You can regret mistakes, can't you?"

"For nearly fifty years?"

"Course you can. I'm not saying he's been sat in a dark room sobbing for all that time. Just that he wishes things hadn't turned out the way they did."

"Yeah, well. It's too late now."

"Why is it too late?" said Tony.

"Come off it."

"Come off what?"

"It. It's over."

"Why is it over?"

"There's nothing left of her. Or there's too much left of her, depending on which way you look at it. She's not Barbara anymore, is she?"

"Are you being deliberately provocative?"

"She was gorgeous."

"And that was all there was to her?"

"Don't worry. I'll write the fucking play with you. They can get back together, I don't care. But really. Between you and me."

"Bloody hell, Bill. You of all people."

"What?"

"You sit in that flat surrounded by empty bottles of Johnnie Walker or whatever, on your own, day after day, miserable as sin, and you can't see the value of companionship?"

Bill sighed and, as he did so, deflated.

"Of course I can," he said. "That's why I don't want to think about it. I want what you've always had."

Jim stayed unmarried.

The big breakthrough came on the next day.

"Hang on," said Bill. "How old is the baby now?"

"Barbara's baby? Timmy? He's not really a baby anymore. He's nearly fifty. He was born at the beginning of the third series—1966, was that? Or '67?"

"Jesus Christ," said Bill. "People who were born in '66 are nearly fifty? I know the show's fifty, but it seems like yesterday. Human years are different. I'd have guessed that Tim was twenty-five or thirty."

"I wouldn't," said Tony. "Roger's more or less the same age."

"Tim," said Bill. "Roger. What were we all thinking of, with those names?"

"What's wrong with them?"

"They're all right now. But did you and June really look at yours and go, you know, 'Coochy-coo, baby Roger'?"

"I suppose we must have done."

Bill shook his head in wonder.

"Anyway. What's baby Timmy doing getting married for the first time at fifty? Who is he, Cary Grant or someone? He's got to have been married before," said Bill.

"What about if he's been living with whatever-her-name-is all this time?"

"They're not going to have that sort of wedding, are

they? Marquees and bridesmaids and a vicar? It's got to be a second marriage, hasn't it?" said Bill. "Have you been invited to many second marriages?"

"I don't know that I have. People tend to slope off, don't they? What about you?"

"I've been to three first marriages in the last six weeks," said Bill.

"Nieces and nephews and all that?"

"No," said Bill. "Don't you read the papers?"

"Who do you know who's famous?"

"Gay people," said Bill. "Gay people are famous. Or they were, when they legalized gay marriage. When was it— March? April?"

"Oh, bloody hell," said Tony. "That's fantastic."

"I suppose," said Bill. "It's only a bit of paper and a booze-up."

"The play," said Tony. "It's a gay wedding."

And they both experienced a familiar prickle of excitement, a feeling from so long ago that it took them a little while to identify it.

The rehearsals were in a Soho club called the Soho Club in Berwick Street, just above the market. They had an hour to talk about the script before meeting the director; the other three cast members—Max couldn't run to more than five—would come in later in the week.

None of them had ever heard of the Soho Club, of course, and they didn't see anyone else over the age of forty all day. A terrifyingly beautiful Slavic girl wearing black lipstick and a tiny skirt signed them in and showed them all up the stairs to a room tucked away at the end of a corridor. Table, chairs, scripts, fruit, mineral water. Bill didn't like it.

"We don't belong here," he said. "And those stairs are no good for me."

"I'm sorry," said Max. "I'm a founder member and I get the room for free."

"Who were all those people downstairs?" said Clive. "And why haven't they got anywhere to go at ten o'clock in the morning?"

"They all work in the media," said Max. "Producers, writers, directors . . ."

"Actual producers and writers and directors?"

"It's tough out there," said Max. "So if you mean, you know, Are they being paid? . . . They're trying. You have to take a punt, don't you?"

It was a different world they lived in now, Sophie caught herself thinking, and then she told herself off. Of course it was a different world. Don't be so banal. Obviously, 1980 was different from 1930, 1965 was different from 1915, and so on. Oh, but dear God . . . To a twenty-two-year-old now, 1965 was like 1915 had been to her when she was starting out. It wasn't like that, though, was it? She saw pictures of the Beatles and Twiggy everywhere. Nobody had wanted to think about 1915 in the 1960s, had they? And then she remembered the Lord Kitchener posters that used to be everywhere. It was all so confusing.

"When were you born, Max?"

He may have been talking about something else to Bill and Clive, but she was lost now.

"In 1975."

"Thank you."

It was a different world because, when they had started out, television and pop music and cinema had had to fight like mad for the tiniest modicum of respect. She had watched Dennis on that *Pipe Smoke* program arguing with Vernon Ditchfield, or whatever his name was, about television comedy, but now she was beginning to wonder whether Ditchfield might have had a point: entertainment had taken over the world, and she wasn't sure that the world was a better place for it. Sometimes it seemed as though all anyone wanted to do was write television programs, or sing, or appear in movies. Nobody wanted to make a paintbrush, or design engines, or even find a cure for cancer.

She emerged from her septuagenarian reverie to find Clive tapping his script with a Biro. To her surprise and delight, she recognized the expression on his face, even though she hadn't seen it for a long time. He was about to say something he knew was going to annoy everybody. There was a particular twinkle in the eyes, an unmistakable lift in the eyebrows, a special jut of the chin.

"I don't think Tim is gay," he said.

She was right. This was fantastically annoying.

"You know Tim, do you?" said Tony.

"I am his father," said Clive.

"You haven't seen him since 1967," said Bill. "You walked out on him. You don't get a say in his sexuality."

"I just don't think fans of the show would believe it," said Clive. "He was such a sturdy little chap."

There were howls of outrage from all round the table.

"I think he's winding you up," said Max.

"I'm afraid not," said Sophie.

"Once a berk, always a berk," said Bill.

"Do you think it reflects badly on you?" said Tony. "Is that it?"

"Don't be ridiculous," said Clive.

"Of course that's it," said Sophie. "That's what it always is."

"Let's just stick to the facts," said Clive. "There's no need to get personal."

"What on earth are the facts?" said Sophie.

"The facts are," said Clive, "that I have two children, and neither of them . . ."

This time, the howls of outrage stopped him from even finishing his sentence.

"Why are you like this?" said Bill. "You must have worked with lots of gay people in Hollywood. You may even have gay friends."

"Of course I have," said Clive. "I love gay people. I love you, Bill. And I don't even feel the need to qualify that."

"How would you qualify it?" said Tony.

"I'm not going to. I don't feel the need."

"But if you had to."

"Well, lots of men would say, 'I love you, but not in that way,' wouldn't they? Not me, though."

"You just said it anyway," said Bill.

"I was made to," said Clive, aggrieved.

"You knew we were going to winkle it out of you. That's why you said you didn't feel the need to qualify it. You wanted to qualify it," said Tony.

"There's a serious point here, though," said Max.

"What's that?"

"Do older people understand gays? Do they want to see a play about a gay marriage?"

"We're older people," said Sophie. "Ask us."

"Would you want to see a play about a gay marriage?" said Max.

"Yes," said Sophie firmly.

"Not really," said Clive.

"Why on earth not?" said Tony.

"I'd be worried that it was going to be too politically correct," said Clive.

"You've read it," said Bill. "Is it too politically correct?"

"It's not politically *in*correct, is it?" said Clive.

"How would that work?" said Tony. "You want lots of 1970s jokes about limp wrists and bending over?"

"Not *lots*," said Clive. "One or two. Just for realism's sake."

"Fair enough," said Bill.

"Don't listen to him," said Sophie, appalled by Bill's capitulation.

"No, I think he's right," said Bill. "Jim's old-school Labor, isn't he? He'd be a dinosaur now. Slightly homophobic, a bit slow-witted, talks about colored people, out of his depth in the modern world."

"You're right," said Tony. "We can play around with that."

Clive looked panic-stricken.

"That's not how I think of Jim at all."

"No?"

"No. I see him as very intelligent, well read, up to date with all the latest, you know, anti-sexism and -racism news . . ."

"That's not very politically incorrect."

"I didn't think Jim would be the politically incorrect one."

"You thought it would be Barbara?" said Sophie.

"Makes sense to me," said Clive. "They were always opposites."

"Let's get this straight," said Bill. "Because you don't like political correctness, you want some homophobic jokes in the play. But because you always want to be liked, you don't want to be the one who makes them."

Clive opened his mouth to say something, and closed it again.

"Tough," said Sophie. "And, Max, we're not old people. Not like that. Remember we're the same age as Bob Dylan and Dustin Hoffman."

"So you'd all run to buy tickets to see a play about gay marriage?" said Max.

"Yes," said Sophie firmly. "All of us."

"It's not about gay marriage, for Christ's sake," said Bill. "Have any of you even read it? It's about a man and a woman making peace with their past, and trying to work out whether they have a future together."

And Clive looked at her, and put his hand on Sophie's knee, and left it there. She thought about moving it, and then decided that she liked it where it was: she had been craving this kind of touch, and had been wondering, over the last year or two, whether she would ever feel it again. She knew what Max meant when he said that people of their age wanted to think about the future, like everybody else, but what they most wanted was to live in the present, rather than the past. She didn't have to worry about what kind of partner Clive would make, or whether their relationship could work, or even whether she was going to sleep with him. That stuff was for the young, and they were welcome to it.

After lunch, they met the director, a sunny, friendly young woman called Becky. As an introductory exercise, she got them all to talk about something or someone important to them, and when it came to her turn, she talked about her wife. Everyone looked at Clive, but he just beamed encouragingly.

There were two previews in Eastbourne before the first night, but the distinction seemed arbitrary: if there were to be no critics and no parties, what was the difference between a preview and what the posters along the seafront called a "World Premiere"?

"Ticket prices," said Max.

"That's it?" said Sophie.

"Pretty much," said Max.

They were drinking tea in the lounge of the Cavendish Hotel, and, rather pleasingly, Sophie had already been recognized. She wouldn't go so far as to say she'd been mobbed. There were a disconcerting number of Scandinavian and German families staying in the hotel and hers was not the kind of fame that had traveled very far. But two or three retired couples—one or two, anyway—had looked over, and then put their heads together, and dropped their voices to a whisper.

"How are the ticket sales?" said Bill.

"Early days," said Max. "We're expecting a lot of walk-ins."

"So to sum up, very bad," said Clive.

"I wouldn't say that," said Max, with the air of a man who was saying precisely that.

"What would you say, then?" said Tony.

"Well," said Max. "It's interesting."

They waited for illumination or elucidation, but Max offered nothing else.

"If you had a disappointment scale," said Bill, "with ten indicating maximum misery, where are we?"

"I haven't got a disappointment scale," said Max.

"I'm saying *if* you had one."

"I haven't," said Max. "I've never had one, don't have any use for one. Wouldn't know what it was if I saw it."

"It's not actually a physical object," said Bill. "You can't put a penny in the slot and stand on it. It's a concept."

"It's not a concept I understand."

"So you've never been disappointed by anything."

"Nope," said Max. "I can't afford to be. Not in my job."

"I don't even understand what your job is," said Clive.

"I'm an independent producer," said Max. "I get things made."

"What kinds of things?"

"Online TV programs. Movies. Shows."

"Would we have seen any of the movies?"

"Not yet."

"Or the shows?"

"You might have seen the online TV program," said Max.

"We haven't," said Tony. "I know I can speak for everyone here."

The younger cast members, Tom (aged forty-six) and James (forty-four), might have known everything about the world of online television, but they were on the beach.

"So . . . this would be a first for you?" said Clive.

It had never occurred to any of them that Max didn't know what he was doing, because he had given every appearance of competence and expertise. Or rather, he had produced money to pay them with, which was the same thing. The old measurements clearly no longer applied.

"Exactly," said Max. "That's why your disappointment scale is no use to me. Ask me about my excitement scale, or my sense of achievement scale, or my self-satisfaction scale."

"You'd score pretty highly on that one, I'd imagine," said Bill.

"If I don't give myself a ten, nobody else will," said Max.

Sophie noticed that the retired couple who'd recognized her had come to a decision and were making their way round the tables to say something to them. Sophie smiled welcomingly, but they weren't looking at her: they made straight for Clive.

"You are Chief Inspector Jury, aren't you?" said the man. "I mean, I know you're not actually Jury, but . . ."

"Clive Richardson," said Clive. "And yes, I played Richard Jury. How nice of you to remember. And how nice to meet you."

He stood up, and shook hands, and though he resisted the temptation to punch the air in triumph and stick two fingers up at Sophie, she could tell that the urge was there.

"We loved you in *Barbara (and Jim)*, as well," said the woman. "We were so sad when you split up."

"They're getting back together," said Max. "Tonight!"

The couple looked confused.

"And here's Barbara!" said Clive.

Barbara waved.

"Oh," said the woman. "Gosh!"

"They're opening in a play tonight. *From This Day Forward*. In the theater," said Max.

"Oh, we never get up to the West End now," said the man. It was 4:45 in the afternoon.

"Here in Eastbourne," said Max patiently.

"Oh, well then," said the man. "We'll look out for it."

"You don't have to look out for it," said Max. "It's here already."

"Can we find a couple of comps for them?" said Clive.

They looked uncomfortable.

"What's it about?" said the woman.

"It's Barbara and Jim. From the TV series. Getting back together after all these years."

"Lovely. And what's it called again?"

"Fuck," said Max.

For a moment, the man looked as though he were thinking of throwing himself in front of his wife to protect her, but he settled for a consoling squeeze of her arm.

"Excuse him," said Clive. "He's young. It's called *From This Day Forward.*"

"Fucking hell," said Max, and this time the couple scuttled off. "We've got the wrong fucking title."

"I like the title," said Bill. "I thought it was very clever."

"It is," said Max. "That's what's wrong with it. The whole point of the fucking play is that Barbara and Jim from the TV series *Barbara (and Jim)* are in it, and we're not telling the old biddies who might want to go and see it. It should be called *Barbara and Jim—The Reunion!* With an exclamation mark. I need to call people. Tell the theater. Get a new poster made. Bollocks."

He was already on his phone to someone before he got out of the lounge.

"Well," said Sophie. "An exclamation mark."

"We've come full circle," said Clive.

"It's not funny," said Bill.

"I like it," said Tony. "Dennis is here with us, in spirit."

"It's still not funny," said Bill.

Sometimes Sophie told Dennis what had been going on. It was as close as she ever came to praying. She knew he would always want to hear everything there was to hear about the children and the grandchildren, even though the news was local rather than national, most of the time; he had never been one of those indifferent, mildly benevolent men who wanted their wives to cut out the dull stuff and reduce long telephone conversations with loved ones to headlines. He was usually the one who made the calls, so she felt that the least she could do was tell him everything, in as much detail as she could remember. She'd never had to talk to him about work before; there hadn't been any since he'd died. He'd be pleased to know that she was doing something.

I'm in a dressing room in Eastbourne, she said. (Not out loud. That would be mad. But she was talking, she knew that, not writing or thinking.) Tony and Bill are out in the theater somewhere. They've written a play about Barbara and Jim, and the young producer is currently walking up and down the prom, barking at anyone old enough to remember us, because the theater is going to be half empty tonight. The play is much better than I thought it was going to be. It's funny, and sad—like life. And Clive is trying to chat me up, and I may well . . . She stopped herself. Dennis didn't want to hear about all that, and she didn't want to tell him, and she didn't know what there was to tell him anyway. So we're all here, she went on. And we'll all be here tomorrow night, and the night after. And if I can't be at home with you, then I want to be with them.

This wasn't quite true, she realized. She didn't want to be at home with Dennis; she wanted to be here, in Eastbourne, with Dennis and the others, or better still in a BBC studio, with Clive next door and Dennis prowling around outside. She didn't want 1964 back; she wasn't nostalgic. She just wanted to work. She picked up the script again. There was something she could do with the teapot in the opening scene, she was positive. She could get a laugh that nobody was expecting, and they'd be off and running.

ACKNOWLEDGMENTS

Thanks to Joanna Prior, Venetia Butterfield, Anna Ridley, Lesley Levene, John Hamilton, Georgia Garrett, Geoff Kloske, and—one last time, sadly—Tony Lacey. The books of Graham McCann were invaluable, especially *Spike & Co.*, which is highly recommended to anyone interested in British comedy of the period. And though David Kynaston hasn't yet reached the 1960s at the time of writing, his three brilliant social histories, *Austerity Britain*, *Family Britain*, and *Modernity Britain*, were an inspiration for *Funny Girl*. Without John Forrester, Sarah Geismar, Sandra Verbeckiene, Hayden Thomas, and Sebastien Alleaume, no work would be done, ever. And finally, the work of Ray Galton and Alan Simpson has been an enormous influence on my own writing, and there are lots of ways in which not only this book but my previous books wouldn't have existed without them.

PICTURE CREDITS

The publishers are grateful for permission to reproduce the following images:

p. 3: Miss Blackpool beauty contest © Homer Sykes/Getty Images

p. 17: Derry & Toms department store logo © Clifford Ling/Associated Newspapers/Rex

p. 26: Sabrina advert © culture-images/Lebrecht Music & Arts

p. 29: Talk of the Town theater © Associated Newspapers/Rex

p. 46: Voice Improvement Programme, Lesson 3. Image courtesy of © Bob Lyons

p. 65: Ray Galton and Alan Simpson © Cyril Maitland/Mirrorpix

p. 69: Gambols strip © Copyright 1967 Express Newspapers. Distributed by Knight Features. Reproduced by permission

p. 83: Tom Sloan at the Eurovision Song Contest © BBC Photo Library

p. 180: Mick Jagger at the Trattoria Terrazza © Mirrorpix

p. 187: *Till Death Us Do Part* cast © Photoshop

p. 278: Lucille Ball shooting *Lucy in London* © Bob Willoughby/MPTV, Camera Press, London

p. 282: Harold Wilson and Marcia Williams © Central Press/Stringer/Hulton/Getty Images

p. 365: Book cover © Penguin Books, designed by John Hamilton

p. 375: *Hair* cast © Central Images/Getty Images

Nick Hornby's inimitable writing—about sports, music, family, life, or love—is original, moving, and insightful.

His first book was a breakout memoir and love letter to the greatest game. His first novel was an international bestseller about a hapless record collector and his romantic woes. His stories explore characters who are sweet, sad, funny, and flawed in a world that is filled with the complications and triumphs of everyday life. These books are remarkable for their warm sense of humor, their psychological insight, and their detailed emotional geography.

Fever Pitch

Nick Hornby has been a football fan since the moment he was conceived. Call it predestiny. Or call it preschool.

Fever Pitch, his first book, is a tribute to a life-long obsession. Part autobiography, part comedy, part incisive analysis of insanity, Hornby's award-winning memoir captures the fever pitch of fandom—its agony and its ecstasy, its community, and its defining role in thousands of coming-of-age stories.

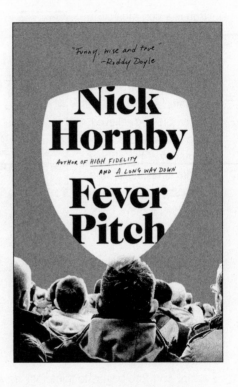

"Whether you are interested in football or not, this is tears-running-down-your-face funny, read-bits-out-loud-to-complete-strangers funny, but also highly perceptive and honest about Hornby's obsession and the state of the game. *Fever Pitch* is not only the best football book ever written, it's the funniest book of the year." —*GQ*

High Fidelity

Rob is a pop music junkie who runs his own semi-failing record store. His girlfriend, Laura, has just left him for the guy upstairs, and Rob is both miserable and relieved. Rob seeks refuge in the company of the offbeat clerks at his store, who endlessly review their top five films; top five Elvis Costello songs; top five episodes of *Cheers*.

Rob tries dating a singer, but maybe it's just that he's always wanted to sleep with someone who has a record contract. Then he sees Laura again. And Rob begins to think that life with kids, marriage, barbecues, and soft rock CDs might not be so bad.

"Mr. Hornby captures the loneliness and childishness of adult life with such precision and wit that you'll find yourself nodding and smiling. *High Fidelity* fills you with the same sensation you get from hearing a debut record album that has more charm and verve and depth than anything you can recall."
—*The New York Times Book Review*

About a Boy

Will Freeman may have discovered the key to dating success: If the simple fact that they were single mothers meant that gorgeous women—women who would not ordinarily look twice at Will—might not be only willing, but enthusiastic about dating him, then he was really onto something. Single mothers were all over the place. He just had to find them.

Will wasn't going to let the fact that he didn't have a child himself hold him back. A fictional two-year-old named Ned wouldn't be the first thing he'd invented. And it seems to go quite well at first, until he meets an actual twelve-year-old named Marcus, who is more than Will bargained for.

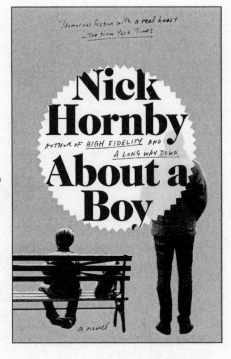

"Hornby is a writer who dares to be witty, intelligent, and emotionally generous all at once." **—The New York Times Book Review**

How to Be Good

A brutally truthful, hilarious, compassionate novel about the heart, mind, and soul of a woman who, confronted by her husband's sudden and extreme spiritual conversion, is forced to learn "how to be good"—whatever that means, and for better or worse…

Katie Carr is a good person...sort of. For years her husband's been selfish, sarcastic, and underemployed.

But now David's changed. He's become a good person, too—really good. He's found a spiritual leader. He has become kind, soft-spoken, and earnest. Katie isn't sure if this is a deeply felt conversion, a brain tumor—or David's most brilliantly vicious manipulation yet. Because she's finding it more and more difficult to live with David—and with herself.

"A darkly funny and thought-provoking ride."

—USA Today

Songbook

Songs, songwriters, and why and how they get under our skin...

A shrewd, funny, and completely unique collection of musings on pop music, why it's good, what makes us listen and love it, and the ways in which it attaches itself to our lives—all with the beat of a perfectly mastered mix tape.

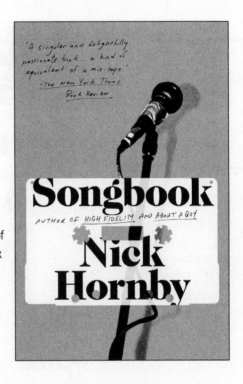

"A singular and delightfully passionate book... a kind of equivalent of a mix-tape."
—The New York Times Book Review

Songbook
AUTHOR OF *HIGH FIDELITY* AND *ABOUT A BOY*
Nick Hornby

"That whole subculture, all those mournful guys to whom the sound of record-store bin dividers clicking by is almost music enough, should love *Songbook*, yet so should anyone interested in great essays, or in the delicate art of being funny, or in how to write about one's feelings in such a way that other people will actually care." **—San Francisco Chronicle**

A Long Way Down

Nick Hornby mines the hearts and psyches of four lost souls who connect just when they've reached the end of the line.

In four distinct and riveting first-person voices, Hornby tells a story of four individuals confronting the limits of choice, circumstance, and their own mortality. This is a tale of connections made and missed, punishing regrets, and the grace of second chances.

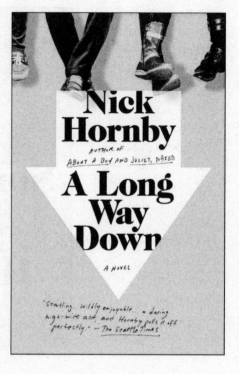

"One New Year's Eve, four people with very different reasons but a common purpose find their way to the top of a fifteen-story building in London. None of them has calculated that, on a date humans favor for acts of significance, in a place known as a local suicide-jumpers' favorite, they might encounter company. *A Long Way Down* is the story of what happens next, and of what doesn't." **—The New York Times Book Review**

"It's like *The Breakfast Club* rewritten by Beckett." **—Time**

Slam

For sixteen-year-old Sam, life is about to get extremely complicated. He and his girlfriend—make that ex-girlfriend—Alicia, have gotten themselves into a bit of trouble. Sam is suddenly forced to grow up and struggle with the familiar fears and inclinations that haunt all adults.

Nick Hornby's poignant and witty novel *Slam* shows a rare and impressive understanding of human relationships and what it really means to grow up.

"We want to hear whatever this kid has got to say—the whole scary, hilarious story…Hornby just makes it look easy."   —*The Washington Post*

Juliet, Naked

Annie and Duncan are a mid-thirties couple who have reached a fork in the road, realizing their shared interest in the reclusive musician Tucker Crowe is not enough to hold them together anymore. When they disagree about Tucker's "new release," an acoustic version of his most famous album, it's the last straw—Duncan cheats on Annie, who promptly throws him out. Via an Internet discussion forum, Annie's harsh opinion reaches Tucker himself, who couldn't agree with her more. He and Annie start an unlikely correspondence that teaches them both something about how two lonely people can gradually find each other.

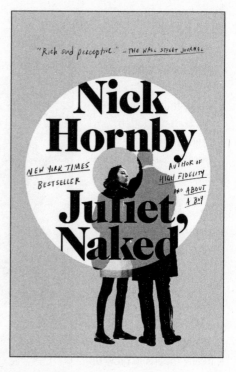

"Rich and perceptive." —THE WALL STREET JOURNAL

Nick Hornby

NEW YORK TIMES BESTSELLER

AUTHOR OF HIGH FIDELITY AND ABOUT A BOY

Juliet, Naked

Juliet, Naked is an engrossing, humorous novel about music, love, loneliness, and the struggle to live up to one's promise.

"Hornby seems, as ever, fascinated by the power of music to guide the heart, and in this very funny, very charming novel, he makes you see why it matters."
                                                    —The New York Times Book Review